> *Hetty had never read a novel; how then could she find*
> *shape for her expectations?*
>
> *George Elliot – Adam Bede – 1859*

Dear Reader,

Have you ever noticed how many great works of art are of women reading? Do a Google search and you'll see what I mean. Do a similar search for men, however, and you'll see a smaller collection, and more often the male is seated at a desk, a hand on a book or scroll, looking straight at the artist or staring thoughtfully into the middle distance, rather than actually reading. They seem to be more about status, power and distance than about immersion and imagination. Why this difference?

It's a question that goes to the heart of women's relationships with books. It's about why women read so many more books than most men, and why they form and join book clubs, swap books with their friends and subscribe to online book discussions and review groups and social media sites. It's about past times in which women had no access to books, and why in countries where they are still banned from reading they will risk their lives to do so in secret. And it's about how women writers speak to other women through the form of the novel; how books start conversations, lead to friendships and to action at an individual and group level. Just like George Elliott's Hetty, many of us need books not just to help us shape our expectations, but also to make sense of a world still shaped by men, and to find ways to be ourselves within it. We use books to talk to each other, to connect with other women, to work out issues in our own lives and, of course, to know that we are not alone.

For a long time, I've wanted to write a non-fiction book about women and reading, but I've been thinking about it and arguing with myself for so long I feared it might never see the light of day. I hoped writing a novel about women and their books might get me started. *A Month of Sundays* is that first step.

My mother was serious about her reading. My earliest memory is of her reading by a window in my grandparents' cottage; a shaft of sunlight captures her, totally absorbed in her book. Through books she made sense of, and peace with, her world. She was equally serious about teaching me to read, and to love and value books. My mother made me a reader and in doing so she also made me a writer.

I hope you'll enjoy this novel and that perhaps you will share it with your mother, your daughter or a woman friend.

Liz Byrski

A Month of Sundays

LIZ BYRSKI

A Month of Sundays

MACMILLAN

Pan Macmillan Australia

First published 2018 in Macmillan by Pan Macmillan Australia Pty Ltd
1 Market Street, Sydney, New South Wales, Australia, 2000

A catalogue record for this
book is available from the
National Library of Australia

Typeset in 11.25/16 pt Palatino Roman by Post Pre-press Group
Printed by McPherson's Printing Group

MIX
Paper from
responsible sources
FSC® C001695

Chapter One

Ros in Sydney, June 2016

At four in the afternoon of the day she is diagnosed Ros stands inside the hospital's sliding glass doors assessing her chances of getting a taxi in the pouring rain, and wishing she had downloaded the Uber app. Outside people scurry past, struggling against the wind that threatens to rip the umbrellas from their hands. *Perhaps if I lie down on the floor and moan pitifully they'll send me home in an ambulance,* she thinks, and she lets out a little sigh of pleasure at the idea of being lifted gently onto a stretcher by strong and youthful paramedics in fluoro vests, transported home in comfort, deposited on the sofa and left in peaceful stillness to contemplate her future.

Beyond the hospital entrance the traffic lights change and as the line of cars moves forward a taxi swings into the hospital car park and stops in one of the drop-off bays. Ros makes a charge for the doors, clutching her bag and stick, and she has a grip on the taxi's rear doorhandle while the arriving passenger waits for his receipt.

'I think this one's mine!' a man in a dark suit, with attitude, says, attempting to elbow her aside. 'I called one ten minutes ago.'

Ros tightens her grip and squares her shoulders. 'Me too, but fifteen minutes ago,' she lies. 'I've been waiting ages. This one's mine.' As the incoming passenger emerges she flings herself onto the back seat and slams the door. 'Paddington, please, driver.'

'You don't look much like Kenneth Bacon who's going to Market Street,' the driver says, grinning at her in the rear view mirror. 'I think you just gazumped my fare.'

'Absolutely,' Ros says. 'But Kenneth Bacon looks more like an Uber person, don't you think? I'm Rosamund Benson, senior citizen, and I just want to go home to Paddington.' And she leans back, impressed by her own speed, dexterity and ruthlessness. Not bad in the circumstances, she thinks, and she closes her eyes and breathes deeply. The small victory makes her feel more like herself again. Fifteen minutes later, she is home, and Clooney is skidding down the passage to greet her.

'Okay, okay. Yes, I'm home,' she says, hanging her stick on its hook and walking towards the living room. 'I was quite my old self this afternoon, with the taxi – bossy, annoying, pushy. The old pain-in-the-arse-Ros, remember her?'

She dumps her open bag on the table and it immediately topples over and discharges a bundle of glossy leaflets that slither out across the wooden surface. Ros stares at them spread out in front of her in full colour – the story of her new life: the symptoms, the treatment options, the lifestyle advice. Photos of healthy young people in white coats, with shiny eyes, clear skin and perfect teeth, assisting hunched and ageing patients along passages, or sharing a cup of tea with them in a sunlit room.

Ros grabs the *Sydney Morning Herald* from the far end of the table and tosses it on top of them. 'Doctors,' she says aloud, flopping down onto the sofa. 'I am so sick of doctors and their sodding tests.' In the last few weeks there have simply been too many doctors, too many needles, tests, scans, X-rays, possibilities, opinions and theories. She knows that only a few years ago she could have taken all this in, thought it through carefully and come home to make plans, but now she just feels overwhelmed, as though she would do anything to avoid thinking about it. She rests her head on the cushions and closes her eyes. She had made notes in the specialist's office, kept cool, forced herself to pay attention. 'Too much,' she murmurs to Clooney, as he jumps up beside her. 'I have brain drain.' He rests his head comfortingly in her lap. *It's a fork in the road*, she thinks, *I can sink into this diagnosis and fade away, or fight it. I can let go of all the things I thought I would do and be in my old age and try to create something new, or I can fall in a heap and hope someone will pick me up.* She strokes Clooney's head and his big, floppy, cocker spaniel ears. 'Do you know how heavy your ears are?' she says, feeling the weight of one in her hand. 'And your feet are enormous. But I've told you that before.' In apparent acknowledgement he licks her hand and they both close their eyes at the same time.

Minutes later the sound of the doorbell has Clooney leaping up and he hurls himself off the sofa and pounds down to the front door. Ros struggles irritably to her feet. The rain has stopped now. As she opens the door a thin slice of late afternoon sunlight forces its way through the clouds, and a bearded young man in a well-worn brown leather bomber jacket and jeans raises a hand to shade his eyes.

'Ros Benson?' he asks.

'Possibly,' she says, 'who wants to know?'

'Tim, Tim Barnaby, Leah's friend. She said you'd be expecting me this afternoon . . . it's about the flat . . .'

Ros steps back and opens the door. 'Of course. Sorry, I only just got home, and I'd completely forgotten you were coming.'

'If it's inconvenient . . .'

'It's not,' she says. 'Come on in.'

Tim Barnaby wipes his feet on the mat and leans his umbrella behind the door.

Ros takes a key from a line of hooks on the hall-stand. 'Did Leah tell you I only rent it to musicians?'

'She did, but not drummers.'

'And you're not a drummer?'

He grins. 'Far from it. My instrument is the violin, and yours – the cello, I think?'

'Indeed it is.' She hands him the key. 'The flat's on the first floor, do you mind going up on your own? Have a look around, see what you think and I'll join you shortly.'

'Sure, thanks.' He takes the key from her and heads on up the stairs.

Ros goes to the small cloakroom under the stairs and splashes water on her face, straightens up and stares at herself in the mirror. *My face,* she thinks, *is moving ever downwards, I will soon have jowls.* It reminds her of the description of an elderly woman in a book. She scrabbles around in her memory and recalls a character described as having 'neatly folded jowls' and there was something else – a long infuriating pause while she grasps at it – 'she would have made a distinguished-looking man', that's it. *Well the jowl bit is right, but I wouldn't make a distinguished-looking anything really.* She takes some deep breaths to loosen herself up, trying to look less like some miserable old bat who would be a terrible landlady. Then she makes her way slowly up the stairs, still trying to remember the title of the book.

Tim Barnaby is standing by the window looking out across the rooftops to the city.

'What do you think?' Ros asks from the doorway. 'People usually either love it or hate it.'

'I love it,' he says, turning towards her. 'It's perfect.'

'Not too small?'

'Small but perfect.'

'My thoughts exactly! I had it converted when James, my husband, died some years ago. Since then it's been home to another cellist, two violinists, a trombone player, and a flautist.'

'Was your husband a musician?'

'No, he was an academic, a historian, but he was also a fine pianist. His piano is still downstairs.'

They stand facing each other, suddenly awkward. He is younger than she'd expected, but these days she finds it hard to tell people's ages because everyone seems to be so much younger than her. Clooney pushes past her, stalks across to the window seat and jumps up.

'No, Clooney, down,' Ros says, and he gives her a sheepish look and slides grudgingly back onto the floor.

'Clooney? Unusual name for a dog.'

'Named after George, of course; I think he has the same sort of look in his eyes. Can you see it?'

Tim crouches down looking into the dog's face, stroking his ears. 'Well actually yes, I can now – a bit.'

Ros thinks he might be humouring her, but that's not necessarily a bad thing.

He looks up at her. 'I'd love to live here, Ros. I have good references, a regular income, and I've known Leah for years; in fact a long time ago, before she married Ivan, we were in a shared flat with a couple of other students. I'm pretty quiet and I understand housework!'

'You understand it or you actually do it?'

'Both. My part-time job at uni was with a cleaning agency.'

An hour or so later they have signed the tenancy agreement and settled on Tim's moving-in date over half a bottle of wine. When he leaves, Ros closes the door behind him and leans back against it sighing with satisfaction. He seems ideal: likeable, respectful, intelligent, with a sense of humour. *I think he'll be fine,* she says, talking silently to James as she frequently does. *It's a relief, I hate the idea of having to organise a new tenant again, but he seems easy and Leah wouldn't have sent me a dud.*

Back in the lounge, the edges of the leaflets peeking out from under the newspaper make her stomach churn again. Hateful things hanging over her, threatening a future for which she is unprepared: a future that could be as distant as a few years or as close as next week. *So I suppose you know about all this,* she says to James. *You should be thankful you're not here; you don't have to be a carer. You'd have done it, I know, but we would both have hated it. On the other hand I wish you were here – it's all very well talking at you like this but I never get an answer. I don't even know if you're listening. I miss you, and times like this I miss you most of all.*

The laptop beeps, announcing new emails, and Ros reaches out and scrolls down the inbox: some junk mail, a couple of bills, and a message from Adele – something about the book club. Adele has somehow become the informal convenor now that there are only four of them left. Not that Ros minds who convenes it, as long as she doesn't have to, but Adele's message can wait until tomorrow.

Getting up from the table she stretches her arms above her head, rolls her shoulders and walks across the room to sit down on the ageing, tapestry-covered seat of her music chair. The weight of the cello is comforting as she draws it towards her, its curves almost human. She flexes her fingers, picks up the bow, and briefly closes her eyes, focusing on what she wants to play. As she draws the bow across the strings the first strains of a Bach cantata float upwards, as though the instrument itself knows what she wants. Seconds later she is absorbed, blood singing in her veins, at one with the music, rising above the anxiety, letting it drop away. Her energy surges, transporting her beyond the room, beyond the depressing outcome of the hospital visit, beyond herself. But as her spirits soar, her right hand trembles, and the bow slips from her fingers, clattering to the floor, dousing the music like water on a fire. Ros crashes back down through disappointment to despair, and folding both arms around the cello, she holds it closer, rocking slowly back and forth in the silence, staring unseeing out into the darkness of the garden.

Adele in Adelaide

As soon as she'd sent the group message Adele had started to worry about it. Did it sound too bossy? Should she have provided more suggestions about how it could work? She'd read it again and it seemed fine, but there was always the worrying possibility that someone would hate the idea. Perhaps she should have invoked the twenty-four hour rule – don't press 'Send' until you've thought about it overnight. She *had* thought about it, but not for twenty-four hours – actually it was only about four hours. *It'll be fine,* she'd told herself again. It's only an invitation, a suggestion really. But she wants it so much she can barely contain herself. Is there anything in it that could upset any of them? Surely not. These women are not mere acquaintances; they're friends – sort of. The three of them, and

Adele herself, are the only remaining members of an online book club started twelve years ago. There were six original members, and it had grown slowly to sixteen – sixteen women in locations around the country. That had been too many to manage online and a few fell away quite soon, others more slowly. Now it has shrunk to just four. Death, illness and international moves have taken some members, while others left to join what they'd hurtfully called 'a proper book club', where food and wine and conversations about things other than books often hijacked the meetings. Adele has been here from the beginning; in fact it was she and her cousin Marian who started it. As a club it does have its limitations. There are no cups of tea or shared bottles of wine; no one prepares canapés or sandwiches, or bakes a cake; not an olive or a scone has ever passed between them. At each meeting they talk energetically about books, the one they've been reading and frequently others as well, but very little else. Since they've been reduced to four it has seemed pleasantly intimate, but they are still just four women, hardly a club at all. Four women who have never actually met, reading and talking books one Sunday afternoon a month on Skype. They have been steadfast in the face of frozen screens, visual distortions, the stubborn refusal of the sound to work and the frequent drop-outs, all of which have irritated but not deterred them.

'I wonder if we'll ever have the chance to actually be in the same room together,' Judy had ventured sometime last year.

'Why risk messing up something that works well?' Ros had responded. 'We don't really know each other, which is possibly a *good* thing, because we don't have to tolerate each other's irritating habits in person. Face to face we could end up loathing each other and dropping out. End of book club!'

It had brought that meeting to a strange and somewhat

awkward close. Adele had thought this was just plain rude, but then Ros could be blunt like that. Adele has often found her quite confronting and wonders if Ros has any idea of how rough it can be to be on the sharp end of her opinions. On this occasion it had seemed that they'd all held their breath for a month wondering whether the tension would bleed through into the next meeting. Adele had feared that this latest thoughtless comment might bring the club to an end, but it hadn't. As soon as they were next assembled online Ros had apologised. 'Foot in mouth, so sorry,' she'd said, and they had laughed about it and moved on.

And now they do have that chance to meet because Marian – who had dropped out of the club years ago – had emailed Adele this morning.

We're heading off in July to visit the children and grandchildren in Germany, and then spend a couple of weeks in Spain, Marian had written. *You mentioned once that you wouldn't mind housesitting for us, so I thought I'd see if you're still up for it. I think you said you were retiring this month so maybe you'd be free to come over here? I know how you love the Blue Mountains. You're welcome to bring a friend or friends with you. It occurred to me that you might want to bring the remaining stalwarts from the book club. Now it's down to four you could easily fit in. Gwenda would still come in to clean and doesn't mind doing some cooking if you want, so you could organise that with her. And Ray is always willing to help out with any mainte- nance problems. We'd be so happy if we knew you were looking after the place for us. Anyway, let us know what you think.*

Adele had read the message through several times. The timing was great – the house would be free from late July until mid-September. She could be there all or part of the time. She pictured herself in that beautiful old house with its glorious views, popping out for coffee or lunch, browsing the lovely little shops in Leura and the galleries in Blackheath. And then she thought more about Marian's suggestion. Should she invite the others – Judy, Ros and Simone – to join her? There were great walks, a huge wood-burning stove and shelves full of books, CDs and DVDs. If she could persuade them to come for four weeks they could each choose a book and discuss one each week. All the things she would do alone they could do together or individually. As she'd thought more about it Adele decided that Judy and Simone would go for it, but Ros . . . well, Ros might be tricky. She was the sort of person who could dismantle any argument, see through the gaps in any plan and give you that sceptical, sometimes withering, look over the top of her glasses. But by then Adele was committed. The more she thought about it the more she liked the idea and she'd whizzed off the email.

Now, as she reads it yet again, she thinks it embarrassingly naive, as though a breathless teenager, rather than a woman of more than a certain age, had written it. She'll be on tenterhooks now until they respond. The old anxiety about what other people might think of her – about looking stupid, or ignorant, or pushy, too assertive or not assertive enough – surges through her. Sometimes she thinks she's overcome this burdensome characteristic, but then she finds herself once again at its mercy.

'Basically it's about wanting, or needing, complete control of what people think of you and that, inevitably, comes down to trying to please everyone, usually at considerable personal cost,' a counsellor had said to her some years ago. The woman's name was Astrid and she was just the sort of person who sent Adele into a flurry of anxiety: confident, eccentric, outspoken and brusque. A bit like Ros, really, Adele thinks now.

'The thing is, Adele,' Astrid had continued, after pausing

to light up a cheroot, 'it's quite hard to get a grip on who you are, because you try to be all things to all people. Someone who might like to get to know you better could find it difficult because you flip flop around trying to please them. There's no consistency. You say you're fine in a role – your job, for example – when you are being . . .' She stopped to consult her notes. 'At work, when you're being the director of the bureau, you know how to do the job, you know what's expected of you, so that's who you become. The same when you're chairing that committee you talked about. It's when you have to be just you, just Adele Grainger, you find yourself in trouble. So what we need to work on over the coming weeks . . . well, months really . . . is who the *real* Adele is. We will discover this together and work on your sense of your core self.' And she leaned back, crossed her legs, took another draw and gazed up at the curl of blue smoke as it drifted towards the window.

Adele had stopped breathing at this point. 'Mmm,' she'd said. 'I see what you mean, Astrid. Look, sorry, could I just pop out to your toilet?' And she'd got to her feet and hurried out of the consulting room, through the waiting room and down the steps into the street, hopped into her car and driven away.

'I knew she was right so I ran away and never went back,' Adele told her daughter on the phone later. 'I couldn't face the prospect of sitting there, baring my soul to her for months, while she smoked her bloody cheroots.'

'Well, I think that says it all really, Mum,' Jenna said. A few weeks later she'd sent Adele a book in a padded envelope. *I think this might help,* Jenna had written on a postcard slipped inside the cover. *Don't worry, it's a novel, not a self-help book – enjoy! Love Jen. PS I love you to bits just as you are! Xxx.*

It was a Canadian book, not surprisingly as Jenna lives in Quebec, by a writer called Carol Shields, and the title was *Unless.*

When Adele read it she felt it was telling her something much bigger than the story, something she sort of knew, so she read it again. It was all there – the feeling that things weren't right, that *she* wasn't quite right.

Adele never knew her mother, who had died from a heart attack just hours after her birth. She often wonders who she would be now had she been brought up by her mother, rather than being caught between the twin powers of her very controlling, widowed father, and the stony-faced woman he had employed to keep his house and raise his daughter. So many women Adele's own age seem confident and empowered, as though they knew something she didn't or had found some sort of guru who taught them how to become their true selves. Adele, always needing approval, always anxious not to cause offence or do the wrong thing, is still struggling to find her own confidence. Astrid had been her attempt to find a guru and that hadn't turned out well at all. She wished she could have talked to Carol Shields – in fact some time ago she decided to write to her about this, but worried for months about saying the wrong thing in the email, and when she actually drafted it and went to the author's website for a contact address, she found that Carol Shields had died years earlier. Adele felt this keenly, as though she had been a personal friend, although she knew that she was confusing the writer herself with Reta, her character. Sometimes the way writers conveyed information could be oblique, and that annoyed Adele, who liked things to be clearly articulated. It's now many years since she first read the book and she still hasn't found a way to switch off her need to please; how to flick the switch of feeling she is answerable to everyone, and always on the threshold of making a wrong decision. Neither her spotless work record, nor the esteem in which her employers and her staff hold her, has changed this.

As she stares at her email on the screen Adele begins to wonder whether, having set this up, she will actually be able to cope with spending all that time in close proximity to these book club friends who are, in many ways, strangers. In her head the spirit of Astrid speaks to her from behind the old cloud of smoke.

So who, or what, will you be in the Blue Mountains, Adele? Astrid asks. *You're retiring in a few weeks, so who will you be in the mountains and beyond? Do you think you're going to find something to fix your life? You've left it very late to establish your identity. This is your big chance to break through, to be yourself. Get it wrong and you may end up still lacking a sense of yourself, but now also without a book club.*

Adele feels the fear creeping up her spine. No one has replied to her invitation yet but it really is too soon. She stands up and paces the room to shake the spirit of Astrid from her. *Calm down,* she tells herself, *they need to think about it before they reply.* But suppose they all say yes and then it turns out to be a disaster? Adele's stomach lurches in horror. Abruptly she logs off the computer and hurries out to the kitchen to pour herself a glass of wine and to solve the more straightforward problem of whether she will have cheese on toast or warmed-up soup for dinner.

Judy in Mandurah, WA

Judy lets herself in through the back door of the shop, puts her handbag on her desk in the rear office, and walks through the stockroom to open the door into the shop itself. From there she can see the glass front door, with the *Closed* sign in place, and beyond it the street. This morning she has deliberately arrived half an hour early to do some paperwork, but the sight of her desk, piled high with catalogues, bills, receipts, spreadsheets and goodness knows what else, has already brought on the sick, trapped feeling that has been haunting her for months. The fact is that she has no idea where to start; there is so much of . . . well, of everything, and it's all a mess. She looks back out to the street, where the postie is making his way towards her mailbox, and beyond him she spots Maddie heading towards the shop clutching her usual bulging plastic bag full of scarves. Judy dives back into the stockroom and closes the door. If Maddie sees she's there opening hours will mean nothing. Judy has, in the past, invested some time and patience in getting Maddie to understand that opening hours are just that and it largely works. But chances are that if Maddie sees her in the shop she will be hammering on the door. Judy is very fond of her, but . . . it's complicated.

'I don't know how you cope with her,' said Pearl, who had helped out in the shop for a few days when Judy had flu last winter. 'She's so demanding and relentless, and she never stops talking. I couldn't get rid of her.'

'That's Maddie,' Judy had said. 'She has no boundaries and she doesn't understand the effect she has on people.'

'I don't know why you bother,' Pearl said. 'You should just ban her.'

Judy smiled, imagining what a process of banning Maddie might involve. 'I like her,' she said simply. 'I care about her and I know that coming here means something to her. We . . . well, we value each other, each in our own way, I suppose.'

Pearl had thrown her hands in the air. 'I give up,' she said. 'Really, I give up. Maddie is the right name, she's mad as a coot.'

'Maddie,' Judy said, inhaling sharply and drawing herself up to her full, but unimpressive, height, 'is an abbreviation of her name – Madeleine. She is not mad, that's offensive.' And she had determined then and there that she would never again ask Pearl to shop-sit, and she would reduce contact with her to a polite minimum.

Feeling treacherous Judy hurries back to the office and switches on the computer. Business has boomed since her early days here, thanks to a revival of interest in knitting. It had come at the right time for Judy, whose basic business was already well established. When the lease on the small shop next door became available, she had grasped the opportunity to expand. As soon as the contracts were signed she cut through the adjoining wall to turn the two shops into one. It gave her more than half as much space again, and soon she had a design and activity room with some tables and chairs and a coffee machine for people to help themselves. Within just a few months she had set up knitting groups and classes, developed an online presence with a website and Facebook page. The surge in the business had initially amazed and eventually overwhelmed her. People come to her shop not only from Mandurah and its surroundings but also from as far away as Perth and Fremantle in the north and Bunbury and Busselton in the south. What she needs now is a person with a commitment to the business. But the right person would be one who would want to share some of the decision-making, and before she can think about finding that person she has to sort out the chaos she herself has created. Melissa, the new part-time assistant who is now working with her two afternoons a week, is young, very bright, and super keen. It's helped, but not enough. When Judy stops to think about it, which she does as rarely as possible, she knows that if she could somehow reorganise and de-clutter the way she runs things, life would be a whole lot easier. She has a management system on her computer, but she doesn't know how it works, and the prospect of having to learn to use it is daunting. She longs to turn her back and walk away.

'The trouble with running your own business,' someone had said to her the year she had acquired the shop, 'is that it never stops. There are no days off, no proper holidays. Not smart for a woman on her own like you, who hasn't got a man around to sort things out.' Judy resented the comment, and it made her more determined than ever to do everything herself. And she *had* done it all herself, and in doing so she is now drowning in her own creation.

In her youth she'd dreaded the parcels of hand-knitted jumpers, gloves, hats and scarves that arrived regularly from her grandmother, who had taught her to knit as a child. In the late fifties and early sixties homemade was not remotely cool, and you wouldn't be seen knitting for quids. Judy had grown up in a small Suffolk town and was nineteen before she moved, with a former schoolfriend, to a shared flat in London. It was there, two years later, that she met Ted, who had been brought along to a party by another housemate. Tall, blond, tanned and fresh off the boat that had brought him to London from Australia, he captured the attention of almost every girl in the room.

He'd grown up, he told her, in the Western Australian Wheatbelt, on a family property where they had wheat and sheep. He talked lovingly about his home, his parents, the neighbours, and the town where they drove to get their shopping. Judy, raised as she was in a small country town, identified with all he said. Despite the fact that she had virtually run away from Suffolk, she knew she was a country – or at least a small-town – girl at heart. Ted showed her black-and-white snapshots of himself with his father alongside a tractor; there were photos of sheep and a sheepdog, and Ted's mother bottle-feeding a sheepdog pup. When he told her it was a long way to town she assumed he meant about twenty miles. When he said the family got on well with the nearest neighbours, she presumed they lived a short walk or bike ride away.

It didn't take long for Judy to fall in love. Ted was gentle and softly-spoken, somewhat intimidated by London, and she took him sightseeing, to the movies, on pub crawls, and to lots of parties.

'He seems nice,' her mother said when Judy took him home with her to Suffolk. 'But Australia is so big, and such a long way away.'

'He's a big man with a big heart,' Judy said. 'I love him and I'm going to marry him.'

And just over a year later they were married in the local church with Judy's family and some of her London friends, celebrating in the parish hall. A couple of months later they were on a ship back to Australia.

'You might find it a bit remote,' Ted mentioned, as the ship approached Fremantle.

'It's exciting,' Judy said, leaning against the rails. 'I'm so looking forward to it all: meeting your family and hanging out with the neighbours, going shopping in town. And the sheep! One of our neighbours back home had a sheep, she kept it tethered in the garden, like a pet.' Much later she remembered that Ted's face had changed when she said this. He'd looked more than surprised; awkward, she'd thought, or perhaps anxious.

'Mmm. Well it's not quite like that, Jude,' he said. 'We don't really make pets of them – there are an awful lot of sheep.'

Judy's naivety, her own ignorance about her future home, still amazes her. How could she ever have convinced herself that it would be similar to her life in Suffolk? The enormity of Western Australia was paralysing – the family property seemed hundreds of times bigger than her hometown. Nothing was as she had expected. They lived by the weather – the heat, the dry, the rain or the lack of it, the fear of drought. The nearest neighbours were miles away; the nearest town more than an hour-and-a-half's drive. The distances and the oppressive silence of this vast country weighed heavily on her.

At first Judy had felt some pride in working alongside Ted and his parents, or spending a day baking with her mother-in-law, and driving miles to take the cakes and scones to the CWA. She made a friend of Donna, the eldest daughter of the Indigenous family who had worked the property with Ted's family for decades. Donna was three years younger than Judy and this was her country, and through her Judy learned more about her new home than she ever did from Ted and his parents. Sometimes they went together on the fortnightly drive to and from town for the shopping, but more often than not Judy did that trek alone. One Wednesday when she had loaded everything into the car she decided to get a sandwich and a cup of tea in the little café and ran into two women from the CWA.

'Come and join us,' they said, indicating a spare place at the table. 'How are you settling in?'

'Oh . . . okay . . .' she said, half-heartedly, and to her dismay she felt her voice break and had to struggle not to burst into tears. 'I'm . . . well, I'm trying to adjust, but it's all very different . . . everything's different, and not at all what I expected.'

One of the women, Edna, reached out and patted her hand. 'I do remember what it's like,' she said. 'I met my husband in

London during the war. And when it was over John had to come back to Australia, and some months later I flew here with a bunch of other girls, all of us war brides. I thought I'd arrived at the end of the earth. But I got used to it, love, and so will you.'

They talked on and when they all got up to go Edna's friend Val said she wanted to go to the haberdashery to buy some wool. 'D'you knit, Judy?' Edna asked.

Judy wanted to hang on to their company a little a longer; they were both a lot older than her and there was something comforting about them. 'I haven't knitted for years,' she said. 'But I wouldn't mind trying again.'

So she'd gone with them, bought several pairs of needles, wool and a pattern book. *I'd be willing to knit my way through the whole book if it means I can spend some time with them*, she thought as she drove home. And that's just what she did. Soon she was knitting blankets, beanies, socks, and jumpers, cushion covers and tea cosies for the CWA. Every fortnight she and Edna would meet for lunch on shopping day, sometimes with Val but more often just the two of them. And for Judy the tedious ninety-minute each-way trek was transformed from a burden to the highlight of her week. With Donna at the farm, and now with Edna's friendship, she began to feel she might yet make it as an Australian farmer's wife. Then the following year she fell pregnant, and baby clothes, blankets, knitted toys and shawls were on her needles. She knitted with almost manic energy and would often finish the last few rows of whatever she was working on long after Ted was asleep. But one night, as she got up from the sofa, she was gripped by spasms of pain that bent her double and she began to bleed. Three weeks later, she was released from hospital, struggling to come to terms with the death of her baby and the knowledge that there was going to be no second chance at motherhood.

From then on each day was a challenge. Donna did everything in her power to help keep Judy's spirits up. Ted's mother – who, although essentially kind and fond of Judy, lacked warmth or empathy – made her special cakes and administered tense, awkward hugs. Edna came to visit her and stayed a couple of nights. Slowly, life returned to apparent normality. Except that it wasn't normal, because every time Judy thought about the future all she wanted was to run away. The following year there was another blow. Edna had a massive heart attack and a few days later, as Judy was packing an overnight bag to go and visit her, Edna's husband called to tell her that his wife had died that morning.

With Edna gone Judy knew in her heart that her days in the Wheatbelt were numbered. Even so she managed to last another year, until one morning she got up, packed her needles, her wool, her cotton yarn and her patterns into a huge crocheted bag and everything else she owned into a suitcase.

'Will you be coming back?' Ted had asked as he stood in the bedroom watching her stuff things into her case.

'Of course,' she said. 'I'll come and visit if you if want me to. I do still love you, Ted, I probably always will, but I can't live here, and you can't live anywhere else.'

They clung together in their bedroom in the sweltering heat, and Judy felt her heart was breaking. 'I'm sorry, really I am,' she sobbed.

In the first couple of years she had gone back to stay with him sometimes and he came to Perth to see her. But distance meant that their lives drifted apart, and they were both just trying to make the best of it. The visits became more infrequent and then, almost three years after she had left, Ted wrote to tell her that Donna had moved in with him. Judy felt an unexpected stab of something like jealousy. Donna was her only real friend in Australia, almost like a sister. She had supported her through the miscarriage and its aftermath, and Judy had grown to love her, and she still loved Ted. So what, she had wondered, was the nature of this jealousy? Did she feel she was losing a part of Ted, or a part of Donna, or both? It troubled her for a while, but these were the two people she loved most in the world and they loved her and each other. They loved life on the land and she hated it. She, on the other hand, had her independence, and a great job in a dress shop in Perth.

Her father had died during her first year in Australia, and when some years later, her mother, still back in that Suffolk town, also died, Judy and her brother Robert inherited the house. He bought her out of the property and thanks to a very favourable exchange rate Judy had been able to buy a townhouse near the waterfront in Mandurah, an hour's drive south of Perth. It was a small town back then, and she had liked the feel of it. It was a neighbourly sort of place on the glittering banks of a beautiful inlet, where families went hunting for crabs on hot summer evenings, and there was an old wooden jetty where the pelicans often gathered. Best of all there was a sign in the window of the rather nice wool shop advertising a vacancy for a salesperson. She had walked in hopeful and out an hour-and-a-half later with a new job, and when she had worked out her two weeks' notice in Perth she began her new life in Mandurah.

'We're an odd sort of threesome, aren't we?' Judy said to Donna one time when she'd driven down to stay with Donna and Ted. And that's what they have remained. Now, when Judy visits, as she does two or three times a year, she sleeps in the bedroom she had once planned as a nursery.

This morning, as Maddie waits at the front door, Judy rummages through the stack of papers on her desk, looking for the bills that are due this week. There are five she knows she needs to pay, but by the time she has located two it's time to open the shop.

'Right on time,' Maddie says to her with a big smile, unfazed by the wait, and holding out the plastic carrier bag. 'I've brought some scarves, and I need more wool.'

Judy pulls out five very long strips of knitting in various colour mixes – in uneven garter stitch. All have scattered holes from dropped stitches, or knots where Maddie has decided to change wool colour in the middle of a row.

'These are lovely, Maddie,' Judy says. 'I'll pop out the back and get you some more wool.' She carries them out to the stockroom, returning with a bag of tightly rolled balls of used wool from Maddie's previous deliveries. In the early days of this strange friendship Judy had recognised that Maddie had little or no money and she began to supply her with new wool. But Maddie knitted very fast and very often, and what she knitted was always unusable. Judy had tried various ways to help her improve her knitting, but Maddie's only interest was in doing the knitting, not in knitting well or in what happened to it when it was done. So Judy began unravelling them and returning the wool to her in tightly wound balls, along with any other odd balls left over in the shop, ends of lines or dye lots. And now there is a ritual: Maddie delivers the scarves, Judy hands over some recycled wool and makes a cup of tea, and Maddie stands around for about twenty minutes regaling her with stories of life in the supervised share house where she lives, and then leaves. But today is different.

'Can't stop,' Maddie says. 'I've got to get back.'

'Really? You don't want a cup of tea?'

Maddie shakes her head and leans closer to whisper. 'I've got a boyfriend. He moved in last week and I can tell that he likes me, because I showed him my scarves and he said he'd like me to knit one especially for him.'

'Well that's very good news,' Judy says. 'You'd better hurry back and get started on it then.' She stands watching as Maddie heads out of the shop and down the street. This unexpected defection from a long-established, if irritating, ritual is strangely disconcerting. Judy checks the shelves and switches on the computer. A couple of regulars wander in and her heart sinks at the prospect of having to listen to their stories of awkward husbands, difficult neighbours, ungrateful children, or the plumber who didn't turn up; and that's before they even get around to telling her about their knitting problems, and asking for advice on patterns. *Some days*, she thinks, *I feel more like an agony aunt than a shopkeeper.* But she puts on her best smile. 'Jane, Brenda,' she says, 'lovely to see you, what can I do for you today?'

It's another hour before she actually has time to perch on the stool behind the counter and check the personal email on her phone.

There are several new messages, some junk and a short message from Ted about some obscure tractor part he thinks she might be able to pick up locally and mail to him. And then there is one from Adele.

Judy reads it, then reads it again.

Quickly she crosses to the door, locks it, replaces the *Open* sign with one that says *Back in 10 Minutes* and goes through to the office. Panic swells up inside her. She tugs at the poloneck of her jumper, stretching it frantically with her hands until it loosens. *I can't bear this anymore, I just can't*, she tells herself, overwhelmed by the need to escape, to find some way out of all that she has built.

In the past her response to feeling trapped has been to run away. But this time she can't just run. She has created a really good business but has let it get out of hand, and failed to build an exit strategy. *You're mad*, she tells herself, *calm down. You need a holiday.* Yes, that's it, a holiday, and that's what Adele's message is about – a holiday. She lets go of her poloneck and hits 'Reply all'.

Yes, yes, yes, please, she types. *I'd love to do this. Just what I need, as soon as possible, so count me in. Thanks so much Adele. Will email again later. Can't believe we're going to meet at last.*

Simone in Hobart, Tasmania

Simone stretches her arms above her head, holds the stretch, releases it gently and sits up, crosses her legs and looks out over the three rows of bodies lying still and silent in front of her.

'Right, everyone,' she says softly. 'Sitting up slowly, take your time, deep breaths.' As the class shifts to sit up she stands, and when everyone is upright she folds her hands in front of her and bows, and the class returns the *namaste* from a sitting position. 'Thank you. Now – standing up carefully when you're ready.'

There is a shuffle of shifting bodies and Simone watches as they cautiously get to their feet.

The seniors classes are a joy to teach; everyone in this particular beginners group has come to yoga late in life, some of them desperate for a route out of stiffness and bodily discomfort, and they are now also discovering how it calms and focuses them, helps them to concentrate more and forget less.

Simone herself started to practise yoga more than fifteen years ago when she hit her fifties. She had sought something different from the morning runs that had always been a source of discipline and refreshment for mind and body. It was a colleague who had recommended yoga and she had been in the mood to try something new.

'You got me at exactly the right time,' she'd told the instructor later. 'I'm notoriously resistant to changing my habits.' But from yoga she had never looked back. She noticed the calm that descended on her in the first couple of weeks. She was never going to be one of those types who attend two classes a week and do nothing in between. She practised every day so that a few weeks into her first course it became a regular habit. She was still teaching high school then and she began to feel calmer and more confident in the classroom.

'I'm loving it,' she'd told her daughter-in law when the classes ended over Christmas that year. 'I'll be back there again the first week in January.'

'Well it obviously suits you, Simone,' Stacey said. 'You're looking wonderful.'

'But you're not going to go all weird, are you, Mum?' Adam asked. 'Not going to start o-mming and chanting and stuff?'

Simone rolled her eyes. 'Quite possibly,' she said. 'I'll be taking it one day at a time and incorporating anything that works for me.'

Adam sighed. 'So I suppose you'll be moving the furniture around and worrying about energy flows next –'

'That's feng shui,' Simone cut in, 'but who knows? I'm open to anything.'

Since then she has changed her diet, learned to meditate and adopted spiritual practices that support her and have helped to rid her of the tension with which she had lived since her childhood. It changed her mind and her body and several years later she took a course that would enable her to teach yoga. When she was taking her first cautious steps towards retirement, the idea of running a class for older people a couple of times a week was top of her list of possibilities. Fortunately it had coincided with the opening of a new leisure and fitness centre, and she had submitted a 'Yoga for Seniors' proposal. It had been snapped up.

'I thought you were giving up work,' Adam had said a few weeks before she officially retired from the rather posh school where she had taught French for years. 'But now you're taking this on.'

'I'll need something when I retire,' Simone said, watching as he mended the lock on her back door. 'I'll only be sixty-five. I want it to be something worthwhile and satisfying and I think it would be wonderful to see some people get what I've got from it.'

'I imagine that if I ever get to retire I will find doing nothing pretty satisfying,' Adam said over the scream of his electric drill.

Stacey had grinned at Simone from her seat at the bench top. 'Remind me to leave home the day he retires,' she said, and the two women had laughed as Adam continued to struggle with the lock.

Simone looks around the room again. 'That's all for today, thank you,' she says. 'Take care and I'll see you again on Friday.'

A few people help her to roll up the mats, collect the pillows and stack them in the storeroom, and Simone is soon making her way out of the hall to the main entrance and into the street, where she sees Adam leaning against his car in the parking bay. She walks towards him, raising her eyebrows. 'This is a surprise. Is something wrong?'

'Not at all,' Adam says, opening the passenger door for her. He takes a large manila envelope from the front seat and hands it to her. 'This arrived this morning so I thought I'd bring it for you and take you to lunch to celebrate.'

'The contract? Really?' Simone says. 'I thought it might be a couple of weeks.'

Adam shakes his head. 'All done, signed, sealed, delivered.'

Simone hugs him. 'Thank you so much, that's wonderful. I'm so pleased, after all this time. Honestly that place had come to feel like a ball and chain.'

'Well you've done it now,' Adam says, 'and done it at a good time, both in terms of the market and in helping you do what you want to do. Congratulations, Mum. The money will be in your account on settlement.'

Simone slides into the front seat of the car, opens the contract and flicks through the pages. 'A celebratory lunch, definitely,' she says. 'What about Stacey, is she coming too?'

'She'll meet us there,' Adam says, starting the engine.

Later, as they toast the sale of her parents' old property in Queensland, Simone feels a sudden and unexpected twinge of nostalgia. It had been her first home in Australia: a small weatherboard worker's cottage, on a citrus growing property where her father had been sent to work when they had arrived from Italy in the fifties. It was owned by the Marshalls, a once wealthy family, by then in disarray and struggling to keep afloat financially. Malcolm Marshall had been paralysed in a car accident that had also killed his son, Graham, a couple of years earlier. Malcolm was confined to a wheelchair and was now descending into dementia. His wife, Dorothy, and daughter-in-law, Claire, were struggling to manage the business along with caring for him and for Claire's seven-year-old twin sons, Geoffrey and Douglas.

Carlo and his French wife Suzette were energetic and hardworking and Carlo proved able to turn his hand to seemingly anything. He was soon sorting out the business, and also doing some repairs to the main house, which had been built fifty years earlier. And Suzette was helping out with the cooking, the housework and the care of the twins.

Simone was just five when they'd arrived in Australia and her first impression of those early days was of a small, rather bleak little house surrounded by citrus trees, and two identical boys, older than her, pulling faces at her from behind the water tank. By the time the boys were despatched to boarding school four years later, the three of them had grown close and Simone, who had attended the tiny local school with them, missed them dreadfully. When they were home for the holidays Geoff and Doug would briefly flaunt their seniority before once again including her in their games. On her eleventh birthday Simone was horrified when her parents told her that she too was going to boarding school. The prospect of going away to live with nuns and other girls in a small Catholic convent was frightening, but to her own surprise she didn't take long to adjust. The nuns were kind and she became a devout, model pupil. Years later when she read of the terrible treatment of some children in Catholic schools, Simone would reflect on her own good fortune.

Each time she returned home for the holidays something in the little house would have changed: once there was a shiny new bathroom with an inside toilet, another time, a shady front verandah, and later two more bedrooms and a dining room. But other things began to change too, becoming more and more noticeable on each visit. Her parents barely spoke to each other, and the house was filled with strained and awkward silence. Simone spent more and more time with the Marshalls and the questions she might once have asked her mother she began to ask Claire instead. Eventually Carlo bought the cottage and some of the citrus orchards from Claire, who had inherited the estate after Malcolm and then Dorothy died, and continued to manage Claire's property as well as his own smaller one.

'I have to admit to feeling a little bit sad,' Simone says as Adam refills their glasses. 'Mama and Papa loved it so much in the early days, but by the time I was in my teens things had changed. And I really missed Doug and Geoff when they went away to uni, they'd been like brothers to me. By the time I left school I just wanted to get away. I was so thankful to have the chance to go to France to stay with Mama's sister. I couldn't get away fast enough.'

Back from Paris almost three years later, Simone was shocked to discover that the Marshalls had all gone, their house had been sold, and there was no forwarding address. Her parents had made no mention of this in their letters, and now they simply stonewalled all her attempts to find out why they had left. The previous year Geoff and Doug had visited her in Paris as part of an extended holiday. She thinks of that now, the walks by the Seine, the visits to the Louvre, Notre Dame, Place du Tertre and Sacre Coeur. How she had loved the weeks they had spent together then. For the first time in their friendship she was the one with the knowledge and the language, the one they turned to for advice and translation. There were postcards after they left, including one sent from a stopover in Hong Kong on the way home, and then nothing. She was disappointed, but assumed they were busy applying for jobs as well as helping with the work in the orchards.

Arriving home early the following year she was stunned by the unexplained disappearance of her dearest friends and hurt by their failure to stay in touch. Why hadn't they told her they were leaving? Why was there no contact address?

'They just left, sold the house and left,' her mother had told her, tight-lipped. 'We don't know why, it's not our business.'

Simone felt she was hitting her head against a brick wall. It was incomprehensible that Geoff, Doug and Claire would have gone without leaving any trace. Her mother's stubborn intransigence on the subject, and the way her father flew into a temper at the mention of them, convinced her that there was more to the story. Then, one night after a blazing row with her father in which she accused him of hiding something from her, everything changed. Within a few weeks she left home. Her parents continued to live there for the rest of their lives. Suzette had died twenty years ago, Carlo the year before last.

From time to time over the years Simone had tried to find the Marshall boys, but it's a common name and she had nowhere to start. They could be on the other side of the world for all she knew. And then, about a month ago, she had decided she would try one more time on Facebook, where she had often searched before. There were always dozens of Marshalls that showed up with the same first names and none looked as though they could be her Marshalls. But this time there was a Geoff Marshall, who looked as though he could be an older edition of the one she knew. What Simone could see from the limited information was that he lived in the Blue Mountains and was an architect. After so many years of wondering, she had almost made a friend request on the spot. But then she'd got cold feet. Would they really want to hear from her after all these years? Had they wanted to find her it would have been easy, as her parents had lived on in the same place all their lives. The part of her that longed to see them again was in conflict with the hurt and resentment she felt that they had never bothered to contact her.

She looked at the bare lines of information and the photograph in which this Marshall's face was half in shadow. Yes, she'd thought again, it could possibly be him. An architect? She remembered that Geoff had been studying civil engineering but he'd always had a passion for drawing buildings – had he moved sideways into architecture? Doug had wanted to be a chef, and when he'd got his undergrad degree he had stayed on in Melbourne with Geoff and got an apprenticeship. She remembered how when they came to Paris, a few years later, he had impressed her aunt by producing Crêpes Suzette, which she had admitted were better than her own. Simone had gone back to the Facebook list several times and checked that the possible Marshall was still there. And then, a couple of days ago, Adele's email had arrived. Simone was keen to meet the other three women face to face, and felt she could do with a change. She had always planned to travel in Europe once she retired and the house was sold. But right now, a few weeks in the Blue Mountains was just what she needed. *And maybe I'll get in touch and see if it really is Geoff, or maybe I won't. I'll see how I feel when I get there*, she thinks.

Chapter Two

Four days have passed since Adele emailed her idea to the others and both Judy and Simone have responded but there is still no word from Ros. *Four days is not much of course, but how long does Ros need?* Adele wonders, driving into the office underground car park. She is wavering, this morning, between anxiety and irritation; she wants it settled, wants to know if it's all going to happen. As she swings into a vacant bay her phone starts to ring. Reaching for it she misjudges the proximity of a concrete pillar and scrapes the front right wing of the car.

'Shit, shit, shit, that's just what I need!' she says aloud, dropping the phone. And she reverses out to straighten up, sacrificing more paintwork in the process. By the time she has safely made it into the bay the phone has stopped ringing and the caller hasn't left a message. Adele sits there staring at the offending pillar, postponing the moment when she will get out and inspect the extent of the damage. The phone rings again, making her jump, and irritably she snatches it up.

'Adele?' The voice is familiar. 'Hello, Adele, it's me, Ros.

I called just now but then I thought I should have left a message so I was ringing again to do that. Sorry to bother you, is this a difficult time?'

Adele sits bolt upright. 'Oh, Ros, how lovely to hear from you, no, it's not a difficult time, not at all.'

'Good, good, look; it's about your invitation. I'm sorry not to have got back to you sooner, I've just had to think about it a bit . . . work out if I can do it . . .'

'You mean you'd actually like to come?'

'Well of course, I'd love to come, but it's the logistics, you see.'

'Logistics?'

'Yes, I haven't been too well recently. I'm not very mobile, I've stopped driving, so I wondered whether . . . I hope you won't mind my asking this, but if you're flying into Sydney and driving up, I wondered if I could come with you?'

Adele is gobsmacked. 'You mean you'd like us to drive up together?'

'Yes, we don't need a hire car; we could go in mine if you don't mind driving. It's a Volkswagen – automatic, very comfortable . . . only three years old, so if you could drive . . .'

'I'd love to, Ros,' Adele says, 'and I'm so sorry you haven't been well. Hopefully you'll be fine again by the time we set off. So if you *do* want to drive . . .'

'I don't think so. It will be so nice to go with you,' Ros says. 'I just want to ask you one more thing, and it's perfectly okay to say no, it's not like it's a deal-breaker, and I know it's a bit of a cheek, but is it remotely possible for me to bring Clooney with me? I mean, I'd quite understand if . . .'

'Clooney, your dog?'

'Yes, I apologise for even asking, but the usual kennels are fully booked. He's a cocker spaniel, very friendly and clean and reasonably well mannered. He wouldn't damage the furniture or anything like that.'

Adele has the strange feeling that Ros is sounding just like she herself frequently sounds: too apologetic, too much explaining, concerned about asking too much, anxious about how she, Adele, might react.

'I think it will be fine, Ros,' she says, with unusual confidence. 'Obviously I'll have to check with my cousin, but she and Brian love dogs, and other friends have taken their dogs to stay there. I'll call them, and I suppose I should check with Judy and Simone too, just in case. Why don't I email them all and then get back to you?'

'Would you? That's very kind, and look, as I said, it's not vital. I have a new tenant moving into the upstairs flat, so I might be able to ask him to feed and walk Clooney . . . but if you wouldn't mind checking . . .'

*

A couple of weeks later, reflecting on her original conversation with Adele, Ros is still puzzling over her own determination to accept the book club invitation. Asking Adele about Clooney had been difficult, as had asking her to drive; she always hated asking favours, but this was especially hard because it had a hint of dependence and neediness about it. The easiest thing would have been to decide not to go at all, but from the moment she'd read Adele's email Ros had known that she would get there, whatever it took. Her determination to go to the Blue Mountains, to be part of this odd little gathering, has surprised her. Ros is not a naturally sociable person; she is an introvert who senses herself dissolving into nothingness if she doesn't get enough quiet time alone to recharge her batteries. The book club was larger when she first joined, and it was the fact that it was online that had attracted her. It meant she didn't have to socialise, and it was easy to sit back and just listen and think about what was said, without contributing much if that suited her. They talked about the books they read each month, and other books as well, but their lives had not become entangled.

The phone call had proved easier than she had anticipated. Adele had always seemed to be a very nice person, but lacking in self-confidence. It's hard in a group like theirs to get to really know someone, and Ros feels that she knows Simone and Judy, who are more recent members, better than she knows Adele who, like Ros herself, has been part of it since the very early days. What she does know about Adele is that she seems to lack the resilience or the confidence to offer a conflicting opinion, and that had been on Ros's mind when she called her. She had been super careful to avoid any of the sort of remarks which, James had once told her, were not half as amusing as she assumed, and sometimes potentially upsetting. But it had gone well, especially the bit about driving there, and she knows that having Clooney with her will make her more confident; not that she would ever admit that to anyone else.

'I thought you didn't like sociable things, getting together, staying in other people's houses, Ros,' Leah says when she pops in later to see both her and Tim upstairs. 'You used to avoid things like that, and be all grumpy about having to find a way to say no.'

'I know,' Ros says. 'Perhaps I'm going soft. Tim's turning out to be an ideal tenant, by the way, pleasant, quiet and very helpful. He even takes Clooney for walks.'

Leah nods. 'He's a really nice guy, I'm very fond of him.' She reaches down to stroke Clooney, who immediately rolls over for a tummy rub.

Leah has arrived tonight wearing a long black dress, a purple jacket, and new purple suede boots. Ros studies her, smiling, thinking how gorgeous she looks, how different from the pale and scruffy fourteen-year-old who, twenty-five years ago, had sat just where she is sitting now, clutching her violin in its battered case.

'Of course you can stay here,' James had said. Leah was his niece and he knew his younger brother's capacity for drunken violence. 'I'll deal with your father.' Then he had marched out of the house and they heard the car roar off down the street. Ros and Leah had been left facing each other across the kitchen bench.

'What about you?' Leah had asked, her eyes dark with misery. 'Will it be all right? Do you mind?'

'Of course not,' Ros said, 'of course I don't mind. Tonight you'll have to sleep in the little spare room. But tomorrow you and I will sort out the back bedroom, the big one that has its own small bathroom. We'll make it into a proper place of your own. You'll be quite safe here, Leah.'

In fact, Ros *had* minded, she'd minded quite a lot. She and James had decided years earlier that they would not have children; they cherished their quiet life, and the freedom that it provided for them both to concentrate on doing the things they loved most. James had just been made a professor, and in addition to teaching was researching a book on British fascism in the pre-war years. Ros was playing with the Sydney Symphony and a quartet, and giving a few private cello lessons at home. The last thing either of them had wanted or needed was a distressed teenager in the house.

Ros drags herself back to the present, pulls out a cheese board, takes brie and cheddar from the fridge and tips crackers from their packet into a small wooden bowl.

'I think I'll enjoy it,' she says. 'After all, a few weeks in a beautiful house in the Blue Mountains is not to be sniffed at, and I probably need a change of scene.'

'It's great,' Leah says. 'You may discover a new talent for sociability! And you'll start going to parties and openings, hosting soirees, and cruising down the Rhine with a bunch of other women.'

Ros chokes on the merlot Leah has just poured for her. 'Don't hold your breath,' she says eventually. 'James used to say that I was already a grumpy old woman when he married me, and I was only twenty-nine then, so I doubt I'm going to become all sweetness and light and hostess with the mostest at this age!'

'Nothing is impossible,' Leah says, 'and this will do you good. You look worn out. Did you get the results of all those tests yet?'

'Not yet,' Ros lies. 'Maybe next week.' And she quickly changes the subject.

Later, when they have polished off most of the wine and Leah has headed off home, Ros joins Clooney, who is now stretched out on the sofa.

'I'm looking forward to it, I really am,' she says. 'You and me and the dames from the book club, up in the Blue Mountains. What d'you think of that?' She tugs his ear and he looks up at her expectantly, and then farts.

'Shit, Clooney, that is truly revolting,' Ros says, waving her hand to dispel the fumes. 'I know you're getting on a bit now but so am I and I don't fart at people. I think I'll have to get you some charcoal tablets before we head off, or you might be banned.'

Ros picks up the television guide, searching for something to watch. *It's all rubbish these days*, she tells James. *You'd go bananas if you could see it.* She discovers a documentary on SBS and flicks through the channels. *So what do you think of this Blue Mountains caper? I bet you're having a sneaky laugh up there, aren't you? Wondering how those three nice women will put up with me? Well I'm wondering that, too, so I shall try to be on my best behaviour.*

*

'I'm leaving in two-and-a-half weeks,' Judy tells Donna on the phone, 'so I won't be down until after I get back. Tell Ted that if he wants anything else sent from here he'd better let me know as soon as possible. I'll be away for five or six weeks.'

'That's quite a long time, considering you barely know each other,' Donna says. 'It sounds like that book you gave me years ago – the one about the four women who rent a villa in Italy and all sorts of strange and wonderful things happen. A husband turns up, and the man who owns the house falls in love with one of the women . . .'

'*The Enchanted April*,' Judy cuts in. 'I have a DVD of that; I might take it with me. Anyway, I don't think there will be any husbands or lovers turning up at this gathering!'

'You never know, Ted might decide to join you.'

They both splutter with laughter at the prospect of Ted spontaneously taking off to the Blue Mountains.

'Well it's up to you to make sure that *doesn't* happen,' Judy says. 'But I doubt you'll have to nail his feet to the floor.'

'I'm so glad you're going, Jude,' Donna says. 'Who's going to look after the shop?'

'Melissa, and her mum. Remember I took Melissa on part-time recently? At the moment she's doing two afternoons a week. She's a single mother with an eighteen-month-old baby, but she's very organised and terrific with the customers.

Her mother, Pam, is helping out with the shop as well, and babysitting for Mel. They'll both do a great job, and –'

'And they do exactly as you instruct them to the letter and are not allowed to have ideas of their own,' Donna cuts in.

'Well . . . well . . .' Judy hesitates. She and Donna have had this conversation before. 'It's complicated,' she says.

'No, Jude, it really isn't. You just need to get things in order and then let go.'

'Oh well, maybe we'll talk about that when I get back.'

'I bet we won't,' Donna says. 'Anyway, I am delighted you're doing this reading retreat thing, darl. It'll be a nice break. What about your Suffolk project, how's it going?'

Judy sighs. 'I was going to take some of it with me, but then I decided to make a little visual tour of it on my iPad to show them – that is, if I feel confident enough when I get there. At the moment you and Ted are the only people who know about it.'

When they hang up Judy stays behind the counter watching a couple of women discussing wool colours. She feels a sudden twinge of envy at their obviously easy relationship, their shared involvement in this decision. She imagines them shopping together for all sorts of things, talking and laughing over lunch or coffee, the way she and Donna had done sometimes years ago when they could both get away for a weekend in Perth. She has missed that, missed Donna; in fact she has missed Donna more than she has missed Ted, ever since the day she left the Wheatbelt, and that was a lifetime ago. But since her recent panic attack she hasn't missed either of them. She has, instead, been entirely focused on getting away, escaping to the Blue Mountains, escaping from Mandurah, the business, and Donna and Ted. *This will fix everything*, she keeps telling herself. *I'll come back rested and refreshed and put this behind me.* And she is intent on drawing up a plan for Melissa, so she can find her way through the business side of things. Fortunately Melissa herself seems undaunted by the lack of proper files, although she does venture in to the office and start tidying things from time to time. One saving grace is that some years ago Judy did get someone to show her how to save things to the cloud, and how to use Dropbox. She's never used them but she's determined to go through the instructions again before she goes.

'We'll be able to read the same things and update them and save them,' she'd told Melissa. 'That'll make things easier.'

'Whatever,' Melissa had said. 'It'll be fine, we'll sort it out.'

But while Judy tries to absorb the information on clouds and dropboxes she daydreams about escape. And her nights are filled with dreams of being trapped in a small dark room, hammering on a door, screaming for help, and she wakes with her head spinning, her bedclothes tangled, hands clasped into fists leaving fingernail marks on her palms.

*

It's a freezing cold evening in Hobart and Simone is curled up on the sofa watching a movie when her mobile rings. She sees it's Adele. *This is a first*, she thinks.

'I hope you won't mind me calling,' Adele says. 'I made a list of dot points from everyone's suggestions, and then I pulled them together as a sort of program, or . . . or something. I'm not sure what to call it. I was wondering if I could email it to you and maybe you'd go through it? I'm going to add some more pictures, maps, ideas for places nearby to visit, once I've got the text right.'

'Sure,' Simone says, wondering why Adele has picked her. 'I'd be happy to if you think it would help. Are you going to send it now?'

'This minute,' Adele says. And sure enough seconds later the email signals its arrival with a beep.

'Okay, I'll read it now. Want me to call or email back?'

'Oh, call, please,' Adele says, and Simone thinks she sounds quite jittery.

Reluctantly, Simone uncurls herself, goes to the computer and opens and prints the email attachment. Back on the sofa she reads it carefully, marking some points to mention and a couple of minor typos. Then she dials Adele's number.

'This is great, Adele,' she says. 'Really terrific. It's so good to have it all set out like this. I must admit I hadn't really thought about all the things we'd need to know, and it's lovely to have the maps and the info on interesting places.'

'Phew, thank goodness,' Adele says. 'I'm relieved you think it's okay.'

'I certainly do, but you really don't need to worry. I mean, it's good to have an indication of what to expect but in the end there are only four of us – we can always change things, swap them around if that's what we think we need to do.'

'But it's very important to get it *right*,' Adele insists. 'And, of course, *clear*, especially the bit about how we manage the reading discussions. We don't want anyone getting upset or annoyed.'

Simone bites her lip to stop herself laughing. 'I really don't think that's going to happen,' she says. 'But I agree, we need to be clear about it and about what we hope to get from the discussions.'

'What we want to *get*,' Adele says, 'is something *more* than a discussion of the book itself: it's also chance to get to know each other better.'

The urgency of Adele's concern about this intrigues Simone. To her it seems obvious that by being together in the same house for what has now been agreed on as a period of five to six weeks, they can hardly avoid getting to know each other better. But she is starting to understand that Adele has more invested in this than she had realised. Simone senses that if the others aren't happy, if someone complains about any aspect of the plan, Adele will see it as a failure on her part.

Simone has not previously thought of Adele as neurotic, but there does seem to be an element of neurosis in the way she's handling this. She wonders whether she's likely to be as het-up as this the whole time they're there, and hopes not because she's not sure how long she'll be able to cope if Adele turns out to be like this about everything.

A couple of weeks later Adele sends them all the final version of the program, which is impressive even when reproduced on Simone's ancient colour printer. The travel arrangements are clear. Adele will drive Ros and Clooney in Ros's car, while Judy and Simone will meet at Sydney airport, pick up a rental car and drive to the house together. They should all aim to arrive between two and four o'clock on Thursday, 28 July, when a friend of the owners will be there to meet them, show them around and explain how everything works.

Friday evening and Saturday will be very relaxed, and on Sunday they will discuss the book that had been picked for their July meeting before any of these plans had been made. *'Tirra Lirra by the River' by Jessica Anderson, make sure to bring your copy with you*, Adele had written. *This should get us in good form for the personal choices to follow.*

After the discussion they will draw lots to determine the order in which the personal choice books will be read.

Please choose a book that will tell us all something significant about you. Be prepared to be honest about why you have chosen it and why it matters to you. This makes it more than just a suggested read, it is an invitation from each one of us to the others to get to know each other better. Do not reveal or discuss your choice of book until it's your turn to introduce it to the group.

Simone had loved the sentiment here, but had been concerned about Adele's prescriptive tone in the first draft. She wondered whether Adele had ever been a teacher, and how this paragraph might go down with, say, Ros, who seemed unlikely to enjoy being told in such firm and specific tones what, and what not, to do. Even so, she understood why Adele had worked it out that way – the structure really was designed to get the best results.

'It's the only way to contain the discussions within their frame of purpose,' Adele had said when Simone raised this with her on the phone. 'If people start chatting about their book beforehand it won't have the same impact. The conversations will be going off in all directions before we start and while we're reading something else. We do have to be quite disciplined about it, Simone. It doesn't matter if someone has read the book before, they can read it again within this frame of purpose.'

And somehow, in the context of a full, well-presented document, it sounded fine.

Reading time for each book is from Sunday evening until the following Saturday. Each of us will introduce her own book choice – don't forget to bring copies of your book for the rest of us, they can be second-hand ones if you wish. Do not reveal your book choice to anyone before introducing it to the group. Keep the introduction short. Then the following Sunday please open the discussion by telling us why you chose the book, what it means to you and why. Then we can all discuss it.

There are other details in the program – stuff about food,

possible cooking arrangements, eating out, keeping the house clean . . . all perfectly reasonable and to be discussed and agreed on the first evening. Lots are to be drawn for the bedrooms. There should be a discussion during the first weekend to deal with *the balance that will accommodate our individual preferences for spending time quietly alone, versus group activities.*

'Are you sure we need that last bit?' Simone had asked of the earlier draft. 'It'll probably work out quite naturally, and we *are* there to get to know each other, after all.' There had been an audible sigh at the other end of the phone line. 'I'm just thinking it's sounding a bit like micro-managing,' Simone ventured.

'Don't you need to know you'll get time alone when you want it?' Adele asked.

'Um . . . well yes, now you've put it that way, I suppose I do.'

'Me too, so that's fifty per cent of the group. There only has to be one person who doesn't get that and it could become very difficult. We need to get it out in the open right at the start.'

When she thought about it later Simone realised that Adele's decisiveness was rather surprising and not what she'd expected. She also thought Adele was probably right and guessed that she might have had Judy in mind when she said that. She was certainly the most talkative, and the one most likely to take the conversation in unrelated directions.

Simone reads the document again now, admiring the beautiful photographs of the mountains, the colourful little maps, perfectly placed between the sections of the text. It's like a high-class retreat or tour brochure, one that's packed with plenty of welcoming messages, useful information, and rules that are not to be messed with. She calls Adele's mobile.

'You've done a superb job with this, Adele,' she says. 'I'm sure Judy and Ros will love it too.'

'I actually got my executive assistant to do the layout,' Adele says, obviously relieved. 'She's a whiz with things like this and she's printing and laminating some hard copies that I'll give to everyone when we get there. I'm so relieved you think it's okay.'

Simone has never considered that Adele might work at a level in which she has an executive assistant. Her apparent lack of confidence and her determination to avoid any sort of conflict have been the central features of her participation in the book club meetings and none of that seems to fit with seniority in the workplace.

'What exactly is it that you do, Adele?' Simone asks, slightly embarrassed that she knows so little about this woman who's been an online friend for several years.

'Oh! Well, I work in a bureau that designs and delivers study tours for a group of universities in Australia and overseas. You know, the sort of academic tours where there are lectures and symposia along the way.'

'Like a travel agency?'

'Only in a very basic sort of way. The bureau is a collaborative project and the groups include academics and some higher degree students who have to do the assignments as credits for their degrees. We plan the tours for them, write all the study materials, recommend the readings and manage the bookings. So it can get quite complex.'

'How interesting, and what's your role there?'

'Oh, well . . . I . . . well, I'm the director.'

Simone catches her breath. 'Really? So you're in charge of all that?'

'Yes . . . I mean, I report to the board of course, but yes, I'm in charge, I suppose.'

'I'd no idea,' Simone said. 'That's a pretty complex job, I imagine?'

'I've been doing it a long time. And actually tomorrow is my last day,' Adele says. 'I'm retiring. So this chance to have a holiday in the Blue Mountains came at just the right time. I hope it's going to break me in gently to the first weeks of life without a job.'

'Wow, that's a big step. You never mentioned it before – retirement, I mean.'

'Er . . . no, well we mainly talk about the books, don't we? But I'm that age – you know how it is – time to make way for the younger ones and do one's own thing; not that I'm really sure what my thing is! So anyway, I'm looking forward to this and it will be nice for us to get to know each other better. If it all goes well, of course . . . if . . .'

'No ifs, Adele. It's going to be terrific,' Simone says. 'We're all going to get along fine. And if anyone does have a grumpy day, or people fall out about something, well, we'll get over it. We're grown-ups, after all.'

'Yes . . .' Adele sounds more nervous than ever now. 'So you think we *might* fall out?'

Simone takes a couple of deep breaths. 'Not necessarily, I'm just saying that if some of us *did* it would all be fine. We have to be natural and relaxed together and sometimes someone gets on someone else's nerves and there's some sulking or an argument. You know how it is among friends.'

There was a long pause. 'Actually,' Adele says, 'I've never been away with friends before. In fact I don't really have friends. It's work, I suppose, I just seem to have colleagues, and well . . . acquaintances, people I know . . . I live alone and I don't seem to meet other people. That's why the club is so important to me. That fixed time once a month to talk with you all about something not related to work. I set this thing up, Simone, and the prospect of it failing is pretty scary.'

Ten minutes later Simone puts the phone down. *Very odd*, she thinks. She's always thought Adele was an anxiety bunny, and then thought she was perhaps a bit of a control freak, and now it turns out that she *is* a control freak *because* she's an anxiety bunny. Simone sits in the silence thinking about Adele, how she will cope with this new stage of her life for which she seems unprepared. Does she have too much invested in this book club in the mountains plan? It sounds as though she may be relying on it to sort out her retirement. Simone thinks Adele would probably be a good candidate for yoga, but then Simone thinks that about most people. It might help reduce her anxiety, which seems more acute to Simone now than it has in the past. She wonders what book Adele will bring. What else she might learn about her, and indeed the other two, from their book choices?

She gets up suddenly and picks up the book she intended to take – the book she'd ordered three more copies of when Adele had first suggested this. It was one of her greatest favourites – Margaret Drabble's *The Witch of Exmoor*. Simone studies the cover, flicks through the pages, then closes it decisively. It's the wrong book, she can see that now. It's a favourite and there's heaps to talk about in it, but what would it tell them about her that they don't already know? She drops it onto the coffee table, hurries through to her bedroom and from the drawer in the bedside table she takes out the book that she has kept there for years, the book she's thought about continually since she read it more than ten years ago. The book that she always felt she would never be able to discuss with anyone.

For a long moment Simone stands there, staring at the cover. It's not quite two weeks until the trip – too late to order it through the local bookshop but she should be able to get three copies online if she pays for express post. She puts down the book, walks over to the computer and types the title into the search bar.

Chapter Three

'So what book are you taking?' Melissa asks, putting two mugs of tea down on the counter.

Judy opens her mouth and closes it again. 'Um . . . well I haven't finally decided yet,' she lies, thinking of the four copies of the book that are sitting on her coffee table at home, knowing instantly that she doesn't want to discuss the book with Melissa.

'Wow! You'd better hurry up,' Melissa says. 'I know! You could take that one we were talking about the other day – you know, the Liane Moriarty one. That's amazing.'

'You mean *Big Little Lies*?'

'That's it. *Everyone's* talking about it. It's going to be a TV series. Nicole Kidman and Reese whatshername are in it. I loved that book.'

'Reese Witherspoon,' Judy says. 'Yes, it's a great book.'

'You know that it was Nicole Kidman who decided to get it made into a series?' Melissa continues. 'She read it and she's friends with Reese . . . thingy, they're both in it. But it was made in America, in California. I mean, why not here? That's what I want to know. I am never going to forgive Nicole for letting that happen.'

Judy smiles. 'Oh well, I'm sure it'll be really good. I suppose it's hard to resist the lure of the US film industry. Anyway, Mel, are you sure you and Pam are going to be able to manage here while I'm away?'

'No worries. Mum and I have got it all worked out, we'll divide the shop and looking after Jack between us. We know who's doing what and when, and we've got my Aunty Chris set up for babysitting too, so we can both be here in the busy times. You don't need to worry, Judy, we'll do a good job for you, we won't let you down.'

'I'm not worried about that,' Judy says, 'but I *am* concerned about you – you have a lot on your plate. I want you to promise that if anything happens and you can't get here one day then you'll just get someone to come in and put a note on the door saying when you'll reopen. It won't be the end of the world if you have to close it for a day or two. Promise?'

'I promise, but no way is that going to happen. So . . . not long now. Are you looking forward to it?'

'Very much,' Judy says, wondering if that's true. 'I'm a bit nervous too. I hardly know the other women. I hope we'll get on all right.'

'Course you will. You said you've been in this club for years? So you must know each other really well.'

'Not really. It's not like a normal book club. Being online means there are limits to how well we could possibly know each other. None of us has ever met other than on Skype.'

'It'll be great, I bet you. Mum says you'll love it; she loves her book club friends. She reckons you'll be ringing us, asking if it's okay if you stay away longer.'

Judy laughs. 'I doubt that. I just hope I can keep up with

them. They're all a lot smarter than me. Ros is a musician; she used to play with the Sydney Symphony Orchestra. I'm not sure what Adele does, I think she might be some sort of manager. And Simone was a teacher. She speaks French and taught it in a very posh school. She's retired now, and she teaches yoga.'

'So she'll have you all doing your *asanas* first thing in the morning.'

'Our what?'

'*Asanas*, you know, in yoga.'

Judy shakes her head. 'I *don't* know. What's an "asana"?'

Melissa pulls a face, then grins. 'Actually I'm not really sure; I just know it's something you do in yoga. I think it might be one of the positions you have to sit in.'

Judy raises her eyebrows. 'And you wonder why I'm anxious?'

'You're not worrying about something like that, are you? I mean, Judy, you are so smart. Mum said this shop was going down the drain when you took it on. She remembers because she was working in the real estate agency when you were trying to take over the lease. And now look at it. You're a natural businesswoman, Mum says. Actually even Dad says it too. You're a legend in Mandurah! Don't look at me like that, I mean it.'

Two women, regular customers, have wandered in from the street.

'She's right, Judy, you're a legend,' one says.

And the other one nods. 'Sure are,' she says. 'You're a Mandurah identity now, Jude.'

Judy's face is on fire with embarrassment. She puts a hand on Melissa's arm. 'Bless you, Mel. Can you look after these dames, please?' And she hurries out to the washroom, shuts the door behind her, splashes her cheeks with cold water then stares at herself in the mirror. *You're getting old, Judy*, she tells herself, patting her face with a paper towel *No, you're* already *old, seventy-three is actually old! And you really look it.* She peers closely at her face, wondering why it is that wrinkles look okay on some women but not on others – Helen Mirren is about the same age, Judi Dench is in her eighties – they have wrinkles but somehow they seem to wear them a whole lot better. 'Make-up, darling!' she says, doing a glamour pose. 'Make-up!' But frankly she can't be bothered, and at least she has good hair. She'd hated it when she was younger, thought she looked like a poodle and had spent a fortune on trying to straighten it, but it remained relentlessly curly and ginger. Going grey had been her salvation, because she'd actually gone more silver than grey, and now, with her hair cut short like this it always seems to look good. *Be thankful for small mercies,* she tells herself, and runs her damp hands through it, watching with pleasure as it springs back into shape.

She thinks about the book she's taking. *If they don't like it, it doesn't matter,* she tells herself; they don't have to like it, they just have to read it and try to understand what it means to her. It's pretty bloody straightforward, and it's a really good read. *What might the others bring?* she wonders. Hopefully they won't be really hard to read. There have been books like that over the years, books that she just didn't *get,* that were way above her head, and she'd put in her apologies and missed a meeting to avoid the embarrassment of trying to be part of the conversation. *Oh well, if there is a book like that when we're all sitting together in a room, I'll have to come clean.*

Quite a long time ago, and certainly well before Adele came up with this idea, she'd read her chosen book again and really wanted to talk about it, but she knew Donna wouldn't enjoy it. She might even laugh at it, it was an odd sort of book, but she's become so fond of it, she wouldn't be able to bear it if Donna thought it was rubbish. She doesn't think the book club will laugh or think it's rubbish. They're used to discussing books, they might not like it but they would never laugh at anyone's choice. *It'll be good,* she tells herself, *such a relief to get away. No shop, no customers, no stupid questions, no one asking me to sort out what they've done wrong in their knitting. Bliss, just what I need and when I get home I'll feel better about everything again, and I won't wake up each morning wanting to set fire to the bloody shop!* But when she thinks of coming back here afterwards she feels the panic start to rise again.

*

'Well if you're staying we could order a pizza or pop down to the corner and pick up fish and chips,' Ros says, pulling a beer from the fridge. 'But Clooney still hasn't had his walk.'

'I'll take him,' Tim says, getting to his feet, 'and I'll have that beer when I get back. I vote for fish and chips.'

Ros puts the beer back in the fridge. 'Thanks, Tim, that'd be good. Yes, fish and chips is my preference. Leah, what about you?'

'Fine by me,' Leah says. 'If we ring the fish and chip shop and order then you could pick it up on the way back, Tim.'

'He is the best ever tenant,' Ros says, handing Leah a glass of wine as the front door closes behind Tim and Clooney.

'Not better than me, surely?' Leah asks, grinning.

'Well no, let's just say more useful,' Ros says. 'After all, you were only a teenager at the time. Tim's a grown-up.'

'He's always been like that,' Leah says. 'Boringly responsible and well balanced.'

'Exactly. Rather like James, totally reliable and responsible, unlike you or me. And you've known him for years and never introduced us before he turned up at the front door. On that first day I thought he was a James-type man, and wondered why you didn't marry *him* years ago.'

'Because, perversely, I married Ivan.'

'Indeed you did, against my advice.'

'I loved Ivan. You can't argue with that.'

'Sure I can,' Ros said. 'Seductive as it is, love is not always enough.' She knows she's sounding like a boring old woman but she's always been edgy about Ivan, despite his good looks, smooth talk and obvious generosity.

Leah gives an awkward laugh. 'I've never really understood why you don't like him.'

'I *do* like him,' Ros insists, 'I just don't quite *get* him. All that dark Slavic brooding. It's always unnerved me. But I suppose it's all in my head. Love is strange, isn't it, and it's often so incomprehensible to other people.'

'It is, although of course James and you – that wasn't incomprehensible at all.'

'No, that was about as straightforward as it comes,' Ros agrees, wishing he were here now to be part of this conversation. It had always seemed so easy for both of them; they were, as James had once said, 'a perfect fit'. 'Mutual love at first sight,' Ros says now, 'and we were just so lucky that, despite some difficult periods, we managed to keep it that way. All this time and I still miss him every day. Especially now in view of the circumstances.'

'What circumstances?' Leah asks, suddenly alert.

'Oh well,' Ros says, mentally kicking herself for not thinking before she spoke. 'Well, you know . . .' She looks out of the window into the shadowy garden to avoid eye contact, gathering her thoughts. 'You know, getting old and doddery and all that stuff.'

Leah leans forward. 'You've heard from the hospital, haven't you?'

'No,' Ros lies. 'No, not yet. I said I'd tell you.'

The silence is loaded with Leah's disbelief. 'It's taking an awfully long time.'

'Mmm. Well there were tests to do, and no news is good news, isn't it? I mean, if I was about to drop off my perch I'm jolly sure I'd have heard something by now.'

Leah takes a deep breath. 'I'm not sure I trust you on this, Ros.'

'I'm fine, honestly,' Ros says, still avoiding eye contact. She really does not want to get into all this with Leah now, not before she goes away, not before she's ready. 'I'll tell you when I know anything. By the time I get back from my holiday in the mountains I'm sure there'll be some news.'

Awkward silence again, a silence weighted with everything that Ros is not saying.

Leah picks up her phone. 'I'll order the food.'

'And I'll get Clooney's dinner ready,' Ros says, relieved to change the subject, flexing her right hand in the hope of stopping the shaking, 'or he'll be wanting to share the fish and chips.'

'So what book did you decide to take?' Leah asks when she has made the call.

'I'm still weighing that up,' Ros says, wondering how many more lies she will have to tell this evening. 'I thought first about taking *On Chesil Beach,* have you read it?'

'Oh lord, yes I have, you lent it to me, remember? I hated it. It's all so uptight and restrained. I almost ended up throwing it at the wall.'

Ros laughs. 'It's because you're so young. You have no idea how difficult anything to do with sex was for those of us who were young in the fifties. And even the early sixties – not all of that decade was swinging, you know.'

'But the book was so *dull*,' Leah insists, 'so grindingly prim and dull.'

'It was spot on,' Ros said, laughing. 'Absolutely spot on and very moving. *Life* was pretty dull then, especially for the young. Anyway, I decided against it, because much as I enjoyed that book and related to it, it didn't really fit the criteria.'

'Which is?'

'It has to be a book that tells the others something about ourselves.'

Leah raised her eyebrows. 'Sounds like *Chesil Beach* would have done that for you.'

Ros studies the dog meat, grips the knife and cautiously begins to chop it. 'There's a difference between the contents of a book being something that you can relate to, and something that actually tells other people something about you – don't you think?'

Leah shrugs and takes a swig of wine. 'Maybe. I'm not sure that I can tell the difference. I might, of course, if you'd tell me what you've ended up choosing – because you obviously *have* chosen something.'

Ros stops chopping and looks straight at her. 'Well okay, yes, I have, and I don't want to talk about it now, because I am thinking about the reasons I feel so connected to it. I'm just not ready to discuss that yet. I'll tell you when I get back.'

She looks away again, hoping that Leah can't see her fear, can't see how vulnerable she feels. Despite knowing that Leah's probing is driven by love and concern, Ros just wants to shake her and tell her to shut up, stay out of it, until she, herself, is ready to talk.

'I see. Like you'll tell me about the test results, which you also obviously already know, when you get back?'

The silence is leaden, and Ros seesaws between fierce resentment and the need to burst into tears and tell Leah everything. She puts down the knife and looks her in the eye again. 'Yes,' she says. 'Exactly that. I will tell you everything when I get back. I promise.'

'Okay,' Leah says, slowly and very deliberately. 'And if there is anything in the meantime, anything at all that I should know, you'll call and talk to me?' She gets to her feet and walks to face Ros across the bench top. 'You're like a mother to me, Ros. You and James were like parents, the best sort of parents that you can talk to, be honest with, totally trust. I was fourteen and heading off the rails, and you dragged me and my violin back from that. I am always here for you, always. I hope you understand that.'

Ros puts down the knife. 'I do, darling,' she says, 'and it means more to me than you'll ever know. But do you remember how long it took you to tell me that you'd actually agreed to marry Ivan? In case you've forgotten, it was seven months.'

Leah's face twitches in an awkward smile.

'Seven frigging months,' Ros continues. 'So you'll understand that sometimes you have to hold back on talking about really important things to the people you love most. And sometimes you really *don't* want them to be the first people you discuss it with because it's simply too hard. It has to be processed elsewhere first, somewhere not so close to home.'

'I suppose.'

'No! You don't *suppose*, Leah, you really do know. So can you let me off this hook and trust me to find the right time?'

Leah nods, looks up at Ros. 'Of course, if that's what you need, of course I can.'

'Good. And just so you know, the other book I had in mind was Julian Barnes's *Nothing to Be Frightened Of*, which is all

59

about the fear of dying, and I didn't pick that either, so I hope you'll find that reassuring.'

'I do,' Leah says, 'I really do. But of course I've never understood why you are so obsessed with some of those English blokes, to me they're boring old farts. What's wrong with Tim Winton or Tom Keneally?'

Ros laughs. 'Nothing, nothing at all, they're brilliant, but they just don't speak to me in the way that Barnes and McEwan, or Blake Morrison, do. Now let's get some plates in the oven to warm. Tim and Clooney will be back in a minute and we'll still be here navel gazing about books.'

*

Adele wanders around her little courtyard, noticing how bare it is: just the paving, a built-in brick trough for plants, a table and a couple of chairs and nothing else. She hasn't really noticed how bleak it looks until now. *That's what giving up work does*, she thinks, *now I've got time on my hands I suppose I'll notice all sorts of things I ought to do. I need flowers in that trough, and some big pots with plants or a small tree or something. As soon as I get back.*

She has been restless since she walked out of the office for the last time a week ago, restless and directionless. It wasn't as though she'd *wanted* to retire, it had just seemed to be the thing she was supposed to do – that she was actually supposed to *want* to do in her sixties. She hasn't given much thought to how she'll adapt to not working or what she wants at this stage of her life. It ought to be exciting but having been locked into working so long, she's more concerned now with how she'll adapt to being without it. How will she structure her days? What will she do now that she can actually please herself? Her habits are so ingrained and some will have to change, but what and when? She is still getting up at six every morning, making tea, and drinking it sitting at the bench top while she listens to Fran Kelly terrorising politicians and captains of industry on Radio National. Adele loves Fran Kelly: she's tough and relentless, and she sounds as though she knows what she wants and how to get it. No one, however internationally famous and important, seems to faze her. Sometimes Adele tries to imagine what it would be like to get up every morning in the wee small hours (does Fran Kelly ever actually sleep?), walk into that studio, put on her headphones and grab the world by the throat. For Adele, the fascinating thing about Fran Kelly is that although Fran can do all that, she also sounds like a nice person. *Just a thin slice of that,* she thinks, *would do me very nicely.*

Adele is well aware that since she gave up work she no longer has to listen to RN sitting at the worktop in the kitchen, drinking tea and eating her two slices of wholemeal toast with sliced avocado, salt and a squeeze of lemon. She could make her tea and take it back to bed with her. Indeed, she could stay in bed all day if she wanted, or sit in an armchair with her feet up in her dressing gown and watch the ABC morning news program. It would, however, be a poor substitute for Breakfast with Fran.

Adele knows nothing about leisure, because she has become a manic workaholic. In recent months she's tried to get to grips with her doctor's suggestion that she was burning herself out. That, and the whole thing of the sixties being the decade of retirement, is why she is home today, retired, but still listening to Fran at six in the morning. So perhaps it's too soon; perhaps the best thing to do until she goes away is to stick with the old routine, and try to change things when she gets back. In any case, she would still always want to listen to Fran Kelly, so maybe she'll get some headphones – or are they called earpieces these days? Whatever! It would mean she could listen while she goes for walks in the mountains, assuming, of course, that she can get a signal. She almost stops breathing at the prospect of not having access to RN, but of course it'll be okay in the house, just perhaps not while walking. Since her conversations with Simone about the program Adele has been feeling pretty comfortable with the arrangements. She is used to making plans for strangers, and feeling confident about them until the final few days, when her anxiety starts to mount. *By the time I get to Ros's I'll be a dithering mass of insecurity again,* she thinks. *Perhaps Simone would teach me a bit of yoga.*

'You are, of course, addicted to this state of confusion and anxiety,' the ghastly Astrid had told her all those years ago.

But Adele had already known that and still does. *You are a lost cause, Adele,* she tells herself now, which was probably what Astrid had been thinking at the time.

Back inside the house she turns the radio off. Fran finished her shift an hour or so ago and The World Today is still a couple of hours away.

'Do you think you might be a bit obsessed with Radio National, Mum?' Jenna had asked when she flew over from Quebec for a month last year. 'You do tend to talk about the presenters as though they're your friends.'

'I know,' Adele said. 'I mean, I do hate the summer when all my favourite presenters go on holiday and I'm expected to listen to strangers. It's like being deserted by one's family.'

'Like your daughter falling in love, getting married and taking off to live in Canada, you mean?' Jenna said, grinning.

'Well yes, I suppose so . . . a bit anyway.'

'Mum!' Jenna said firmly. 'It's time to get a life.'

'When I retire,' Adele said. 'When I retire I will get a life but I'm not yet clear about what that life will be.'

Since then not much has changed. Although she has now retired, she still has no idea how to get a life, or what sort of life she wants. And although it feels quite odd, not having work to go to, she realises she's not actually missing it, in fact she might even be a bit relieved.

'It's great that you're going to this book club thing,' Jenna had said when she'd Skyped at the weekend. 'It hasn't been healthy for you, this focus on work to the exclusion of everything else. I mean, when did you last go out to lunch with a friend, or go to the movies, or do something normal like that? And please don't bother trying to answer that because I know it's been an unbelievably long time, years probably. Please, Mum, now you've retired just try to work out what you want. Something that will be good for you, something that will nourish your soul.'

Adele wonders if Jenna has any idea how daunting, how totally beyond her that sounds. *Simone*, she thinks, *maybe she could help*. She'd been so nice and helpful on the phone, and Ros was nice too. And quite suddenly Adele does something that is so out of character that she can barely believe she's doing it. She goes to her contacts, brings up Simone's number and writes a text.

Any chance you could give me a bit of coaching to start me on yoga? She clicks 'Send'. She is immediately so horrified by what she's done that her neck and armpits begin to prickle with sweat. Fortunately Simone replies straight away.

Love to. Looking forward to it. x

Adele blinks and looks again at the message, or at least at the little *x* at the end. Simone has sent her a kiss, just as Jenna always does, though Jenna sends about ten. How unexpected is that, a kiss from Simone? It makes her feel stronger somehow. What a relief it will be to be able to think about just one thing at a time.

'What book are you taking?' Jenna had asked.

'The one you sent me when I flunked out with Astrid,' Adele said.

'Really? That's great. That's just what you need to talk about with book club friends. It's the start of getting a life.'

Is it really? Adele wonders now. Will the next few weeks help her find out how to change? And she is suddenly so anxious about it that she has to run upstairs to the spare room, where all her travel stuff is lined up neatly on the bed, and check that all four copies of *Unless* are still there, although of course they were all there when she checked them last night, and earlier this morning.

Chapter Four

The Blue Mountains, end of July

Judy wheels her suitcase into the bedroom and closes the door behind her. They'd agreed to draw lots for the bedrooms, this being a house tradition done with coloured marbles drawn from a small black velvet bag. They had removed the white marble, which was the master bedroom and which they'd all agreed should be left unoccupied. Judy had dreaded the possibility that she might draw a pink room – she loathed pink, loathed it so much that if she did draw pink she felt she would have to ask someone to change with her. But there was no pink room, and she'd drawn green. There are three white walls and the fourth is painted to look like pale green seawater with ridges and flecks of crisp white foam above a line of pale sand. In the fading light from the nearby window the water has a luminous quality and she reaches out to touch it cautiously, as if expecting it to be wet. There are full-length curtains in pale green with white tassels, and a green velvet armchair, a white dressing table, and pale green and white bed linen. *Heaven,* she thinks, *I must have died and gone to heaven.* She kicks off her shoes, flops down on top of the doona and lies there relishing the comfort and the silence.

She and Simone had arrived half an hour after Adele and Ros, who were already ensconced in front of the fire with someone called Gwenda who, it seems, is a sort of caretaker in the owners' absence.

'Thank god you've arrived!' Ros had said, as she and Adele got to their feet. 'Gwenda's made scones but wouldn't let us start on them until you got here.'

There was laughter, and handshakes turned into awkward hugs, and as they settled near the fire Gwenda had wheeled in a tea trolley laden with scones, sandwiches and a carrot cake. They fell upon the food as though they hadn't eaten for days, while Clooney sniffed around, checking them all out, and then gazing mournfully up at each woman in turn, as if trying to decide who was the best bet for titbits.

Judy had found it quite confronting to be suddenly face to face with all three of them. Meeting Simone at the airport had been pretty straightforward. Their flights had been due in at about the same time but Simone's from Hobart was twenty minutes late, so when the carousel for the Hobart flight was announced Judy had moved closer to watch the passengers coming down the escalator to the baggage hall. Simone was easy to spot. On Skype she had always looked immaculate: her thick, dark hair, heavily streaked with grey, perfectly even features and those wonderful dark eyes, thanks, no doubt, to her Italian heritage. She was just as immaculate in person and taller than Judy had expected, but as she herself admits, everyone over twelve is taller than her. Simone was wearing tight-fitting jeans and a soft white shirt under a charcoal jacket. She looked stunning, calm, confident and so casually fashionable, like an advert for Country Road. Judy had felt her confidence evaporating, but Simone's smile as she spotted Judy, and the way she had immediately waved and then headed towards her, made her seem more familiar.

'Sorry about the wait,' she'd said, hugging Judy. 'Was your flight okay? Shall we get a cup of tea before we go?'

They stopped, with their baggage trolleys, at the small café and Judy found it helped to sit there and chat about the ordinary travel things, the crowd of pre-weekend travellers, the inflight meals, and she began to relax.

'So shall we go and get the car now?' Simone asked eventually. They set off for the hire desk, signed the paperwork, picked up the keys and headed out to the car park. 'Would you like to drive, Judy?' Simone asked, turning to her.

'I'd really rather not,' Judy said. 'I'm totally stuffed – all the running around to organise things has suddenly crept up on me, so if you wouldn't mind . . .'

'I love driving,' Simone said. 'But I probably can't talk until we get out of the city traffic. I think it'll be a bit of a challenge compared to Hobart!'

Judy rested her head on the back of the seat in relief and they travelled in comfortable silence until they were clear of the city.

'I'm really looking forward to this,' she'd said eventually. 'It's so long since I had any sort of break or holiday.'

'I think it would be incredibly demanding to run your own business,' Simone said. 'And your shop looks great, I had a look at your website.'

'It's going very well,' Judy said, 'but it's too much for me really. I recently took on a lovely young woman, but I'm not good at letting go of things, so I keep checking on her, to see that she hasn't missed anything. It probably drives her mad but she's very sweet about it. She and her mother are looking after the shop while I'm away.'

'So when did you last get away for more than a few days?' Simone had asked, negotiating a bendy stretch of road.

Judy hesitated. 'Well, not at all since I took over the lease on the property next door,' she admitted.

'And that was when?'

'Um . . . well that would have been the late nineties. I sometimes go down to the Wheatbelt for a long weekend, or my friend Donna comes to Perth and we get a couple of hotel rooms and have a weekend in the city. That's about it, really.'

'You're kidding,' Simone said, turning to stare at her and swerving perilously. 'But that's ridiculous, that's more than twenty years. Why? Why on earth have you done that to yourself?'

'It's just . . . become my life,' Judy said. 'I created it, and now I'm stuck with it.'

'It sounds as though you need to make a change. Could you sell the business? Retire?'

Judy hesitated. 'I do love the shop, the customers – at least most of them.' As she said it she realised she was talking rubbish. Many of the customers drive her absolutely bonkers. And while she is very proud of it, she no longer *loves* the shop. She wondered if Simone detected her lack of conviction. 'Oh, and admittedly I'm a bit of a control freak . . . and I've let everything sink into a bit of a mess, really. We look good in the shop but behind the scenes the business side is chaos. I think I'd have to sort all that stuff out before I tried to sell it. Sometimes I feel as though I'm drowning. So when Adele suggested this I jumped at it, and of course I've always hoped we'd all be able to meet one day.'

Now, lying on her bed, Judy wonders what it was that had made her suddenly confess all this to Simone, whom she barely knows, so soon after they'd met. She has never said any of it to anyone. Simone must have thought she was loopy, but she was such a good listener, and she had seemed genuinely interested and concerned. *Maybe admitting it is good though; maybe it'll do the trick, get it out of my system, help me relax,* she thinks. *And maybe I should change my style. I'll have time to go shopping here. I should study Simone, stick to simple things instead of all these bright colours, wash and wear things, fewer frocks, something more casual. I look like a shopkeeper from the fifties.*

'Judy? Judy, are you okay?'

There is a tap on the door and she wakes with a start and sits bolt upright. 'Yes,' she calls. 'Yes, I'm fine, come on in.' Blinking and yawning, she rubs her hands over her face and picks up her glasses from the side table.

'We thought you might be asleep,' Ros says from the doorway. 'Supper's ready. Don't feel you have to get up but Gwenda has made a very yummy-looking fish pie, enough to feed an army. But if you'd prefer to . . .'

'No, no, definitely not,' Judy says, swinging her legs off the bed and getting shakily to her feet. 'Goodness, I've been asleep for almost two hours. I must wash my face and tidy up.'

'Simone said you were exhausted. We're all pretty tired so it'll be an early night,' Ros says. 'No one else has washed or tidied, I don't think. I certainly haven't. Anyway, take your time, no rush.' And she backs out of the door, closing it behind her.

Judy sits down again on the bed, longing to get back into it, to burrow down and sleep. The peace that she'd felt a couple of hours ago has evaporated to be replaced by her old fear about being away from home and the business. She is sick of the shop, but at the same time she yearns for it as the old fear of being elsewhere grasps her. Having longed to get away, all she longs for now is sleep, and then, in the morning, to find some pretext to escape; call a taxi, get on the next available flight home from Sydney. Being here in this gorgeous house, these lovely friendly women, and the prospect of the book discussions, it's overwhelming. Everything that holds her life together is so far out of reach. She is now reliant on a group of comparative strangers for the next few weeks. Her chest tightens; she is giddy with panic, and her heart races. *There's no way I can do this,* she thinks. *I have to go home.* Why did she think coming here would make things better? She considers leaving tomorrow but changes her mind immediately, knowing she is just too tired to cope with travelling again so soon. She'll go to dinner, and tomorrow she'll come up with some sort of reason why she has to leave on Saturday morning. In fact, she'll book a taxi to pick her up; that will make her feel better. And tomorrow she'll search for a flight. She grabs her phone, searches Google for a local taxi service and makes a booking for nine-thirty on Saturday morning to take her to Sydney airport. She puts her phone back in her bag with a sigh of relief. It was madness to come here, but she'll be home in time to open the shop on Monday morning.

In the bathroom she grips the edge of the hand basin and stares at her reflection in the mirror. She looks like the walking dead: her hair messed up, her face grey with exhaustion, the panic obvious in her eyes. In a distant part of the house she can hear Ros calling to her dog to come inside. The bathroom starts to spin and she leans against the wall and lets herself slide down to sit on the floor, resting her head on her knees. The panic starts to ease almost as rapidly as it arrived. Getting up again she pours a glass of water and gulps it down, sloshes water on her face, dries it, brushes her hair, and sits for a moment on the toilet lid. 'Am I actually going mad?' she whispers. *I just have to get myself through this evening and then I can think about how to tell them that I'm leaving.* She takes a deep breath and, feeling as though some connection between her head and her body has gone on strike, she walks out to join the others.

*

A little cheer goes up as Judy takes her place at the table.

'Sorry, I just went out like a light,' she says.

'Don't apologise,' Ros says. 'You'll probably need to do a lot more of that in the next few weeks. Maybe we all will.'

Despite the lightness of her tone Ros is watching Judy closely. They are the oldest of the group; Judy, at seventy-three, is four years younger than her. Earlier, Simone had mentioned a conversation in the car from which it seemed clear that Judy was close to breaking point. Ros feels for her, she knows how hard it is to be with strangers when you're worn out. She's feeling a bit that way herself; getting all her own and Clooney's things packed had been tiring, and then there'd been the journey. A few years ago she started to accept that not only can she not do what she once could, but also that the things she *can* do take longer and require more energy. And for Ros, being with other people adds new levels of exhaustion. She had anticipated this when she made the travel arrangements with Adele, and she'd been prepared for the effort of making conversation on the drive up. But although Adele had obviously felt awkward and ill at ease when she first arrived to collect her, by the time they were on the road she'd seemed more relaxed.

When she'd arrived Ros had made tea and as she sat opposite Adele she could both see and feel her tension, from the obvious stiffness in her shoulders to her neatly crossed ankles and her hands which, when not holding her teacup, she constantly curled into fists, stretched out and then curled again. Those fists fascinated Ros, because she can no longer make strong fists like that. Now, glancing at the varied pairs of hands around the table, she fears her own shaky ones will soon be noticed, and she grips her knife and fork as tightly as she can to steady them. But of course it's not just her hands. Ros wonders if her own state of health is as apparent in her face as Judy's is in hers. She thinks not, but the loss of muscle strength and stability that had sent her to the doctor some weeks ago has slowed her down dramatically. She knows she is walking differently, and generally moving more slowly. For so long she's assumed that she appears to others as she has felt within herself – an ageing but energetic and competent older woman. But she is no longer that person, at least in a physical sense. What others see now cannot but be an old woman who walks and moves cautiously, who no longer trusts her physical self, who, and this is the worst part for Ros, is clearly vulner- able. How desperately she hates that word – vulnerable – and the others that cluster in its wake: unsteady, frail, wobbly and fragile. Losing it. She tries to focus on the fish pie.

*

Adele is telling them that some weeks ago, knowing she was about to retire, she decided to stop colouring her hair. 'It seems like a significant thing to do,' she says, 'but it's difficult to get used to it. It's pretty noticeable. I'm trying to get myself to accept that it's okay to look my age, to be a retired woman of sixty-five with greying hair.' What she doesn't tell them is how strange and out of character it is for her to be revealing this.

'I think your hair looks great,' Simone says. 'It looked a

very solid chestnut colour on Skype, but this is softer, more flattering.'

'I've given up on mine,' Ros says. 'In fact I've got used to being completely grey and I quite like it – it's fairly forgiving, I think. It was already quite grey in my fifties. And it's one of the things I remind myself of when I think about getting old – life just seems to get better as one ages. We all worry about it, but I try . . . have tried always to think positively about old age, and about making the most of it. It can be a really precious and enjoyable time of life.' She's tempted to add *until some blasted twist of fate kicks you in the gut* but restrains herself.

'No doubt about that,' Simone chips in. 'This is certainly the best time of my life.'

'Really?' Adele says, startled. Every woman she knows seems to think that the most important thing is to stay young and hide any signs of age, and she wonders what it is, what special quality Ros and Simone have, that she does not. What gene makes them so positive about ageing? 'I feel as though it's all downhill from now on,' she says, 'as though I need to hang on to youth, or rather to middle age, and not let go. I even thought about cosmetic surgery but I'm hopeless with pain, and frightened of looking like those "worst celebrity facelift" photographs. I know it's silly and unrealistic, and I thought the hair thing might help me face reality.'

'The trouble is,' Simone says, 'that wherever we look there is so much crap about old age, particularly about women, our bodies, our faces. I think it takes an effort to resist that, and . . . well . . . claim oneself and one's age: be in the moment and stop worrying about what people think of us, what they see when they look at us.'

Ros smiles. 'Simone, I have to say that most people looking at you would see someone tall, elegant and beautifully dressed, and many women would be somewhat intimidated or envious.'

'Goodness, I hope I'm not intimidating,' Simone says, laughing, 'and I'm certainly no fashion plate. I spend very little on clothes because these days I mostly wear the same things all the time. Look, I know I'm lucky. I've always been slim and had good hair. But it's really about how you *feel* that matters.'

Adele drains her glass of wine. 'I'd love to stop worrying about how I look and particularly what people think of me. But I don't know how to do that. ' She hesitates, wondering if she really wants to go ahead and say this, but if she doesn't do it now she might never get the courage. 'For years,' she says, 'I've run a really significant organisation. It's been a huge responsibility, a big budget, forty-odd staff, a board of academics and business people, mainly male. It's been very demanding and I've organised the rest of my life down to the most neurotic small details so I can fit everything in, make it all work seamlessly. Somehow I was that person, and now I'm not, and I'm supposed to work out what's next, and who I am without all that. I don't really know who I am without the job, never have done, I don't know how to be comfortable or confident with myself.' She stops suddenly, feeling bewildered. 'I can't believe I just said all that . . .' she says, feeling her face glowing with embarrassment. 'Sorry, I shouldn't . . .'

'It's all related, Adele,' Ros says. 'How we look in relation to how we think we *ought* to look and how we ought to be. And the pressure comes on in so many ways.'

'Yes,' Judy cuts in, 'I was thinking just the same earlier, that I should try to find a style, like Simone has, simple but elegant, and then maybe that would help me sort out the rest of my life because I'd feel better about myself! Single female of seventy plus! What does it mean, what does it look like? It's just something else to worry about.'

Simone glances at Ros and then at the other two. 'Well *I* have no formula,' she says, 'no plan. But I can tell you that in the time I've been teaching yoga to older people I've heard a lot of them say things like this about wanting to change their lives, their looks, the way they feel about getting old. It's the reason some of them come to yoga in the first place. And what I've learned from it is that you have to create space for yourself, spiritually, mentally and physically, to allow new positive energy to come in so we can embrace our age. And I really do love getting old and observing it and seeing what I can get from it.'

Ros helps herself to more fish pie. 'I remember trying to push it away – age, I mean – even though I'd always looked forward to getting older. But I learned a lot from James, who was older than me. He did what you said, Simone, deliberately set aside time to think about it, talk about it. He wrote in his journal what he wanted for his old age. The sad thing is that he died before he could really put it into practice. It made me determined not to postpone making a move to save my own life and get it into the shape I wanted. But of course I *did* keep postponing it, I should have started years ago. But when I got your message, Adele, I knew that this was a chance to kickstart myself. I felt it was the right thing to do at the right time. If your invitation had come even three months ago, I would probably have run a mile.'

There are murmurs of agreement around the table as Adele gets to her feet and fetches another bottle of wine. She can feel herself starting to loosen up and relax – it's a very unfamiliar feeling. 'We should stock up on wine tomorrow,' she says, 'and make a shopping list.'

'Aha!' Ros says. 'The director of the bureau speaks.'

Adele hesitates, feeling a flood of heat through her body. Her muscles are tensing again and her face is burning. They've only been here a few hours and she's already offended Ros. 'Oh goodness, I'm so sorry for being bossy, I . . .'

Ros holds up a hand. 'Stop, Adele! I'm teasing you. You're quite right, and it's good to have someone thinking ahead, taking charge. We should definitely replace this wine and stock up on some of our own.'

'Oh good . . . I thought I'd . . . well, never mind, just me being silly. But on the subject of organising, I did wonder whether it might be good to draw up a roster for the cooking and housework and so on. I'd be happy to do that, and I . . .'

Ros wails and sinks her head in her hands. 'Not a roster, oh no, please god, not a roster!'

Adele feels the breath fly from her body again. 'Oh . . . well no . . . of course not . . .'

Ros looks up, smiling at her. 'Just kidding, Adele, just kidding. I'm all in favour of a roster, as long as I don't have to be the one to draw it up.'

*

'I've been thinking about what you said earlier, Ros,' Judy says, as Adele tops up their glasses. 'About how this is a most unlikely thing for you to do – have a holiday with people you barely know – because really it's much the same for me. I came because I felt it was right for me now, at this time. But unlike you, I've been blindly turning my back on the fact that I'm getting old and struggling on, trying to do more and more and getting totally worn out. I don't know how to change. I don't even know what sort of change I want.'

'So you've done the right thing, Judy,' Simone says. 'You've made space for yourself to think, and consider the future. From what you told me earlier, if you hadn't made this space I think you would soon have fallen right off your perch and crashed.'

'You're probably right, but I feel so odd, I've never done anything like this before, and just now, in my room, I . . . well I had a panic attack.' She stops, takes a deep breath, her heart pounding so fiercely she feels they must be able to hear it. 'Please don't take this the wrong way, but I haven't unpacked my case, because I've decided to go home on Saturday.' Everyone stops eating and she sees their faces drop.

'Oh no, Judy,' Ros says. 'Please don't do that.'

'I should never have come, there's the business and every-thing, and I am . . . I'm not good at doing social things like this. I really can't cope, and actually I'm exhausted. I was feeling I couldn't cope while I was at home but it's worse now I'm here.' She stops, hearing the tremor in her own voice. 'Sometimes I wonder about my own sanity.'

There is silence around the table.

Simone reaches out and puts her hand on top of Judy's. 'I don't want to discount your feelings because they're obvi-ously profoundly real and distressing. But please don't go. I think this sort of intimacy with strangers is bound to be discomforting until we adjust to it. We have to take it one day at a time.'

Judy grips her hand. 'I . . . I don't know.'

'Could you just give yourself a few days' rest?' Ros suggests. 'I think you need that. You've had a very long day. You said you left at five this morning to get to the airport, then the flight and the drive here. It's a lot, Judy, at our age especially. I'm exhausted and I only had to come from Sydney. Stay the weekend, rest and relax, we'll have some nice meals, some laughs, you can get lots of sleep and we can venture out somewhere if it ever stops raining. See how you feel on Sunday evening.'

'Ros is right, Judy,' Adele says. 'If you rush off on Saturday you'll be totally stuffed by the time you get home – you might get really sick. And you'd miss out on *Tirra Lirra by the River*, you said you were looking forward to that.'

Judy nods slowly. She's moved by their concern and their kindness. It's years, decades, since anyone – with the possible exception of Donna – has shown this sort of affectionate concern for her, and her eyes fill with tears. She brushes them away, clears her throat. They're right – it would be stupid to make the journey back while she feels so wiped out. 'That sounds sensible,' she says cautiously. 'I'm probably not thinking straight. It *would* be silly to travel feeling like this. So thank you, yes, I'll stay the weekend. It would be so nice to talk about *Tirra Lirra by the River* with you. Tomorrow I'll have a look online for flights. Meanwhile I'll have a good rest and make the most of your company.'

She hopes she sounds rational and in control now, and she does indeed feel a little better. It's a decision, and they all seem okay with it. She'll have a nice little break and can leave on Monday with her friendships intact.

*

Later that evening as she climbs into bed, Ros gazes at the sprigs of bougainvillea that decorate the pale lavender wall in her room. She had drawn the purple room, which, she felt, could have been designed especially for her. Turning off the light she lies there in the darkness, thinking about the conversation over dinner, and how they all grew more relaxed as the evening progressed. *Something important happened this evening*, she thinks. *Already we feel more like friends than acquaintances.*

She sighs, thinking of James, of how lucky they were to find each other all those years ago. *It's certainly not that I think a woman* needs *a man*, she tells him now. *You know I don't think like that, it's just that what we had was so special. Anyway, I like these women. I was worried I might not like Adele, that her desire to please might drive me bonkers, and it still might, but she's interesting. Lord knows how things will work out, whether we'll get on each other's nerves. You know how rapidly I can end up wanting to punch someone in the face! We'll just have to wait and see.*

From his bed on the floor Clooney lets out a series of small yelps, his legs twitching as though chasing something in his dreams. 'Shh,' Ros whispers softly, 'shh.' She leans down over the side of the bed and puts her hand on him. He lets out a great sigh and is perfectly still again. Ros plumps up her pillows, lies down and closes her eyes. *Not a bad start*, she thinks. *Not a bad start at all.*

*

On the other side of the house, Adele sits in front of the dressing table mirror brushing her hair and wondering how long it will take to grow out the colour, how much grey there will be, and what it might do to the colour of her skin. Ros – or was it Simone? – said it looked softer with the grey. Did they think that was flattering? Is softer good? Is going grey taking control of her life or just submitting to being old? She wonders if she'll need different make-up, different-coloured clothes. Someone had told her that there was an app that you could use to take a selfie and then try out different hairstyles and colours on the photo to see how they would look. She thinks she might try to find it tomorrow, but sadly she knows she will not look at all like Simone, whose hair is perfectly cut and parted fashionably on one side so that it sweeps dramatically across the side of her face and ear. She thinks of Ros, also seemingly at ease with her iron-grey hair; Ros, whom Adele thinks is possibly struggling with mobility, who thinks her seventies is a good time of life despite the obvious disadvantages. Ros has obviously worked out how she wants to look, and probably doesn't think much about clothes, but appears strikingly interesting and eccentric with her messy hair falling out of whatever holds it up, and in her long, shapeless dress with a big scarf around her shoulders.

Adele thinks of her own wardrobe at home, packed with neat business suits and shirts in a narrow range of muted colours, all essentially the same: the straight black pants and skirts and the shoes with heels that she is still trying to wear, despite the discomfort. For the last few years she has feared that she may look as though she has been upholstered in those suits. *I want something different,* she tells herself, *something to help me feel and be different.*

Packing her bag had been difficult. She has so few things that are suitable for a holiday in the Blue Mountains. A pair of designer jeans, a couple of warm black jumpers, and a short black coat which, while very warm, looks rather too formal – too city-ish. *I need an anorak,* she thinks, *and more jumpers.* Shopping, tomorrow. She might have to sneak out on her own into Leura. Ros has said that she is welcome to use the car, as are the others, whenever they want. The difficulty might be in going alone. It's quite likely that others might want to come with her. Lots of women go shopping together, but Adele never has, and the prospect of starting it now is challenging. As a teenager she went shopping with the housekeeper who looked after her father and herself, and she suspects that Mrs Richards' severe and matronly tastes are still to some extent influencing her own wardrobe. The jeans are the only thing that would have shocked Mrs Richards, and this realisation makes Adele think that she might just buy a second pair, and maybe something else more colourful.

Adele gets up from the dressing table and stretches, thinking now about Judy. She'd felt really concerned about her this evening but at the same time Judy had helped her to feel more confident. Adele thought it was brave of Judy to admit she wanted to leave – she'd felt like that herself when she'd arrived at Ros's place and then again when they got here. But Judy's anxiety is something else.

She climbs into bed, looking around her room, the one she had drawn on the two previous occasions when she'd stayed here; turquoise, one of her favourite colours, but one that she has never worn. *Perhaps that's what I'll buy first*, she thinks, *something turquoise and totally unlike anything I would have bought in the past*. As she draws the doona up to her chin, Adele has a rare and wonderful moment of feeling she is in exactly the right place at the right time, and with the right people.

When the taxi had drawn up outside Ros's house that afternoon, she'd been close to shaking with anxiety. All it would have taken to send her into a complete spin would have been for Ros to make one of her familiar caustic comments, or even to seem a bit frosty. But Ros had greeted her warmly, like an old friend, had actually ignored Adele's extended hand and hugged her, urged her inside.

'Sit down, make yourself comfortable. You must be tired – flying is exhausting, isn't it, and airports are just the pits. Would you like tea or coffee or something stronger?'

She was introduced to Clooney, and while Ros made tea he had joined her on the sofa and put his head in her lap. His warm shape beside her was comforting. *Perhaps I need a dog*, Adele thought – company, warmth, unconditional love – and she relaxed, stroking his head.

'He's taken to you very quickly,' Ros said, putting the tea

down beside her. 'He can be quite picky when it comes to whom he'll join on the sofa.'

'I'm so glad he's coming with us,' Adele said. 'He's gorgeous, and he'll have some wonderful walks up there. Will we need to restrain him from chasing the wildlife?'

Ros shook her head. 'No. He would have done years ago, he was a terror for it and it drove me crazy. But since he's got older he can't be bothered.'

By the time Adele had helped Ros get her luggage and Clooney into the car she was feeling very different. In some ways she had been glad that she and Ros would travel there together. It was, she thought, probably easier to arrive at the house with someone rather than alone. But then, in the infuriating way she had of always expecting the worst, she'd worried about being alone with Ros in the car. How awkward it might be. What would they talk about? It was quite a long drive, and she wanted to make a good impression. The last thing she wanted was to annoy Ros before they even got there. The previous night she had dreamed they were driving up winding roads and she swerved and Ros shouted at her, told her she was a hopeless driver and shouldn't be behind the wheel. She'd woken up sweating and had to get up and make a warm drink to calm herself down. So by the time she'd arrived at Ros's house she was at her most tense, making fists all the time, and she was sure Ros had noticed, although she didn't say anything. She'd noticed that one of Ros's hands seemed a bit shaky – surely Ros of all people couldn't be nervous. On the drive they'd talked about books, and music, and Ros had told her about the quartet she played with, and about playing with the Symphony Orchestra, and it had all been fine. So here they are, and here she is in her favourite room and Adele feels herself unwinding, her muscles softening, relaxing, her eyelids heavy, and she knows that as per usual she has worn herself out with pointless anxiety.

What would it be like to feel relaxed like this all, or at least most, of the time? Who would she be if she wasn't always struggling with what other people might think about her? Yawning, she turns on her side and stares at the narrow sliver of night sky between the gap in the curtains and wonders what the others might be thinking as they lie waiting for sleep.

*

In the yellow room Simone sits in darkness, the curtains drawn back, gazing at the starlit sky. It's been an interesting day in all sorts of ways, she thinks: her conversation with Judy in the car, the glorious but unfamiliar landscape of the mountains, the sense of moving out and away from her normal life and step-ping into something new. But most interesting of all are her companions. From the day Adele's invitation arrived she has been imagining this; considering the extent that it's possible to know people solely through an online medium like Skype. *Did we all prepare for those meetings?* she wonders. *Did we all check our hair and what we were wearing? Did we all manipulate the height and distance of the computer camera, the background that reveals something of our homes and therefore of ourselves?* Simone has done some of this herself, stage-managing, in small ways, both what could and couldn't be seen.

The scar on the left side of her face and the disfigured ear alongside it are always her first thought, even though they are largely concealed by her hair, which is parted on the opposite side so that the heavier hair masks it. She doesn't think she's particularly neurotic about it. People do see it every day – they catch a glimpse as she turns her head, or the wind lifts her hair. Simone thinks she manages it quite well, and if she's asked about it she tells the truth. 'It's a burn,' she says, always careful to sound casual and uninterested. 'From a long time ago, in my twenties. I was lucky, it could have been a lot worse.' It works, people rarely ask any more after that. She thinks the others will not have noticed it before now but may have caught sight of it sometime today. Accustomed to managing this, as well as having a strong sense of what she wants others to see when they look at her, Simone is also rigorous in maintaining what she thinks of as a 'classy casual' look and chooses her clothes accordingly.

People, of course, are not always what they seem, especially on a computer screen. It's not necessarily how they look but who they are that can be misleading; a brief period of internet dating had shown her that. She'd thought about this during the drive here with Judy, who had always appeared to be a confident and energetic businesswoman but had today revealed herself as a woman in crisis, poised precariously on the edge of a cliff.

And then there's Ros, who for so long had seemed to be brusque and sometimes lacking in both empathy and tact. As she sits here now in the darkness Simone realises she has very little evidence for that opinion. Over time there have been a few examples of what Ros herself calls her 'foot-in-mouth moments' and she's certainly very straightforward, and Simone likes that. But she can also be too blunt, too harsh, and maybe a bit prickly. Yet from the moment she met Ros today Simone sensed vulnerability. She wonders whether this is new or something she simply hasn't noticed before. Is this what Ros does to protect herself and, if so, from what?

Simone is pretty good at reading people but she is still confused by Adele – conservative in style and dress, obviously intelligent and well read – who has for years held down a very senior position, but who has always seemed to be so uptight, lacking in confidence and anxious to please. Today she had seemed a little more confident. These anomalies are fascinating to Simone, and she wonders whether the others are watching her with this same forensic interest. Ros, she thinks, is the only one likely to be doing that and, if so, Simone would love to know what Ros sees in her.

She has taken to Ros in a big way, although she's pretty sure Ros is a yoga sceptic. Not that this bothers Simone; she meets them all the time. People must be free to do and think what they want, but Simone feels Ros might benefit from what yoga has to offer. And she's certain she'd take well to meditation. It's not that she sets out to convert people, but she is never backward in suggesting some of the things she herself has learned. *So will I take Ros on about this, in a light-hearted sort of way?* she wonders, and she decides she will. Adele is already interested, and if she can get Ros on side, that might encourage Judy, if she's here long enough. Simone still thinks Judy will succumb and stay on. She smiles at the thought of them all lined up on yoga mats in the big downstairs games room. *That would be so good*, she thinks. *That would be the best energy ever.*

Chapter Five

Clooney stands by the open door, hesitates, then steps cautiously outside, looking back hopefully to see if Ros is coming with him.

'No way,' she says. 'You have to do this on your own.'

He stands still, ever hopeful.

'Does he have a raincoat?' Simone calls from the kitchen.

'He does, but I'm not taking him out in this.'

'If you put it on I'll take him for a walk. Adele says there are boots and Drizabones for visitors in the storeroom.'

'Really? Well that's very good of you, Simone. But it's awful out there. D'you think it'll ever stop?' In the two days and nights since their arrival the rain has barely ceased.

'Tomorrow, the forecast says, then three days of clear skies and sunshine,' Simone says, joining her by the door. 'But I quite like walking in the rain if I've got the right gear. I'll take Clooney and then I'm going to drive down to Leura, have a nose around, so I can do the shopping if we put together a list.'

'I'd like to go with you,' Adele calls. 'Not walking, but into town, if that's okay.'

'Sure,' Simone replies. 'Let's do the list when I get back from the walk. Anyone seen Judy yet?'

'I haven't,' Ros says, zipping Clooney into his red tartan raincoat. 'She was really zonked out last night, probably best to let her sleep.'

Adele appears at the entrance to the kitchen. 'I might just start preparing things for breakfast. How long d'you think you'll be, Simone?'

'I thought I'd do that walk to the waterfall, the one you told me about. So you tell me.'

'Oh, about half an hour.' She checks her watch. 'So shall we say breakfast at nine-thirty? Eggs, bacon, toast? Gwenda has stocked up on those for us.'

'I'm in,' Ros says. 'Breakfast is my favourite meal but I'm too lazy to cook it at home. I'll give you a hand. Shout when you're ready. But I think we should leave Judy to sleep as long as she wants, don't you?'

'Definitely,' Simone says, backing out of the storeroom clutching a Drizabone and a battered Akubra. 'And definitely yes to eggs and bacon too. Are you actually going to do a roster, Adele?'

'Am I?' Adele looks at Ros, who grins back at her.

'You don't need my permission,' she says, 'but since you ask I think that would be a very good idea.'

'Okay, Clooney,' Simone says, 'off we go. See you in about half an hour.'

And with Clooney wagging his tail furiously, she opens the door and steps outside.

'You are probably insane,' Ros says, handing her the lead, 'but Clooney and I are nonetheless grateful.'

Simone is glad to be out. She was first up this morning and has already done her yoga practice and made tea for herself,

Adele and Ros. Yesterday, Friday, had been an odd sort of
day. Everyone had been tired and slept late, and Gwenda had
arrived at ten to cook brunch for them, which is something,
Adele had explained, that Marian always organised for visitors the first morning after their arrival. It poured with rain
most of the day and they sat around talking, watched a movie
on TV, napped, and Judy, when she finally surfaced, looked a
little better, and got out her knitting. None of them had energy
for anything more.

'This is adjustment day,' Ros said, late in the afternoon. 'We
don't have jetlag, it just feels like it.'

Judy had brought a DVD with her and they watched it after
dinner. It was *The Enchanted April*, which they'd all seen before,
and Ros had also read the book. The story of four women
taking time out from their early twentieth-century lives, in a
glorious Italian villa, had struck just the right note.

'It's still pissing down,' Ros said at ten o'clock when she let
Clooney out for a late night pee. 'We should have gone to Italy
instead.'

Simone walks briskly now, sticking to the path, splashing
through and around puddles, hands in her pockets, watching
Clooney running joyfully between the trees, sniffing, peeing,
bounding off in different directions. She opens the rear gate of
the property and continues on for some time, watching out for
the stone marker that Adele had told her points to the waterfall. They finally turn alongside it onto a narrow path with
a handrail. Clipping on Clooney's lead she walks cautiously
until the muddy path widens, the trees thin out and she can
hear the sound of rushing water. Clooney tugs on the lead but
she holds him back.

'Wait,' she says. 'Just wait. We're nearly there.' And suddenly
they are out of the cover of the trees and the landscape opens up.

She catches her breath at the sight of the white water tumbling and foaming over walls of dark rock to a depth she cannot safely see.

Simone holds on to the handrail, mesmerised by the sight and sound of the water, barely noticing that the rain has almost stopped, until a crack in the clouds opens up and a narrow shaft of brilliant sunlight makes her gasp as it transforms the rock and the water to every imaginable shade of green laced with white foam.

'Well look at that, Clooney,' she gasps. 'Isn't that simply glorious?'

Clooney, at the limits of the lead, cocks his leg on a nearby fern.

The rain has stopped now and Simone inhales the fresh, damp air, captivated by the sound of the rushing water and the magical effect of the sunlight on the drenched landscape. This moment feels like some sort of blessing, a moment sent to make her stop to think, to feel its importance. She stretches out her arms, turns her face to the sun and closes her eyes. The surge of freedom that had come with the sale of the house is reignited. Energy rushes through her veins like water against the rocks and she fills her lungs with the clear air. *This*, she thinks, *is the start of something new, something special – I must make the most of every moment from now on.*

There is a seat made of old logs and she sits down on it. Clooney jumps up beside her. She puts her arm around him and drags him closer, and he tilts his head up and tries to lick her face. 'No thanks,' she tells him, 'but I appreciate the sentiment. I like you too.' She fishes in her pocket for a few dog treats that she took from the tin Ros has put in the kitchen. 'Here,' she says, 'this is to cement our friendship.' Clooney swoops and gulps them down in seconds.

For a while they sit there, the two of them, Clooney alternately sniffing the air and sniffing Simone's pocket for more treats as she gazes out at the waterfall, listening to it, narrowing her eyes at the sparkling landscape. But soon the rain returns, slowly at first, then building fast as the clouds crowd out the sun. She gets to her feet. 'Come on, Clooney,' she says, turning back down the path. 'Let's get home before we drown.'

*

'Judy's up and seems in good spirits,' Adele says when Simone appears in the kitchen. 'Did you get to the waterfall?'

'I did,' Simone says, 'thanks for telling me about it. It's just glorious. Wow, that bacon smells good.'

'It tastes as good as it smells,' Adele says, 'take my word for it. We should get some more when we go shopping.'

'Is Judy really okay?'

'She seems pretty good to me,' Adele says. 'I'm hoping if she gets through today and tomorrow she'll decide to stay on. Going home is probably the worst thing she could do. She really needs to rest and relax a bit.'

'Fingers crossed.'

Adele cracks eggs into a bowl and begins to whisk them with a fork. 'Could you let the others know that it'll be ready in a minute?' she asks. Simone wanders out and Adele hears her rounding up Judy and Ros.

Adele is glad she rostered herself on for the first breakfast. When she'd suggested a roster for the cooking and housework, she failed to mention that she'd already drawn it up and stored it on her laptop. She'd deliberately put herself down for the first breakfast so she could feel useful, and as though she was pulling her weight right from the start. Later she'll print it out on Marian's printer. Telling the others that she'd organised it two weeks in advance might make them think she was obsessive and trying to control things, both of which she knows are true, even if only in a small way. It would be nice if the others didn't find that out too soon.

A couple of minutes later she is spooning scrambled eggs onto slices of toast and Simone is adding bacon and grilled tomatoes and setting them on the table. It's just as they are starting to tuck into the food that the doorbell takes them by surprise.

'I'll go,' Simone says, pushing back her chair.

Ros raises her eyebrows. 'Visitors already?'

'Probably Gwenda,' Adele suggests.

Simone appears back in the kitchen doorway. She clears her throat, smiles and Adele thinks she looks as though she's trying not to laugh.

'Taxi to Sydney airport for Judy Castle?' she says.

Judy's eyes widen; she drops her fork and it clatters onto her plate. She pushes back her chair and gets to her feet. 'Oh my god! I forgot,' she says. 'I completely forgot.'

Ros gives a short burst of laughter. 'Forgot to run away?'

'Forgot that I ordered the taxi. I did it the first night, before dinner, before we talked about staying longer . . . oh my goodness,' and she hurries out of the kitchen past Simone.

'D'you think she'll make a run for it?' Ros asks, and the other two collapse into laughter. 'She may have one booked for Sunday morning, too. Who knows?'

Adele moves briskly towards the door. 'I'm going to make sure she doesn't run and that she hasn't got any more secret escape plans up her sleeve.'

Simone drops back into her chair. 'Poor Judy. She's all over the place. She must have been feeling pretty desperate, but I think we need to keep her here as long as possible. She'll get through this crisis, I'm sure she will.'

A few minutes later Adele and Judy are back and Judy sits down again, red in the face and obviously very embarrassed. 'I'm sorry,' she says. 'I was in such a state when I arrived. But I do intend to stay, definitely for tomorrow, and leave on Monday.'

Ros leans across to her. 'One day at a time, Judy,' she says. 'Just one day at a time.'

*

'Shall we do the shopping last?' Simone asks as Adele drives them to Leura in Ros's car.

'Yes, I'd like to have a wander around. Shall we make a time and meet for a coffee later, then go to the supermarket?'

'Perfect. You said you wanted to buy boots?'

'Yes, and I'm looking out for a jumper. I'm going to be daring and look for something in turquoise, inspired by my turquoise bedroom.'

They park just off the main street, and set off in different directions. Simone takes her time, browsing the shelves of a bookshop, then walks on, passing and then turning back to a small but interesting-looking fashion and gift shop to examine some leather handbags. The leather is beautifully soft and hand-stitched but, torn between two bags, neither of which she really needs, she decides against both. As she's about to leave the shop she spots a turquoise jumper on a model just inside the window. It has a soft cowl neckline and when she touches it she realises it's cashmere, but it's way too small for Adele. She goes to the counter to enquire about the availability of larger sizes.

Heading out onto the street again she walks on, gazing in shop windows. This morning she'd returned from her walk full of positive energy, determined to get straight onto Facebook and send a friend request to Geoff Marshall, but since then her mood has changed. She's nervous about it now. What if he doesn't respond? And why is she fussing about it now, as soon as she's got here, when it could easily wait – after all, she's been looking at what she thinks is his profile for months. Perhaps Judy is not the only one feeling out of place. She walks on up the street, gazing in various shop windows, stopping to buy a beautiful scarf for Stacey in one place and some brightly coloured socks for Adam in another. The combination of a longing to make contact with Geoff, and the fear of doing so in case she is ignored or rebuffed, is growing, pushing everything else into the background. The more she thinks about it the more she is drawn back into the past, to her relationship with the Marshalls, and to their importance to her; an importance that had grown as her parents had seemed increasingly estranged from each other, and her father became more volatile, and less able than ever to control his temper. Eventually she reaches the café where she is supposed to meet Adele in twenty minutes' time. She pushes open the door, orders some tea, sits down at a table and takes out her phone.

She looks once again at the limited profile of the man she thinks could be Geoff, and opens Messenger.

Hi, she types, then hesitates. *I'm looking for Geoff Marshall and his brother Doug whom I knew in Queensland from the fifties to the seventies. My name is Simone Ricci, if you remember me and would like to meet again I would love to hear from you.* And she hits 'Send' before she can change her mind.

Her heart is thumping in her chest as though she has done something momentous, taken some huge risk, and she is almost giddy as she stares at the phone, willing it to reply instantly. *For heaven's sake, relax*, she tells herself. *He's hardly sitting there waiting to hear from you.* It could be days or weeks before he responds – maybe never. She stares hard at the photo-graph again, the face half-masked by shadow. She imagines the Geoff she knew hearing a beep on his phone, picking it up, staring at her message. What would he feel when he saw her name: excitement or dismay, pleasure and anticipation or mere irritation?

'I'm early but you beat me to it anyway,' Adele says, slip-ping into the seat opposite her.

Simone feels as though she is physically struggling to drag herself back to the present.

'It's pouring out there now, we should have stayed home, but I managed to get some boots,' Adele continues, sticking a foot out from under the table. 'Flat boots with thick soles.'

Simone stares at her, trying to muster a response. She looks down at Adele's extended leg and nods approvingly. 'They're great, ideal for the paths around here. I thought you might succumb and fall for heels.' *How amazing*, she thinks, *I sound like a perfectly normal person.*

'I almost did,' Adele admits, 'but the assistant persuaded me otherwise. These are wonderfully comfortable. What about you?'

'I just mooched around and window-shopped. And then . . .' She hesitates, looks up. 'Actually I've just messaged that man I told you all about last night, one of the Marshall boys I was friends with . . . and now I feel really stupid.'

'But why?' Adele says. 'It's good – it's more than good, it's great. There's not much point spending ages staring at a photo you can't really see and wondering whether or not it's him.'

'He . . . they . . . may not *want* me to find them.'

'In which case you won't get a reply.'

'But I won't know whether that's because I've got the wrong person, or the right one and they don't want to know me.'

'Simone,' Adele says, reaching across the table to put a hand on her arm. 'You can't have it both ways – you can't find out without trying, so you have to risk confusion, rebuffs, or the fact that you'll never know, in order to have a chance at the jackpot. You've done it. So stop staring at your phone, put it back in your bag and drink your tea.'

'You sound so sensible and well balanced,' Simone says, 'not at all like . . .' She stops, horrified by what she was about to say.

'Not at all like the neurotic, anxious person you know me to be,' Adele says, smiling. 'Actually, I'm really good at other people's stuff. It's just my own that brings me to my knees.'

'Oh my god,' Simone says later, as they stroll back to the car and the clouds start to clear. 'I almost forgot. There's something I want to show you in this shop.' She grabs Adele's arm and draws her to the window. 'Look! A beautiful turquoise jumper.'

They push open the glass door of the shop, and Adele walks over to the model. She stares at the jumper, gently fingering the fabric.

'It's so light and soft.'

'Exactly. Cashmere and something else, so it'll be warm too.'

'But it's tiny.'

'They have other sizes, I asked.'

Adele looks at the price tag. 'Crikey, it costs an arm and a leg.'

'Of course, it's cashmere. Do you like it?'

'I love it, but . . .'

'Then go and try one on, come and show me.'

Adele blushes. 'Oh I don't think –'

'Why not?'

'It's just that I'm . . . I usually go shopping, trying things . . . well, on my own.'

Simone hesitates, and then laughs. 'Oh Adele, you are such a mystery! Shall I go and wait for you in the car?'

Adele hesitates, takes a deep breath. 'No,' she says, 'my daughter would say I'm being ridiculous. Stay right there. There's a first time for everything and I suppose this is it.'

*

Just inside the front door Adele and Simone divest themselves of their coats, and Adele dries her boots very carefully as she doesn't want to take them off just yet.

'I want to show them off to Judy and Ros,' she says, feeling emboldened by the experience of trying on the jumper and walking out of the fitting room in front of Simone.

'Good on you,' Simone says, 'swagger off and do just that. And I mean swagger – "look at me in my cool new boots and my lovely turquoise cashmere jumper".'

'Oh, I won't put the jumper on,' Adele says, blushing furiously. She had been horribly anxious about stepping out of the fitting room in the shop, but she'd made herself do it and, strangely, it had felt fine. She tries to think of the last time she paraded something she'd bought in front of someone. It really was too long ago for her to remember, but it would have been Jenna because she'd never have done it with anyone else. 'You know I can't do that,' she says now.

Simone catches her arm. 'Maybe not today, but soon. It *is* allowed, you know, to do something, to say something, that's all about you. Something that draws attention to yourself and how much you love these new things that make you feel good. We will all enjoy it, we'll laugh and clap and celebrate it with you.

It's what women friends do. But you have to stick your neck out to make it happen.'

Adele is about to laugh until she realises that what she wants is to cry. She swallows several times, to hold it all back, to lock down the desire to be the woman Simone describes, striding out into the middle of the room in her new clothes, flinging out her arms, twirling around and demanding to be looked at. Doing all that without embarrassment, without the everlasting concern that her hips are two sizes bigger than her bust, that there is a stubborn roll of fat that sits like a shelf above the waistline of her jeans, and the bulge of her stomach below it; most of all without the fear that she is showing off or making a spectacle of herself.

Simone must have realised that she has touched a sensitive spot, because she moves closer, puts a hand on Adele's shoulder. 'You're a beautiful woman, Adele. And before we leave here we'll have you shaking your booty.'

Adele laughs.

'You may laugh now,' Simone says, wagging her finger, 'but booty shaking is on the agenda. You mark my words.'

'And just what's going on out here?' Judy asks, appearing from nowhere. 'There seems to be a lot of giggling.'

'Indeed there is,' Simone says, taking Judy's arm. 'How are you feeling now?'

'Better,' Judy says, 'quite a bit better. I slept for three hours! I think it's what I needed. Perhaps I was just exhausted, and then that stupid stuff with the taxi ... anyway, I'm feeling more like myself now, just seem to have developed a bit of a cough. And I'm starving – did you bring anything for afternoon tea?'

Adele thinks Judy does not look as good as she sounds. This morning she had started coughing after breakfast, and now she looks pale and there are dark hollows under her eyes. 'We did, but it's a surprise,' she says. She hurries through to the kitchen to help Ros with the tea.

In the kitchen she puts a carrier bag down on the table and Ros raises her eyebrows and opens it. 'Goodies? Crumpets! Oh my god, crumpets,' she says, ripping open a packet of six. 'Heaps of crumpets, *three* packets! Goodness, how wonderful, I'm drooling already. I hope we have enough butter.'

'We bought some more,' Adele says. 'And I know that there are several toasting forks in one of the drawers so we can open the stove, toast the crumpets and let the butter run down our chins.'

Ros grins. 'You are a wise and wonderful woman, Adele. Did you get the things you wanted? The boots?'

'I did, look.' Adele walks over to Ros and thrusts out her foot. 'In fact I wore them home. They're really comfortable.'

'They also look great,' Ros says. 'And flat ones are the thing this year apparently. So Leah tells me – Leah's my de facto daughter, and she's very cool. She's just bought some purple suede ones with flat heels. Did you buy anything else?'

'Yes. A lovely cashmere jumper.' She hesitates, realising that Ros is waiting for something from her. 'It's . . . it's um . . . well it's really nice.'

'So are you going to show me?'

Adele feels herself blushing again. 'Er . . . okay, if you want . . .'

'Of course I do,' Ros says, lifting the kettle with both hands to pour boiling water into the teapot.

Adele picks up the glossy carrier bag and takes out the jumper that is wrapped in two layers of white tissue paper. She puts it down on the end of the table, carefully folds the bag two ways and smooths it flat, then unfolds the tissue.

Ros walks over to the neatly folded jumper and feels its softness. She lifts it up and shakes it out, then looks at Adele and smiles.

'Beautiful,' she says. 'Go and put it on!'

Adele flinches. 'Put it on?'

'Yes, why not?'

'Well I . . .' She feels her face has flushed a deep red. 'I'm not, um . . .'

'Good lord,' Ros says. 'It's not like I'm asking you to get your tits out, Adele! It's just trying on a jumper.'

Adele stands there paralysed with embarrassment.

'Okay,' Ros says, 'sorry, I didn't mean to embarrass you.' She holds the jumper close to Adele's face. 'This is a fabulous colour for you, do you often wear it?'

Adele shakes her head, still blushing. 'Never, it's . . . well it's a bit bright.'

'Bright! I think you mean it's just not black or navy! It's gorgeous, and it does wonders for your skin.'

She hands it over carefully and Adele folds it back into the tissue and then the bag. 'It was awfully expensive,' she says, 'but once I saw it . . .'

'Of course,' Ros says. 'And every time you wear it, you'll feel more than a little bit special.'

Adele watches as Ros piles the crumpets onto a plate, then adds butter, plates and knives to the tray which is already loaded with the teapot, milk and cups.

'Could you carry this please, Adele?' Ros asks. 'I'm not very reliable with trays.' She walks briskly out of the kitchen with the plate of crumpets.

Adele stands there for a moment, staring at Ros's retreating back, thinking how different, how much nicer it is to be here with these women than when she has stayed here with Marian and Brian, both of whom she is fond of. 'Weird,' she murmurs under her breath. And she picks up the tray and follows Ros into the lounge.

Chapter Six

The first Sunday

Judy is surprised to find herself still here and enjoying herself. Staying over until Monday morning was the right decision, she'd really needed the rest, and now she's looking forward to their first book discussion.

'So here we are – face to face,' Ros says as they settle in. 'We should get started, but I've got a housekeeping suggestion first. This house is gorgeous but it's making me nervous – the Chinese vases, the crystal birds over there on the low table, other ornaments. Frankly I'm concerned that either Clooney or I will knock something over and break it.'

'Oh, thank goodness,' Adele says. 'I always feel like that here.'

'We could probably put some things out of the way,' Simone says. 'There are heaps of cupboards.'

'Exactly, rough it up a bit,' Ros says. 'As long as we remember where things go so we can put them back.'

'Let's do it in the morning,' Adele suggests, 'and next time

I see Gwenda I'll explain. She knows the place so well I'm sure she'd help us sort it out again before we go.'

'That'd certainly make me feel more relaxed,' Ros says. 'Anyway, let's get going.'

As Ros tells them something about the author, Jessica Anderson, and that the book is considered an Australian literary classic, Judy leans back in her chair and thinks how very different this is from switching on the computer and hoping that Skype won't bomb out and disconnect them midway through the conversation.

'It won the Miles Franklin Literary Award in 1978,' Ros says. 'And I'm ashamed to tell you that despite having been born in Australia and spending most of my life here I had never even heard of it until I saw an article in the weekend paper a couple of months ago. Do you want me to read the cover blurb? No? Okay then, who's going to go first?'

There's a brief silence.

'I will,' Judy says, thinking that this is a book she understood and really enjoyed so she might as well do her bit now and if she doesn't make a complete fool of herself they may remember her kindly when she's gone.

'I loved this book,' she says, 'and for all sorts of reasons. Primarily I think it's because Nora, the narrator, is an old woman who has lived away from her original home for a very long time, and comes back towards the end of her life. It made me think about the time it was written, and how interesting it is that a book by a woman, about an old woman's life, won that award then.'

'I thought that too,' Ros says. 'Most of the awards went to men in those days, probably still do.'

'I looked that up,' Adele says, putting on her glasses. 'Did you know that since nineteen forty-five only three women had won it – Thea Astley, Christina Stead and Elizabeth Harrower. Imagine that – only three women in thirty-three years, and then in nineteen seventy-eight Jessica Anderson won it, and Helen Garner won a big national award for *Monkey Grip*, which I guess we've all read at some stage since then because we all love Helen Garner.'

Judy feels her confidence growing. 'I think it's great that this book made it, because it's a real treasure. I took to it because I left my home in England in my early twenties and I've never been back, so I understood that part of Nora. She grabbed me right from the start. I love this way of telling her story too, that she's old and she's returning to her original home to take stock of things, to reflect.'

'I do too,' Simone says. 'And I especially like it that Nora's life is not exceptional, but the way the story is told, the insights into her inner life, make it fascinating. She's tough and persistent, she survives and escapes from the awful marriage and the mother-in-law, at some cost to herself, but she carries on. And in the end she's working out what she knows about the past and trying to fill some gaps. Because, after all, we all forget things about the past and if you're in an entirely different place, a different country, there are gaps, and things are hidden within them.'

Judy listens to what Simone is saying; she herself has been here in Australia for half a century and her memory is full of holes, fragments she can't recall, most of all gaps about the actual place she came from, how it felt to be there, how she once knew it so intimately that it was always home. She wonders what sort of place it is now, how it would look and feel to go there.

'For me,' Ros says, 'this is a perfect example of what I love about novel: the fact that you get the character's inner life, their thoughts. I mean, we can all know Nora better than we could have done had she been a real person, because we can see inside her head. Sometimes that sort of insight makes me wonder what was actually going on in the writer's head when they wrote it, whether it says something about their own state of mind at the time.'

'I think Nora is really trying to discover who she *has* been and who she *is* now,' Judy says, realising as she does so that she is actually talking about the questions she is trying to answer for herself. 'She needs to do it before she dies, although even when she gets sick she doesn't seem to realise that this might be sooner rather than later. I particularly loved the significance of her work, her craft or art – call it what you wish. She's a dress-maker and an embroiderer – personally I believe that makes her an artist, although that sort of work is often described as craft when women do it!'

'Too right,' Adele says. 'Whether it's tapas or tapestry, when the men start doing it it's elevated and professionalised.'

'That aspect of Nora's life, the times when it's almost hand to mouth, was really interesting,' Ros says. 'It's the creative work that keeps her going and makes Nora who she is. It's what gets her up in the mornings, this compulsion to make beautiful things, whether they are clothes or hats or wall hangings. They're her mark on the world . . .' She hesitates. 'It's a classic story of a woman's life at the time – that struggle to make meaning in her life, to rise above the disappointments and the hardships and simply do what matters to her.'

'As a rule,' Adele says, 'I'm not keen on books that use that device of an old person looking back on their life. But I suppose that writers sometimes do it because having the person reflecting means they don't have to tell the whole story from start to finish, just sort of illustrate it with significant moments and turning points. By about the third chapter I realised that I started to read this book a long time ago, and I stopped because I was bored. But this time it grabbed me from the start. I wonder if that's because I'm older, because that's a thing you do as you get older, isn't it? You start asking yourself questions about the past but, as in Nora's case and my own, the people who could actually help you to answer them are gone. I also wonder if one just becomes a slightly more sophisticated reader with age too. What do you think?'

'I think both are true,' Ros cuts in. 'But why does anyone actually make the physical journey as opposed to . . . well, I suppose an inner emotional journey? I mean there are lots of books in which a character goes back to a place of childhood, or where something dramatic happened. I wonder if it solves anything? Does it actually solve anything for Nora?'

Judy has stopped thinking about Nora. She had seen vague parallels with her own life in Nora's, and she is now taking it all more personally. She is about to step back into the conversation when Adele cuts across her.

'Of course it does!' Adele says. 'It enables her to see herself and her life retrospectively. But are you talking about whether it works in the book or in real life?'

'Oh I think it works beautifully in the book,' Ros says, 'because the story is crafted to *make* it work for Nora. But does it work for people like us, for example, as opposed to fictional characters?'

'I think it does work in real life, sometimes in quite dramatic ways,' Adele says. 'You can see that on television when people are interviewed about the war and they go back to places where they were imprisoned, or perhaps a relative died, something like that. It helps people to deal with their memories, and their losses, even if it's only in terms of laying a few ghosts.'

'Yes, and finding out about families is important too,' Judy cuts in. 'Like on that program *Who Do You Think You Are* where people don't even know what they are going back to, but when they make the journey they find that all sorts of aspects of their lives are drawn together by threads and then they have to think not only about the past, but who they themselves are because of that, or perhaps in spite of it.' She's been coughing a lot today and it starts again now. She's almost thankful for it because the others won't think it's her emotions but the cough that's responsible for the tears in her eyes.

'That's exactly right,' Adele says. 'Are you okay, Judy? Do you want something for that cough?'

Judy shakes her head. 'No, no I'm fine, thanks,' she says.

'I think this journey for Nora was like completing a jigsaw puzzle,' Adele continues. 'She tried to come home earlier, she couldn't afford it and then when she could she got sick. She always wanted to make sense of the past, to get some clarity and resolution around it. I understand that completely. Haven't you ever wanted to go back to where you came from, Ros?'

Ros smiles. 'I suppose I'm being unreasonable in this because where I originally came from is two streets away from where I live now and have done for most of my life.'

'But haven't you lived in some other places?' Adele asks.

'Well yes, a year in London in my twenties, and then James and I lived for a couple of years in Germany, when his research took him there. We did the same again in London, it was supposed to be for two years so –' She stops abruptly.

'So don't you ever think of going to one of those places?' Simone asks. 'Lifting up the lid and peering inside again, so to speak?'

Ros hesitates, and Judy watches her, wondering what Ros is feeling, if she too is experiencing this in a very personal way.

'I *have* thought about it in that way, yes, I've thought about going to London . . .'

Judy can see that Ros is trying to get past this moment, and she almost stops breathing.

'You see, James died while we were there,' Ros continues. 'It was a horrible, sudden, accidental death and I was devastated, and I came home, perhaps too quickly. So I have thought about going back, to . . . well, to think things through, I suppose, to honour him. But I am not sure whether I would find any meaning . . .'

There is a brief and slightly awkward silence.

'What I think Nora's life demonstrates,' Simone says, 'is the subtle and not so subtle ways that, back then, women were put down and trivialised, and not always by men but often by other women. This really gets under my skin, because I think we all do it from time to time. We try to find someone to look down on, in order to feel better about ourselves. That has to be one of the nastiest things people can do to each other. To me it's as bad as physical violence because it can destroy your sense of who you are.'

'Yes, I agree with that,' Judy says, 'and one of the lovely elements of Nora's character is her sense of herself. She's getting physically frail, but her ability to know herself enables her to withstand that sort of undermining, as well as the challenges of her age. She has great endurance and dignity, and you can really see both of those characteristics very clearly by the end of the book.'

As the conversation continues and broadens, they laugh and argue, cutting across each other, apologising, punching the air, burying faces in hands. At one point Simone doubles up with laughter, and as she straightens up and throws her head back Judy catches a brief glimpse of a big scar down the side of her face that is usually hidden by her hair. She is about to say something and then stops herself. If Simone wants to tell them about it she will, she decides. And she looks around again and senses a change, not only in herself, but in the group. So much of what's been said has struck home for her. She'd really enjoyed the book but this conversation has made it all seem more significant.

'How are you doing, Judy?' Ros asks.

'Okay thanks,' she says. 'I'm glad I stayed for this.'

It's almost two hours before the last word on Nora's story is spoken.

'Great choice, Ros,' Simone says. 'I'm tea lady today. Ready for it now?'

The rain has stopped at last, and while Simone makes the tea Clooney leads the way into the garden and bounds off through the sparkling grass and fallen leaves. The wind has dropped too and the scent of the sodden ground – of damp old logs and dripping branches – fills the air. The light has almost gone and the trees are slowly becoming silhouettes against the sky.

Ros inhales deeply. 'At last,' she says. 'I love that smell and the wonderful stillness. I hope it's a clear bright day tomorrow. Maybe if it is you'll be tempted to stay a bit longer, Judy?'

Judy smiles, thinking about the book she's chosen. When they go back inside they'll draw the marbles to decide who'll be first to introduce their book. She almost wishes she'd be here to be a part of it – almost, but not enough. Although she'll miss them; they've listened and heard her, and they understand how she feels. Best of all they've made her laugh, even at herself.

As they go back into the house she pauses, admiring, for the first time, the beauty of it, the thick stone walls and the dark polished timber floors, the soft light from the lamps on side tables and the glow of the wood stove alongside the huge basket of logs. It really is a lovely place. She sighs as she admits to herself that today she is feeling a sense of calm that she hasn't felt for a long time. As she heads for her chair nearest the fire she notices that they are all returning to the places where they'd sat earlier, the same places they had sat in yesterday, and when they had arrived on Thursday afternoon: Ros in the big armchair, Adele on one side of sofa, her legs drawn up to one side, and Simone at the other end, though often also cross-legged on the floor. *How strange*, she thinks. They're like a group of nuns who have their own special places on the pews and never sit anywhere else. *How easily and naturally this has happened.*

Adele fetches the bag of marbles. 'Who wants to go first?'

'I will,' Ros says, and she draws the same purple marble she drew before. 'Breathing space,' she says with a smile. 'Who's next?'

Simone reaches for the bag. 'I'll do it.' She draws pale green, then turns to Judy. 'Yes or no?' she asks, about to pass the bag in front of her to Adele.

'What happens if no one draws white?' Judy asks.

'We'll start again,' Adele says.

Judy hesitates, raises a hand to the bag, and then drops it. 'I won't be here,' she says.

'Go on, just for the hell of it,' Ros urges.

Judy laughs, reaches into the bag, takes a deep breath and is shocked to find the white marble in the palm of her hand.

'Fate,' Simone says. 'Perhaps it means you are meant to stay a week and talk about your book.'

Judy, frozen with shock, looks around the room. The others are smiling at her, waiting for her, and she can see that they want her to stay. She buries her face in her hands.

'It's just a white marble,' Adele says. 'You *can* put it back and pass the bag on.'

Judy looks up again, swallows several times. 'I don't know . . . it's complicated,' she says. 'I don't know how to explain . . .'

'Take your time,' Ros says. 'And you don't actually *have* to explain anything. But there is a question I'd like to ask you. Is that okay?'

Judy nods.

'What will going back solve? To me it seems it would just drop you back into what you've described as a mess of your own creation, and one that's draining the life out of you. Do you think there's a chance that by staying away you might be in a better position to find a solution? To find ways of changing things?'

'That's three questions,' Adele says, 'but they *are* good questions, Judy. And I know quite a bit about business management and budgets and so on. We could talk about it, try to get to the root of the problem or problems. Only if you want to, of course.'

Judy leans forward, forearms on her knees, hands clasped, staring down at the floor, trying to work out what she feels, and what she wants to say. Everyone else is silent, waiting.

'I'll try to explain something,' she says eventually, looking up. 'You'll think I'm stupid but you might understand.'

'We all know you're *not* stupid, Judy,' Simone says. 'Just tell us whatever you want.'

Judy takes a deep breath, sits up straighter. 'Okay, well, I have a history of running away. It began on my second day at school. I hated it, and we lived really near the school, only a few minutes' walk away. So at lunchtime on the second day I just walked out and ran home, no one even noticed. My mum had a fit when I walked in the back door and told her I'd run away from school like a girl in a story she'd once read to me. It didn't go down well. The next time I ran away was when I was nine. My best friend Margie and I were in the Brownies and there was a four-day camp at the seaside. Margie wanted to go so I said I'd go too. But when we got there I decided I didn't like it and told the Brown Owl. She said I had to stay one night and see how it went, but I sneaked out to the phone box and called my dad, and persuaded him to come and get me. Margie was terribly upset. I saw her crying as Dad drove out of the car park. It was weeks before she spoke to me again after that.'

She stops, feeling slightly stronger, takes another deep breath and sees that the other three are all listening to her attentively. 'It's pathetic, I know,' she says, 'and it doesn't stop there. I ran away from my first job. It was a Saturday morning job in the local grocer's shop. I was thirteen or fourteen, and I hated it, so I ran away after four Saturdays but I didn't dare tell Mum, so I just went out as though I was going to work and stayed out all morning until it was time to go home. I got found out then too.'

Ros laughs. 'So you really do have form!'

'I do,' Judy admits, even managing a smile. 'And it gets worse. I ran away from the little town where I lived and went to London. I didn't tell my parents I was going, just phoned them when I got there. In London I fell in love with an Australian from the Wheatbelt, married him and came here to live, then I ran away from him and that life too. I guess . . . I guess that when things get tough I've never learned the art of staying put and finding a different solution. You could even say that in coming here I was running away from my life with the shop. And now I want to run away from here. It's my first reaction to feeling out of place, being an outsider, not being able to cope.

Run, run, run. But I guess there has to be a time when I stop running, although I've left it rather late in life, haven't I?'

'But not *too* late,' Ros says.

Judy nods, and very slowly takes more deep breaths. 'So yes, I will, I'll stay a bit longer and maybe, Adele, it might help to talk about the business. Thank you, all of you, for being so kind and patient. And I'm sorry for being such a "soppy date", which is what Mum called me when I ran away from Brownie camp.'

'And you don't have a taxi, or a helicopter rescue, booked for tomorrow?' Ros asks.

Judy feels something heavy lift from her chest and she laughs, a lot now, laughs until tears run down her face and the others laugh with her. 'Nothing, Ros,' she says, 'nothing booked at all. You don't need to start building barricades.'

'And you'll be okay going first with your book?' Adele asks. 'We can always draw again.'

'I'll be okay,' Judy says. 'I'll go and get it now.' She gets to her feet and goes slowly up the stairs to her room. She is still on the verge of tears, but it's a good feeling, as though she has got past something that was standing in her way. Talking about the shop with Adele might really help. This morning she had taken the three copies of the book out of her suitcase and put them on the dressing table. She'd intended to give them to the others before leaving; just hand them out and ask that they consider it for the reading list sometime. She glances at her face in the mirror. *I look at least a hundred,* she tells herself. She's had a bit of a rest but it probably isn't enough. Feeling she's made a good, if somewhat scary, decision she picks up the books and heads back down the stairs.

'Okay,' she says, standing still, holding the books in front of her, marvelling that she now feels so comfortable, and . . . what else is it? Thankful, yes, thankful – that most of all. 'So here are the books,' she says, handing each one a copy. '*Sacred Country* by the English writer Rose Tremain. It's set in a small Suffolk town, similar to the place where I spent my childhood, and it starts on the fifteenth of February nineteen fifty-two, which was the day that the whole of England stopped for two minutes' silence in honour of the king, who had died about ten days earlier at Sandringham. Sandringham, in case you don't know, is in Norfolk, so actually not very far away from Suffolk.' To her own amazement she thinks she is sounding different, stronger and more confident.

They study the cover, flick through the pages, stare at the author biography.

'I think it might be one of those books that people either love or hate,' Judy says. 'Of course I love it and I've read it several times. So . . . I hope you enjoy it. And thanks for being so patient with me.'

'My mum used to call me a soppy date too,' Ros says quietly. 'I think that's our vintage, Judy. I'm looking forward to reading this.' She picks up the champagne bottle and holds it out to Judy. 'Why don't you open this? Your turn to pour.'

Chapter Seven

It's still dark when Simone gets up on Wednesday morning and she takes her time, enjoying the early morning stillness of the house and focusing on her body: the way she is moving, walking without shoes, monitoring her breathing and being absolutely in the moment with no other distractions. In the kitchen she pours herself a large glass of water and sips it slowly, standing by the window and gazing out towards the narrow line of pale dawn light on the horizon. Clooney joins her; he has taken a liking to her because she is usually good for a walk and always has treats in her pockets. She, in turn, has fallen in love with him. She opens the back door to let him out, watching him as she finishes her drink. When he wanders back inside Simone gives him some treats, then he follows her to the games room and sits on the bottom step watching as she rolls out her yoga mat. Once she is sitting cross-legged on the mat he gets up and walks over to lie down beside her.

At the sound of footsteps on the stairs Simone looks around to see that Adele has come to join her.

'It's only me,' Adele says softly. And she picks up a mat from the stack by the wall and rolls it out so that she is horizontal with Simone, with Clooney in the space between.

'I'm so glad you decided to come,' Simone says. 'Have you done any yoga before?'

Adele shakes her head. 'No, but when you said you'd help me I started reading quite a lot about it, so I'm not totally ignorant.' She names a couple of books and Simone nods approval.

'That's a really good start. So let's begin with some breathing exercises . . .'

She leads Adele through the basics, demonstrating each position and then watching as Adele follows. For the next half-hour they work through a range of moves and positions and Simone is impressed by how intently Adele listens, retains information, and can then put it into practice. 'I don't think I've ever had a person new to yoga who took to the basics as quickly as you're doing, Adele,' she says. 'Your schoolteachers must have loved you.'

Adele laughs. 'Not really. I didn't have the same powers of concentration in those days – besides, I'm very motivated to learn now and I want to make the most of the time we're here.'

'Okay,' Simone says. 'Let's do it all again.'

It's almost an hour later when they make their way back up to the kitchen.

'I'm not sure I like this,' Simone says, studying the breakfast roster. 'We all get up at different times, and I don't always want a cooked breakfast anyway. What say after today everybody gets their own breakfast when they feel like it, except perhaps for Sundays, when we could all have breakfast together?'

'Fine by me,' Adele says. 'I'd like to walk some mornings

too so it would be good not to be tied to a particular time. I didn't allow for that when I set up the roster.'

'Which, of course, you did weeks before we got here,' Simone says, turning to her with a smile.

Adele blushes. 'How did you *know*?'

'I didn't, but I'm getting to know *you*, Adele, so it was an educated guess.'

'Please don't tell the others,' Adele says. 'They'll think I'm a complete control freak.'

'I won't. But I think they'd just tease you about it,' Simone says. 'And I'm on the roster for today, so I'm going to make lemon pancakes.'

*

When Adele gets back to the kitchen after a quick shower upstairs, Simone is whipping up the batter, squeezing and slicing the lemons and hunting for the caster sugar. Ros is sitting at the table reading yesterday's paper and looking rather glum.

'I drank too much white wine last night,' Ros says when Adele asks if she's feeling okay. 'I should know better, it always upsets me. I can drink red until it comes out of my ears, but white is no good for me.'

'Then we'd better stock up on red next time we go shopping,' Adele says and Ros gives her a wan smile.

Outside in the passage she can hear Judy heading for the kitchen, coughing.

'Morning all,' Judy croaks, dropping into a chair opposite Ros. 'Oh pancakes, Simone, what a treat.'

'Still coughing, Judy?' Ros says, glancing up. 'Do you feel okay?'

'Not too bad. I might get something for it if we go out later.'

'I was thinking,' Simone says, flipping the first pancake onto Ros's plate, 'about going into Blackheath. When we were in Leura the other day I picked up this flyer for an exhibition by local artists, and today all the artists are going to be there in the gallery to chat about their work. Anyone fancy coming with me?' She pulls a flyer from her pocket and drops it onto the table.

'Oh yes, I will,' Adele says. 'I picked up one of those too and then forgot about it. I'll definitely go with you.'

Judy draws the flyer across the table, stares at it and turns it over.

'Yep, looks good,' she says. 'I'm in, what about you, Ros?'

'I might see how I feel after breakfast,' Ros says. 'This might be a staying home day for me.' She picks up her knife and fork and tastes her pancake. 'This is delicious, Simone, thank you. Absolutely perfect.'

'Simone and I were talking about changing the breakfast arrangements,' Adele says when they've all had one pancake and Simone is back on her feet cooking the second round. 'We're wondering whether it might be better if we all do our own thing for breakfast except for perhaps on Sundays. We all get up at different times, after all – sometimes we might not want to get up at all.'

'Good idea,' Ros says. 'We eat our other meals together, so independent breakfasts make a lot of sense.'

'I agree,' Judy says. 'I'm actually better if I stick to my usual cereal for breakfast. I seem to have more energy after that. Mind you, I'm loving the pancakes this morning, Simone.'

Simone has cooked another small stack of pancakes and she puts the plate in the centre of the table. 'Help yourselves,' she says. She flips a pancake onto her own plate and sprinkles it with lemon and sugar. 'Here you are, Clooney, just a taste for you.'

Adele looks nervously at Ros, who doesn't approve of titbits at the table. But Ros just rolls her eyes and says nothing.

They sit for a while, sipping their coffee, and Adele feels herself relaxing into the conversation, noticing how normal it feels, how different from the other occasions when she has been away from home with her work colleagues. In the past she has set up brief planning retreats for the bureau staff when they would all go off to a hotel together and spend two or three days sorting out new options for the study tours, matching them to specific partners, and deciding how and when to schedule them. She would always try to bring in a guest too, either a local celebrity, or a motivational speaker of some sort. It was clear the staff enjoyed this mix of work and socialising for a few days, free of other domestic responsibilities. Adele always booked the best facilities where they could use the swimming pool and the gym; everyone seemed at ease, they worked well together and she felt it strengthened the sense of goodwill and trust that she wanted to foster. Everyone looked forward to the retreats – everyone, that is, except Adele herself, who always felt awkward and exposed outside the safe, predictable confines of the office and the regular pattern of working. Adele had thought about this while planning the book club retreat. She'd been pretty sure she could organise it so that the others would enjoy it, but the anticipation of being in such close proximity to people she barely knew had borne down on her in the last few weeks and only now is she starting to truly relax; even to feel a little bit confident that there will be no nasty surprises and no awkward cases of people falling out.

Ros has finished her pancakes and coffee, and she gets to her feet and starts rummaging for something in the pantry. 'The red and black tin,' she says, 'the one with Clooney's treats in it, has anyone seen it?' She pushes jars and packets around trying to find it. 'I'm sure I put it in here but now I can't find it.'

'It's on the next shelf down, Ros,' Simone says.

Ros bends over, retrieves the tin, straightens up, and backs out of the pantry, holding it up with a puzzled expression. 'That's odd,' she says, shaking the tin. 'I could have sworn it was about three-quarters full the other day. But this feels almost empty.' And she carries the tin to the table and opens it. 'It is, it's practically empty!' she says, shocked. 'I must have . . . no . . . no, I remember quite clearly it *was* more than half-full, so where . . . ?'

'Sorry, Ros, my fault,' Simone says. 'I always put some in my pocket when I take him for a walk. And I've slipped him some at other times too. I'll replace them, get some more when we're out.'

Ros turns to face Simone, and Adele can see that she's really pissed off.

'It's not about replacing them, Simone,' she says. 'You feed him at the table, every meal time. I haven't said anything earlier, because I don't want to nag, but now this – *so many* treats! What I put in that tin would normally last him about three weeks, but now there's only a couple left.'

'It's not only Simone,' Judy says. 'I've been sneaking him some too, every day.'

Adele takes a deep breath. 'Me too,' she says sheepishly. 'He always seems so hungry.'

'He is NOT hungry!' Ros is really angry now. 'He's a dog, and so by definition a natural scrounger. I can't believe you would do this, especially as I specifically asked you all, on the day we arrived, not to feed him at the table, and only occasionally to give him treats. Every meal I've seen you slipping stuff to him. But now the treats as well! Yesterday I saw one of you – you, I think, Adele – give him a piece of cheese. Well did you know that a small cube of cheese, smaller than the one you gave him, is the equivalent of a Big Mac for a human? No, of course you didn't, but you do now, so don't do it. Clooney has two perfectly good meals a day. He's old, and this is very bad for his health. It could make him really sick.'

Clooney looks mournfully up at Ros and the tin. There is deadly silence and Adele can see that she's not the only one who can't look Ros in the face. 'I'm so sorry, Ros,' she says, making herself meet her eyes now. 'I wouldn't want to do anything to hurt him.'

'Well that's just what you *are* doing,' Ros says, glaring at her. 'It's what you're *all* doing.' Adele hears the crack in her voice and sees for the first time that Ros is not simply angry with them, she is also deeply upset.

The others are murmuring more apologies, but Ros picks up the tin and calls to Clooney, who has been looking from one to the other with a grave expression. He gets up and follows her as she marches towards the door.

'Ros,' Simone calls, standing up now. 'Really, I'm so sorry.'

'Just go off to your blasted exhibition and leave me in peace,' Ros snaps, then stamps off down the passage with Clooney following her.

'Oh dear,' Judy says once Ros is out of earshot. 'That was pretty awful. What do we do now?'

'Nothing,' Simone says. 'We just do as she asked. We leave her alone to get over it.'

'One of us could go and talk to her,' Adele suggests.

Simone shakes her head. 'I think that would be a very bad idea, Adele. Let's just clear up, put everything in the dish-washer and go out. A little walk, the exhibition, a nice coffee somewhere . . . by the time we get back, she'll still be annoyed, but she'll be over the worst of it.'

'Do you really think we've made Clooney ill?' Adele asked. 'I've never had a dog. I know nothing about looking after them but I have rather fallen in love with Clooney.'

'Me too,' Simone says, 'and I doubt we've done any damage yet, but Ros is right, and we do have to stop. I thought it was just me.'

'Me too,' Adele says. And Judy nods.

Simone starts to stack the dishwasher. 'Come on, let's get going, everyone, there's some shopping to do.'

*

Ros sits by the window in her bedroom, staring out at the rain and savouring the silence, with Clooney stretched out on the rug in front of her snoring very softly. The others have been gone for some time and she relishes the sense of being alone in the house. She had come back to her bedroom seething with what she can now see was probably an unreasonable level of outrage, and it then took her some time to calm down. On reflection, she can see that it was fear more than anything else that fired her outburst. Feeling she had lost control over Clooney's diet, and potentially his health, had totally spooked her. It's made her realise how much she depends on the reliability of his habits and their regular routine. He is her constant, faithful companion, hugely comforting and entertaining, and so predictable. Although, she admits to herself, maybe in addition to the fear of losing him, she also didn't like the thought that the treats and titbits would mean sharing his unconditional love. She smiles slightly, nudging Clooney with her socked foot. 'So, maybe I was jealous,' she says. 'Competing for your affections, I said, and I'm the most fiercely competitive of all.' Clooney yawns, readjusts his position slightly and starts snoring again.

The house is blissfully quiet. It's not just the silence that she relishes; it's the lack of movement that enables her to feel at one with herself. Constant movement and conversation eats away at her equilibrium, leaving her feeling like an old plaster statue slowly being chipped around the edges, the colours peeling off and flaking away. Living with three other people was always going to be a challenge, and she'd felt relieved when she heard the car crunching off down the gravel this morning.

When, after James's death, she had converted the first floor into a separate flat Ros had insisted on soundproofing it. 'I don't want to hear people moving around,' she'd told the builder. 'And I don't want them to hear me. The only sounds that should be audible to both of us are those around the front door.' Even the staircase was insulated. It had turned out to be mightily expensive but to Ros it was worth every last cent.

Ros has not always sought stillness and silence. In the late sixties and well into the seventies, she had shared a large and chilly apartment with three other musicians. It was a grubby sort of place that allowed for deteriorating standards of house-keeping. The sink was always full of unwashed crockery, it was rare to find a clean plate in the cupboard, and tea towels would be discovered balled up in odd places gathering dust and fluff. Ros could cope with all of this, and make her own contribution to it. She grew accustomed to strangers sleeping on the sofa, or to discovering them in her bed if she came home late. She became immune to late night encounters with some-one's naked boyfriend raiding the pantry; to discovering her hairbrush had accrued someone else's hair, and to unknown persons pilfering the curry or pasta that she had left in the fridge. But as time passed living with others became oppressive, and she craved her own space. Eventually she moved into a flat over a greengrocer's shop, and there she discovered the pure joy of living alone.

She was twenty-nine when she met James, who was a few years older and much more mature. He was a calm, organised person, with high domestic standards – to him cleaning and cooking were things that one just did daily without fuss; a rare find in this respect as in many others. He was also something of an introvert and Ros, in those days, was inclined to adapt to her surroundings. She had grown up in a really well-ordered household; her mother was a true domestic goddess and perhaps the shared flat had been a reaction to this. It was easy for her to adapt to James, to adopt his standards and live in peace with order, cleanliness and agreed personal boundaries that helped her to stay calm and centred. She moved into James's larger flat within a few months, and they lived there for several years until he eventually inherited his parents' home in Paddington where she still lives now, and where they had shared their love of stillness, of music and books and good, simple, well-cooked food. Ros had felt that James was the only person who had ever bothered to find out who she was; who knew her, and who accepted the whole package. He made her real to herself, validated her idiosyncrasies, tolerated her more irritating habits and loved her just the same. It was easy for her to reciprocate. Ros reflects on this now, on her extraordinary good fortune in finding another introvert, falling in love and living largely in peace for so much of her adult life.

But James died. He died when he should still have lived, earlier than either of them had imagined. He was on a two-year residency as a Visiting Fellow at the University of London, and they were almost halfway through their stay there when, on an icy February morning, he caught a bus along Euston

Road, close to the apartment the university had provided for them. Ten minutes later, as the bus slowed down to approach the corner of a busy junction he jumped off, slipped on the ice and crashed down, hitting his head on the kerb. He was dead before the ambulance arrived.

Ros thinks of this now, fifteen years later, as she does at some point every day. She thinks of James: blood seeping from his skull staining the ice crimson, the clamour of people around him, their breath making clouds in the cold air, and the ambulance siren growing closer as the driver weaves through the commuter traffic, unaware that it is already too late. She'd tried to make sense of it. Why? Why then? Why James? Why couldn't she have had the chance to be with him at the end? What was the meaning of such a banal death for such an extraordinary man? How could she live with it? But she has, of course, lived with it every day for almost fifteen years, and there are no answers. It happened, it's done; it was all over a long time ago. Why, then, does it all seem so unfinished?

Ros is an only child who learned how to live her life through reading, and so she believes that one day she will find an answer in the pages of a book. She believes this despite knowing that there *is* no answer. It is simply what it is. But where there are books there is hope. Isn't there? The hope that one day she will land on a page and there will be resolution at last.

She had left London as soon as she could and in the meantime avoided going anywhere near the place where James died. Somehow she had kidded herself that by staying away she would find an answer to her questions. But what answer could there be? And what would resolution look like? Some years ago she started to read some of the classics she had neglected in her youth. She had begun with the Russians:

Tolstoy, Dostoyevsky, Turgenev. It was hard but rewarding work, though if resolution was tucked away in the pages Ros couldn't find it. Eventually, searching for something completely different, she began to read Proust and staggered through *In Search of Lost Time*, by turns loving and hating the author and his alter ego hero; wanting some days to sit down and talk with him for hours, and on others itching to punch him in his calm, pretentious face. What it clarified for her, though, was something she unconsciously understood but had never thought much about: that experience is only fully lived through memory, through true imaginative recollection. When, back home a few weeks ago, she had first read *Tirra Lirra by the River*, she saw that Nora was, in a way, reliving – perhaps remaking – her own life in this same way. It was a very short book compared to Proust's three hundred thousand words, but Jessica Anderson had created something similar and, in Ros's view, more beautiful, thanks to its simplicity. She had been captivated by this seemingly perfect example of revisiting the past to make sense of it; not just in the mind and the heart but also the power of physically going back to a place. And since their conversation about it she has realised that this is what she has being trying to do for a long time – make sense of her own life, both with James and since he has gone. She has more in common with Nora than she realised: the observation and reflection through the lens of old age, the attempt to see her life as a whole, coordinated entity, rather than a jumbled mess of experiences. It has made sense to her to try to work out why she did, or did not do, certain things at certain times, why she had been selfish or cruel when she could have been generous or kind, why she had been blind or indifferent when she could have shown compassion. It wasn't a simple rehashing of the past but it was showing her a way to think about the future and how to live a good life in her old age.

It seemed tied in somehow with the changes in her body. Even before the diagnosis she had begun to feel physically old, weaker and more vulnerable, and to tire easily. She lost her balance a few times and had to grasp the back of a chair or a table to steady herself. Her feet sometimes seemed to be heading in completely different directions from each other and she came close to falling as she tried to correct them. And then her hands started to shake from time to time. Even her feisty, often obstructive nature seemed to soften and thin. It was her shaking hands and her disobedient feet that had eventually compelled her to talk to her doctor. And so began the whole battery of tests, followed by the delivery of information, of certainty.

Parkinson's, they said, thus transforming her image of the future with a single word. Parkinson's. And now, each day, try as she might to pretend that if she doesn't tell anyone it isn't real, she recognises that this is the second time in her life that she has been faced with the unchangeable, and that she is stuck in a place in which she cannot summon imaginative recollection to her aid.

In their discussion of Jessica Anderson's book she had raised questions about the value of returning to a place of memories. The others had looked at her strangely, as though she was suggesting it might be a waste of time. But what she had really been asking was – *should I go back? If I went back to the Euston Road, if I stood in the spot where James's head cracked so sickeningly against the kerb, would that provide resolution? And how could going back help me now that my future is disappearing in a blurry haze of incapacity and dependence?* She pictures him doing what he always did; getting to his feet, walking to the back of the bus and standing on the open rear platform, near the conductor, hanging onto the rail until they reached the stop.

Why, she asks James now, *why did you have to jump off? Why the hell couldn't you wait until it turned the corner and stopped? It was only a few metres, for goodness sake. What sort of idiot does that?* And she can almost hear him answer: *People do it all the time, Ros, you know that. I was just unlucky.*

The rain has stopped now and she can hear the sound of an engine and tyres splashing through the mud. They'll need a cup of tea, she thinks, and she gets to her feet intending to go and put the kettle on, then stops. *No,* she tells herself. *You need this time – sit down, stay here. They can make their own tea.*

Chapter Eight

The second Sunday

Judy wakes on Sunday morning with a sense of energy and purpose. She has enjoyed a whole week of rest and finds now that she is actually looking forward to discussing *Sacred Country* this afternoon. Only the wretched cough remains to cramp her style. The weather has cleared and she decides on an early walk. For the first time since they arrived she is up before the others, standing in the kitchen in her tracksuit, drinking a cup of tea, when Adele wanders in.

'Really?' Adele says, when Judy tells her she's going for a walk. 'Do you think that's a good idea? You're still coughing and it sounds rough. It's cold out there, and look at the sky.'

July reboils the kettle and gets out a mug for Adele. Then she peers across the sink to study the sky through the window. 'Looks okay to me. Not all bright and clear like yesterday, but I think I can beat the rain.'

'Well I don't like the look of it,' Adele says.

'I need some fresh air and a bit of exercise.'

'You could wait until a little later,' Adele suggests. 'We could all go with you.'

The last thing Judy wants is company. 'It'll be fine,' she says again. 'And I'm looking forward to this afternoon.'

She hands Adele a mug of tea, hurries to the front door, pulls on her boots, her anorak and a beanie and closes the door behind her. The coldness of the air takes her by surprise; it catches in her throat and she coughs, tightens her scarf, and looks up at the sky again. Maybe Adele is right; it does look as though it could rain later. *Anyway*, she thinks, *I'm not going far, just a gentle stroll.* But Judy has spent at least a couple of decades rushing everywhere, trying to fit the various aspects of her growing business into a working day. How a gentle stroll might feel has been erased from her memory by her need to keep on the go. She sets off at a rapid pace, taking a steep track down and away from the house.

She walks on for some time trying to focus on the book, what it means to her, and what choosing it as her special book might tell the others about her. The last part is difficult – what could it tell them? Why hasn't she asked herself this before? She stops abruptly. 'That's ridiculous,' she says aloud. 'I can't just say it's about my home, the place, the characters, and so on.' She feels the same sharp stab of failure that she remembers from schooldays, especially from exams, when she would invest considerable thought and effort in answering a question only to realise, as the final bell rang, that in her haste to begin, she had misread the question.

Okay, she tells herself now, *this is all perfectly okay, this is not an exam, it's fine for me to pick a book simply because I love it and it means something to me about my old home. That alone must tell them something about me.*

There is a wooden seat ahead of her and she stops and sits

down for a moment to get her breath. Thinking about the book has distracted her and she realises she has walked further than she intended, and her breath is uncomfortably harsh in her chest. As Adele predicted, it's now starting to rain. Judy checks her watch and is amazed to see that she has been out for more than half an hour. She gets to her feet and starts back up what seems like a different, wider and rougher track towards the house. Her pace is slower now and the tightness in her chest has worsened. She puffs and wheezes. *Idiot*, she thinks. It's going to take her a lot longer to get home again. It's raining heavily now and she pulls up her hood and feels her hair pressed wet and cold against her head. Fifteen minutes later, the effort of pushing back, uphill, against the forces of wind and rain compels her to stop and rest. Her legs are aching horribly and her knees are particularly sore – as though someone has hammered nails into them. Somehow she has lost track of how much further it is to the house, and has ended up on a different path; in fact it's a dirt road. She just knows she needs to keep heading for higher ground. It's hard to see through the downpour and she struggles against the wind that keeps ripping the hood from her head. A sudden sense of helplessness overtakes her, a feeling of weakness that tells her she can't go on. She sinks down onto a fallen tree trunk on the edge of the road, eyes closed, face buried in her hands, willing her lungs to get her home while struggling to breathe normally. She hunches her shoulders, trying to sink her neck deeper into the protection of her anorak, and doesn't hear the sound of a car engine until it stops alongside her.

'Judy,' Adele says, jumping out of the passenger seat. 'Judy, can you get up? Can you get in the car? Come on, I'll help you.' She slips her arm through Judy's and urges her to her feet.

'Wow, you're a godsend,' Judy says, getting up slowly, steadying herself against Adele. 'I think I overdid it a bit.'

'You're soaked,' Simone says, leaning across from the driver's seat to take her hand. She hauls Judy into the car, while Adele slides into the back seat.

Judy leans back, her breathing more normal now. 'Were you going somewhere?' she asks.

'We were looking for you,' Simone says. 'Adele came and got me because she was worried about you. But we didn't know which way you'd gone. We tried three other tracks before we found you.' She slips the car into gear and goes a little further on down until there is space to turn and then heads cautiously back up towards the house. 'Okay,' she says, pulling up outside the front door. 'Can we trust you not to do this again? Or do we need to chain you up?'

'I promise,' Judy laughs. 'It was a really stupid thing to do. Sometimes I feel compelled to just rush at things.'

'Come and do yoga with us,' Adele says. 'Simone is a great teacher. I already feel calmer, more centred.'

'Maybe,' Judy says, unconvinced. 'But for now I might just go and have another lie-down.'

*

'Are you sure you feel up to this, Judy?' Simone asks as they settle around the fire that afternoon.

'I'm sure. I really want to,' Judy says, looking out through the big windows to the garden, which is still taking a beating from the rain, then she turns back to the others. 'Okay,' she says, picking up her familiar, dog-eared copy of the book and stroking the cover. 'This is my book, *Sacred Country*, and as I think I told you last week it begins in nineteen fifty-two with the two minutes' silence for the king. It was the day of his funeral, just like it says on the first page, and it began to snow that afternoon, and just like the family in the book, we – my younger brother Robert and I – stood with our parents at the bottom of the garden to honour the king. So you can imagine how it felt when I opened this book and, on page one, found a place and a time and a feeling that was entirely authentic and personal.'

'I imagine it was a bit strange to read something so close to your own experience,' Adele says. 'Almost as though the writer had been watching you.'

'Yes. Sonny, the father in the book, made his family go outside because he believed that prayers worked better if said out of doors. And my dad was the same; he maintained that even churches, with their high ceilings, could get in the way of messages getting through to God. So it really felt as though Rose Tremain had been there with us.'

Simone, who had been intrigued by *Sacred Country*, is watching Judy closely. She really wants to know more about why this book is so important to her. There is also something about it all that reminds her of her own childhood: the way that the people in the book struggle to cope with the place where they live, their limited choices. It is nothing like her childhood home, but parental controls based on religious beliefs – whether Baptist as it had been for Judy, or Catholic as it had been for her – was something familiar to her. And above all there was the sense that all important life was happening elsewhere . . .

'When I was out this morning –' Judy says.

'When you tried to escape and were brought back by the guards,' Ros interjects.

'Exactly!' Judy laughs. 'So, when I tried to escape, I was trying to work out why I had actually chosen this book, other than the fact that it is incredibly important to me. Is that enough reason to select a book that fits the brief that Adele gave us?'

'Oh, I didn't mean you had to stick to –'

'I know why you suggested it, Adele,' Judy says, 'and it was a brilliant idea, because we all know each other but, at the same time, we don't. What better way to fill the gaps than by talking about books, this time more personally? Anyway, on that first page there's that mention of the way the buses stopped at that moment, that people wept, not just for the king but also for themselves and for the country. It says *the silence was heavy with eternity.* And when I read that line halfway down the first page, I swear my heart stopped, because I was right back there with the snow falling, and the utter stillness and the enormity of the silence. I thought that the whole world had stopped breathing. And as I read on it seemed as though some of the people I'd known then were in the book. Not that they are exactly the same, but versions of them.'

'Not that awful man who lives in the bus and has cancer in his nose, I hope,' Ros says.

'Not exactly. But the local butcher's widow was very like the wife of the baker in my village. And there was a woman who was said to have gone mad with grief when her husband was killed at Dunkirk. Her name was Beattie Hindmarsh and she was supposed to be responsible for the flowers in the church, but she would often disappear completely for weeks on end, and my mother had to do the flowers instead. Beattie, I later discovered, was frequently taken off to what was then called "the asylum" until she stopped crying and calling for her Arthur. I can remember that when I was in my teens she would wander around the village knocking on doors, asking if Arthur was there. To me, Estelle, in the book, is Beattie Hindmarsh – she even looks like her.'

This strikes a chord for Simone. 'I loved that character,' she says. 'She was being driven slowly insane by hardship and the awful implacable husband, but I think she actually retreated to a sort of peace in her stays at the asylum – in a way she used it to escape. And of course, as time goes on she uses television in the same way.'

Judy nods. 'I think she's not unusual,' she says. 'She lived a life without hope. And as I read on there were other characters that felt familiar, like Mr Harker, who works in his cellar making cricket bats. He, to me, was Stitch, a tailor who lived in a tiny cottage and ran his tailoring business from a shed in the garden. It had a long rail on one side, for hanging the customers' suits or jackets. And he had a workbench with a sewing machine at one end, and at the other end he would sit up, cross-legged on it, to do his hand-sewing. He must have been between seventy and eighty, and he could still get up there like a little gnome, taking in waistbands, shortening cuffs, putting leather patches on the worn elbows of old sports jackets and tweeds and . . . well, sorry, I'll stop going on about this, it's not what we're here for. But I think you can see that when I read *Sacred Country*, it brought the past back to life for me in a very vivid sort of way. I wondered if Rose Tremain had grown up in the same area.

'But if any of you thought I picked this novel because Mary stands outside in the silence on that first day and realises that she is in fact a boy, that is not the reason. I have never wanted to be a boy, nor thought I was one. It's all about the place, and the people who live there; whether or not that is home and, of course, what it's like now.'

'It sounded grindingly miserable,' Simone says. 'People were trapped in all sorts of ways – poverty, hardship, tradition.'

'I thought that too,' Ros says. 'It's a very different picture of rural life in England in the fifties and beyond from what we're used to seeing. It's hardly *Miss Marple* or *Midsomer Murders* country, is it?'

Judy nods, puts her hand up to her face and realises that it's quite hot. She moves back a bit from the fire.

'No, you're right, both of you. It was a tough life. People were really hard up. England was still recovering from the war; the early fifties were pretty bleak. We had the big advantage that Mum and Dad owned the house. It was small and quite plain, it had belonged to my grandparents, and a lot of the furniture was theirs and was old and well worn. My dad was a clerk in the bank in town, and Mum used to do some cleaning and laundry for a couple of women who had big houses a few miles away. She rode there on her bike. It certainly wasn't an easy life, and of course the weather was pretty awful, cold and wet and often very windy, at least that's how I remember it.'

'This place is obviously important to you,' Adele says. 'You've told us all the negatives but you speak about it really affectionately.'

'Yes, because as a child I was happy there, perhaps because it was all I knew. We seemed lucky because we were better off than a lot of the people around us. And in those days it would never have occurred to me to question things that seem alien to me now. I was probably eighteen before I began to hate my father's involvement with the chapel, for example, and to protest about the rules at home – not talking at meal times, not being allowed out to play on Sundays. Things like that were part of life. And the people I knew then came into my life again through the characters in the book. It made me long to go there, to stand in our old garden for just a few minutes and feel that place, because it is part of who I am.'

'And did you go back?' Simone asks.

Judy shakes her head. 'Never. I haven't been to England since Ted and I left in nineteen seventy.'

'But why not?' Ros asks. 'It means so much to you.'

Judy laughs. 'Wasn't it you who asked the other day *why* people go back? Now you're asking me why I *didn't.*'

'Of course,' Ros says. 'I'm asking because when you were talking I could hear a longing for that place and that time. And I feel you're really sad about it. So what stopped you?'

Judy sighs. 'Well, to answer that I need to tell you about why I left and what followed that. But I need a break before I get into all that. Anyone want another cup of tea?'

In the kitchen Judy fills the kettle and switches it on. She is suddenly exhausted by the effort of talking about herself so much. She's unused to discussing her personal life and now she feels rather as though she's been doing that ever since she got here.

'How are you going?' Adele says, appearing in the doorway. 'Want a hand?'

'Thanks, that'd be good. I'm okay but it all feels a bit full-on.'

'I'll say! I was sitting there thinking how glad I was I didn't draw the white marble. Going first is really tough.'

'It is,' Judy says. 'But it also feels good. I don't get much chance to talk about the past or what matters to me. Things seem different when you say them out loud, don't they? All that stuff I told you the other day, about running away – it was so good to put it out there, get your reactions. Just sharing it made a big difference. But it's also exhausting.'

Adele nods. 'Are you okay to go on? You can just say, no more, draw a line, and leave it to the rest of us to talk about the book.'

Judy turns to her. 'I want to go on, because when I think of stopping it doesn't feel good. Perhaps I've wanted to tell my story for a long time. That's how it feels. And you've set this up in a way that lets me do that. So I'll hang in there until you all tell me to shut up.'

Adele laughs as she starts adding milk to the mugs, remembering to keep one milk-free for Simone. 'Well that's great,' she says. 'I hope I can handle it as well when it's my turn. This coming week we could have a look at your business situation, if you like.'

'Please,' Judy says. 'I really have to do something and I'd appreciate your help and advice.'

'So you'll stay on with us?' Adele asks.

'I will, I really will. I'm determined to make the most of it now.'

Once everyone is settled back in the lounge room a natural silence seems to take over. Judy puts her tea on the side table, closes her eyes and inhales deeply. She can feel the warmth of the fire in front of her and the comforting presence of the other women, and knows she is in the right place. *Thank you,* she says silently to whatever power might be listening. *Thank you for bringing me here and persuading me to stay.* And she sees that this is where she might mend herself, where she will stitch together the seams that are strained or have already come apart. And she feels enormously relieved and grateful.

'I'm so glad I'm here,' she says, opening her eyes. 'Thank you for encouraging me to stay. It feels a bit like a nursing home for the soul and it is obviously what I needed. You could all see that but I couldn't.'

'Well, we are very wise,' Ros says, her face absolutely straight. 'Actually we're a coven. But a reasonably benign one. So we're glad you're here too. And Clooney is pleased, too, even though his consumption habits have been cut back. Are you ready to go on?'

Judy smiles and straightens up. 'I am,' she says. 'My parents were staunch chapel people, and very conservative. I think of them now as being scared of authority – not any particular sort of authority, just anyone in charge, a sort of threatening, shapeless entity that had them under surveillance and could, at any time, turn up and find them in the wrong about something, despite their always having done their best. They were very controlling and in my teens I did start to kick against that. Apparently I was quite bright – the headmistress told them I could get into university, but no one in our family had ever been, and I don't think Mum and Dad actually knew what I could do at university that might get me a job. I wasn't good at maths or science, just art and sewing, although I did write good compositions. I said I wanted to be an artist, but if you expressed ambition, or the desire to do something other than being a wife and mother, or maybe a secretary or a nurse, you were pushed back into your box. It wasn't just grown-ups, even the other girls would whisper about you: "Who does she think she is?"

'So, I did my GCE, and then worked in a small, very old-fashioned dress shop until I decided to leave home.' She fills them in on her time with Ted, the loss of her baby and how she eventually left him, ending up in Mandurah and starting the knitting shop.

'So what about Ted?' Adele asks. 'Do you still see him?'

'Of course,' Judy says. 'From time to time.'

'And your friend Donna?' Simone asks.

Judy tells them about Donna and Ted being together, and finally admits that she and Ted are still married. There is absolute silence in the room. Judy sees the others exchange glances. 'You think it's weird, don't you?'

'Well, it is a bit . . .' Simone begins cautiously. 'Don't you think so?'

'Oh I *know* it's weird. Which is why I've never told anyone else; and at the same time, despite that, it's been fine. I go down there for the occasional weekend, and sometimes Donna comes up to town and we have a weekend together in a posh hotel in Perth. Although that's pretty rare these days as we've all grown older. The thing is, I love them both, and they love each other and me. Oh, and of course there's no . . . well, no . . . it's not a threesome.'

'No hanky-panky,' Ros says.

'Exactly, well not for me!' Judy pauses, then begins again, unnerved by the silence. 'I suppose that this, and the business, is why I haven't really made friends, why I haven't had holidays. Ted and Donna are a sort of mainstay, even though I don't see them very often. I just concentrated on working. And recently things have been getting on top of me. I've been struggling to cope. Quite a few of the customers drive me mad, I don't want to be bothered with them, some are just hangers-on who want to talk at me.' She tells them about Maddie and her scarves. 'I'm very fond of Maddie, I can cope with her, but there are others who come into the shop for more than just wool, and patterns and needles. They just seem to want someone to unload on! It's become overwhelming.'

There is silence and it's clear no one knows quite what to say.

'So how do you actually feel about this, Judy?' Simone eventually asks.

Judy looks at her hard, saying nothing, just nodding, then looks away. 'I feel trapped,' she says, a lump forming in her throat. 'Trapped by my own failure to make a proper – a *balanced* life for myself. I left home because I needed freedom, and like several of the characters in this book I also wanted more than home could offer, although I didn't know what that might turn out to be. Walter, in the book, desperately wants to be a country and western singer – his every waking moment is filled with this longing, this dream, and he makes it.'

The others nod, remembering Walter's story.

'And Mary fulfils her dream of becoming Martin. Those were big dreams, and there were people I knew then who had big dreams and made them come true. And others whom you knew would be there forever, who would somehow fight to keep things the same. My only dream was escape. It's only since we talked the other night that I've begun to see that this has been a pattern throughout my life. I fight my way out of something because I feel trapped, but I always step out into the darkness without a plan, without a torch, and then fall into something else. My last trap, of course, is the one I'm in now. The one where success traps me and starts to suffocate me. And at the same time I've felt great nostalgia for the past. My parents are both dead, of course, and my brother too. So there is no one left of my family there now.'

'Would you like to go back?' Simone asks.

'Yes,' Judy says decisively. 'I feel I should have done that years ago.'

'To live?' Ros asks.

She shakes her head. 'No, only for a visit. I think it would help just to be there again, a day or two, a week perhaps.' She pauses. 'May I show you something?' She takes her iPad out of her knitting bag, which is on the floor beside her chair. 'You'll think I'm crazy . . .'

'No worries about that,' Ros says, 'we already do!'

They all laugh with relief, Judy hardest of all.

'Well,' she says, 'after I read *Sacred Country*, I was longing to be there, but there was no way I could afford the time or the money. So I decided to knit my hometown. It's taken me a very long time but I've almost finished it.'

She hands the iPad to Ros, who is sitting beside her.

Ros puts on her glasses and studies the screen. 'This?' she says in amazement. 'You mean you've knitted all this?'

Simone and Adele both get up to look over her shoulder.

'Good heavens,' says Simone, 'a knitted town. I've never seen anything like it.'

'How big is this, Judy?' Adele asks.

'Well, it occupies the whole of my spare bedroom. It's on a big board, on trestles, and there is just enough space on all four sides for me to squeeze around it to put new bits in place.'

'This is extraordinary,' Ros says. 'I mean, I've seen stuff about men setting up and making huge war scenarios or even train sets that occupy whole rooms, but I've never seen – never imagined I *would* see – a knitted town.'

'Look,' Simone says, 'there's Stitch, sewing on his bench.'

'And this must be Beattie Hindmarsh,' Adele says, 'you can see her wild hair and . . . you knitted all these people and their houses. How big are the figures?'

'They're bigger than toy soldiers, about the size of finger dolls, that you'd give to a small child.'

'But the detail . . .' Ros says. 'It's so beautiful. And are you there, Judy?'

'Yes, look,' Adele says, 'in the corner, Judy and her little brother and their parents.' She points to where two adults and two children are standing on green knitted grass, their faces turned to the sky. 'See, they're in the garden staring upwards, to see their prayers for the king going up to heaven.'

*

'I think our first discussion was a remarkable success,' Ros says at dinner that evening.

'But we didn't talk much about the book,' Judy says.

'No, but the book did exactly what Adele suggested,' Ros says. 'It told us more about you. Or rather, you told us through the framework of the book. We've learned more about you than we would otherwise have known. It's not a book I would have thought I'd want to read. But I am so glad I have. And now, because of what you've told us, I'll read it again.'

'I enjoyed it,' Adele says, 'although I got a bit fed up with some of the characters, and some of the more gritty bits. But I did like Mary/Martin's story. It was very poignant that when Martin finally goes back he knows he no longer belongs there and that's because he has changed in so many ways while the place itself and so many of the people are just the same. That might be how it would feel if you went there, Judy?'

'You know, Judy,' Simone says, 'I don't think I can actually talk about this as we might ordinarily discuss a book, because I can't separate it from you. I feel we're talking about your life, and what you valued in that place and what you didn't like.'

Ros is about to make some sharp remark about Simone going all touchy-feely when she realises that Simone is saying exactly what she herself feels. She clears her throat and sits back, listening.

'It's become very personal since you explained your rationale for choosing it,' Simone continues. 'I admire your honesty, and your willingness to put yourself on the line with us, especially going first, given the way you were feeling a few days ago. It was a real act of trust.'

Ros is again immediately tempted to come back with some sharp or funny remark but again she manages to stop herself. *Why do I always want to do that?* she wonders. *Simone is quite right, so why do I feel so embarrassed and awkward when she goes all earnest like this? She's genuine. What's wrong with me that I can't*

be comfortable with hearing that without trying to make a joke of it?
She shakes her head and looks up.

'Me too,' she says. 'It's that thing about a novel being a demonstration of the human condition, telling us who we are. I know that I've learned something about you in reading and discussing it, and I'm starting to feel I've learned something about myself from it too.'

Simone picks up on this and continues to talk about it, but Ros feels herself slipping away from the conversation. What she feels, but isn't yet able to say aloud, is that she, like Judy, has in some way failed herself. By not going back to England, to the spot where James died, she has cut herself off from his death. And so that imaginative recollection of their life together remains incomplete.

The other three are still talking. Ros leans forward and the wineglass in her hand shakes, splashing a little wine onto the table. Quickly she grasps the stem of the glass with the other hand, lowers it to the table with both hands, and reaches out with her napkin to blot up the wine, hoping that no one noticed. She gets to her feet and heads for the kitchen.

In the kitchen she puts her hands flat on the marble bench top and leans forward to look more closely at them. They are wrinkled, speckled with age spots, but at least they are still now. *I used to love my hands*, she reminds herself, *but now they keep betraying me.* She looks up suddenly and sees Simone in the doorway.

'Just getting some water,' Ros says.

Simone walks over to her and puts her right hand on top of Ros's. 'Parkinson's?' she asks.

Ros feels her breath stop, while Simone's hand stays warm and somehow reassuring on hers. She nods. 'Did you see it just now?'

'Yes. Actually, I already saw it the afternoon we arrived, and a few times since, but you didn't say anything, so I didn't either.'

Ros nods, draws a deep breath. 'Thank you. I haven't felt ready to talk about it yet, although it's one of the things I came here to do.'

'Of course,' Simone says, 'and you don't have to anyway if that's what you want.'

'But it's clearly more obvious than I realised.'

'Not necessarily. I teach yoga to seniors – a couple of them have Parkinson's, and a couple of others have late onset multiple sclerosis, so I'm used to looking out for what's happening.'

'I haven't told anyone yet,' Ros says. 'I'm still trying to get to grips with the fact that this is happening to me.'

'What about the cello? Can you still play?'

'Sometimes. But I can't rely on it. And I feel terrible because for years I've played with a quartet and I haven't been able to make myself tell them yet. Telling them I won't be able to play with them anymore will be the end of something that's very special to all four of us.'

Simone nods. 'This must be so hard.'

'It is. Please don't say anything to the others yet.'

'Of course not. But you know that Adele asked me to teach her some yoga, and we're practising every morning in the games room? Think about coming to join us. A lot of people with Parkinson's find it helpful, physically and mentally. You don't have to explain it to Adele, just come on down and join in.'

'Maybe,' Ros says, 'maybe I will,' although she's thinking, *No, I probably won't.*

Together they head back to the table.

'Time to pick the next book,' Adele says, holding out the black velvet bag of marbles to Judy. 'You'd better do this, Judy. The odds are shorter today because you're not in the draw.'

Liz Byrski

Judy takes the bag. 'Who wants to go first?'

Ros is suddenly short of breath; she is not ready for this, just as she knows Judy was not ready last Sunday.

'Ros?' Judy holds the bag out to her.

She reaches into the bag and pulls out green and is so relieved that she barely worries that the marble slips from her shaking fingers into the deep pile of the carpet.

'I'll go,' Simone says, as Judy bends to retrieve Ros's dropped marble. She reaches in and draws the white marble. 'Okay. Another lamb to the slaughter. I'll go and get the books.'

Ros stares into the fire as they wait. So, Simone knows what's happening to her, but what about the others? Somehow Simone knowing seems okay. She didn't make a big fuss about it, accepted it as a fact of life, but at the same time Ros had felt that she grasped the enormity of it, the way it hangs over everything she does. She dreads telling Leah, who will be devastated; who will try to make her feel better, try to manage things, who will worry herself sick about it. More than ever now Ros believes she has done the right thing in giving herself time to learn how to talk about it, with people to whom she is not any sort of mother-figure: not the woman who rescued a talented teenage violinist from an abusive, alcoholic father and a helpless mother, and gave her a home. Far better to talk about it first with someone unaffected by their love for her.

'So this is the book,' Simone says, handing out the copies, *Truth and Beauty*, by the American writer Ann Patchett. It's a memoir, not a novel. Ann Patchett's best friend was Lucy Grealy, who was a poet and died quite young. This is the story of their friendship. It's also about writing, love, ambition and a whole lot more.'

Ros, who for some time has felt antagonistic towards all

things American, says nothing. She flicks through the pages, smothers a sigh.

'I'm not an Ann Patchett fan,' Adele says, 'but it'll be nice to read some non-fiction, especially about a friendship between writers.'

'For several reasons I was really captivated by it,' Simone says. 'But did I like it? It's odd, unusual; I both loved and hated it and since I read it it's never let me go.'

Ros stares down at the book on her lap, thinking about what's been said about liking or not liking a book. 'I suppose that this is part of the magic of books, you can read something you don't actually like but still be impressed or moved by it. And even something that is quite distasteful can strike some profound note within you, so you still read on. That's how I felt in the eighties when I first read *The Handmaid's Tale*. I hated it but couldn't stop reading it. Liking or not liking is not always the most important thing about a book, is it?'

Chapter Nine

dele is making coffee for herself and Ros. After yesterday's late night following the book club, she's had a perfect start to her day. Yoga with Simone, followed by a short, treat-free walk with Clooney, followed by yoghurt and an apple in her bedroom, where she even got to spend a bit of quality time with Fran Kelly.

'Have you had breakfast, Ros? I could make something – scrambled eggs, a bacon sandwich?' she asks.

Ros looks up at her. 'Adele, we're all doing our own breakfasts, remember?'

Adele's face goes very hot. 'Yes, but I just thought, as you're there . . .'

'Well, don't,' Ros says. 'Don't think about making breakfast for the rest of us. Look after yourself. You kindly offered to make coffee and I accepted. That's all. It's wonderful that you organised all this – our coming here – everything. But you don't need to look after us, you really don't.'

'Okay, yes, sorry,' Adele says. 'Sorry about that.'

'And don't apologise, you haven't done anything wrong.

You are a very fine person, Adele. I like you a lot, and I also admire you. If I need anything I know I can ask you. So just relax. And if I upset you it won't be deliberate and you are welcome to say, "Shut up, Ros, you grumpy old bat."'

Adele is horrified; the mere thought of speaking to Ros like that makes her chest tight with anxiety. 'Oh my god, I could never do that.'

'I do need people to call me out from time to time, so you should try it, and see how you feel after you've done it the first time. I think you'll find it helps.'

'What helps?' Simone asks, wandering into the kitchen.

'I'm simply explaining to Adele that she might feel better if she considers saying "Shut up, you grumpy old bat" to me when I . . . well, when I'm being a grumpy old bat.'

'Oh yes, I think that would be excellent,' Simone says. 'Take note, Adele, you may be very glad of this before too long.'

'Anyone seen Judy this morning?'

Ros shakes her head. 'I haven't. I tapped on her door earlier to see if she wanted a cup of tea but she didn't answer. I think she must be sleeping in. Unless she finally managed to escape.'

Adele starts breathing again at the change of subject. 'Her knitting bag is on the sofa,' she says. 'I don't think she'd leave without that.'

'No way,' Simone says. 'Anyway, I think she's pretty convinced to stay now, don't you?'

'Oh yes, we're going to sit down together this afternoon and talk about the shop and I'll see if there's anything I can do to help.'

'So do you think she's okay?' Ros asks. 'That cough was pretty nasty yesterday.'

'It was,' Simone says, 'but I think we should let her sleep a bit longer, she really needs the rest. Last night she asked me to get her something for the cough and the sore throat, so I might just pop down into town and get those, so she'll have them when she wakes up.'

Ros picks up the coffee Adele has made for her. 'I'm off to do some email and pay some bills online. D'you think it's okay to use the study, Adele? I could take my laptop in there.'

'It's fine. Brian put something about it in the house notes he left for us. Just go ahead. Would you mind if I came with you, Simone? I need to find a birthday card for my former assistant and get it in the post.'

'Sure,' Simone says, glancing at her watch. 'Fifteen minutes okay? I just want to call Adam before we go.'

'I'll be ready,' Adele says. She finishes her coffee sitting at the table, thinking about the conversation with Ros. *I really am going to have to try and get a grip on this,* she tells herself. Ros had been kind, though Adele knew that her own fussing had really irritated her. She had seen signs of it in the others too over the last few days: seen Simone take a deep breath and turn away, seen Judy's mouth twitch in amusement at something she'd done which was unnecessary or over the top.

She closes her eyes. Knowing she is making fists again, she concentrates on putting her hands flat on the table just as she has seen Ros do, presumably in an attempt to stop hers from shaking.

So this is it, Adele, Astrid whispers in her ear. *They like you, they admire you, they want you as a friend. It's all up to you now. Are you going to step into yourself or are you going to spend the rest of your life worrying, fussing, apologising, wearing yourself out in the hope that people will find you acceptable?*

'Shut up, Astrid, you silly old bat,' she says aloud, standing up suddenly and taking her coffee mug to the sink. 'Shut up and get out of my head. If I'm going to do this I have to do it on my own.' And she walks out of the kitchen and goes upstairs to fetch her coat and boots.

*

It takes Ros a couple of hours to pay her bills, respond to emails, read *The Guardian*, and download and read the latest edition of her monthly music journal. Finally, she logs off, stands up, stretches, and gives Clooney a gentle nudge with her foot. As she pulls on her boots she notices the time: almost quarter to twelve and there is still no sign of Judy. *I don't like the look of this*, she thinks. *I really don't*. She goes upstairs and taps on Judy's door.

'Judy,' she calls. 'Judy, it's Ros, may I come in?'

There is a sound of movement in the room, some coughing, then, 'Yes, come on in,' Judy says.

Ros opens the door. Judy is sitting upright in bed, eyes closed, her head resting against the bedhead. Her face looks grey except for her cheeks, which are a bright, feverish pink.

'Oh, Judy,' Ros says, 'you're really not well.' She crosses the room and puts her hand on Judy's forehead, which is hot and damp. 'You've got a fever. How long have you been like this? Why didn't you call us?'

'I didn't want to be a nuisance.'

'You're not. I'm going to find a thermometer.'

'There's one here,' Judy says, reaching out to the bedside table. 'I found it in the bathroom of the main bedroom earlier on. It seems a bit high, my temperature, but I can't read it properly without my glasses.'

Ros shakes the thermometer and puts it in Judy's mouth. 'Don't you dare move from there,' she says, picking up an empty glass from the bedside table. 'I'm going to get you some fresh water.' A couple of minutes later she returns with a freshly filled glass.

'Okay,' she says, taking the thermometer from Judy's mouth and handing her the glass. 'Drink this, but slowly.' She puts on her glasses and reads the thermometer. It's almost forty-two degrees. Ros goes to the bathroom, wrings out a flannel in cool water and returns to gently wipe Judy's face.

'Oh that feels good,' Judy says, starting to cough; it's a rough, hacking cough, punctuated by wheezes.

'You need to see a doctor,' Ros says. 'I'm going to –'

'It's okay,' Judy protests, 'I'll be okay. I'll go when I feel better.'

'You're either going today, or I'll get a doctor to come here. I'm going to make you some tea and I'll ring Gwenda and ask her to recommend someone.'

'But . . .'

'Please, Judy, don't argue, you're sick, you need a doctor.'

Judy stares at her, stonily at first, then looks away and back again. 'Okay,' she says, 'you're probably right, I do feel pretty rough.'

'Okay, so keep sipping the water and I'll be back in a minute.'

In the kitchen Ros picks up the house phone that has Gwenda's number keyed into it with a little red light beside her name.

'Ah, Gwenda,' Ros says with relief, 'thank goodness you're there. Sorry to bother you but I need some advice about a doctor for Judy . . .'

Fifteen minutes later Ros hears the car pull up outside the house and hurries downstairs.

'Judy's really sick,' she says to Simone and Adele. 'Gwenda put me on to the Blue Mountains Hospital, and they said to bring her in. We need to take her there straight away and pack a bag to take with us in case they admit her.'

'Admit her?'

'Yes, it's possible that when they have the X-rays they may admit her for a few days. They said it sounds like a chest infection or possibly pneumonia.'

Ten minutes later they are all packed into Ros's car, Adele driving, Judy in the back seat, wrapped in blankets, her legs stretched out on Simone's lap.

'You didn't all need to come,' she says weakly. 'It seems such a fuss.'

'We just have to be sure you won't make a dash for it,' Simone quips. 'This way we can keep an eye on you.'

Judy laughs and coughs, and then coughs a whole lot more.

'Don't make her laugh again,' Adele says. 'I'd like to get her to the hospital conscious and in one piece.'

'You are all mad,' Judy says wearily. 'But you are also rather wonderful.'

'You sound drunk,' Ros says. 'Close your eyes, and stop talking.'

*

Simone takes the spiraliser, secures a zucchini in it and starts winding the handle. 'It's weird without Judy,' she says. 'We haven't been here long and already the three of you feel like my family.'

'Me too,' Ros says. 'What on earth are you doing?'

'I'm making zucchini noodles,' Simone says. 'We're having them tonight with peas, bok choy and fish in ginger.'

Ros shakes her head. 'That's serious vegetables,' she says. 'But what is that spiral thing again?'

'A spiraliser. I use it almost every day at home.'

'Hmm. So what's wrong with good old pasta?'

'Nothing,' Simone says, 'except this is much healthier,

cheaper and easier to digest.'

'And I bet it –'

'Stop!' Simone says, holding up her hand. 'I know you were going to say "I bet it tastes like shit!" So don't even think about it. Don't you dare comment on it until you've finished your meal and then you can say whatever you like. I will not be terrorised while cooking.'

Ros laughs. 'Fair enough. I reserve judgement. Poor old Judy, thank goodness she's in the right place.'

Judy had been admitted to hospital a couple of hours after they arrived there. The X-rays confirmed that she had pneumonia and although she had protested and Simone had been close to believing that they might not be able to persuade her to stay, the doctor had insisted.

'A couple of days,' he'd said, 'maybe three.'

'But I didn't bring my phone with me,' she protested. 'I won't be able to call Melissa.'

'Well that might be a good thing,' Simone said. 'Have you been calling often?'

'Twice a day,' Judy said. 'Suppose something goes wrong?'

The doctor had looked up from his clipboard. 'You do need to let go of work and other responsibilities, Mrs Castle,' he said. 'All the signs are that you are quite rundown, and that's partly why you're so unwell now. You really need to rest or we'll be keeping you here for at least a week, maybe more.'

Simone wondered how Melissa felt about getting calls from Judy twice a day.

'I could call for you, if you like,' Adele said. 'I'll just say you have a bit of a sore throat. I doubt she'll panic. From all you've said she sounds really competent.'

'Oh she is, she's terrific,' Judy said between bouts of coughing. 'I just don't want her to worry or feel cut off.'

Simone exchanged glances with Ros and Adele. 'You know what, Judy?' she said. 'I think it's you who's worried and cut off. I suspect Melissa is efficiently doing her job and enjoying having the shop to herself. She might even be wishing that you wouldn't keep phoning.'

'Exactly,' Ros said. 'She might feel you don't trust her.'

'Well that's just rubbish,' Judy said angrily, her face reddening by the minute. 'Of course I trust her.'

The doctor raised his eyebrows. 'Look, it really would be best for you to stay calm and discuss this when you're well again. You need to rest and relax. I'm sure your friends will look after things for you. Meanwhile you'll be able to go up to the ward in about fifteen minutes and you can use the telephone there if you need to.' With a nod to the other three, he'd walked off through the sliding doors.

'Okay,' Judy said reluctantly, 'you're probably right. So would you ring her please, Adele? But don't say anything that would make her panic.'

'Let's hope she's settled down a bit this evening,' Simone says once they're seated at the dinner table.

Adele sighs, helping herself to fish. 'It'll be interesting to look at the business with her. Some people fall into the trap of thinking that because their computer is in a mess their work or business is too, but sometimes it's just a matter of tidying things up.'

'Wow! These noodles are terrific, Simone,' Ros says. 'Really delicious, as is the fish –' She's interrupted by the buzz of a mobile phone, reaches into her pocket, then shakes her head. 'Not mine,' she says.

Adele rummages in her bag, which is on a nearby chair. Simone reaches down to the end of the table where hers is sitting on top of today's newspaper.

'Oh! Oh my god, there's something . . . a message – a Facebook message from . . . Geoff.' She sits there rigid, phone in hand, looking at the other two.

'Open it,' Adele says.

'It might not be him . . . it could be another Geoff Marshall, it's a very common name and I'm not sure –'

'Oh for heaven's sake,' Ros interrupts, 'open the bloody thing, I can't stand the suspense.' And she leans across to Simone, takes the phone from her hand, taps the icon on the screen and hands it back to her. 'Now – tell us what he says!'

Chapter Ten

Adele walks out to the hospital car park, gets into her car and starts the engine. After a couple of days in the hospital she could see a definite improvement in Judy, who looks better, less feverish, more relaxed. The nurse had told Adele that she was doing well and Judy said she was making progress with *Truth and Beauty*, although it's hard for her to concentrate.

'I can only take in a bit at a time,' she said, 'it must be the antibiotics.'

'No, it's that sort of book,' Adele said. 'I have to keep putting it aside because it makes me uncomfortable.'

'Simone said it might be like that,' Judy said. 'It's very intense in some places.'

'And intensely annoying in others.'

'Well, a bit, but it's pretty interesting and strange too. The more I read it the more I like it. I'll have finished it by Sunday,' Judy insisted.

'But if you aren't home by then . . .'

'Of course I'll be home.'

'Whenever it is we won't start without you,' Adele had promised.

She drives out of the car park now and heads for the town centre. They need tomatoes and broccoli, Ros has asked her to get her a monthly magazine that's due out today, and Simone has lost the earpieces for her phone. But what Adele needs first is a cup of coffee. She parks the car, heads for a small café where she had once been with Marian, settles into a corner by the window and sits, sipping her coffee, gazing out onto the street, where the late morning sunshine has brought people out to the street after so many days of rain.

How strange this all is, she thinks, being in the house with people she is only starting to know, and yet feeling so much at ease. As Astrid had pointed out, being the director of the bureau gave her confidence in her working life, something that she didn't have outside it. But at the same time the energy and stress involved in performing that role had left her little space to find out how to be herself. Despite the toll it had taken on her, she had loved it, and she knows she was good at it. It was a stressful job made more stressful by her own reaction to it. She was always on the alert waiting for the moment when she would be unmasked as incompetent; always wondering how people were judging her. That feeling of having to live up to unspecified expectations has haunted her all her life. She has always assumed that it came from her relationship with her father, but she is also intimidated in this way by certain women – Astrid for one.

'I think the yoga might help. I'm feeling different, more at ease,' she'd said to Simone this morning as they rolled up their yoga mats. 'No one is judging me, it's safe to be myself here.'

'Was it not like that at work?' Simone asked.

'No, not at all. But I'm wondering now if that was real or all in my mind. Whether what I thought was coming from other people was actually coming from within me. It got so bad that when Jenna came home for a holiday last year, I even felt that way with her. I started to fumble with things, apologise unnecessarily, I kept expecting her to find something wrong with me.'

'And did she?' Simone asked.

'Of course not. I realised later, when she'd left to go home, that it was all in my head. She's the least critical person you could imagine, and she was incredibly patient with me. Just told me it was time to break my obsession with Radio National and get a life, but in the gentlest possible way.'

'So where do you think it comes from?' Simone asked.

'I'm still working on that,' Adele said, and she'd changed the subject.

She sits here now enjoying being alone, enjoying the feeling of being okay with herself. Eventually, she finishes her coffee and walks out into the street to do the shopping. In the nearby newsagent she finds Ros's magazine, and a new set of earphones for Simone. Heading for the greengrocer she passes a wool shop, then turns back and looks in through the window. It's decades since Adele bought wool or knitted anything – in fact the last thing she remembers is struggling with a matinee jacket just before Jenna was born, and making a terrible hash of it. The shop looks really inviting and she pushes open the door and walks in.

It is not remotely like the poky little shop where she'd bought skeins of white three-ply and needles for the jacket. It's bright and warm; the walls are mainly lined with white pigeonholes each packed with different yarns in a huge variety of shades. There are casual tables with patterns spread out on them, and in a small alcove there is a coffee machine with a sign on it inviting customers to help themselves. Nearby, two women who have done just that are sitting at one of the tables comparing patterns as they drink their coffee.

Near the front window of the shop, where it can be seen from the street, is a spinning wheel set up with sheep's wool and a sign that says *Spinning classes every Tuesday 6–7.30pm, enquire at the counter*. And at the far end half a dozen women and a couple of men are sitting at a big worktable with their knitting, watching something on a large wall-mounted television screen. Adele is amazed to see men at the table but then remembers that Judy had said something a few days ago about men becoming interested in knitting, and that it actually began with men. Adele wishes she'd listened more closely now.

On the screen a woman is demonstrating the use of some form of stitch that Adele, not surprisingly, has never heard of. There is something familiar about the woman on the screen. Adele walks closer, gets her glasses out of her bag, stops, blinks, moves closer still and clasps her hand over her mouth.

'Can I help you?' a voice says beside her. 'Did you want to join the group?'

Adele points at the screen. 'That's . . . is that . . . ?'

'It's Judy Castle,' the woman says. 'Great, isn't she? We love her here. You must be a knitter?'

Adele can barely drag her eyes away from the screen. 'Er . . . no, not really, well actually not at all,' she says finally, looking at her. 'It's just that I know Judy and I didn't expect to see her in here.'

'Oh, her videos are brilliant,' says the woman. 'I'm Linda by the way; I'm the owner of the shop. Yes, we have people in every day following the videos. In fact, if you're interested we're having our own little Judy Castle promotion.'

She steers Adele to the opposite side of the shop where there is a poster-size photograph of Judy holding a knitted hat with two ears and beneath it the words: *Special Offer: Free Judy Castle Pussy Hat Pattern when you buy the wool.* And below it is a basket of needles and wool – mostly fleshy pinks, browns and yellows, but also brighter colours – and alongside them laminated patterns with a small picture of Judy in the top left-hand corner.

'It's for those pussy hats that those girls in America are wearing to protest about Donald Trump.'

'Yes,' Adele says, 'I see that.'

'Judy's pattern uses a fantastic two-colour brioche stitch. It's selling like hot cakes,' Linda says. 'She's great for business. Get yourself a coffee and sit and watch the video if you like. I must go and talk to that lady at the counter.' And she hurries away.

Adele sits down, still watching the screen where Judy is now showing some examples of a particular design used first on a scarf, then on a baby's blanket. She puts the examples down and starts talking about the pussy hats, holding one up just as shown on the poster. Then she puts it aside and goes on to describe how knitting has played a role in various political protests throughout history.

'Beanies,' she says, 'scarves and gloves, jumpers and waist-coats, but also some different and more complex forms.' She shows photographs of knitted wall art on public buildings, a VW Kombi entirely covered in green and white knitting, the words *Green Peace* cleverly worked into it. She talks about groups of men 'yarn bombing' for peace in America, and other protests and support movements that use knitting as a tool in their campaigns.

'Of course,' Judy says, winding up, 'there were also women knitting at the guillotine in the French Revolution, although I guess they were there for the spectacle rather than the knitting! Bye for now, and good knitting.'

For some time after it finishes Adele sits there watching the knitters pack up their wool and needles, gather up their coats, and wander out into the street. Finally she gets to her feet and walks over to the counter.

'Do you have a business card for the shop?' she asks. 'I'd like to give it to Judy next time I see her, tell her I saw one of her videos here.'

'Of course.' Linda opens a drawer, takes out a couple of cards and hands them to her. 'Please tell her it's Linda from The Knittery. I often email her. Tell her if she's ever here we'd love her to come to the shop.'

'Thanks, I'll tell her for sure,' Adele says, slipping the cards into her bag. 'Lovely shop, by the way, almost makes me want to knit again.' And she walks out onto the street and has to stop to think about what she's doing and where she was heading.

*

Simone pushes open the door of the restaurant and looks around. Geoff had offered to pick her up but she'd insisted she could find her own way there. It's a small Italian restaurant: white tablecloths and low lights. Being Friday evening it's nearly full. In the far corner a man gets to his feet and raises his hand in greeting and, taking a deep breath, she walks towards him, head spinning, heart thumping with anticipation.

I could barely believe it when your message arrived, he'd said in his message. *Doug and I have talked of you so often and hoped one day we'd hear from you. You didn't send your phone number, Simone; we both want to talk to you, see you again if possible, our numbers are below. I'm in the Blue Mountains, Doug's in Melbourne. Where are you? Is it remotely possible that we could meet again? I have tears in my eyes as I write this. Please call me or Doug as soon as possible.*

We've missed you so much. Love from both of us. And beneath it were their two phone numbers.

She had called him straight away, barely able to speak with the joy of being in touch again. He lived, he told her, very close to Leura.

'Well that's near where I'm staying,' she said, and described the house.

'That sounds like Marian and Brian's place.'

'It is,' she said.

'They're away, aren't they? I remember him saying a group of women were going to stay there. A coven, he said.'

She'd laughed. 'We're actually quite harmless. Just the remaining members of an online book club.'

He was calling, he told her, from Sydney.

'I came down here last Friday for my granddaughter's wedding,' he'd said. 'I'll be back late tomorrow, could we meet? Maybe have dinner together on Friday?'

An hour or so later he had texted the name of the restaurant, and a time to meet. *Can barely contain myself,* he'd written. *Doug, green with envy, is trying to arrange a visit soon.*

For a moment they stand facing each other, neither of them able to speak or take the last couple of steps, caught as they are in a time warp of more than forty years.

'You look just the same,' Geoff says. 'No, actually you look more beautiful than ever. I'm so happy to see you.' And he takes the step forward that breaches the gap between them, reaching out to her, hugging her. 'I've missed you so very much, Simone, I'd almost given up hope of seeing you again. We both had.'

'So, how was the wedding?' she asks when they are settled at the table and Geoff has ordered a bottle of wine.

'Lovely,' he says. 'I must be getting old and sentimental; I had tears in my eyes during the ceremony, and again at the reception when my son-in-law, father of the bride, made a really lovely speech. Then I cried again when I saw your message and replied to it. And here I am in tears again!'

They talk about their respective children, in Geoff's case two and in Simone's just Adam. It's all much easier than she had anticipated, for despite the pure joy she felt at connecting with him and Doug again she had also wondered if it would be difficult to navigate the gap of the many years since they last met.

'And you . . . your husband?' Geoff asks.

'I was never married,' she says.

'Okay, well Adam's father . . . ?'

She sighs. 'I might leave that for another time. But if you're asking if he's around now, no he's not. I've been on my own for decades.'

'I see,' Geoff says. 'Well actually I don't, because I can't imagine how someone like you would be alone other than by choice. But yes, there's lots of time ahead for us to talk about our lives over all these years.'

'And what about your wife?' Simone asks. 'I thought she might come with you tonight.'

'Eva died nine years ago,' Geoff says, 'skiing in the Snowy Mountains. She was a very confident and competent skier, but she had a nasty accident. She fell and broke her neck, suffered some brain damage. She died in hospital, a couple of weeks later.'

He tells it in a flat, matter-of-fact way that makes it all the more shocking, and Simone puts down her menu.

'Geoff, I'm so sorry, what a terrible thing to happen.'

He nods, grasping her hand. 'It's been a very hard few

years, and I'll tell you more about that some other time too. It is so good to see you again. Doug sends his love; he and Steve have a restaurant in Melbourne.'

'Steve?'

Geoff nods. 'His partner, they've been together for thirty-two years. He was so delighted when I told him I was meeting you tonight.'

'Doug is gay?'

'Didn't you know?'

She shakes her head. 'Since when?'

'Well – since always,' Geoff laughs. 'Did you honestly not know? Not even when we were in Paris?'

'I had no idea.'

'Well you were always a bit of an innocent, Simone. He came out to me on our seventeenth birthday but I'd already guessed. It was a while before he told Mum, though.'

They order their meals and talk on, working out how many years it is since they last met.

'It was Paris,' Simone says, 'you came to visit me, and that was the last time I saw you. I remember you'd just finished your PhD. I think Doug had just finished his apprenticeship. When you left you were going to Spain and Portugal, I think, and maybe Greece. You sent postcards from several places – the last one came from Hong Kong – and after that I never heard from you again.'

He nods. 'It's such a long time. Can we really be this old?'

''Fraid so,' Simone says. 'But what happened? Where did you go? Because when I finished my degree and went home the following year you'd all gone. Claire had sold up and there were new people in the house. Mama and Papa said you'd moved away and hadn't left an address.'

She pauses as the waiter arrives with their meals, then refills their glasses.

'I couldn't understand it. I kept asking where you'd gone, but every time I asked they shut me down. Mama was all tight-lipped. Papa got really angry. I was so upset that you hadn't left an address or written to let me know. You had my address in Paris, you'd actually been there.' She feels the emotion rising, hears it in her voice as she recalls how painful it had been at the time. 'Why did you do that? Why did you both abandon me?'

Geoff puts down his glass. 'I'm truly sorry. It was a very difficult time . . .'

'So difficult that you couldn't even leave a message or send a postcard? You'd managed to send me postcards when you were swanning around Europe, but once you were home – nothing. Was it really so hard that you couldn't even send me a note?'

'Well we did send a letter to your aunt's address before we left, but clearly you didn't get it. And frankly, yes, it was that hard,' Geoff cuts in.

But Simone is angry now, the old hurt and disappointment spilling out as raw and painful as ever. She puts down her knife and fork, and lifts her hair. 'See this?' she says. 'This scar, Papa did this. I kept on at him trying to find out where you were. I was sure he knew. You and Doug were like brothers to me. And then you just disappeared. I was so upset and frus-trated that one evening I went out to the shed where he was working on the truck. I'd been crying, and I lit a cigarette and marched out there and started shouting at him. He yelled at me to shut up, and of course I wouldn't and he was yelling back at me. And then he suddenly stood up and picked up a bottle from the work bench and threw it at me –' She stops abruptly, needing to draw breath, her hand automatically moving up to her scar. 'I turned away to dodge it and put up my hand with the cigarette to shield my face but the contents splashed out – it was methylated spirits. My face caught fire.'

Geoff gasps. 'Oh my god, Simone, I'm so sorry . . .'

She shakes her head. 'God knows why, he'd never thrown anything at me before. He said he'd thought it was a juice bottle. He certainly didn't mean for this to happen. But it just confirmed for me that something really bad had happened with you guys, or Claire. I was burning up with anger all the time in hospital and as soon as they let me out I went home, packed a bag and left. It was two years before I went back there again and no one ever mentioned it. By that time I'd given up on ever finding out what had happened, or where you were.'

Geoff looks at her for some time, takes a sip of his wine. 'So you don't know,' he says. 'They never told you?'

'No one *ever* told me *anything*. It was as though you'd all gone up in smoke, or been abducted by aliens. Mama died some years ago, she had Alzheimer's. Papa stayed on there. He died the year before last and I still know nothing.'

Geoff reaches inside his jacket and brings out a mobile phone, scrolls down the screen.

'What are you doing?'

He holds the phone out towards her. On the screen is an obviously recent photograph of him and his twin brother standing either side of a much younger woman, their arms around each other.

'What's this?' Simone asks. 'I mean, it's a lovely picture of you and Doug, but who's this woman?'

'Doug and I have a half-sister. She was born in January, nineteen seventy-three. Her name is Paula.'

Simone studies the photograph. 'A half-sister, really? But how . . . ?'

'Simone, Paula is also *your* half-sister.'

Chapter Eleven

The third Sunday

Judy has been home for twenty-four hours. She'd expected to be discharged on Friday but it was Saturday morning when the doctor finally said she could go as long as she promised to rest.

'And I mean real rest, Mrs Castle,' he'd said. 'I hope you understand how serious this is for someone of your age. You're not in good health; frankly you show all the signs of extreme stress and I urge you to think seriously about how you can take better care of yourself in future.'

Adele was there at the time, sitting beside her, nodding in agreement, so Judy knew she was in for more of this once they got back to the house. A couple of days earlier Adele had suggested that she could have a look at some of the documents on the computer so they could discuss the situation when Judy was released. Judy, who had been enormously relieved by Adele's original offer of help, was suddenly paralysed by the prospect of her coming face to face with the chaos. Long ago she had created files for all the various suppliers, GST documents, outgoings, tax assessments and payments, notes about her videos, and correspondence from all sorts of people. But most of those folders are empty because a few weeks after setting them up there was a particularly busy time when she also had a mild dose of flu, and she'd started keeping everything on the desktop and when it all got too crowded she would just drag and drop everything into an unnamed folder, to get it out of her way. In the past she'd managed to pull things together well enough to file a tax return, but the latest is now a couple of months or more overdue and she suspects she's probably already incurred a fine.

'So you see I ought to do something about that before you even look at it,' she'd said to Adele. 'I think you'll have a fit if you look at it now.'

Adele had leaned back in her chair, selected one of the chocolates she'd brought and considered the situation for a moment. 'Mmm, I see,' she said, and then stopped, obviously running her tongue over her teeth. 'Oh, this is soft toffee, with some sort of alcohol in it – delicious. Simone chose these, she has such good taste. Anyway, it sounds to me as though this is something that has to be done before I can get a sense of how things really are. So, how would you feel if I go in there and start sorting it out? It would be a great way of helping me to get an overall picture, and it will mean that once you're back in the house I'll have some sense of what's involved.'

Judy felt herself turn white. 'It really is a mess.'

Adele shrugged. 'As I told Simone recently, I'm quite good with mess – as long as it's not of my own making. I won't be judging you on the basis of your filing system or lack of it, Judy.'

Judy sat there in bed, staring at Adele as she tried to decide what to do.

'Perhaps that seems intrusive,' Adele went on. 'I'm sorry. It wasn't meant that way.'

'No!' Judy said. 'No, Adele, it's not that. I just . . . well it's a big thing, sort of handing it over, but what you say makes sense.'

'Okay, well if you change your mind . . .'

'No, this is silly. I'm embarrassed, you see. You'll think I'm very unprofessional, not businesslike at all.'

'Well you must be doing something right,' Adele had said. 'There's a shop in town that looks like an outpost of yours, because they're using your shop design, your patterns, showing your videos and they have pictures of you plastered all over the walls.'

'That'd be Linda at The Knittery, I suppose,' Judy said. 'You didn't tell her I was here, did you? That woman can talk the rust off a tin kettle.'

'I didn't tell her,' Adele said. 'Judy, I suspect that the only thing wrong with your business is that you need a management system so that you have everything organised and easy to find. You can see at a glance what you've got, what's on order, when things are due.'

'I think I've got one – it's on both computers but I haven't activated it. It seemed too complicated.'

'It might be as simple as me showing you how to use it. Are you making a profit, Judy? Once you've paid yourself and Melissa, and covered all the costs?'

'Oh yes, quite a lot, I think.'

'And what's happening to that money?'

'It's in the bank.'

Adele nodded. 'Not in any sort of investment account or anything like that? Didn't your accountant suggest that?'

'He said I should talk to a financial advisor but I haven't done that. The thing is, Adele, talking about that sort of stuff paralyses me. I can't understand half of it, can't make decisions. It's so intimidating, so it's easier to keep things as they are. Suppose I put it all in the wrong account?'

Adele had laughed then. 'Sounds like you're already keeping it in the wrong account!' she said. 'I reckon this is less complicated than you think, and if we get going on it soon we can get things fixed up. And we can sort out your tax return too – even lodge it. I am actually a certified tax accountant, so we might get it stitched up before we go home.'

Parting with her password had, in the end, felt like something of a relief. It seemed to be a small step forward and as the next couple of days passed Judy had stopped thinking about it and relaxed, dozing, watching television and ploughing through *Truth and Beauty*. And even though Simone had brought her phone to the hospital the day after she was admitted, Judy held off on calling Melissa. It was difficult, but she managed to stop herself. 'I think you might be right,' she'd said to Simone, 'it's me who was feeling worried and cut off, and I'm feeling less like that now.'

So now it's Sunday, book club day, and Judy lies on her bed in the green bedroom contemplating the impact of last Sunday's discussion. No one had thought her reasons for choosing *Sacred Country* were naive or trivial. They hadn't even laughed at the idea of a knitted town; in fact they'd really admired it, thought it was remarkable. She remembers now how Ted and Donna had looked at each other in amazement and then burst out laughing when she'd shown it to them on the iPad. It wasn't that they were being unkind; they just couldn't imagine what could have made her embark on something like that. Judy had been surprised because she was intimately aware of Ted's deep attachment to the Wheatbelt and his little share in it. It had shaped him, and she'd known he would never leave. But it was Donna's reaction that had surprised her more. Donna's family, her wide group of relatives, were deeply connected to the land both physically and spiritually, going back thousands of years. But she didn't seem to understand Judy's lesser, but still strong feeling of connection to this small English town. But Ros, Simone and Adele had understood it instantly, respected it, and encouraged her to think again about going back.

A green vase filled with white chrysanthemums was standing on the dressing table when she got home yesterday, the room had been cleaned and tidied, her bed remade with fresh linen. To Judy, who has done everything for herself for more years than she can remember, it feels like the height of luxury, especially as she has been banned from cooking and housework for the next two weeks. She thinks of the two women in *Truth and Beauty*: friends united by their passion for writing, and their love for each other. It's a bit one-sided of course, one of them is doing all the heavy lifting and the other is so desperately ill and needy, but it's love that keeps their friendship alive, and that love seems to have all the dimensions of what people would call a relationship. But then love comes in so many shapes and sizes, how can you define it or make rules about it? *And why*, she wonders, *is it missing from my own life?*

As she lies here now, the sunlight from the garden pouring in through the windows, she sees and feels the complete change that has come over her this week. And she sees that the care and concern that her new friends have lavished on her here is love. The sort of love she had felt for and from Edna all those years ago. She's read about it, seen movies about it, and at times her friendship with Donna has come close to it, but the Ted factor is inclined to get in the way. For years she has isolated herself while surrounded by people who would have been willing, keen even, to move beyond acquaintance to friendship. Now she knows she needs and wants something more, and the prospect of going back to her old life horrifies her. *Awareness*, she thinks, *changes everything, but unfortunately it doesn't come accompanied by a guidebook.*

*

Simone sits on the end of her bed holding her copy of *Truth and Beauty*. Since her evening with Geoff the whole landscape of her life seems to have been rearranged. Geoff had told her that Carlo demanded that they never try to contact Simone, and never tell her about Paula. Their fear of shattering her relationship with her parents compelled them to agree to this. 'We thought it was the safest and fairest solution for you, Simone,' Geoff explained. 'We believed that Carlo would settle down and eventually tell you the truth, or some of it, or if he didn't, then Suzette would. They knew we had gone to Mum's family in London. Obviously now that we've met again we wish we'd done it differently, but Doug and I and Mum did what we thought was best.'

Claire, pregnant at a time in her life when she'd thought she could no longer conceive, wanted to go back to her home in London. Doug and Geoff had sought advice from a friend's father who was a solicitor and he had recommended selling the property. He thought a nearby citrus farmer who had once been a friend of Malcolm Marshall, their grandfather, would be interested in buying it. When the deal was complete the solicitor advised Carlo that the property had been sold and he no longer had access to it. He had no option but to remove anything of his that remained there within seven days. From then on he must run his own operation without using the respected Marshall name. Both Geoff and Doug had scrapped their own plans and gone with Claire to London. Simone thought there was more he was not telling her but when she tried to draw him out about Claire's pregnancy and her relationship with Carlo, or even about her own mother's part in this whole thing, he was reluctant to tell her any more.

'Doug wants to come and meet you,' he'd said. 'He's trying to arrange things at the restaurant, and then he'll come up here for a few days. Let's sit down and talk it all through together then.'

It had seemed enough for the moment, she already had plenty to think about.

Putting down her book Simone once again scans the photographs that Geoff has sent her. Paula as a baby, as a toddler and starting school; there are pictures with Claire on a beach somewhere in England, and as a teenager with her much older brothers in the garden of the house that she and their mother shared with their grandmother. Simone remembers the day that she, Doug and Geoff adopted each other as siblings, pricking their fingers to share their blood as a bond. She'd been nine then, Geoff and Doug eleven, and she'd thought they would always be together. She wonders now whether her father had any idea of the loss he was inflicting on her when he insisted on their silence. And now, Simone wonders whether they can ever get that connection back again. And then there's Paula; how will she react to this?

'Tea's made,' Ros calls, tapping on the door. 'Book club time.'

Simone takes a last look at her sister's face, switches off her phone, and walks into the lounge clutching *Truth and Beauty*, wondering what she will say, and whether talking about any of it will help or simply make it all more difficult and confusing.

Chapter Twelve

They have done this only twice before but already it feels like an established ritual. This time it is Ros who has prepared the tea and made a loaf of dark, moist banana bread.

'This is for you, Simone,' she says. 'It's paleo banana bread, so I think it fits your hippy eating regime.'

They settle once again into their usual seats.

Simone sips her tea, puts her cup and saucer down on the side table and picks up the book.

'Okay, let's do it,' she says, 'Ann Patchett's *Truth and Beauty*. I'm sure you're wondering why I chose it. You'll either have loved it or hated it, and frankly I've done both! Many years ago I read a book by the American poet Lucy Grealy, called *Autobiography of a Face*. As you now know from reading this book Lucy had a form of cancer that severely distorted her face. And she had a seemingly endless and horrendous series of treatments and operations that never succeeded in fixing it, and on some occasions made things worse.'

Simone hesitates, then lifts up her hair to reveal her scar.

'You've probably already noticed this,' she says, 'although none of you has asked about it because,' she pauses, smiles and looks around, 'well, because you're all so well mannered! It's a burn; it happened in my early twenties and I was lucky, it could have been a lot worse, and I'll tell you later how I got it. It's difficult to adjust to having any form of facial injury, and I've never lost my awareness of it, so I wanted to read Lucy's book. The damage to my face is minimal compared to hers, and I loved her courage and extraordinary endurance that come through very strongly in her own book. Then, later I discovered *Truth and Beauty*, which is Ann Patchett's memoir of their long friendship.

'But before I tell you more about my other reasons for choosing it, perhaps we could talk about it? You don't need to worry about trampling on my feelings, in fact your honest reactions will help me.'

There is a murmur of agreement.

'Fine by me,' Ros says. 'Okay if I start? I actually have quite a lot to say – yeah, I know – as always! But I think this book is extraordinary. Ann Patchett writes so fluently and with such apparent ease that I began by loving it for just that, for involving me immediately in a true story that I might otherwise not have read.'

'Me too,' Judy says. 'I was right into it from the start.'

'I also like learning about writers' lives,' Ros continues, 'how they manage to earn a living and so on. As a musician I understand that sort of hand to mouth existence, and how hard it is. So I was very enthusiastic about it at first, but then I started to feel that I was being drawn into something else that I didn't much like.'

'Yes,' Adele says, 'me too. There was a point at which it started to feel creepy.'

'Creepy?' Judy cuts in. 'But why? How could it be creepy?'

'Even bearing in mind the awfulness of Lucy's condition I felt she was increasingly narcissistic and demanding,' Adele says. 'And I was really uncomfortable with the way Ann constantly responded to that. The relationship seemed oppressive – but also oppressive for me as a reader.'

'Me too,' Ros says.

Simone leans back in her chair, listening and watching. She had thought it might be contentious, she has had mixed feelings herself ever since she first read it, and those feelings seem to change from time to time.

'I felt entangled and resentful because of that,' Ros goes on. 'I was in there *with* Ann, a fellow traveller. She became *my person*, I was on her side. But then there were no "sides" because she wasn't complaining about Lucy's devouring need to be the centre of everything and to have Ann at her emotional and practical beck and call. That began to feel very dark for me and then I got annoyed with Ann; I wanted her to stop being so noble and patient, and to give Lucy a big dose of home truths about her self-obsession, her thoughtlessness, her selfishness.'

'Oh my god! I thought Ann was amazing,' Judy says. 'Lucy's problems were huge and she'd try something and it would fail and she'd bounce back and try again. I can't believe . . . I mean, wouldn't you *want* to help a friend in that situation?'

'Of course,' Ros says, 'but I don't have the patience or the capacity to be entirely unselfish to the degree that Ann Patchett appears to have been. And frankly I started to lose faith in that. I ended up feeling it was quite manipulative. I was wavering between two positions. Either Ann *wanted* to be a doormat, or she was manipulating readers in the way she told her side of the story. And because she is obviously a highly intelligent woman and a very skilful writer I felt it was the latter. It was the skill of the writing, and the judicious selection of snippets from Lucy's letters, plus her reconstruction of their conversations, that formed my understanding of Lucy, and of their friendship; a friendship in which Lucy really ended up looking like a basket case, and Ann was the perfect friend and selfless Good Samaritan. She's a very fine writer and I find it hard to believe she could not have known what she was doing in writing it this way.'

Simone shifts her position, though her discomfort is not simply physical. Quite suddenly she feels ill at ease with what's happening, with Ros's vehemence, but she can't explain why because she has felt exactly the same at times.

'I got to a point where I disliked both of them quite a lot and thought they deserved each other,' Ros says.

'I did too,' Adele says. 'I also wondered if Ann had deliberately set up that sort of position so that she came across as the best possible, noble friend. I agree with you, Ros. She must have understood the impact of her characterisation of Lucy, who comes across as selfish, self-indulgent, needy and demanding. And perhaps she was, but Ann's portrayal of her was pretty brutal.'

'Exactly,' Ros says. 'I also realised that Ann was not just creating a reader's response to Lucy, but that she was enabling Lucy's narcissism. So for me that made it worse. Bearing in mind that she wrote it very soon after Lucy Grealy died, it felt as though she was getting something off her chest. It's so well written, but I felt I couldn't really trust the writer's motives. Even so I still couldn't stop reading it, which, I suppose, says something about the power of the writing, because despite all that, and despite longing to give up on it, I was compelled to hang in there to the end.' She stops, raises her eyebrows, looks around the room. No one speaks. 'I've gone over the top, haven't I?' she says.

'I think you have. Way over the top,' Judy says.

'No,' Adele says.

'Go on, Ros,' Simone urges. There is some relief now in hearing Ros's passionate excoriation of the book, and relief too in Judy's defence of it. She had expected this to come up in the conversation but it's not the aspect of *Truth and Beauty* that had made her choose it; that is one side-step away. She had wondered briefly if she would feel hurt or diminished if there were strong negative responses from some of the others, but in fact it helps her to hear it.

'Okay, I'm nearly done,' Ros says. 'I ended up feeling that this *friendship* became a struggle for supremacy in both their writing and their emotional lives. And I wondered which one would finally ring the bell, get off the bus and walk away. I started out feeling it was a story of friendship, and then that it was actually a love affair, and finally that it was a story of two people held together by two very destructive forces: Lucy's overwhelming neediness, which would never be satisfied, and Ann's own need to be, or to be seen to be, the perfect, stoic and always-loving friend.'

'That sounds right to me,' Adele says.

'I feel as though we've been reading different books,' Judy says. 'Honestly, none of this even entered my head and I can't really see what there is that makes you quite so worked up about it, Ros.'

'Oh, Judy, don't be so wet!' Ros says. 'It's obvious, how can you not have seen it?'

'Ros! Really . . .' Simone interjects.

Ros flushes and shakes her head. 'Sorry, sorry, you're right, that was thoughtless and rude, Judy, I'm way out of line. I apologise.'

'It's okay,' Judy says. 'It's interesting to see how worked

up you are, because your reaction seems out of proportion to the fact this is simply a book we're reading for book club. I think you're completely wrong about this, and you too, Adele, if you're agreeing with her. You're reading a whole lot of stuff into it. I think you should stand back, try again, read it for what it is: a love story, recounted by one party after the tragic death of the other. I think you are . . . yes, way over the top.'

Simone has been on the edge of her seat during this exchange. How amazing it is to see Judy come back at Ros with such confidence. Simone almost wants to cheer her! Adele is obviously surprised too; Simone sees her glancing down at her notes.

'I think a significant question here is *should* Ann Patchett have written this?' Adele says. 'Is it a betrayal to have revealed the extent of Lucy's neediness and her often manipulative and irresponsible behaviour? Because that is basically what she does and Lucy's not able to speak for herself. I looked for reviews and I found a piece written by Lucy Grealy's sister. She makes the point that there is no real mention of Lucy's family, and that she and her other sister were deeply upset by this book both for themselves and for their mother. Certainly before I read that I assumed that Lucy's family were not there for her, but it seems that wasn't the case. I suppose writers have the right to recreate a very singular version of someone else, but Lucy is dead, she can't respond. I think it's a clever piece of work but also a narcissistic one.'

Ros is nodding firmly. 'Yes. And I think this is a classic story of co-dependence,' she says. 'Lucy's dependence is on love and approval that almost amounts to adulation. That's her drug, both the sort of love she gets from Ann, and to a lesser extent from other friends, but also on sex, which she confuses with love. She could never have enough of either. But is that who she really was? Ann Patchett wrote this very soon after Lucy's death. Maybe she should have put it away in a drawer for a year or two and then rethought it. It might have ended up being very different, and have had more integrity.'

Simone has been leaning forward, listening attentively. 'You've both raised everything that I felt in my various readings of it. Particularly – did Ann Patchett really understand how it might be read? And even if it is her right to write it, should she actually have done so?'

They are all looking at Judy.

'Well, you all know what I think. To me it was a deeply moving love story. It made me long to have a friendship like that with another woman, someone who would always be there for me, always have my back. Not a sexual relationship, just love, care and honesty. You know, sometimes I read reviews of a book I've already read and wonder if the reviewer and I have been reading the same book. That's how I feel now. But – and it's a big but – I do believe it's true that we all bring something of ourselves to what we read, we've discussed that before, and so, with respect, Ros, Adele and you, Simone, I wonder what personal baggage you might be bringing to this very lovely book.'

There is a moment of absolute silence.

Ros draws breath, then lets out a short burst of laughter. 'That's a really good question, Judy, and you've absolutely floored me with it. Of course you're right. Reading is so personal, as are our reactions to what we read. I still feel, though, that Ann Patchett warned Lucy about the drugs, threatened to withdraw her friendship, threatened to leave her, but didn't do so until she was in really dire straits. Had she done so earlier – set some boundaries and stuck to them – *that* would have been true friendship. Instead she just enabled all

Lucy's dependencies, turned up to rescue her all the time, until the end when Lucy was in more trouble with the drugs than ever and Ann switched off.'

'That's not the book I read, Ros,' Judy says. 'Or are you just stirring me now?'

'No. No I'm *not* stirring you. And I really do think you made an excellent point about baggage. I'm not sure where mine is coming from on this, but you've certainly got me thinking.'

'She'd tolerated it as long as she could.'

'That is a very benign interpretation.'

'Maybe, but it's my interpretation.'

'Okay, you two,' Simone says, 'wind your necks in.' She glances across at Adele, who appears frozen in dismay. Clearly being up close to this minor spat has been very confronting for her.

'I'm only saying that friendship is hard work,' Judy says.

'It doesn't *have* to be,' Ros snaps. 'What it *does* have to be is authentic, and it can't be co-dependent – if it is it won't survive.'

'Okay, I understand that. But I think this was authentic, and it survived a long time. I think it was love, so we just have to agree to differ. And what I wanted to say is that it made me see that I haven't made room . . .' She pauses, looks down at the floor. 'Since I left Ted I haven't made room in my life for love and friendship, and now it's too late.'

Ros turns to her. 'Now *that is* authentic, Judy,' she says. 'I don't know how you got there from this book, but what you're saying is really important. And if you don't mind my saying so, I really don't think it's too late. If it was I don't think you'd be here with us now.'

Judy looks surprised. Her eyes, Simone thinks, are a little glassy. It's clear the conversation has taken its toll on her, and they haven't yet got to the questions Simone wants to ask.

She gets to her feet. 'I think that's enough fisticuffs. Let's have a break and then I'd like it if we could change direction a bit.'

'That sounds like a very good idea,' Ros says. 'I'll make some more tea. Shall we call a truce, Judy?'

'Let's do that,' Judy says. 'Although, Ros, I must tell you that you are not half as scary as I thought you would be.'

'Well I suppose that's a good thing,' Ros says. 'On the other hand, *you* are a great deal more feisty and challenging than I ever expected!'

*

Judy looks around as the others get to their feet. Simone automatically stretches her arms above her head and Ros almost drags herself up, clinging to the arm of the chair and steadying herself briefly before heading for the kitchen. Meanwhile Adele seems more anxious than ever. Judy stays put for a moment, feeling pretty good about the way she'd handled Ros.

'Well, that was interesting,' Simone says. 'You were pretty impressive, Judy.'

'I was gobsmacked,' Adele says. 'I don't think I could have held my own.'

'I'd been dreading something like that with Ros,' Judy says, 'but it was okay. And you would be too, Adele, in fact . . .' she lowers her voice slightly, 'I think Simone is right, Ros is really a pushover. She believes what she's saying but her way of saying it is just bluster.'

Simone laughs. 'I think that's right – honestly, you take this stuff too seriously. I don't think Ros has any malice in her, she's just outspoken and not in the least diplomatic. Look how quickly she backed off.'

'But she came back again,' Adele says, 'still quite fiercely.'

'She's a very passionate person with strong views. I'm sure there'll be some more outbursts. You just need to see it for what it is. I suspect it's a way of protecting herself, keeping people at a safe distance. It's odd though, because she's also warm and forgiving, and hugely supportive. She's a bit of a puzzle, isn't she? Anyway, that discussion was really good, and it makes it easier for me to talk about why I chose the book, even though in the last few days it seems to have lost some of its significance anyway.'

'Because of Geoff?' Adele asks.

'Because of something Geoff told me.' Simone shivers, folds her arms across her chest, rubbing her upper arms with the opposite hands. 'I'm thankful I'm here with all of you to talk to.'

'To me it feels as though this is real life,' Judy says, '*my* real life. The one I was living until we got here seems like another world.'

Simone nods. 'Yes, a bit like waking up on another planet!'

'Maybe we should go and see how our fourth inhabitant is getting on with the tea,' says Judy.

Ros looks up as Judy and Simone enter the kitchen.

'I'm glad you came in,' she says to Judy. 'I've been thinking about what you said. You reminded me that there is more than one way to read a book. You read it as a love story and you spoke from the heart and told us how it affected you. I know I often get too analytical, try to pick holes in the writing, or make big assumptions about a writer's intention, and I couldn't get past that. So I think you're right, Judy, it *is* a love story, and Ann Patchett may simply have wanted to convey its intensity and importance in her own life, but I still think she should have taken time to stand back and think more about *how* she wrote it and how it could be read.'

Simone sighs. *Oh, Ros,* she thinks, *you are so complex, and often a bull in a china shop. But you are also so generous and wise.*

'I'd like to talk about another aspect of this book, and it's the part of it that made me choose it,' Simone says when they are back in their seats. 'The question in the cover blurb is about Ann and Lucy's relationship.' She turns it over in her hands and reads. '*What happens when the person you promise to love and honour for the rest of your life is not your lover but your best friend?* What I want to talk about is whether this was love or friendship or both; were they *in love;* was it a battle for supremacy between two writers? Is it unusual, or are there lots of friendships like this?'

'Oh good,' Ros says, 'that's on my list too, and it's so relevant to Ann's motivation for writing it and the way she wrote it.'

Simone takes a deep breath. 'My personal connection to the book, and what I want to talk about now, goes back to just that – the love between Ann and Lucy and why it was important to me.

'Years ago I had a very close friendship, a loving friendship with a woman called Colleen, that ended abruptly after almost eight years. I've never seen or spoken to her since the day we parted.' She stops to focus her thoughts, looks down at the book.

'When I first read *Truth and Beauty* I thought it was going to tell me something about my friendship with Colleen. We were both in our twenties when we met. I'd left home after a huge falling out with my parents and I wanted to get away. I eventually got a teaching job at a posh high school for girls in Melbourne. That was where I met Colleen, we started there on the same day. I taught French and history, Colleen taught maths and geography. We liked each other straight away, and we ended up sharing a house. It was a very close friendship. We shared everything, our hopes and fears, our clothes, our books, even our darkest secrets, which weren't really dark at all, but we never shared our beds.'

Simone suddenly has misgivings and stops abruptly, staring down at the floor, wondering what they will think of her – a woman in her sixties who sounds like a teenager.

'Are you okay, Simone?' Adele asks. 'You don't have to go on if you don't want to.'

'Of course not,' Judy adds. 'We can stop this anytime.'

'I don't want to stop,' Simone says firmly. 'I really don't, but it's difficult, I've never talked about this before.'

She looks around, manages a smile, and begins again. 'I think we were both pretty emotionally naive and needy, me more so than Colleen, probably because I was learning to live with the scar on my face, which I'd acquired some months earlier. Boyfriends came and went, but never seemed significant. I assumed, I suppose, that we would always be together. She filled a gap in me that made me a better, more complete person. I never had a sister, not even a really close female friend before. Just Geoff and Doug, when I was young.'

'So this Geoff is the person you had dinner with on Friday?' Judy asks. 'Sorry, but I missed out on some of your conversations this past week.'

Simone nods. 'Yes, that's right.'

'And you said that he's told you something that made this more confusing.'

'Yes, and I'll get to that in a minute. One evening Colleen came home with another girl – Lorraine. I'd met her a few times and didn't like her much, and they'd had a bit to drink. I was just about to go to bed, so I said hello and disappeared into my bedroom.

'The next morning, when I got up, I saw that Lorraine's shoes were still where she had kicked them off, so I realised that she must have stayed the night in Colleen's room. Anyway, it was a Saturday, and I had a shower and dressed and went out and didn't think any more of it. But that evening Colleen told me that she and Lorraine were in love, and she'd asked Lorraine to move in with us. They'd been seeing each other on and off for several months. They were a couple.'

The silence when Simone stops speaking is laden with anticipation. The three other women are staring at her, willing her to go on.

'I was devastated, and outraged, paralysed by the most overwhelming jealousy and hurt. I was mad with it. I wept, I shouted. And Colleen was clearly stunned. She kept saying, "But I've been out with other people, and that didn't bother you. It's no different, you'll still be my best friend." She didn't seem to understand that it *was* different because Lorraine was a woman, and that had she fallen in love with a man I could always be the most important woman in her life. I felt I'd been robbed of my primacy in her life because her lover was another woman.'

'So what did you do?' Adele asks. 'Did you explain that to her?'

Simone shakes her head. 'Foolishly I didn't. I was young and stupid, and obviously impulsive. I packed everything and moved out the next day. I actually think I flounced out. I wouldn't speak to her, wouldn't say where I was going. I avoided her at school, handed in my notice and left at the end of that term. I never spoke another word to her, despite her efforts to try and talk to me. I've never seen or heard from her since I left the school. And for months I was lost and grief stricken, and deeply confused. My overwhelming feeling was that something fundamental had been ripped away and I would never get it back. I believed I had lost the love of my life.' Simone stops again, shrugs and sighs.

'And you and Colleen were never lovers?' Adele asks. 'Not ever?'

Simone shakes her head. 'Never. There was never anything sexual between us. And much later, a year or more after I walked out, I was still asking myself the same questions. What was this? Was it love or friendship, what did it all mean? Can you actually be *in love* without it being sexual? Why did I feel and behave like a spurned lover when I had never wanted to be her lover? And why did she wait so long to tell me – they'd been seeing each other for months and she'd never spoken about Lorraine in anything other than a casual way until she brought her home that night. I still don't know the answers to those questions.'

'I think it was pretty outrageous to have invited Lorraine to move in with you both when she hadn't even mentioned it to you,' Ros says. 'Have you ever tried to contact her?'

'No. I couldn't bear to at the time, and then I just left it too long.'

'Would you try to find her, if you could, like you found Geoff?' Judy asks.

'I don't know. I don't see any point now. All I know is that she went back to Ireland at some stage, with Lorraine. I heard that from one of the other teachers I bumped into when she was on holiday in Hobart. What I want to know and what Colleen wouldn't be able to answer anyway is, what was wrong with *me* that I couldn't bear not to be the only woman in her life? Am I actually a lesbian, and if so, why can't I fully inhabit that identity? If not, then why couldn't I let Colleen have this love and still retain our friendship? I didn't know the answers then, and I still don't know them now. And the only friendship between women that in any way mirrored the intensity of what we'd had was the friendship that I read about in *Truth and Beauty*.'

'But that seemed to me to be such an unequal sort of friendship,' Adele says, with obvious caution. 'This wasn't the case with you and Colleen, was it?'

'No, that's right,' Simone says, 'but it doesn't explain my reaction . . . does it?'

'It doesn't, but . . .' Ros hesitates.

'Go on,' Simone says.

'I don't want to presume . . .'

'Presume all you want, just talk to me.'

Ros raises her eyebrows. 'Okay then, perhaps you were *in love* with Colleen. You had a love affair without sex, which I'd call a relationship. Perhaps Lucy Grealy and Ann Patchett had something similar.'

'Does it *matter* what you call it?' Judy asks.

'It only matters in that it's confusing,' Simone says. 'I suppose I've questioned my sexuality because – and now you are going to think I am totally weird – because I feel no sexual desire for either sex, and although I can flirt with both men and women, flirting is a game in which I never want to score a goal. It's a step towards something that doesn't interest me. Something else drives me, a different sort of connection that I can't define.'

'But you have a son,' Adele says, 'so presumably you had a relationship after you left Colleen?'

'No,' Simone says. She puts down her cup and looks away, staring out of the window to the garden. 'I had my son without having sex. I desperately wanted a child, but had no man in my life and didn't want one. My son is the result of an accommodating male friend and a turkey baster.'

Adele gasps, claps a hand to her mouth. 'You didn't really?'

'Really,' Simone says. 'Is it so very odd?'

'Well . . .' Adele hesitates, blushing, 'it's . . . it's pretty unusual, isn't it?'

'I don't think it's odd,' Ros says. 'Back in the early days of the women's movement – the early seventies – I knew a few women who used the turkey baster, but they were pretty cagey about telling anyone. They were committed to the idea that being a single parent was the best solution for a woman, and for her children.'

'Hmm,' Adele says, 'I didn't realise that.' She turns back to Simone. 'But do you really mean that you haven't had a relationship since Adam was born?'

'Well actually I've never had a *relationship* with a man at all,' Simone says. 'I had some casual sex when I was young, when I lived in Paris, and then later, when I first lived with Colleen and after that. I had a few brief and unenthusiastic interludes, but nothing serious, nothing that lasted more than a couple of months. And it was never something that I sought out.'

'Crikey,' Judy says, 'I thought I was odd because I've only ever had a couple of brief relationships and a few casual flings since I left Ted.'

'But why, Simone?' Adele asks.

Simone hesitates, torn between needing to talk about this and wishing she'd never started to. She's struggling to behave as though she is totally cool with talking about it, while simultaneously discovering that she is actually not cool at all. 'I am asexual,' Simone says. 'It's not as uncommon as you probably think. There are lots of people who simply don't feel sexual attraction to anyone. But there are various forms of asexuality – I mean, some people have romantic but not sexual attractions to others of the opposite sex or same sex.

And we're all capable of, and frequently long for, a full and rich lifelong relationship as much as anyone else.' She stops suddenly, seeing the expression on Adele's face. 'Oh, Adele, I can see you are amazed by this.'

'I am,' Adele says, 'amazed and fascinated. I'd no idea.'

'Me neither,' Judy says. 'I've always been a bit half-hearted about sex, but I thought that was just me.'

'I was never half-hearted,' Ros says, and everyone explodes into laughter. She smiles. 'Actually I was enthusiastic and always considered myself rather good at it, and James and I had a very robust sex life, I'm glad to say. But I do know several women who feel, like Judy says, half-hearted about it, especially once they've had children. And I know one woman who, like Simone, is asexual and very much at peace with it.'

'It's easy to live without sex,' Simone says. 'I've never missed it, I never really think about it and I've never sought it. But I have sometimes cooperated out of politeness!'

There are more hoots of laughter.

'I can't believe you said that,' Adele says. 'That's hilarious.'

'Hilarious but true.' Simone smiles. 'And since I stopped being polite the year I turned fifty, I've felt much better about myself. There's a feeling of congruence that comes with it. Accepting who you are feels quite powerful. My only problem is trying to understand what happened with Colleen, because I loved her, but I felt no desire for her. It all made more sense when I actually started to explore asexuality. I've sometimes wondered if I'm homoromantic, which is having romantic but not sexual feelings for someone of the same sex. But while I loved Colleen it wasn't a romantic sort of love, more like I imagine you'd love a sister. I'd always had the feeling that someone was missing from my life, and I believed that Colleen was that person.'

Judy nods. 'I certainly don't feel I've lost out on anything by not having had a sex life for years. I feel I've missed out on love and friendship, but not sex.'

Adele shakes her head. 'I am so ignorant,' she says. 'I knew none of this. I've always been,' she hesitates, flushing, 'um . . . enthusiastic about sex but often found it very disappointing.'

'Many men are hopeless lovers,' Ros says. 'Not that I have vast experience, but I've been involved in many conversations with lots of women.'

'I've wondered . . .' Adele says cautiously, looking down at her feet, '. . . well, I've thought it might just be because I'm embarrassed about my body. I've always been big, and never in great shape. There have been times when I've felt real shame when a man looked at me as though I wasn't what he was expecting. That certainly curbs one's own enthusiasm.'

Simone listens as the conversation continues, wondering whether, in fact, revealing herself like this was wise. No one actually freaked out. But has it changed the way they see her? *Perhaps*, she thinks, *this is just who I am and perhaps that's the answer. What else was I hoping to get from this?*

'This is fascinating,' Judy says, 'but, Simone, you did say that there was something else, something that Geoff told you – can you tell us about that?'

Simone nods. 'Sure,' she says, and she begins to talk about her childhood, her friendship with the Marshall twins, their closeness, Claire's kindness, and the strain that had developed in her parents' relationship. She tells them how the boys had visited her in Paris and how, when she got home the following year, their house had been sold and the boys and Claire were gone.

They listen as she tells them of the fight with her father, the methylated spirits, the subsequent stay in hospital and the fact that she left home as soon as she could after that. 'And that's when I moved to Melbourne and met Colleen,' she says.

'Does your son know about the turkey baster?'

Simone laughs. 'Yes, he knows. We joke about it as the virgin birth. He's met his biological father and they get on well together.'

Ros smiles. 'But, Simone, what did Geoff tell you that was so important that you've been brooding on it ever since?'

'He told me that the reason they left was that my father got their mother pregnant while all us kids were away. My mother found out, there were terrible arguments, tantrums, threats, and eventually Claire sold the property and she and her boys went back to her family in England. So what Geoff told me, and what I've been brooding on, is that I have a half-sister, young enough to be my daughter – and more than ten years older than my son. Her name is Paula.'

She takes out her phone, shows them the photograph of Paula with her brothers.

'Before they left my father begged them never to tell me. But Geoff told me that he and Doug wrote to me in Paris, not saying anything about Paula, just telling me where they'd be. They sent it care of my aunt in Paris, but she was my mother's sister, and I can only assume that either Mama must have told her to destroy it, or perhaps she sent it to me at home and my parents destroyed it.' She looks down at the photograph. 'When Geoff showed me this I felt an extraordinary sense of recognition – she does look like my father and I feel joined to her. I grew up as an only child. Adele, you and I have talked about this, about how being an only child is quite distinctive in the way we think about ourselves, and how we relate to other people.'

Adele nods. 'Yes, of course – it's central to who we are.'

'So imagine you suddenly discover that you are, in fact, a sister, even if just by fifty per cent.'

Adele is obviously taken by surprise. 'I can't imagine how I'd react to that,' she says. 'It would challenge everything I think I know about myself. I have no idea if I'd feel a connection as you do, Simone, or whether I'd feel anger or resentment, freak out, or want to run away. It would throw my understanding of my past and myself into chaos.'

'Exactly,' Simone says. 'And now what I want most is to meet Paula. But I have to face the fact that she may not want to meet me.'

'But Simone, how did all this happen?' Judy asks. 'I suppose your father and Claire had an affair?'

'They must have. Geoff said he'd fill me in on all the details when Doug gets here,' Simone says. 'I do think he's holding back and is a bit edgy about it. Anyway, I'll know soon.'

'This is all getting away from what Simone was asking about the nature of her relationship with Colleen,' Ros says. 'History and literature are packed with instances of passionate friendships between women, and how threatened men were by them and the steps they took to separate the women friends. Of course some of those passionate attachments were sexual, but many weren't. So, I stick with my belief, Simone – that you were perhaps in love with Colleen, just as you might be in love with a sexual partner of either sex. I don't think sex defines love or being in love. We make things what we want them to be – if we're brave enough, that is.'

'I'm getting awfully hungry,' Judy says, suddenly.

'Me too,' says Ros. 'Shall we continue this over dinner? Who's night is it?'

'It's mine,' Adele says, getting to her feet. 'I made a chicken pie, and the veggies are all ready to go too.'

'I'll come and help you,' Judy says, getting to her feet and following Adele out to the kitchen.

Simone sits silently. She feels drained, but relieved to have spoken about this at last.

'That must have been quite hard,' Ros says quietly. 'But sometimes just airing something helps, doesn't it?'

Simone nods. 'It does, it has. Although I don't understand how or why!'

'Time to draw lots,' Judy says later, when they have cleared away the dinner plates. 'Only Ros and Adele left. Which of you will go first?'

They look at each other across the table. 'Shall we toss a coin?' Ros asks.

'Good idea,' Adele says and she fetches a dollar coin from the housekeeping money they keep in a box in the kitchen.

Judy takes the coin. 'Ready? Adele, you're heads; Ros, tails. Here we go.'

The coin falls to tails.

Ros pulls a face. 'Okay,' she says, 'where are the marbles?'

Judy holds out the black velvet bag. Adele reaches in and draws white.

'Oh dear!' Adele says, sighing. 'Okay, I'll go and get the books.' She heads for her bedroom and picks up the books from the side table, turns, then stops at the bedroom door, remembering the moment she had left her house, locked her front door, got into the taxi and headed for the airport for the flight to Sydney. So much seems to have shifted since then. *I've changed*, she thinks. *Just being here with these three women has changed me.* And she runs back down the stairs.

'Here you are,' she says, handing round the copies. 'The book is *Unless*, by Carol Shields, a Canadian writer who I think is brilliant. Perhaps you've read some of her others . . . ?'

They shake their heads, study the cover, read the back cover blurb, fan the pages. Then Ros looks up.

'Actually I *have* read one of hers,' she says. '*The Stone Diaries*. I really loved that.'

'My daughter, Jenna, sent me this some years ago after I had fled . . . yes, I actually did physically run away . . . from a terrifying therapist called Astrid who wore very heavy make-up and a turban, and smoked cheroots all the time. I excused myself to go to the bathroom in the middle of a session, ran downstairs, out to my car and drove away.'

'Sounds like she was a good one to run from,' Ros says, amid the laughter. 'Have you regretted it since?'

Adele shakes her head. 'Not for a moment. I mean, I think a therapist might have helped me, but not Astrid. How can you talk to a counsellor about being uptight, intimidated and feeble when it's a person who seems so judgemental and intimidating that you can barely open your mouth?'

'Impossible,' Simone says. 'This looks interesting.'

'Jenna sent me this after I told her about Astrid; she said she thought it might help. So I read the book and really enjoyed it, and then read it again. Then I thought I understood what it was saying but I couldn't see how I could take that understanding and make it work for me.'

'So what did you say to Jenna?' Ros asks. 'Did she ask you what you thought about it?'

'She asked me if I enjoyed it, and I said I had, and that I'd read it a couple of times.'

'You didn't ask her anything else?'

'No.' Adele shakes her head, pulls a pitiful face. 'I didn't want her to think I was a complete idiot.'

'That makes it sound like a tough read,' Judy says.

'That's the odd thing, it's not hard at all, because you can enjoy it for the story and the characters very easily. I suppose for me it all made sense but I couldn't quite articulate why. I mean, I enjoyed it and was really moved and a bit disturbed by it. Normally when I've read a book I like to sum up in one clear sentence what it's about, but when I try to do this with *Unless*, I feel it's about so many things, all linked, that I can't quite draw them all together.'

'We could try to do that,' Simone says, 'if you'd like? Each write a sentence.'

'Oh yes! That would be really good,' Adele says. 'We could nut it out a bit first and then everyone say how they had summed it up.'

'Stone the crows,' Ros says. ' Homework! What a bunch of girlie swats we are!'

Chapter Thirteen

'Judy, there you are!' Adele says. 'I was looking all over for you. Are you sure you're warm enough out here?'

Judy is sitting on the front verandah in a patch of sunlight wearing a thick hand-knitted jumper, a beanie and knitted gloves, and reading *Unless*.

'I'm fine thanks, Adele. I promise to come in if I get cold, but the air is lovely this morning, and I'm wearing several layers of pure wool!'

'So I see,' Adele says. 'I just wondered if you're feeling well enough to come for a drive with me?'

Yesterday, Adele had spent some more time exploring Judy's laptop, which appears to be her dumping ground for stuff she simply hasn't had time to deal with. It's a pretty straightforward business – the mess Judy mentioned is extensive but not serious, so it will be simple if tedious to fix.

'A drive?' Judy says. 'Does it include coffee and croissants?'

'Oh you *are* feeling better! Well yes, it certainly could involve that.'

'Let's do it,' Judy says. 'How's the plan going?'

'Pretty good. I'll talk you through it either tomorrow or the day after,' Adele says. 'In the meantime there's something I want to show you.'

'Okay,' Judy says. 'When do you want to go?'

'What about now?'

Judy hesitates, closes her book, and gets to her feet. 'Sure, why not? Where are the others?'

'Simone's taken Ros to get her hair cut. I won't keep you out long.'

Judy laughs. 'I feel a bit like the ancient demented relative being taken out for an airing.'

'Exactly,' Adele says, 'just what I had in mind.'

Fifteen minutes later Adele is parking the car in the centre of town. She snaps off her seatbelt, reaches into her bag and hands Judy a large pair of sunglasses. 'I need you to keep your beanie on and wear these,' she says.

'Whatever for?'

'Trust me for just a few minutes, you'll soon see.'

Judy shrugs, and puts on the glasses. 'Am I in danger of being recognised?' she jokes.

'Actually yes, so I want you to have the choice of whether or not you reveal your identity. And I'd like you to hold on to my arm and try to look as though you need my full attention.'

Arm in arm they stroll out of the car park. In the main street, Adele stops and points across the road. 'Look,' she says, 'The Knittery.'

'So it is.' Judy reaches up to take off the glasses.

'No, no, keep them on a bit longer,' Adele says. 'I want you to come in there with me.'

'Is that really necessary?' Judy asks, taking the sunglasses off and stepping into the road. 'Let's go. Are you going to take up knitting, Adele?'

Adele grabs her arm and hauls her back. 'Wait, Judy. I want you to go into this shop and have a good look around. I know you like reading crime and spy novels, so think of this as an undercover fact-finding mission. I want you to wear the sunglasses in case Linda is there. I called the shop earlier to ask whether she was in and was told she always takes Tuesdays off. That's why I wanted you to come today. Linda is a big fan of yours; if she sees you she will overwhelm you with enthusiasm, so best to hope she doesn't unexpectedly turn up. I don't think you are ready for Linda yet.'

They cross the street arm in arm and Adele pushes open the glass door.

'Lovely shop,' Judy murmurs. 'A bit like mine.'

'Very much like yours,' Adele says. 'Because as I told you earlier, it's obviously modelled on the online images of your shop on your website, even down to the spinning wheel in the window. Let's get closer to the screen.'

A group of women at the worktable are following the instructions on a video, checking the commentary and then checking their needles.

'Oh my goodness,' Judy hisses, 'it's me, how embarrassing, one of my lessons for beginners. It's called Casting On.'

Adele nods. 'It is. And look over in that corner.' She points to the pussy hat patterns on special offer with a large poster of Judy above them. 'And look around the walls.'

Judy stares open-mouthed. 'Lots of my patterns. Wow.'

A young woman wanders up behind them. 'Good morning, ladies. I'm Narelle. Would you like to join the beginners group? I can get some more chairs brought in.'

'Thanks,' Adele says, 'we can't stay today; we might come back another time. Lovely shop, though.'

'Yes, it's always been popular but last year Linda did a big

Judy Castle promotion, and it worked so well we've kept it going. Made a huge difference to the business.'

'How often do you show the videos?' Judy asks.

Adele flinches at the rather plummy English accent Judy is putting on.

'Oh they run every day – usually we start them around ten and run them on and off until about four.'

'I see you have the Judy Castle patterns,' Adele says. 'Are they going well?'

'Incredibly well,' Narelle says. 'Linda bought a laminator and we print and laminate them on the premises. They're five dollars each or you can get five for twenty dollars.'

Judy makes a choking noise and Adele kicks her sharply on the ankle.

'Are you both knitters?'

'Not me,' Adele says.

'I do knit a bit,' Judy says, 'but I'm having trouble with my eyes at the moment, hence the sunglasses.'

'Of course, cataracts, is it?'

'Yes, had them both done a couple of days ago,' Judy says.

'I thought they only did one eye at a time,' Narelle says. 'But much better to get them done in one go, if you've someone to look after you for a couple of weeks.'

Judy smiles, pats Adele's arm with her free hand. 'My sister's looking after me, she's a saint. I don't know what I'd do without her.'

'How lovely! Well, I must get on. Feel free to browse, won't you? I hope you'll be back when your eyes are better, Mrs . . . ?'

'Grainger,' Adele says rather too quickly. 'We're the Grainger sisters, you may have heard of us?'

'I . . . I'm not sure . . .'

'You're too young, dear,' Judy says. 'Forget it. Come along, Adele, time we were getting home.'

'You were outrageous!' Adele says, doubling up with laughter once they are out of sight of the shop. '"Both eyes done at the same time." I thought I was going to wet myself!'

'Excuse me!' Judy says. '*You're* the one who started it. I just got a bit carried away with the disguise. And what about "We're the Grainger sisters"! You made us sound like a cabaret act from the seventies. We were awfully good at it though, weren't we?'

'Too good,' Adele says, steering her into the café. 'You can take the glasses off now.'

'You don't think I'll be recognised in here?'

'You're not *that* famous. Coffee or tea?'

'Hot chocolate, please.'

'Honestly, Adele,' Judy says once Adele has returned from the counter, 'that was the best possible medicine.' She leans back in her chair smiling. 'I love being with you and Ros and Simone. And you've all been so kind to me . . . I'm not going to want to go home when the time comes.'

'I was thinking the same thing,' Adele says. 'I feel like a different person from the one that left Adelaide. I'm afraid the feeling will evaporate when I get home. We *could* stay longer, you know. Marian and Brian won't be back until mid-September.'

Judy's face falls. 'That would be wonderful but I don't think I could. I mean, I can't just not go back.'

'Well obviously not forever, but maybe a week or two?' Adele sees the furrows forming on Judy's forehead. 'Don't stress about it, but you could ask Melissa if she and her mum would like to stay on a bit longer. You said yourself that she needs the work, and from what you've said she's doing a really good job. Think about it – we can talk to Ros and Simone too.'

'And you, Adele,' Judy says. 'Could you stay on?'

'Easily,' she says. 'There's nothing and no one waiting for me at home except a couple of plants that are already half-dead.'

*

Ros is trying to find a comfortable way to read in bed. For most of her life she has had choices about this: lying down propped on pillows, holding the book in both hands or alternating hands, lying on her side with the book in one or both hands, sitting up with plenty of pillows behind her – knees drawn up, or legs outstretched with a pillow to rest the book on. But slowly some of these options have been eliminated from her repertoire. It seems that however she tries to settle herself to read, or sleep, nothing is truly comfortable anymore. Arthritis plus the onset of Parkinson's is a horrible combination. *No one tells you*, she thinks, *how time consuming and frustrating it is to find new ways of doing the things you've done all your life without even having to think about it. And then you have to add in the issue of glasses.*

'If you got a Kindle,' Simone had said when Ros complained about it in the car earlier today, 'you'd find it much lighter to hold, and you could enlarge the font – in fact you might not even have to use your glasses to read.'

'No way! I did try it, I actually bought one, but I hated the measly little screen. And I could never remember how to flip back and forward to re-read bits. I couldn't get as involved in what I was reading as I usually do. I like a book, a pencil and a nice firm bookmark, so I can underline things, add exclamation marks and asterisks, mark sections or whole paragraphs, write comments in the margins and turn down the corners of pages.'

Simone was aghast. 'That's sacrilege,' she said. 'I never write in a book or turn down a page.'

'Then I have to tell you that you are missing one of life's great pleasures.'

'The nuns at my school would have sent you to the naughty corner, got the priest in to hear your confession and then assigned the number of Hail Marys required to absolve you of these terrible sins.'

'Bring it on,' Ros said, 'and I'll tell the priest exactly what I think.'

Simone, who was driving at the time, laughed out loud. 'Now that sounds like the old Ros,' she said. 'Rebellious and awkward, the one I was slightly nervous of meeting, the one who hasn't been too obvious here.'

'There *was* the dog treats crisis.'

Simone shrugged. 'That was entirely understandable. We all behaved badly.'

'So did I. It rattled me, you see; Clooney . . . well it seems a stupid thing to say about a dog but he's sort of – my rock, I suppose. It was about more than just the treats. Feeling physically unstable and vulnerable isn't confined to the body, it gets into your head as well.'

'Of course,' Simone said. 'What exactly have they told you about looking after yourself with the Parkinson's?'

'Very little so far. I got the diagnosis and was supposed to go back to a special clinic the following week, but I decided to pretend it wasn't happening and postponed it. Now, of course, I realise it would have been better to get advice sooner, so that I could chew it over with the three of you.'

'That would have made sense.'

'I've only skimmed the material they gave me. Stupid, isn't it? Obstinate – like a difficult child. I also left it too long before I even went to the doctor. By the time I talked to her I had symptoms on both sides of my body. And I already had arthritis, which doesn't help. I was going along pretty well until the start of this year.'

Later, once Ros had emerged from the hairdresser and they were on their way home, the subject came up again.

'So do you think you'll be able to manage shorter hair more easily?' Simone had asked.

'I hope so. It's too hard to hold the hair dryer and the brush – I often drop one or both. But the shorter cut and this marvellous spray the hairdresser sold me mean that I can just scrunch it into shape and let it dry naturally. I may end up looking like an old witch, although she says I'll look really cool. Ha! Bet you never thought of me as cool before, Simone, but there you go.'

'I think you are very cool,' Simone said, turning her eyes from the road to look at her. 'Your hair certainly looks very cool now. And I think it would be super cool if you called the clinic today to see if you can go this week.'

'Nice idea, but I can't drive that distance, I don't feel safe.'

'I'll drive you. It's only an hour-and-a-half each way. I could come into the consultation with you too, if you like. Sometimes it's good to have someone else there, it's so easy to forget what they tell you. Think about it.'

So now Ros sits on the bed thinking. She has been dreading going to the clinic and particularly going alone. Leah, she knows, would take her, but she would worry and perhaps be overprotective. Besides, Ros is not ready to tell Leah yet, not until she's got to grips with it herself. She picks up her phone, dials the clinic, and to her amazement is told that someone has just cancelled an appointment for Thursday.

Well there's a thing, she says to James. *I did it. I can just imagine what you're thinking – About effing time, aren't you? You would've had me down there weeks ago. Anyway, it's done now. Roll on Thursday.*

*

'How's it going today, Melissa?' Judy asks. 'Everything okay?' She is in her room, calling on video chat that enables her to see not only Melissa but the shop as well.

'Hi, Judy, we're doing fine,' Melissa says. 'Hope you're still on the mend.'

Judy hasn't told Melissa that she's had pneumonia and been in hospital for several days. She had asked Adele to call her and simply say that she was a bit under the weather with a very sore throat that made it hard to talk, especially on the phone. Appearing vulnerable or weak is not an option; neither is letting her recent lack of interest in what's happening there leak through to Melissa. After just two days without calling she had totally lost the desire to know what was going on, and her interest in the shop and what might be happening has been draining away ever since.

'Shall I give you a little iPad tour of what we've been doing?' Melissa asks, and the images on the screen swirl around as she organises herself to do a walk-through. 'So over here, we've created a special baby corner, and Jack is modelling some of your patterns – but he's doing it in his sleep at the moment!'

Tucked in his pusher in a corner by the window, Jack, looking adorable in blue and white, thumb in mouth, is the centrepiece of a display of baby patterns, and several knitted examples that have been fitted onto some of Judy's collection of baby mannequins as well as on Jack himself.

'And over here,' Melissa says, 'Mum and I have knitted up some of that big batch of rainbow wool from some other patterns – the gloves and scarves have been very popular. We thought it was a nice theme for winter, cheerful, warm and colourful. We've sold lots of the wool and the patterns. By the way, we haven't seen Maddie for a while, but I guess she'll be back soon.'

'You and Pam are doing a terrific job,' Judy says a few minutes later when Melissa returns to the counter. 'Look, I hope you won't mind my asking, and you must say no if it's not possible, but I was wondering whether you and Pam might be able to stay on a bit longer . . . another couple of weeks perhaps?'

'Really? That's brilliant, we'd love to. More if you like. We'll stay as long as you want, Judy. We love it. The customers miss you, of course, but business is really good.'

'You don't want to check with Pam?'

'Don't need to. We've already talked about it. Mum thought you might want to stay longer. She says you haven't had a break for years, so take as long as you need.'

When they finish talking Judy closes her iPad and flops backwards onto the bed. She and Adele weren't out for long – the recce in The Knittery, coffee and croissants, then home – but it's taken all her energy. As Ros had pointed out, she is not just recovering from pneumonia but from years of driving herself too hard, neglecting her health and denying herself the opportunities of a more balanced life.

On Monday she had stared at her knitting, put it in her bag and dumped the bag on the floor by the fireplace, and when she went to bed that night it was still there. It is still there now. The last thing she wants to do is to knit anything, ever again.

Judy pulls the duvet over her and wriggles into a more comfortable position, thinking about Donna and Ted. She hasn't called Donna since she left home and now she doesn't want to.

Why do I have to be the one who always phones, who holds things together between the three of us? I make the calls, I make the effort to go there. When did Donna last come to Perth – nine . . . ten months ago? Actually it's almost a year, she realises, and Ted never comes, and neither of them ever comes to Mandurah these days. *So what will happen if I don't call? Will they even notice? Do they keep it going just for me? Do they tolerate me because they know I have no one else?* Years ago, several months after Ted had got together with Donna, Judy had asked him what he wanted to do about a divorce.

'Oh, no worries,' he'd said in his usual laconic way. 'We haven't talked of getting married. I guess we'll sort it all out eventually, but I'm harvesting right now.' It was a typical Ted conversation. Judy could almost see him shrugging his shoulders, hands in his pockets, or sitting on the bench on the verandah rolling a cigarette before heading off to the tractor shed. But of course they never had sorted things out. *Why not?* she wonders now. Is she the elephant in the room? Ros would probably say that they are a co-dependent triangle. Perhaps, in the past, it provided her with some reassurance, the feeling that someone was there for her. But now she feels the stirrings of resentment. They are fine, the two of them, down there in the Wheatbelt, snug as bugs in a rug. They're fond of her, but their world is complete without her. *So what about me?* she thinks. *What about my world?* She remembers that Simone said something recently about how fascinating it is to discover the inner lives of characters in books, because no one can ever know the inner life of another person, however close you are to them. 'Where is my inner life?' Judy murmurs angrily. 'Does it even exist? No one would put me in a book.'

*

At the sound of the doorbell Simone, who is sitting reading in the lounge, glances up from *Unless*, wondering if anyone else will answer it.

'I'll go,' Ros calls from the kitchen, and Simone hears her heading for the door, with Clooney behind her. She returns to the book, wondering why she has never come across it before. It's written in first person and the voice is distinctively female – a woman who is thoughtful, well organised, professional. She's a writer and translator, and Simone is fascinated by this woman who is acutely perceptive and intelligent but who has for a long time been blind to the reality of a bigger picture, and what that means in her own life. *Of course,* Simone tells herself, *that's the case with a lot of us, I suppose.*

'Come on in,' Ros says to whoever it is. 'Don't jump, Clooney, get down. She's in here, I think. Simone, your friend Geoff is here.'

Jolted out of her thoughts Simone starts up and drops her book.

'I hope you don't mind me barging in like this,' Geoff says, hesitating.

'Of course not.'

'See, I told you she wouldn't mind,' Ros says. 'I'm making coffee, will you join us?'

He looks at Simone as if asking for permission.

'Yes, do,' she says, 'that would be nice.'

'Excellent! Won't be long,' Ros says, and heads back to the kitchen.

Clooney is watching Geoff with interest.

'Hello,' Geoff says, reaching out a hand. 'You're a handsome sort of chap.' He bends down to stroke Clooney, and retrieves Simone's book at the same time. 'Good read?'

'Yes, it's our choice for book club this week.' She drops back into her chair and Geoff settles on the sofa.

'Simone, I know you said you wanted time to think things through, but that was Friday evening, and now it's Wednesday and I was concerned that I haven't heard from you. Are you okay?'

Simone is about to say that she's fine but then stops herself. 'Not really, I'm still pretty shaken by all this. I can't get Paula out of my head and . . . I was going to call you today anyway.'

Geoff nods. 'It must be very difficult, I'm so glad you're with friends.' He hesitates, looks around the room. 'It feels different in here,' he says, 'more homely. It's all slightly formal as a rule, unbelievably tidy, a bit display home-ish.'

Simone laughs. 'Yes, we thought it was all a bit too perfect so we packed away some of the things that looked expensive and breakable. Gwenda says she'll put them back in the right places when we leave. Do you know Gwenda?'

'Of course, Gwenda and Ray look after my place too when I go away.' He leans towards her, puts his hand on her arm. 'This must have been such a shock, Simone.'

She nods and takes his hand. 'It was, still is. Friday night, when I got back here, I couldn't stop crying. And then I felt so sad about all that I've missed with you guys, and of course with Paula. Do you really think she and Claire will be okay about meeting me? I keep thinking that perhaps Claire won't want to, or maybe it will upset Paula.'

'Honestly, it'll be fine, Simone,' Geoff says. 'I'm confident they'll both be thrilled. But look, let's talk it through with Doug and then we'll tell them after that. We both feel that it will be better to tell them on Skype rather than on the phone, after we three have talked. It will be a big thing for both of them but

I'm sure it will be wonderful for them too. One reason I called in was to let you know that Doug is organising his visit. It's a bit awkward because he and Steve run the restaurant together and Steve is away in New Zealand for his niece's wedding right now, but Doug is confident he can be here early next week. Meanwhile he sends his love. So I'll ring you as soon as I know when he's arriving. We'll have dinner at my place and we can talk things through then.'

'I'd love that,' Simone says. 'It'll be great to see Doug and catch up on everything. Unless you want to have a chat now.'

He fidgets awkwardly. 'I'd love to stay for coffee, but as far as filling in the details . . . it's long and messy and complicated and best to do it together with Doug, I think.'

She shrugs. 'Okay. Claire was always wonderful to me, I would so love to see her again.'

'She's doing well for her age, a bit frail physically, but she's sharp as a tack otherwise. Forgetful of course, but that's understandable. She always thought the world of you. So, you're okay with dinner when Doug gets here? One of us will pop over and pick you up and run you back again.'

'Of course.'

'Coffee's ready,' Ros says, walking in with a plate of Anzac biscuits and putting them on the coffee table. 'Adele's right behind me with the tray. Help yourselves to these, they're still warm.'

'I'll help,' Geoff says, getting to his feet as Adele comes in with the coffee tray. 'Those Anzacs smell amazing, they're –'

A door slams, stopping him in mid-sentence. The four of them look up as Judy charges into the room and, apparently unaware of them, goes straight to her knitting bag which is lying between an armchair and the hearth, picks it up, opens the door of the wood stove and slings the lot inside.

'Fuck you!' she shouts, staring as the flames lick around the wool. 'Fuck you, fuck you, knitting, fuck the shop, fuck Ted and Donna. Fuck everything.'

They stare at her in silent amazement, and then Ros walks slowly over to her.

'Coffee time, Judy,' she says, taking her arm. 'This is Simone's friend Geoff. Come and have an Anzac biscuit.'

Chapter Fourteen

For many years Adele has been delivering high-level presentations and all the evidence indicates that she is very good at it. Whether for the board of a travel company, a bank, a hotel chain or airline, or the senior executive team of a university, she knows that success lies in thoughtful, disciplined preparation. Unturned stones do not exist for Adele – she will turn every one of them, and has always had enough nervous energy to keep her on her toes. It was she who had developed the concept for International Educational Tours Bureau, having been approached by a man with whom she'd once had a brief affair. Some years after their liaison ended he'd been promoted to a senior executive position in his university and he remembered conversations with Adele in which they had imagined an operation that combined learning, research and international travel. He contracted her to develop their discussions into a plan he could take to his executive.

Three years later Adele, then aged fifty, was appointed as director of the entity she had visualised and established. It had come at a time in her life when she was bored stiff by her job in a major bank and was thinking about dropping out of any sort of corporate life, selling her house, and moving from Adelaide to Byron Bay, or Noosa, or somewhere easygoing and relaxed, where she could simply hang out. Jenna was in Canada, and Adele imagined a totally different life. It amazes her now that she ever believed she could make that sort of change. She would never have survived the imagined opprobrium that would be heaped upon her by her father and, she realises now, she would have stuck out like a sore thumb in Byron Bay.

Bernard Grainger was a man who could not be satisfied. He had wanted a son and been landed with a daughter, which he blamed on his wife, Sheila, who had died so soon after Adele's birth. He hired a housekeeper–nanny to look after Adele, cook the meals and do the laundry and housework. And he made up his mind that his daughter would be brought up to be a credit to him in the same model he had imagined for his son. Hardworking, confident, corporate minded, astute, a high achiever. Being that person, having that identity drilled into her, had shaped Adele's teenage years and adulthood. She was locked into her father's plan, and fear of the shame of failure has haunted her all her adult life. Now, twelve years since her father's death and a few weeks into her retirement from corporate life, she senses that the shell she created, and into which she forced herself to please him, is starting to fragment, and that is both liberating and terrifying. Freedom beckons, but unfortunately Adele has no idea what to do with it.

When Judy had given her access to the computer Adele knew it was a big step for her, and she appreciated the trust involved. The situation was, as she'd expected, messy but not very complex. Whoever had set up the computer system had done a great job. And she or he had also installed various management tools, very few of which Judy had put to use.

And so this morning, as she checks again through the list of things she wants to talk to Judy about, Adele is surprised to find herself feeling strangely nervous. Judy has put her future in Adele's hands and is not in the best state to question the possibilities, engage in serious discussions, or make life-changing decisions. Adele thinks it's quite likely – in fact it's almost certain – that Judy will want brief information, a couple of options and to make a decision immediately. The responsibility of advising someone in her seventies, who is unwell and trying to hide her desperation under a cheerful facade, seems much more intimidating than fronting up to a board of men in suits and women in pearls. Yesterday's burning of the knitting bag had not been reassuring. Judy is still unwell, and Adele knows she must find a way to delay the decision-making.

*

Judy is sitting on the sofa, reading the final chapters of *Unless*. It has 'taken her out of herself' as her mother would have said, and out of herself is definitely where she wants to be. Reading this has reminded her that there is such a thing as a slow pace in life, and of the pleasure of savouring words and sentences and thinking about what they mean, instead of charging rapidly through to the end.

'I'm ready when you are, Judy,' Adele calls. 'Shall we set ourselves up on the big table and go through it together?'

Judy puts down her book and joins her at the table. 'This is exciting,' she says. 'I'm so grateful, Adele.'

'I'm glad to be able to help,' Adele begins, 'and it's good that Ros and Simone are out – no one to distract us.'

'I don't think we'll need much time,' Judy says. 'I'm sure I'll be able to make a decision very quickly.'

'Yes, but that might not necessarily be a good idea. You need to take time to think through all the options.'

'I know what I want, Adele.'

'Of course you do, but there are different ways of getting that. You shouldn't be rushing into anything at present.'

'Don't patronise me, Adele,' Judy says, feeling herself bristling. 'I know I'm still not well but that's my *body*. My capacity to think things through and make rational decisions is unimpaired. I am not some temperamental, irrational old woman who needs humouring.'

There is a long pause and Judy can almost feel Adele thinking hard about how to respond.

'There are a couple of things about that,' Adele says. 'The first is that if Simone were here I think she would remind us that mind and body are inextricably linked, and a struggling body translates into a struggling mind – only she'd probably put it better than that.'

'Well that may be true for some,' Judy says, hoping she has mustered a truly icy tone, 'but my mind is not struggling with anything. And your second point is?'

'In view of what you've just said then I suppose you consider yesterday's shouting, swearing and burning of the knitting, followed by floods of tears when you realised it was irretrievable and you'd even burned your only copy of the first draft of the pattern, was an example of a calm and untroubled mind?'

Judy feels as though she is a balloon into which Adele has just stuck a huge hatpin. She buries her face in her hands. 'Oh don't remind me, I feel terrible about that, and with that nice Doug sitting there too.'

'It was Geoff who was there, Doug lives in Melbourne.'

'Whatever – they both look the same in the photograph.'

'That's because they're twins.'

'Do you think Simone will ever forgive me?'

'She already has, not that there's much to forgive. It was, as we said at the time, rather entertaining.'

'I must have looked ridiculous.'

'No,' Adele says, 'you didn't look ridiculous, Judy, you looked upset, unwell and at the end of your tether, which is just what you are. And that's not a state in which you should make life-changing decisions. There's plenty of time.'

Judy nods. 'Yes,' she says, 'there is, especially if we all stay on a bit longer. Have you asked the others?'

'Not yet. I wanted to wait until they got back from the hospital.'

Judy feels the relief of no longer being the subject of discussion. 'Of course, that makes sense. Do you know what's wrong?'

'No, but my guess is Parkinson's. Ros might tell us more when she gets back.'

'Oh I do hope it's not that – poor Ros, it's such a horrible disease and she lives on her own too. And that'll be goodbye to the cello, I suppose. That's awfully sad. Sorry, Adele. You're right, of course. I will listen carefully, and take time to think about the whole thing, so let's do it.'

'Good,' Adele says, and she turns the laptop screen towards Judy. 'So, first of all I've tided up, transferred documents to the correct files and relabelled some of them. It's a very simple system, so it should be really easy for you or anyone else to use. It would be good if you, and Melissa and Pam, can try and keep filing daily from day one. I know that sounds tedious but it will save you quite a lot of heartache later. It's an excellent system that's in there, all you need to do now is use it effectively, and I can show you how to do that. And if you *do* decide you want to sell . . .'

'Yes, I have decided that already.'

Adele sighs, raises her eyebrows and continues. '*If* you do decide that, you will have all the information that a potential buyer would need, very easily accessible. See, here in this file called Business Overview . . .'

Judy's phone rings and she gives it a sideways glance. 'Oh, it's Melissa. It's the first time she's actually called me, usually it's the other way round, so I think it must be important.'

Adele leans back in her chair. 'Of course,' she says, 'go ahead.'

Judy picks up the phone.

'Hi, Judy,' Melissa says. 'How are you?'

'Good, thanks. And you?'

'Yes, yes, fine thanks, but there's something I have to tell you.'

Judy thinks Melissa sounds awkward, reluctant.

'Oh look, if you feel you can't stay on . . .'

'No, no, it's not that. But . . . you remember I said the other day that we hadn't seen Maddie for a while? Well a care worker from the place where she lives came in this morning with the usual bag of scarves. And . . . oh dear, I don't know how to tell you this . . . Maddie, she's . . . um. She died, Judy. The week after you went away, she'd been out to buy some liquorice allsorts for an elderly gentleman who'd moved in there recently, and she was hurrying back and she stepped out into the road without looking and was hit by a car. She died in hospital the following day. I'm so sorry to have to tell you this, Judy . . . I know you were very fond of her . . . I wonder if there is anything you'd like me to do?'

*

'Is there anywhere else you need to go while we're here, or would you prefer to head straight for the hills?' Simone asks as they walk out to the hospital car park.

'I'm a bit peckish,' Ros says, 'and there's a lovely little café in the same street as my house. I thought we might have lunch there and I could pop in and pick up my mail.'

Simone drives out of the car park and follows Ros's directions to Paddington. 'It's years since I was in Sydney,' she says, looking around with interest as they wait at the traffic lights. 'I might just spend a few days here catching up on the city when we leave the Blue Mountains.'

'Oh yes, do,' Ros says. 'You could stay with me, if you like. I have a lovely studio room upstairs.'

'I thought you had a flat that was let to a violinist?'

'I do, but that's on the first floor. When I had that converted I also had the roof space insulated and lined, and then opened it up into a studio. It's just a really big space with a double bed and a sofa that opens out into a second bed. And it's got a small kitchen area and its own little bathroom with a toilet and shower. I thought the rent from the flat and maybe the studio would help boost my very small retirement income. So far I've kept the studio for friends, but recently I've been thinking of putting that on Airbnb as well. The views of the city are great from up there.'

She thinks back now to when she made those decisions about the house, a few years after James died. At the time a couple of friends had told her she would regret it. 'What if you meet someone else and want to live together?' one had asked, while the other said, 'You should sell your house now and buy something more suitable, move to a retirement village.' Ros had ignored both and for her it had also spelled the end of these two, never very important, friendships. It was suddenly clear to her that these women had no real sense of who she was, or what she cared about. Couldn't they understand that there could never be anyone after James? Couldn't they see how unsuited she was to living in the very sociable environment of a retirement complex?

At the time she still had plenty of regular work with the Symphony Orchestra and the quartet, certainly enough for her financial needs, even if not enough for lots of travel, which was something else they had both mentioned. 'Come on a cruise with Len and me,' one had said. 'It's wonderful, lots of things to do, dancing, games on the deck, and lots of the cruise ships have groups for table games – cards, mah jong, even Monopoly.' 'Best to downsize first,' said the other, 'and those villages have the same sorts of social activities, as well as sports and walking groups, that sort of thing. You'd be well set up in one of those places and you'd have heaps of cash left over to go cruising.' But for Ros the prospect of organised social activities was the kiss of death. Doing anything with a group of people, or being out at sea on a ship and having to dance and play games, sounded like hell on earth. Converting the house and staying put as long as she could was her plan and she'd stuck to it.

'At the clinic this morning I got the feeling that I'd be able to live independently for quite a while yet,' she says now. 'They did say that deterioration could be quite slow, didn't they?'

'Yes, they did,' Simone says, sounding cautious. 'But they said it *sometimes* happens that way. I don't think they meant that it happens in most cases. Hopefully it will be slow for you, but I think you have to accept that at any point it could accelerate, so you need to plan for that.'

'Oh yes, I understand that, but going there today was a good thing, because it has allayed my *immediate* fears. You were right when you said that once I had more information I would feel I had more control. I just have to make the long-term plan and start changing the way I do things. And of course they did say about yoga being valuable, so I really will join you and Adele to get myself started. I said that before but every day since then I've found an excuse not to!' She indicates a couple of parking bays. 'The café is right here and my house is just across the street.'

It's good to be back on home territory, Ros thinks. Not that she is ready to come home, but there is a pleasant reassurance in seeing that life goes on as usual. The Italian couple who run the café are delighted to see her, especially when she introduces Simone. Hearing her surname they lapse immediately into Italian, and Ros is happy to be left for a while with her thoughts while the three of them talk.

'What nice people,' Simone says later as they stroll across the street to Ros's house. 'And the food was great.'

Ros nods. 'I'm so at home in this area, I just love it. It'll be really tough if . . . when I have to move.' She goes up the four steps to the front door, unlocks it, and drops her keys on the hall table alongside the pile of mail that Tim has left there. 'Come on in, Simone,' she calls, beckoning her through to the lounge. 'I just have the ground floor, which is quite enough for me.'

'This is lovely,' Simone says, walking across to the French windows, looking out onto the garden. 'Do you look after the garden yourself?'

'I always have done, but when I come back I'll have to start rethinking everything, I suppose. The big decisions will be the garden, the car and, of course, the cello. The quartet I play with has a gig in late October. I should've let them know by now that they'll need to find a new cellist, but I haven't been able to face doing that yet because it's so . . . so final. But they really need to know.'

Simone walks back to the table. 'Why don't you call someone from the quartet while we're here? Then it'll be done. I know it's a big thing, but it's also the *right* thing to do. And you need to do something significant to make yourself feel you're taking control of the situation.'

Ros sighs, looks up at her. 'I suppose . . .'

'I'll have a wander in the garden while you think about it,' Simone says, and she squeezes Ros's hand, turns and walks out through the French doors.

For a moment Ros watches her as she crosses the small paved terrace. Simone has thrown down the challenge, and everything she said is right, but just the same . . . She watches as Simone looks around the garden, hesitates, then stoops to pick up the basket where she keeps the gardening gloves and secateurs, and heads towards the three rosebushes. *This is the right thing to do,* Ros tells herself again. *I've barely left them enough time to rehearse.* The change will be as disruptive emotionally and musically for them as it is for her. She sucks in her breath, picks up the phone and dials Donald, the leader and first violin.

It takes time to explain, to allow him his shock and dismay when it registers that she is not just withdrawing from this performance, but that they will not play together again and the reason why. She and Donald have played together for more years than she can remember, so it seems impossible to both of them that they won't do so again.

'I just can't believe it,' he says. 'Dear Ros, I'm devastated, and so very sorry. What will you do?'

'Whatever I can,' Ros says, trying a small laugh. 'Keep going, work with it, adjust to it and hope that the progress is slow . . . that's all I can do, really.'

'We *will* play together again,' Donald says eventually. 'I *know* we will. I will come and sit in your lovely room looking out on the garden, and we will play together.'

Ros sighs. 'You'll have to contend with me shaking, messing up the fingering and probably dropping the bow,' she says. 'You know how you hate working with incompetent musicians, and how cross you are when anything goes wrong.'

'But this is *you*, Ros,' he says, 'and we will play for our own pleasure for as long as you have the strength and the desire to do so. Dearest friend, I will only stop making music with you when you actually kick me out of the door.'

They talk on some more, and she warns him not to tell Leah if he should bump into her, and asks him to tell the other two members of the quartet not to mention it either. 'I will tell her soon,' she says. 'I have to now that I've told you. But she must hear it first from me.'

'Of course,' he says. 'And are you back home now, Ros?'

'Only today to go to the hospital clinic. Simone, one of my friends from the book club, kindly drove me down, and now we're heading back to the Blue Mountains.'

When she puts down the phone, Ros presses a handful of tissues to her eyes and walks over to James's piano and picks up his framed photograph. *You would've made me do it sooner and you'd have been right. You'd have managed everything for me, and I know it's probably character building to have to do it myself, but who needs more character at my age?* She holds the photograph clasped in her folded arms against her chest and crosses to the open door. *Look*, she says, *Simone's pruned the roses. You'd like Simone; she's your sort of person. You'd like the others too. We laugh a lot*. She moves to return the photograph to its place, then changes her mind and puts it in her bag. *I'm taking you back with me,* she says, *not that I'd forget what you look like, but just because.* She watches as Simone carries the basket of clippings to the far end of the garden, tips them into the bin and turns slowly back towards the house.

'I've done the roses,' she says, gesturing towards them. 'They're all ready now for new life in the spring. And what about you, Ros?'

*

Ros is quiet on the drive back. She seems to be watching intently as first the city and then the suburbs disappear behind them, and Simone, who well understands the need for silence, knows that Ros will talk if she wants to. Making the call to the leader of the quartet had obviously been tough; Simone could read the signs in her face. 'Let's have a cup of tea,' she'd said, and she had made it while Ros walked out to the terrace, wrapping a scarf around her shoulders. They sat there, drinking their tea, for a while in silence.

'You were right,' Ros had said eventually, 'it was awful, but it was the right thing to do, for them and for me. It was irresponsible not to have done it sooner. And it is a sort of marker, a sign of acceptance, I suppose.'

Later Ros had taken her up to the third-floor studio.

'Oh my god, it's gorgeous,' Simone said. 'Much nicer than I imagined, and it's huge!'

'Well, not huge, but it's a good size,' Ros said. 'I thought I might ask Adele about putting it on Airbnb, what sort of rate I could charge for it, what to look out for. She seems to know all about these sorts of things.'

'Adele has no idea how much she knows about so many things,' Simone had said, laughing.

'Her choice of book is significant. I haven't quite finished it, but I could almost write my sentence about the story now and it would be Adele's story too,' Ros commented.

'I haven't got very far with it yet,' Simone says. 'I need to catch up ready for Sunday. But I know what you mean – Adele's managed to be part of the group and still hold back. But I like her so much more than I expected to.' She'd turned away from the window then. 'Would you really rent this to me for a couple of weeks when we leave the mountains, Ros? It would be the perfect place to stay.'

'I won't rent it to you,' Ros had said. 'You can use it for as long as you like, and the car too. It would be lovely to have you here in the house.'

As they went back down the stairs Ros had hesitated and then tapped firmly on the first-floor door. 'If Tim's is in I'll ask him to show you the flat,' she said, but there was no response.

A few minutes later they headed out through the front door and Ros was about to lock it but then seemed to change her mind. She opened it again, stepped back into the hall and appeared to be staring down at something on the floor.

'Everything okay?' Simone had called from the pavement.

'Yes,' Ros replied. 'Yes, everything's fine.' And she stepped outside again, and locked the door.

'Did you by any chance notice a pair of purple suede boots just inside the front door?' Ros asked as they were getting into the car.

'I did, and I meant to say how cool they were. Did you mean to bring them with you? I can run back and get them for you.'

'No . . . no thanks, they're not mine.'

'Not your tenant's though – they were women's boots.'

'Exactly. And they looked damp, didn't they?'

'I didn't look that closely.'

'Did you get the feeling that there might be someone else in the house?'

'No, not really, but you did say some areas were sound-proofed. Why? Is there a problem?'

'No. But I do know exactly whose boots they are.'

Now, as she drives out of the city, Simone realises that several hours have passed since she thought about Paula, who has been on her mind almost exclusively for the last week. She imagines the evening she'll spend with Geoff and Doug, for the first time in more than forty years, the three of them together again with the chance to recapture something of what they shared in the past, maybe to discover if they can share it again.

She remembers the time before she went to Paris, when the Marshall boys had both left for university and she was growing rapidly critical of her parents' relationship. It was then that she had been more aware of how ill-matched they seemed – Carlo so domineering and, in her view, narrow-minded, and Suzette's tight-lipped, shrugging adherence to his rules. She had lived with their tension for so long that she had taken it for granted. Now she wonders what sort of demons haunted her mother, what else she had had to cope with as well as what was, presumably, Carlo's affair with Claire. *Were there other women?* Simone wonders. She feels now that she should have done more, made more effort to know her mother better, both at the time and in the long, difficult years that followed.

She had been an exceptionally obedient and dutiful daughter, and had craved physical affection, but that was lacking both at home and in the convent, where physicality among the girls was strongly discouraged. It was Claire who dispensed the cuddles when Simone was small, the warm supportive hugs and maternal advice as she grew older.

How hard it must have been for Claire, she thinks now, a pregnant widow with adult sons. *Perhaps, if Mama and Papa had told me the truth, if they hadn't cut me off from the Marshalls, we could all have recovered from it*, she thinks. At least it would have been better than the years of silence and the awkwardness each time she saw her parents. She'd lost her parents, as she had lost the Marshalls, and some years later she had lost Colleen as well. *Is it me?* she wonders now, *is it something about me?* But these things had happened *to* her and in each case she had felt herself helpless – a casualty. Is that it then? *Is that what I am – a casualty, a loser?* she thinks. *Will I always be that person? Is that who Paula will see when we meet?*

They are back in the mountains now, just a few kilometres from what feels like home. Simone looks across at Ros, fast asleep in the passenger seat. She thinks of Adele and Judy back at the house, and feels a great wave of affection for all three of them. *They matter to me*, she thinks, *they really matter. I trust them and I want them to be part of my life, always, just as I want my sister and Claire and Geoff and Doug.*

Chapter Fifteen

I t's Friday morning and Adele is reconsidering her relationship with Radio National. She recognises that in recent
years it's become somewhat excessive: a prop that enables
her to get herself in the right state of mind to face the world
every day. It's only really in the last week that she's realised
how vital it was for her to listen every morning to a strong
woman confronting leaders, asking probing questions, taking
on anything that her producers put in front of her. By doing
her job in this way Fran Kelly made Adele feel strong, well
informed, even reasonably confident in her own job. This
morning it occurs to her that perhaps it's not as odd as it seems,
and that other people also need to kick-start their working
selves, especially if they live alone. *We all find our props and
our stepping-stones*, she thinks. She remembers now that Roger,
who had been instrumental in getting her to set up the bureau,
had always insisted he was unable to start or end the day
without classical music. It reinforced his belief that there were
things in life greater, more important and enriching, than the
idiocies of the administrative demands of life in a university,

he said. His bedside radio was always tuned to Classic FM, while Jenna, when she was at uni and then later in her first job, seemed unable to start the day without Triple J. 'Music to arm myself with,' she had insisted. *Music for them, words for me, so maybe I'm not so different after all*, Adele thinks, *even if I did take it all a bit too far*. She looks down at her hands; she's hardly made any fists in the last week. That has to be a very good sign.

Since yesterday afternoon when Judy took the phone call from Melissa and promptly ended their discussion, Adele has been thinking how alike she and Judy are in the ways they have organised their lives. Judy had spoken of cramming her life with work and other responsibilities that left no room for love, and when Adele heard that she'd felt winded, as though she'd been punched in the chest, for she knew instantly that she had done exactly the same thing. She had once longed for love, for a lasting relationship, what people thought of as a 'normal' family, but her fear of rejection always held her back and when she did meet someone she saw as 'a person of interest', she seemed unable to relax and became, instead, her most awkward and self-protective self. But while Judy has been suffocating under own chaos, Adele knows that she herself has been trapped by her own neurotic orderliness.

In Judy's case she sees that business success is the result of a lively imagination that not only comes up with ideas but can also visualise and create ways of realising them. In contrast her own success with the bureau has been ruled, and probably limited, by her own self-protective control mechanisms. She can see the contrast between being driven by creativity and vision, rather than a commitment to process, systems and restraint. *Who would I be*, she wonders, *if I had even a small percentage of Judy in me? And who would she be with a small percentage of me? Maybe we'd be one well-rounded person!* She can see the possibilities for Judy to escape from the business completely or partially, but it is not so easy to see how to free herself from her own chains. Astrid could have a field day with the two of them, Adele thinks.

This morning, to Adele's surprise, Ros has joined them for yoga. She turned up in a pale grey tracksuit, her hair newly styled – from scruffy to stylishly scruffy. Simone, who on day one had discovered yoga mats in the cupboard, fetched one for her and Ros lowered herself cautiously onto it.

'I will give it my best shot,' she says now, 'but I might need some help.'

'I'm learning very slowly,' Adele says, 'but I'm already feeling the benefit.'

Minutes later the three of them are lying side by side on their mats, with Clooney alongside Simone, and Adele and Ros following Simone's instructions, when the door at the top of the steps opens and in comes Judy.

'Is it okay if I join in?' she asks softly, moving swiftly down the stairs.

'Of course,' Simone says, fetching another mat.

Adele lifts her head and looks across at Judy. They had postponed their discussion about the business yesterday when she got the news about Maddie. Judy had disappeared into her room for some time and emerged later, quiet but clearly not grief stricken. Adele wonders if her arrival in the games room this morning is somehow related.

Before Simone can get them started, Ros lifts her head too and looks across at Judy and Adele.

'You may already have guessed that I have Parkinson's disease,' she says without preamble. 'When Simone took me to the clinic yesterday yoga was one of the recommended activities, so that's why I'm here.'

'And I'm here,' Judy says, 'because Adele thinks I am of unsound mind, and I think she's probably right.'

*

'I'm glad I bit the yoga bullet,' Judy says later, leaning against the worktop in the kitchen where Ros is making coffee. 'It felt good just being there, very calming.'

'Me too,' Ros says. 'It's odd that we should both have chosen this morning to do it, isn't it? Now I wish I'd started sooner. Simone said that I should think about "owning" the Parkinson's – her language of course, but I know what she was getting at. I have to accept it and start planning, rather than trying to pretend it's not happening.'

She puts a mug on the table for Judy and then picks up her own, and they sit down together.

'It's a horrible thing for you to cope with, Ros,' Judy says. 'I had noticed that you never carry a tray. If you ever need to talk about it, or need help or support, please let me know. I'm hoping I can sell the shop and that I'll have a lot more time available then. I may also decide to move away from Mandurah. I need somewhere different, where I won't be the woman in the knitting shop.' She lowers her voice and glances over to where Simone and Adele are sitting on the rear terrace outside the kitchen door, the steam from their mugs curling upwards in the cold air.

'I came to yoga because of Maddie. I'm so ashamed of myself, Ros, and I feel I must confess to someone. When Melissa told me what had happened, all I felt was shock, and I went into my room and lay on the bed and fell asleep almost immediately. When I woke up my first thought was of Maddie, and I sat bolt upright and said, quietly of course, "Well, one less problem." Can you believe it? What an awful thing to think, how callous and selfish. Please don't tell the others, they might not understand, but perhaps you do? I knew Maddie for years and I did whatever I could for her. I was fond of her, but in that moment I just didn't care. I felt I was struggling so hard to get well again, and to sort the future for the shop, that I was unable to really feel anything. Does that make sense to you?'

'Absolutely,' Ros says. 'And I do think it's to do with age. Death becomes a very personal reality in ways that are probably quite selfish. I noticed that as I got into my seventies.'

'Before I came here,' Judy begins, and then stops, not clear where she's going with this, feeling her way. 'It was just too hard to . . . to let anyone else get close to me. Melissa comes quite close, she and her gorgeous baby, but in a way I need to keep them at arm's length.'

'I know what you mean,' Ros says. 'It's a horrible thing to have happened, you won't forget Maddie, but you actually *feel* very little. If it had been Ted or Donna, it would be different, even though you're a bit conflicted about them right now. And wouldn't it be true to say that Maddie was something of a burden? Someone you felt responsible for when you are already barely able to cope?'

Judy raises her eyebrows, shrugs. 'Well yes, that's right.'

'So when you knew what had happened you could put that burden down. You didn't *want* it to happen, you would never have wished for it, but it *did* happen, and you felt relief.'

'That is just what it was,' Judy says.

'I was devastated by James's death,' Ros continues. 'I still am, but I've learned to live with it, and without him. But I notice that these days I might read a death notice of someone I've known and liked for a long time, and I'm sorry about it, and sad, but in a detached sort of way. Somehow it doesn't touch me as it might once have done. I do think it's about conserving emotional energy. Saving it for ourselves and for people whom we're really close to.'

'I suppose, yes,' Judy nods.

'Don't beat yourself up about this, Judy,' Ros continues. 'You showed extraordinary patience and kindness to Maddie for years. Respect and affection are sufficient ways to honour her and keep her in your memory.'

*

On Saturday morning Ros, alone in the house, is sitting by the window with her copy of *Unless* but not reading it, even though they're discussing it tomorrow. She is thinking about the damp purple boots tucked just inside the front door at home. They are Leah's boots, of course, but what were they doing there on Thursday afternoon? It was not a wet day; in fact it was cold, clear and bright, although there had apparently been a storm with torrential rain the previous afternoon. The Italian couple who own the café had mentioned it when she and Simone were having lunch.

The more Ros thinks about this the more she wants to know under what circumstances the boots arrived there on Wednesday afternoon, presumably wet, and why they were still there the following afternoon. She can think of only one explanation. When she'd knocked on Tim's door as they came down the stairs she'd felt a very odd sense of tension, the sort of tension that comes when someone is holding their breath to avoid emitting signs of life.

Ros has a pretty good idea of what they might have been doing that would make it impossible, or at least inadvisable, to answer the door, especially as they would have known who was knocking. What she doesn't understand is how this has happened. How this situation has developed without her knowing anything about it. Does Ivan know?

She thinks back to the time Tim went to get fish and chips for the three of them, a few days before she'd left to come here. She tries to remember her conversation with Leah in the kitchen; they had talked about Ivan, how Ros liked him but had never thought him right for Leah. About how nice Tim was, how like James, and so what a splendid husband he would have made. 'But I love Ivan,' Leah had said – or had she? Did she actually say that, Ros wonders now, or did she say, 'But I *loved* Ivan,' past tense? *I think that's what she said*, Ros tells herself now.

More important, though, is what she should do about it. Some people might say she should do absolutely nothing; it's not her business. *That's what you'd say, I suppose*, Ros murmurs to James, *and I see your point. But Leah is my daughter . . . whoa! Sorry, darling, she's your niece, our de facto daughter. We were only ever in loco parentis, but she feels to me like a daughter. And you, my darling James, are not here and your absence makes Leah more important than ever. She's the person who will pick me up if I stumble and fall, and I mean that in every possible sense of that phrase. Besides, I love her to bits and I don't want her to be hurt.* She waits in the silence hoping that James can hear her, wishing that she could hear him. *Sure*, he'd say, *I understand that but it's still not your business.*

Ros sighs, thinks it through again. Leah might get hurt! Yep! She will leave Ivan and he'll go berserk . . . or at least he'll be devastated. Who knows what might happen, what he might do?

Ros closes her book in frustration. *None of your business*, she tells herself for the umpteenth time, and stands up. Clooney thumps his tail on the floor at the possibility of a walk.

He's been restless since the others went out a while ago. 'You've been spoiled here,' Ros says, bending down to stroke him. 'Walks, walks, and more walks. You won't get this when we're home. Come on, let's just have a stroll around the garden.' She grabs up her big scarf from the back of the chair and wraps it around her shoulders.

In the hall she hesitates in front of the umbrella stand where she has parked her walking stick. The garden paths are rough and stony and there is now no reason to conceal her occasional reliance on the stick. She picks it up, laughing. 'Madness, really,' she says aloud to Clooney, 'relying on the ability of a stick held in a very shaky hand to keep me upright.' They walk out into the luscious green of the garden where the sun feels remarkably warm, and the air is filled with the scent of the gum trees.

Ros strolls cautiously on the uneven ground while Clooney trots happily between the bushes in an ecstasy of sniffing. She stops and gazes out over the landscape of darkly glistening rocks and verdant slopes stretching into the misty distance. Eventually she turns her back on the view and walks up the path and in through the back door to the kitchen, where she fills the kettle and switches it on. At the sound of a car moving slowly over the gravel at the front of the house Clooney pricks up his ears and to Ros's surprise the doorbell rings. She puts down the coffee canister and walks through to the hall.

'Did you forget your keys, Simone?' she calls, unlocking the door. And she opens it to find Leah standing there, in jeans, a black leather jacket and her purple suede boots.

*

This morning, while Simone is doing the shopping, Judy and Adele are finishing the discussion that had been interrupted by

Melissa's phone call and they are doing it on the move, walking to the waterfall. They'd been tempted to take Clooney but eventually decided against it, as they needed to concentrate and didn't want to lose track of him. He had stood in the doorway with Ros looking deeply offended, and even let out a long and agonising howl just as they disappeared out of sight of the house.

The conversation with Ros yesterday has helped Judy to understand her own reaction to Maddie's death, and the yoga has helped her to focus. As she lay there in the silence this morning, following Simone's instructions, and then standing, stretching, bending and trying to *find her centre*, as Simone had said, Judy felt almost frighteningly calm. *Is this really me?* she wondered, and she had let the sensation wash over her until she thought she must be glowing with it. An hour or so later, when she was standing in the shower, Judy realised that she felt calmer, almost peaceful, as though she had been given permission to slow down, pull back. *Poor dear Maddie*, she thought, *she's laid something to rest for me*, and in that moment she was determined to keep that in her mind, to remember Maddie with gratitude for closing a door so that a different door could open.

'You mentioned when we went to Linda's shop that it looked like yours,' Adele is saying. 'It does, and that's deliberate. You have lots of pictures of your shop on the website – Linda has replicated it, even with the spinning wheel in the window. Remember all the ways that she used your ideas and your materials, the patterns, the pictures with quotes, the videos, everything?'

'Okay,' Judy replies, 'but do you think that matters? I mean, do you think Linda is doing something wrong? It's not illegal, is it?'

'I think some of it is borderline. This is your *brand*, you created it, you own it,' Adele says. 'My understanding of copyright law is minimal. It's complicated, and online work and social media make it even more complicated. Printing the patterns and charging for them, without your permission, is probably a breach of copyright. It seems dodgy to me, as does the use of the videos. But we'd need proper legal advice on that. I don't think that copying the look of the shop is wrong – in many ways it's very flattering – but I do think that the extent of the copying overall is a bit cheeky and she should have checked this out with you, especially as she's in regular email contact. What concerns me is that Linda, and any other shop owners who use your work in this way, are making money out of it and you aren't.'

When they reach the boundary gate Adele opens it and ushers Judy through. They turn onto the waterfall path.

'Yes, yes of course, I see what you mean,' Judy says. 'But there's nothing I can do about it. I wouldn't know how to stop it.' Judy hopes Adele will let it drop now. She feels like a smoker who, having given up the habit, can't bear to think they were ever addicted to tobacco. Talking about it makes her feel slightly sick.

'You don't have to stop it,' Adele says, 'you just have to make it work to your advantage. You make them pay.'

'But how would I do that?'

'Well one thing you could do is charge for downloads of the videos, or set it up to pay per use. You could also charge for downloading the patterns. That's all possible, but we'd have to get advice on it.'

'It sounds awfully complicated,' Judy says, 'and they'd think I was a really horrible person.'

Adele sighs. 'I knew you'd say that. I've done some research and discovered there are a number of knitting shops modelled on yours, and they are raking it in free of charge, thanks to you.

Your videos and patterns – and *your name* – bring customers into the shop, keep them there, and deliver an increase in turn-over. Linda takes a small amount from a lot of people. She's a businesswoman, and she'd understand exactly why she had to pay. The Judy Castle brand has real value and Linda knows that, as do all the others. The only person who doesn't seem to get that is Judy Castle herself. If you decide to sell the business a buyer might want to own that Judy Castle brand even if you were no longer involved, and that could mean a better deal for you. How many knitting shops are there in Australia?'

'No idea, but hundreds, maybe more. I don't know. And I don't care, Adele. I just don't care if they're ripping me off.' As soon as she's said it she feels terrible. Adele is trying so hard to help her, but even thinking and talking about the business is encroaching on this new sense of calm and distance in which Judy wants to immerse herself.

'Okay, look,' Adele says, 'I know you don't want to talk about this, but whether you decide to keep the business or sell it you need to fix this part of it. You should benefit from what you've created. So I would just say we need legal advice on how you maximise the Judy Castle factor, whether you stay or sell.'

Judy walks on, staring hard at the ground in front of her, wishing Adele would stop. 'I can see you're probably right, Adele. And you are so kind to help me like this, but I wouldn't know where to begin, and my heart isn't in it anymore. It just isn't.' To her dismay her voice breaks and her eyes fill with tears.

Adele stops abruptly. 'Oh lord, I've been bullying you, Judy, haven't I? I'm so sorry.'

'No, I'm sorry, for being pathetic,' Judy says. 'But you see, I wouldn't know how to do any of that. I'd have to get some sort of business consultant, and that would cost me a bomb. And I honestly don't think I could bear to go through it all.'

'I'm not suggesting you do it yourself, and you don't need to hire anyone. I could easily do most of this for you, and it wouldn't cost you anything. It would probably be best if I did it in Mandurah so we're both in the same place and I can actually see the shop. And I imagine there's quite a bit of paperwork floating around in your office, so we probably need to go through that and get it sorted.'

Judy looks up. 'You mean you'd come to Mandurah with me?'

Adele nods. 'Why not? It would be easier. I can do some research from here and then I can have a look around the shop as well, and we can match the system in both computers. And I have a lawyer friend who deals with this sort of thing – I could get some free advice from him on that or anything else we need.'

Judy stares at her, a lump forming in her throat. Adele had said *anything else we need . . . we.* 'Are you serious?'

'Of course.'

'You'd do that for me? You wouldn't mind?'

Adele laughs. 'Of course I wouldn't mind. I'd love it, actually, love to see how we can add value to the business for you and set you free from it, if that's what you want. Besides, I have some very happy memories of Perth and I've never been to Mandurah.'

'I'd love you to stay with me.'

'Isn't your spare room occupied by a knitted town? I don't want you to have to move that and I really want to see it! I could probably get an Airbnb place.'

'The town is in the small spare room,' Judy says. 'My townhouse has three bedrooms, and two bathrooms. The second bedroom is nearly as big as mine.'

'Well then . . . I'll come to Mandurah?'

'Yes, yes please, that would be wonderful,' Judy says, trying not to cry again. 'Even if you came back with me and did nothing, it would still be wonderful. I've been trying to visualise going back. I didn't know how I would make myself get on a plane, go into the shop and start working again. But if you went with me . . .'

Judy had felt her new calm sliding away into the abyss of the shop, but now the tension in her chest begins to dissipate. It's crystal clear to her that she has made a decision to sell, to escape, to have a different sort of life. There is no going back.

'Yes, Adele,' she says, 'please, please let's do that. Yes, yes, yes.'

*

'Well this is a surprise,' Ros says, opening the door wider. 'You're the last person I expected to see.' Surprise and embarrassment, she thinks. Is Leah here on the doorstep because she knows what Ros has been thinking? The prospect makes her feel small and petty, like a teenager caught out behaving badly.

'A nice surprise, I hope,' Leah says, hugging her. 'I thought I'd come and see how you are. What a gorgeous place.'

'It sure is, come on in,' Ros says. 'Coffee, tea, something to eat?'

'Yes please, tea and food, I'm starving, but can I have a look around first? Are your book club friends here?'

'Of course you can. The others are all out.'

Ros leads Leah around the house, taking her finally to the games room.

'Simone does yoga here and I joined in yesterday and today, it feels good.'

They make their way to the kitchen and Ros takes the remains of a chicken and some salad from the fridge and begins to make sandwiches, aware of a new and awkward tension between her and Leah. There are things she wants to say, but she can't open up the subject, and likewise she senses that Leah is here for a purpose. She puts the sliced chicken on a plate, rewraps the carcass and pops it back into the fridge.

'So I guess you'll be home in a couple of weeks,' Leah says, perched on the corner of the kitchen table. 'It'll be good to have you back.'

'We're probably going to stay on a bit longer,' Ros says. 'An extra week or two.'

'Really? I thought you'd be bored by now, champing at the bit to get away.'

'Well, you were wrong,' Ros snaps, and she can almost hear a sharp intake of breath from James.

Leah shrugs. 'I thought it because this is not really your sort of thing. You don't hang out with women for weeks at a time. You're a loner, an introvert, and you hate being out of the city.'

'Well maybe I've changed,' Ros says, seriously irritated now. 'Maybe I've found out that hanging out here with three terrific women *is* my thing after all.'

'And is that due to the Parkinson's?'

Ros stops buttering bread, puts down the knife and continues to stand with her back to Leah. 'How did you know about that?'

'There was an information pack from the Parkinson's clinic in the mail. Tim left it with the other mail on the hall-stand, but you know that because you were there the other day and you collected the mail.'

'And you have a problem with that?' Ros asks, and resumes buttering the bread, her back still turned towards Leah.

'I have a problem with the fact that you didn't let me know you'd be back in town. We could have met for lunch.'

Ros turned to face her. 'I came back to go to the clinic. Simone took me there and came in with me, and then we had lunch at Stephie and Marco's place and called in at the house.' She is caught between anxiety about what she thinks she knows, and surprise at the hostility she felt when Leah suggested that being here was not her sort of thing, because right now it feels like the thing that will save her life.

'But you didn't let me know,' Leah says.

She sounds, Ros thinks, petulant and sulky, as she so often did as a teenager.

'Why would I? I'm not under any obligation to let you know when I go in and out of my own house.' The conversation is deteriorating into something she really doesn't want, but she feels unable to let go of it. 'Of course I *might* have warned you had I known that there was a possibility that you'd be there bonking Tim in the flat. I assume that's why you both ignored my knock at the door.' She turns round to face Leah. 'If you don't want to be caught out, don't leave your boots in the hall.'

The silence is sudden and weighted with mutual resentment, and Leah has flushed crimson.

'So was I supposed to get your permission to bonk the tenant?'

Ros slams her fist down onto the worktop. 'Don't get mouthy with me, Leah. You obviously feel guilty, because you sound just as you did when you were sixteen and I found you'd hidden that awful Nick in your room overnight.'

'It's actually none of your business,' Leah says. 'I'm a big girl now.'

'You are, and you're married to Ivan, whom you claim to love.'

The silence is longer this time and Ros senses a change of atmosphere.

'Ivan and I have split up,' Leah says. 'We split up two months ago.'

Ros stares at her in amazement. 'What? Why didn't you tell me? We talked about him in the kitchen, a couple of nights before I left, when Tim went to get the fish and chips.'

Leah shakes her head, shrugs, and stares down at the kitchen floor. 'I couldn't. I felt so stupid because we broke up . . . I left him for all the reasons you had laid out for me before we got married. You were right all the time, and I suppose I resented that. Also, I thought you might think you'd have to stay home for me if you knew.'

'I probably would've done,' Ros says. 'And of course you resented it. I always interfered, right from the start. Are you all right, darling?'

Leah moves around the table, hugs her, hangs on to her, pressing her face into Ros's shoulder. 'I am,' she mumbles. 'And I know it's the right thing for me, but I feel really stupid and sad.'

'So did you leave him for Tim?'

Leah shakes her head. 'I split up with him because he was sleeping with his PA. The fair girl from Brisbane with the huge tits? You said they were probably full of plastic, remember?'

'How could I forget! Is it serious?'

'He says not, but she wasn't the only one. He was also getting it on with a pianist who plays in the jazz club on Sunday nights. And that *was* serious, he's moved in with her now.'

Ros hugs her tighter.

'Tim and I . . .' Leah goes on, 'we've always been friends, and he's been so lovely. We've been seeing quite a bit of each other, though that was the first time I'd stayed at his – your – place . . . and then we heard you.'

Ros sighs. 'I was sure there was someone in the flat, and on the way out I noticed your boots. I've been thinking about it and getting grumpier ever since, so I'm sorry too.'

'You know I would have gone with you to the clinic.'

'Of course.' Ros goes back to the sandwiches, and switches on the kettle. 'So what now?'

Leah shrugs. 'Not sure yet. Ivan has gone to live with the pianist. I'll stay in the house for a while until the lease runs out, and consider my options then. As for Tim and me . . . well, I don't know what will happen there yet. Are *you* okay, Ros?'

Ros puts the plate of sandwiches on the table. 'Yes and no,' she says. 'I came out of the clinic feeling quite hopeful because they'd said that deterioration is sometimes quite slow. But since then I've had to admit to myself that my symptoms are more marked now than they were a couple of months ago. It's been wonderful being here with Simone, Adele and Judy, and, as you said, most unlike me. They'd all worked out what was happening for me before I told them. When I get back home I'll have to start making changes, but I don't really have any sense of how long I'll be able to live independently.'

'I'm so sorry, darling Ros,' Leah says. 'I didn't only know through the mail from the clinic, I actually ran into Donald early this morning, and he burst into tears when he saw me. He made me promise not to tell you he'd told me, but I already knew, and I know you'd understand why he did.'

Ros nods. 'He took it very hard; we've been together for such a long time. How will I cope without playing with them? I'm struggling to look ahead, to see myself in six months' time, a year, five years . . . but right now I really have no idea where to begin.'

Chapter Sixteen

The fourth Sunday

Since daily breakfasts were abandoned the group meal on Sunday morning seems to Adele to have become something quite special. It's Simone's turn again today and they all begged for more of her pancakes.

'Are pancakes going to be my signature dish then?' she asked, searching for the whisk.

Adele watches her as she beats the batter and heats the pan. She loves the graceful way Simone does things; there is something almost balletic about the way she moves between the pantry, the stove and the table, just as when she walks or stretches, or slips down into a chair. Adele wonders if Simone has always moved like this or if it's a result of yoga. She hopes it's the latter, because if it is maybe it will work on her too. But then Simone is tall and willowy, while when Adele looks in the mirror she sees a short dumpy woman, passable in appearance when her clothes and hair are just right, but pitiful when something is out of place. How does Simone always look so magnificent even when her hair is a mess and she's wearing a crumpled shirt and has spilled coffee on her jeans? *It could make me hate her,* Adele thinks, *but of course I don't. I like her more every day.* But there is still that gap between them, the dark, yawning gap filled with her own negative sense of herself, a gap she feels could never be bridged, although she knows Simone is probably unaware of it.

Adele is sitting across the table from Ros's de facto daughter, Leah, who arrived yesterday while they were out, and whom they later persuaded to stay for dinner. By the time they'd finished it was quite late and Leah was too tired and had drunk too much wine to drive back to Sydney. It's nice to have a new face at the table, Adele thinks, and Leah is interesting. She shows them a side of Ros that they've not seen before – Ros the de facto mother, who took on a difficult but talented teenager. Adele watches them with interest, observing how the relationship works, wondering what it would be like to have Jenna here with her. *Would I embarrass her with my awkwardness, my tension, by being so ordinary and uptight while the others are such interestingly complex women?* As she watches Leah and Ros, Adele misses her daughter more than ever. *I should go over there,* she tells herself, *soon. Now that my time is my own, there's nothing to stop me.*

Simone puts a stack of pancakes on the table, sits down and reaches for her own plate. 'You're looking so much better now, Judy,' she says. 'We were all very worried about you for a while there.'

'I'm feeling heaps better too,' Judy says. 'So much better that last night I rang Ted and told him I want a divorce.'

'Oh well done!' Adele says. 'What did he say?'

Judy laughs. 'He said, "What for? We're in our seventies, for god's sake!" So I said, "I don't care, I don't give a shit, I want a divorce and I'm letting you know so that when the papers arrive it won't come as a shock."'

'Good for you,' Adele says.

'Mmm . . . Well then I hung up and a few minutes later Donna called and asked what the problem was. So I told her – no problem except I'm still married to Ted and I don't want to die married to him. No hard feelings but please, Donna, just make sure he signs the papers when they arrive.'

'That was a really good move, Judy,' Ros says.

'It certainly was,' Adele says. 'In fact you all seem to have grown and changed in the last few weeks. I feel I'm the only one that's stuck somehow. I don't know what I want, where I want to be, nor even who I am since I retired.'

Judy looks at her with an expression of total disbelief.

'Don't look at me like that, Judy,' Adele says, 'you know it's true.'

'No I don't. Really, I don't know anything of the sort. That is absolutely not how I see you.'

Ros leans towards her across the table. 'This book, *Unless*, there's so much of you in it, and something of all of us,' she says. 'So let's all just trust the process, the one you created when you told us to choose books through which we could get to know each other. It's working so far.'

'By the way,' Simone says, helping herself to a pancake, 'I found this flyer for a craft market. It looks like it's a big annual event, bigger than that one we went to in Katoomba, and it's on all day.' She pulls a folded flyer from her pocket. '*Annual Winter Crafts Market*,' she reads. She pushes the flyer into the middle of the table. 'Anyone else want to join me before this afternoon's book club?'

'Definitely,' Judy says, 'sounds great. I'd like to find gifts for Melissa and Pam, and for the gorgeous Jack.'

'Me too,' Adele says.

Simone turns to Ros. 'You piked out last time, Ros,' she says.

'I did and I regretted it,' Ros says. 'So yes, I'll come too. Leah?'

'I'd love to,' Leah says, 'if you guys don't mind. I don't need to head off home until later.'

*

By the time they head for the market it's past midday and the sun has emerged to brighten the spirits of both the artists and the visitors. Some have set up in the big hall while others are spread out along the narrow pedestrian mall, putting their faith in the forecast of a clear bright day.

Ros, walking slowly behind the others, her hand tucked in Leah's arm, is relishing this unexpected opportunity to spend time with her in the company of the other three. 'So what do you think of them?' she asks, nudging Leah with her elbow.

'Great, aren't they?' Leah says. 'There's some really original stuff here. I love the fabric handbags – I might not be able to leave without buying one.'

'I meant my friends,' Ros says. 'What do you think of Simone, Judy and Adele?'

'Oh! Sorry,' Leah laughs. 'I love them – what terrific women. It's so good to see you all together.'

Ros squeezes her arm. 'I feel good with them,' she says. 'And they've already survived a couple of my hissy fits.'

Leah raises her eyebrows. 'Even Adele? She seems a bit vulnerable to me. I think that's what she was trying to say at breakfast.'

'Yes, there's a way to go yet. It's her book we're talking about this afternoon, so if you want to stay I'll need to check with her first.'

'No,' Leah says, 'thanks. I'd love to but I do need to get back.'

An hour or so later, they find a café table big enough to accommodate all of them. The day is drifting gently on and Ros feels exceptionally relaxed as she watches Adele, who does seem to be getting more nervous as the time to head home for the book discussion approaches. She's wearing her turquoise jumper for the first time and Ros thinks it does wonders for her. The colour is strong but not harsh and enhances her pale skin, giving it a new glow. And the grey in her hair is definitely softer and more flattering. She looks different, despite the anxiety that still seems to haunt her.

Alongside her Leah gets to her feet. 'I'm going to head off now,' she says. 'Thanks so much for inviting me to stay, it's been great to meet you all.'

They all get to their feet, hugging her, promising to get together again.

'We'll try and keep Ros out of trouble,' Simone says. 'It's a big responsibility but the three of us are up to it.'

'Good luck with that,' Leah says, 'and if it works let me know your secret. Love you to bits,' she says, hugging Ros. 'I'll see you soon. Take care and when you get home we'll talk about what lies ahead.' She walks away towards the car park, turning back once to wave before she's out of sight.

Ten minutes later they are on the move themselves. 'Shall we have a nice cheese and wine evening after the book club discussion?' Judy suggests. 'It'd be good to do something different.'

And they agree to stop for wine, nuts, cheese and nibbles before walking back to the hire car.

'While you get that I'll just pop into the seven-day

pharmacy,' Adele says. 'I really want to get something for indigestion, it's been particularly bad the last couple of days.'

'D'you think it's food or anxiety?' Ros asks her quietly. 'It can do that, you know.'

'Yes, I know, and I'm sure it's that,' Adele says. 'Hopefully it will disappear after we talk about *Unless*. I feel I've got so much hanging on that, as though it's going to open a door for me.'

They stroll together down the street until they reach the supermarket.

'Shall we meet you outside the pharmacy?' Simone suggests.

'Perfect,' Adele says.

And Ros watches as she walks away from them, crossing the street.

'That colour really suits her,' Simone says, nudging Ros. 'What do you think it would take to get her to go clothes shopping with me?'

'Rather less effort than it would have done three weeks ago,' Ros says. 'I think you should make that your mission, Simone. But it still won't be easy.'

*

The pharmacy shares its large premises with a small sub post office which, it being Sunday, is closed. Stainless steel rails divide the two queues and today the sole queue for the pharmacy is longer than Adele expected; clearly the craft market has drawn a lot of people to the town. At the top of the steps behind the counter the pharmacist is dispensing the prescriptions, while his assistant deals with business at the counter.

Adele glances at her watch hoping she won't have to wait

too long and standing as far back as she can from the man in front of her, who reeks of stale alcohol.

The assistant serves a woman with a packet of Panadol, then takes the next customer's prescription from him and hurries up the steps to hand it over to the pharmacist while the customer joins a couple of other people standing to one side, obviously also waiting for scripts to be filled. Adele remembers now that this young woman had served her recently when she came in to get a prescription filled for Judy, and that she had been struck by her beautiful dark eyes and pale caramel complexion framed by the hijab.

The man in front of her is getting restless as the assistant serves a woman who wants to speak to the pharmacist. He turns to look behind him at Adele, stares at her then turns away again. Adele thinks he's hungover – he certainly smells like it, his eyes are red, and although he's wearing an expensive-looking suit it's severely crumpled, as is his shirt, and the end of a silk tie is sticking out of his jacket pocket.

Adele watches as the next customer moves down to the counter. Now there's only the man in the suit, then it's her turn. She hitches the strap of her handbag, which she's wearing crossed from shoulder to the opposite hip, and glances back at the door. No sign of the others yet.

The man in front of Adele grunts and swears. *Charming*, Adele thinks, taking a further step back from him, and she watches as the assistant takes the payment for the prescriptions and hands them over. Then at last the man in front of her moves down to the counter.

Adele checks over her shoulder past the people in the queue behind her and back by the door she sees Ros, Simone and Judy waiting. She waves, points to the counter then points at her chest. Judy waves and gives her the thumbs-up.

At the counter the man in the suit pulls a handful of crumpled papers from his pocket, singles out two dog-eared prescriptions and slams them down on the counter.

'About fucking time,' he says to the pharmacy assistant, pushing the prescriptions towards her. 'I'll have one of each of these.'

'There'll be a bit of a wait for the prescriptions, I'm afraid,' the assistant says, and Adele, straining her eyes at the badge she's wearing, remembers that the name on it is *Neha*. 'We're very busy today and there's only one pharmacist on duty. Would you prefer to come back later, or tomorrow perhaps?'

'For fuck's sake, I want them *now*, so get a wriggle on. And while you're at it you can open up the post office, I want to pay a bill and some other stuff.'

Neha maintains a completely neutral expression. 'The pharmacist is working alone,' she repeats. 'I think yours will be ready in about twenty minutes, and we can only dispense this one, I'm afraid.' She pushes the other prescription back towards him. 'This other one has expired; you'll need to get a new prescription from your doctor. And the post office is not open on a Sunday.'

'Listen to me,' the man says, leaning forward, and Adele thinks he sounds quite menacing. 'I want my fucking tablets and I want them now. And I want things from the post office, so open it up.' He is leaning as far as he can over the counter and reaches out to grab her wrist, but Neha sees it coming and steps back. 'You people, you bludgers come here whenever you choose and think you can treat Australians like shit.'

Neha flinches.

Adele turns to the man behind her. 'Could you go and say something to him,' she says, 'wind him down a bit?'

He stares at her briefly, then turns on his heel and heads out to the entrance.

'Well thanks a lot for that,' she calls after him, and the other people in the queue shuffle forward and avoid eye contact with her. Adele feels her anxiety mounting.

Neha's face is flushed and there is fear in her eyes. 'I can't open the post office on Sunday,' she says again. 'It's not allowed, and there are no post office staff here on Sundays. And we can't dispense an expired prescription. I'm sorry . . .'

'You're sorry, are you?' he says, pushing his face towards her.

Neha glances around as though in search of help, then looks back to where the pharmacist is now on the telephone. 'I'm sorry,' she says, her voice shaking, 'we can only fill the one prescription.'

Adele feels a chill creeping over her – something nasty is going to happen and no one is doing anything about it.

'Open the Post Office!' the man barks, reaching out in an attempt to grab her again, but she is too quick for him and steps back out of reach. Adele sees the fear and horror on Neha's face. She feels the fear throbbing in her own chest, but there is something else, something stronger happening too. Rage is building in her now, overwhelming the fear. She steps forward, so that she is standing just behind him.

'Hey you,' she says loudly, 'leave her alone. Shut up and leave her alone now, she's only doing her job.'

He jerks back in surprise, turns and looks her up and down.

'Mind your own business,' he snarls, turning away again.

'I *said* leave her alone.'

'And I said *fuck off*,' he growls with his back to her.

Behind the counter Neha seems rooted to the spot.

Adele, rage seething within her, takes a step closer to him and waits, somehow knowing instinctively that he will eventually turn around again. Sensing her presence, he turns to find her still looking at him. She stares him in the eye.

'Who do you think you are, bitch?' he shouts, poking her in the chest with his forefinger.

She can feel his foul breath on her face, and it's as much as she can do not to turn away, to flinch, to step back. She slips her hand into her bag, feeling for her keys, grasping them and jiggling them around until the ends of some of them protrude between the fingers of her clenched fist.

'I'll tell you who I am,' she says in a voice she doesn't recognise. 'I'm the bitch who's going to call the police and get you arrested.'

He makes to poke her chest again, but she holds her ground.

'Don't even think about it!' she snaps. 'Take your foul mouth, your foul breath and your disgusting racist attitude out of here.'

Everything seems to be happening in slow motion. There are just the two of them now locked in this standoff. Neha, the people in the queue watching transfixed, her friends who were heading towards her and have now stopped in their tracks, all seem irrelevant. It's a battle of wills, and no way is she going to back down. He makes a slight move towards her and she pulls her hand out of her bag, the metal keys jutting towards him.

'Make one more move and I'll have your eyes.' She sees a flicker of uncertainty cross his face.

There is a moment of absolute stillness between them, and Adele maintains her unwavering eye contact. Then, quite suddenly, he shoves his way past her and strides back out through the shop.

Adele stands there, unable to move; the fear is surrendering to relief and then, quite suddenly, she is consumed in a fierce and powerful rush of triumph that leaves her reeling.

As it subsides she sighs, like a rapidly deflating tyre, rocking back on her feet, swaying perilously, and Simone grabs her arm and steers her to a nearby chair.

'Did I do that?' she asks. 'Did I really do that?'

'You did it,' Simone says. 'You were amazing.'

'Amazing,' Judy says, looking anxiously into Adele's face.

Neha drops down beside the chair and reaches for her hand. 'Thank you so much,' she says, with tears in her eyes. 'I was terrified and you were so brave.'

'You were so strong and calm,' Adele says. 'That made me strong too.'

Neha shakes her head. 'In my heart I was dying,' she says. 'And you were the only person who would speak for me.' She looks up at the other three. 'I will always remember your friend,' she says, getting to her feet again. 'Always,' and she bursts into tears and rushes off behind the counter to the back of the shop.

For Adele everything now becomes a bit blurred. People are patting her on the back, shaking her hand, talking about what happened, but she is longing to get out of there, to be in the fresh air. Finally they escape and wander slowly back to the car, where they pack their market purchases, along with the wine, cheese and other nibbles, into the boot, and climb into their seats. Since they left the pharmacy silence has descended on them and Adele feels strangely flat, as though all her energy has been sucked from her.

Simone buckles her seatbelt and starts the engine. 'So – is it home now?' she asks, and they mumble in agreement. She slips the car into reverse but Ros, in the passenger seat, puts a hand on her arm to stop her.

'Hang on,' she says, 'hang on. You just did an amazingly courageous thing, Adele: you took on a nasty, vicious bully and you won! That's a triumph, and we're all sitting here like half-dead fish when we should be celebrating, not sloping quietly off home.'

'Good point,' Simone says, twisting round in the driver's seat to look at Judy and Adele.

'We should go to the pub, get plastered, dance on the bar,' Ros says.

Adele laughs. 'I don't think I'm quite up to that,' she says, but her mind is revving up again now and she is starting to feel the satisfaction of having won something significant. 'But I'd love a gin and tonic or three. Judy?'

'I could murder one,' Judy says, 'but what about the book club?'

'We can talk about *Unless* in the pub,' Ros says. 'It's pretty straightforward, and it's very pertinent to Adele's victory this afternoon.'

'Is it?' Adele asks.

'Of course it is.'

'Oh do let's do it,' Simone says. 'We'll probably be in time for the Sunday session, and the prospect of gin has got me going.' And she swings the car around, and they roar off out of the car park and up the hill to the pub.

'I hope you all wrote your sentences about *Unless* and can remember them,' Adele says, feeling the excitement bubbling within her.

'I have mine,' Ros says.

'Me too,' says Simone.

'Mine's on a piece of paper in my handbag,' Judy says.

A few minutes later they pile out of the car, and Ros fronts up to the bar and orders the first round.

Chapter Seventeen

As Adele sips her drink she wonders if the way she feels is what people mean when they say they feel *unworldly*; not out of body or anything like that, but as though the world has dislodged her, thrown her up in the air and she is still suspended somewhere, waiting to land. A bit like a plane circling an airport waiting until it can descend onto the tarmac. The incident in the pharmacy runs through her head again, and she remembers not just the relief, but that sudden brief flash of triumph that raced like a bolt of heat through her body and left her reeling.

'We should start on *Unless*,' Ros says, eventually, 'but we should get another round in to see us through it.'

Adele wonders whether she is capable of talking about the book and, glancing at her watch, she sees that they've been there for half an hour and she hasn't heard any of the conversation so far.

'Another gin for you, Adele?' Judy asks. 'Are you still with us?'

'She's in there somewhere, in shock probably,' Simone

says. 'Do you think you'll be all right with another drink?'

'I'm feeling fine and I definitely want another drink,' Adele says, forcing herself into the present, and putting her empty glass down on the table.

'My round,' Judy says, getting up. 'Same again, everyone?'

'I think we should also have some food to soak up the booze,' Ros says. 'We can do cheese and wine another night.' She scans the menu and stands up. 'How about I order a big bowl of fries and some chicken nuggets, then we can all pick at those?'

'Meanwhile I'll just pop out to the bathroom,' Simone says, getting up.

Adele is left alone at the table, thinking of the moment when, standing transfixed, she suddenly decided to act. *But did I actually decide?* she wonders now. *Did I stand there making a decision or did it just happen?* She can't remember weighing it up and thinking, *oh yes, I'll do this now.* She can't remember whether she even paused for a second thought. All she can remember is the compulsion that drove her, and the way she felt when he turned on his heel and walked away. *What really happened to me, what did he see in me in that moment when he backed off?* she wonders. And she holds that moment in her head: the fear, the triumph, the way he turned away looking straight ahead, past the onlookers and out of the door. And she feels again the sense of power that surged through her just before her legs seemed to weaken and she thought she was going to collapse. *That was me,* she tells herself, *really me, no one telling me or urging me, it was all me. And that's who I could . . . who I can be.* And the realisation makes her feel at first giddy, then joyous, as though something that has for so long been bearing down on her has suddenly lifted and set her free.

'Off you go then, Adele,' Ros says when they are all back at the table. 'Food will be along shortly.'

Adele takes a deep breath. 'I've had trouble working out where to begin talking about this book,' she says, 'because although I love it I feel something in it is evading me. I can't quite pull it together. But maybe I'll start by telling you something about myself, so you'll understand why it's so significant for me. I'll start with my father. He was very much a man of his time and his need for control was of epic proportions. He was the youngest of three brothers but his older siblings both died during the war. He'd wanted to join the air force, but because of a weakness in his lungs none of the services would sign him up. I think he saw that as failure, because he seemed obsessed with trying to prove himself in other ways, and although he was very successful in business and civic affairs it was never quite enough. He couldn't bear to be in the wrong, couldn't tolerate disagreement, or having anyone question him. He believed that my mother "let him down badly", and I'm emphasising that because those were his exact words every time he spoke of it. "She let me down badly."' Adele she sighs, shakes her head. 'What actually happened was that she had a heart attack and died just a few hours after I was born. And of course she had also let him down by producing a daughter when he'd desperately wanted a son.'

'Oh my god,' Ros says, 'that's appalling. Your mother *let him down* by dying?'

'That was his reality,' Adele says, realising that she is now actually enjoying telling her story. In fact she's enjoying being the centre of attention. 'He liked women, but only when they were doing what he wanted, and when they "knew their place".

'He hired a woman to live in and look after me. Her name was Barbara, and she was a very sweet person. She lived with us until soon after I started boarding school when I was twelve; I came home for the holidays and Barbara was gone. Dad said she'd had to leave to go back to her family in Perth. I was sure it wasn't true, because she'd been writing to me until two weeks earlier and she would have warned me if she was making a choice like that. I was sure he'd sent her away. When I was in my twenties and living with my aunt, my mother's sister, in Perth, I managed to find Barbara. She told me that they'd had an affair and he apparently thought she must have told someone because people started talking in the bank. One day he was in the men's toilet and the chairman of the board came in, slapped him on the back and made a joke about him fucking the help. He told her about it that night and said she had to leave the next morning. He paid her fare back to her family in Perth and gave her money to stay away. He told her he couldn't have it known that he was involved with a *servant*. A servant! This was the early sixties! I should have mentioned that he was a terrible snob, as were his parents, and appearances were everything.'

'It sounds like an Edwardian novel,' Ros says.

'Anyway, I was devastated, especially as he replaced Barbara with a much older woman, Mrs Richards, who is the only person I've ever met who could honestly be described as hatchet-faced. She was humourless, haughty and behaved as though it was beneath her dignity to have taken the job.'

Adele pauses, realising that until now, the only person to whom she has told all this is Jenna. She has a strange and rather pleasant sense of the story unwinding, and herself unwinding along with it. The others are watching her, waiting for her to go on. There is no disapproval or embarrassment in their faces.

'Dad stayed out of the house whenever he could,' she continues, 'and I had to eat most of my meals with Mrs Richards. She took me shopping for clothes that seemed to be made for someone of her age rather than mine. I was always hugely relieved when it was time to go back to school and I could wear my uniform most of the time.'

'Was he kind to you, though, your father?' Judy interjects. 'Was he at all loving?'

'I believe he loved me in his own way, which was stern and demanding. He had no idea of fun, or how to be with a child or a teenager, he wasn't physically affectionate, but I do believe he wanted to do his best for me,' Adele says. 'But he was a hopeless man in many ways; for example, he had an unfortunate habit of saying that I must never think that it was my fault that my mother died as she did. He said it so often that it had the opposite effect! Oh, and he named me Adele because he had recently won a seat on the Adelaide City Council, and he was confident he would become mayor, which he eventually did.'

'Crikey, that all adds up to a pretty stressful childhood,' Ros says. 'You must be tough to have emerged from that, Adele.'

'Well emerge I did, but I'm sure you can understand where my anxiety and my need to please everyone comes from. I wasn't the son he wanted and I could only ever be second best. I tried very hard, for a very long time, to be what he wanted, although it was far from what I wanted, which was to have a husband and a big family, and live in a comfortable house where people were always welcome. I envied the other girls at school who went home in the holidays to what I thought of as normal homes, with parents who were kind and funny, and took them to the zoo or the beach or away on holidays. Parents who cuddled them and praised them; mothers who cried when they dropped them back at school after the holidays.'

'The holidays must have been a nightmare,' Simone says. 'I liked boarding school but I also loved going home, though admittedly that was mainly thanks to the Marshalls.'

'Yes, the holidays were deadly,' Adele says. 'I spent most of the time at home, with Mrs Richards, studying stuff that Dad wanted me to learn, about business practices, economics, the stock market, accounting, all of which was incredibly tedious. Occasionally I was sent to stay with my mother's sister, Alice, who lived in Perth. She had a slightly older daughter, Marian, whose house we're staying in now. Those were good times.'

'I'm not surprised you've suffered from anxiety, and found it hard to . . . well, to be confident about who you are,' Judy says.

'Well, you get the picture now. Like *your* father, Simone, his love was conditional on compliance, good behaviour, top results. And like you I was usually able to deliver. Finally, I escaped to university.'

'And I bet you came top of everything,' Judy says.

'Pretty much; but it never compensated for not being a boy!' She says it lightly but that endless struggle to be good enough, to make up for being what and who she was, still remains. *Why?* she wonders? *He's been dead for years, and it's me, just me, who's keeping this alive, kicking it along all the time.* She hesitates, shakes her head, stares down blindly at the table.

'Are you okay, Adele?' Simone asks, putting a hand on her arm.

Adele looks up, tries to smile. 'Yes, fine, sorry, lost track for a moment,' she says. 'Anyway, to cut a long story short, I finished uni and got a job in a bank. Mrs Richards had gone by then. I was still living with Dad and still very much under his thumb, but he was out a lot, and so was I, so we got on all right, probably because I rarely stood up to him, and on the occasions I did I soon backed down. I managed to have a bit of a life of my own, boyfriends, and quite a bit of casual sex, which, some time later, meant that I ended up pregnant.

When I told Dad I was pregnant he was quite pragmatic, and I've wondered since if at some time he'd got someone pregnant. Anyway, I'd expected him to go berserk and in fact he was reasonable. But he knew people high up in the bank and didn't want them to find out his single daughter was pregnant. So he packed me off to stay with Aunty Alice, and I had Jenna there, and stayed on in Perth for several years, got a job there in the same bank. Eventually I moved back to Adelaide largely because Dad developed early onset dementia. Then I was invited to set up the bureau. Jenna and Jean-Claude had met by then, they lived with me for a while but when they got married they went to Canada, to Quebec, which is his home. So, there it is. I thought it might help you to understand why I am as I am.'

A waiter arrives with huge bowl of fries, deposits them on the table and disappears, only to return immediately with an equally large bowl of chicken nuggets, cutlery and pile of plates.

'Enjoy your meal, girls,' he says with a big grin. 'All on a diet, are we?'

Ros looks up at him and Adele sees anger flood her face. 'Just sod off, you fatuous, sexist twit,' Ros says.

The waiter freezes. 'Sorry,' he says, flushing. And he turns away and heads rapidly back to the kitchen.

'That was a bit rough, Ros,' Judy says. 'He was only joking.'

'He was,' Ros says, 'but we're not girls, we're probably the age of his grandmother, so it's actually demeaning, and I really resent jokes that rely on ridiculous stereotypes of how women look or *should* look and what we eat.' She turns her fierce gaze to the food. 'Let's get stuck in to this.'

They are all really hungry now and the fries are to die for. Across the room a dozen or so women of a similar age to them are celebrating a birthday. There's a lot of noisy laughter, and they sing 'Happy Birthday' three times without stopping for breath.

'Let's get back to the book, shall we?' Simone says eventually, tossing her crumpled serviette onto her empty plate. 'Do you want to tell us something about it now, Adele?'

Adele nods. She reminds them that the main character, Reta, is a forty-four year old writer with a loving husband and three beautiful daughters, and that the book begins with Reta saying, 'It happens that I am going through a period of great unhappiness and loss just now.' One of her daughters, Norah, disappeared recently and turned up sitting on a street corner in Toronto with a begging bowl and a sign around her neck simply saying *Goodness*.

'So,' she says, 'I started reading this as a family story but as it moved along I began to feel it was telling me so much more, and this continued all the way through. I loved it, but I felt I was always missing something. I still do, and I am not sure what it was I missed.'

Ros nods. 'Yes, it's haunting and in its own gentle way it doesn't let you go. It's intimate and utterly believable and I felt it was like something I had as a child: a packet of flat coloured pieces of paper that you drop into a glass of water and they open and swell into beautiful, colourful paper flowers.'

Adele clasps her hands together. 'Exactly, Ros, but I felt I was just not getting the flowers to open.'

'Reta spoke, I listened and didn't want her to stop,' Simone says. 'By the end I felt she had cast a spell on me. I emerged from the book feeling calm and serene . . .'

'That's not the book, Simone,' Judy says. 'You're always like that.'

'Not really, but I try to be.'

Adele takes a breath to speak, but Judy continues before Adele can begin.

'It *is* like a spell, she . . . well, the author, through the character of Reta . . . made me feel that this was a very simple story, but I slowly realised that I was reading something much more complex but I couldn't actually join all the dots. So I'm with you on this, Adele.'

Adele looks around. 'I'm relieved that you felt that too, because so much is packed into these simple, elegant sentences. It is not overtly literary, because it feels as though a friend is telling you something, because she talks about small things that are so familiar, things that slip below the radar but leave us feeling crushed, or impotent, all so small it seems petty but adding up to something so much more significant. Is that how you felt?'

'Absolutely,' Simone says.

Judy nods in agreement.

Adele is enjoying this now, enjoying the way they are engaging with it and with her. 'Reta starts recognising the ways that she is powerless through this awful experience of her daughter disappearing and cutting herself off from the family. It's every mother's nightmare, and it makes Reta examine her comfortable and predictable life. I mean, it's almost a picture-perfect family: the mother intelligent, thoughtful, writing books, poetry, short stories, translating the work of an eminent feminist writer, the father a kindly doctor. He's a bit obsessed with his study of trilobites but I don't think we can hold that against him. Although he does seem to be one of those nice men who is absent while being physically present. The sisters are dutiful and loving, and then Norah disappears without warning, and when they eventually find her she won't talk to them, won't engage at all with any member of the family. I thought that this was so inexplicable that it almost amounted to violence.'

'Yes, well the thing about Reta,' Simone says, 'is that her happy and predictable life is thrown up in the air. She's a very reasonable woman and that reasonableness is also fundamental to her writing. What she writes is mild, like Reta and like her life, not in any way contentious or challenging, she never rocks any boats. And it's interesting that while *she's* so reasonable, the woman whose work she's translating, Danielle, is a tough and challenging French feminist and quite *un*reasonable.'

'Could I just stop you there?' Ros asks. 'Adele, do you think it would be a good idea if we each read out the sentences we wrote? It might help to clarify things because I think you may actually have *got it*, but maybe you just can't name it.'

Adele looks puzzled. 'Really? Okay, sure, let's go with the sentences. Who wants to go first?'

'I will,' Judy says, pulling a folded piece of paper from her bag. She puts on her glasses. 'Here's what I wrote. "This is a lovely story of a really nice woman called Reta, with a beautiful family, and they are all shaken to bits because one of the daughters has left home and is doing something truly weird, and Reta feels helpless and powerless and she writes letters of complaint to important people but never sends them."' Judy stops reading, looks up. 'Oh dear, very long sentence with no punctuation. And I forgot, I was going to add a second sentence if that's allowed, which was going to be about how Reta is puzzled by the way her happiness has been totally disrupted. But you already knew that, didn't you?' She laughs.

'We did,' Ros says, smiling, 'but you've got it all there to focus us.'

'Okay,' Adele says, 'here's mine. "This is the story of Reta, who feels powerless in every aspect of her life, despite loving that life, and she only really recognises this when her daughter leaves home to pursue a life on the street, which Reta can't understand.'"

Ros nods, and looks at Simone.

'I suspect that you and I are the same on this, Ros,' Simone says. 'You go first.'

'Okay.' Ros rummages in her pocket, smooths out a piece of paper and begins to read. '"When Reta's beloved daughter, Norah, takes dramatic action because she feels powerless in the face of widespread injustice and inequality, Reta realises that Norah's political position mirrors her own more personal sense of disenfranchisement in her everyday life, and she starts to recognise that her ambivalence has led her to collude in her own powerlessness."' Ros stops and looks around. 'Simone?' she says, raising her eyebrows.

'Spot on,' Simone says, 'only I couldn't have put it so succinctly.'

'Hang on,' Adele says. 'Could you read that again please, Ros.'

Ros reads it again and sees that Adele still has the stunned mullet look.

'Look,' she says, 'you could say that through Norah's *public political* action, Reta finally sees that she has lived her life doing all the things that are expected of what we might traditionally call *a good woman* or *a good wife and mother*. She's lived with and accepted it, been irritated and maybe sometimes angry or resentful, but she has never done anything to change it. Her only form of protest is in the letters she writes, but she doesn't post them. She resents it but she doesn't rock any boats. Reta's daughter, on the other hand, is overwhelmed by inequality and justice on vast scale. She takes it very personally and her response is to reject the comfort zone of privilege and to live from hand to mouth on the street corner, to draw attention to what matters to her. She's channelling her concern, her distress, maybe her rage into a form of public protest. So – Nora makes the personal political by making it public, whereas Reta never really acts or does anything remotely contentious.'

The pub is noisy but there is complete silence at the table. Adele stares at Ros, her head spinning. 'And the woman at the end,' she says, 'the immigrant woman who sets fire to herself, she's doing the same thing?'

'Exactly,' Ros says, 'she takes control of her life in a horrific way because she has no alternative.'

'Crikey,' Judy says, 'I really will have to read it again now, in a different way, just as I will *Truth and Beauty*.'

'Can I ask you something, Adele?' Ros says. 'Are you seeing what I'm seeing about what happened this afternoon?'

Adele nods slowly. 'Yes,' she says. 'I think so. My own confrontation with the political and the personal. It feels . . . powerful.'

'It *was* powerful, and important,' Ros says. 'You took control in a remarkable way. You were truly awesome, and as you know I consider that word to be appallingly overused and misused but in this case it feels right.'

Adele is trying hard to get to grips with all this and retreats again from the conversation, examining once more what happened and how she feels. Eventually she gets to her feet.

'Ready for another round?' she asks. When they all nod, she walks to the bar with the empty glasses and stands there, watching the musicians in the small jazz band that has been playing on and off since they arrived, and who have now started to pack up.

Back at the table they talk more about the book, and Ros suggests that they are all part of some sort of transitional generation of women who were aware of the rise of feminism in the late sixties and early seventies but let it pass them by.

'I hooked into it quite late in the seventies,' she says, 'but I know heaps of women who simply thought it wasn't for them. They thought it was too aggressive, or meant they shouldn't have relationships with men, or it would destroy their families. Some thought they just didn't need it and only comparatively recently discovered what it could really mean.'

'That's me!' Judy cuts in. 'You know what finally did it for me? It was that misogyny speech when Julia Gillard took Tony Abbott apart. I sat there listening to that and something really powerful seemed to be whizzing around inside me and I thought – *oh yeah!* This is what it's about, and I couldn't believe I'd only just caught on.'

Ros nudges Adele. 'Look over there,' she says, 'this might be a bit of a laugh.'

Two of the women from the birthday group are setting something up on the karaoke machine and as the others turn their chairs to see what's happening the first notes of 'Mamma Mia' float out and the group at the big table whoop in delight. Soon the room is swaying to the music of ABBA, and the two women – probably, Adele thinks, around her age or a little older – are belting out the lyrics.

What have I been doing all this time? she thinks. *How can I have got into my sixties without ever feeling what I felt this after-noon, what I feel now?* A great surge of frustrated energy seems trapped inside her and she wishes some of that lovely noisy group of women would get up and dance so she could join them. *You don't have to wait for them,* something tells her, *you can just get up and dance,* but she's still locked in her chair. The women finish to shrieks of laughter and wild applause and then begin again, this time with 'Dancing Queen'. Swinging their hips, waving their arms, twisting and turning; Adele feels the wildness infecting her. These women are not worrying about how they look, or what anyone might think of them, they are simply having a wonderful time.

She feels as though she is about to burst out of her skin.

*

Ros is enjoying the karaoke, she loves the uninhibited way the two women are singing and dancing and the others are urging them on. She wishes now that she hadn't made that unkind retort to the waiter. His remark *was* fatuous and sexist, but he probably didn't know that, and she didn't have to do it and embarrass him and the others in the process. As James would have pointed out had he been there, the young guy wouldn't really understand what he'd done wrong and there's not much point in complaining or picking up on things like that unless you explain why. The waiter was simply trying to be matey. But Ros is still partially caught up in the incident in the pharmacy. Adele's handling of it really was a triumph, but she is disappointed in herself for not stepping up to support her. It's not so long ago that she would have done that without thinking twice, but today she'd come face to face with the fear of her own vulnerability. When she was younger she had thrown herself into the fray of feminist and anti-nuclear demonstrations, struggled with police and been arrested on marches for Indigenous land rights, and on industrial relations issues and, most recently, against the government's treatment of refugees. But today her own physical condition had held her back; she feared being hit or pushed and falling down, perhaps getting injured in some way that would further reduce her independence or mobility. *I was pathetic*, she tells James, *and you'd have been ashamed of me.* And she can almost hear him saying,

You don't have to front up for everything, Ros. But for Ros this has struck at the core of who she believes herself to be.

The singers have had enough now; they laugh, do some exaggerated curtsies and head back to their table. Judy and Simone are deep in conversation now about Julia Gillard, and Adele seems restless. Ros imagines that Adele will have a sleepless night in which she will circle the events of the day and what they mean for her. She turns to speak to her, touching her arm, but Adele pats her hand absent-mindedly, gets to her feet and walks away.

Is she going to cry, or throw up in the toilet? *I'll check on her in a minute,* Ros thinks, and she turns to join the Julia Gillard conversation.

'She did have a very hard time,' Simone is saying, 'and the Gillard government managed to pass a lot of important legislation. I don't think she ever got sufficient credit for that.'

'It's an awful job, politics, I reckon,' Judy says, 'and the top job would be the worst.'

Ros opens her mouth to speak but a loud electronic beep followed by a blast of something else from the karaoke machine makes the three of them look up.

'Oh my god!' Judy says. 'It's Adele!'

Ros blinks, wondering if she's seeing things, but it is indeed Adele up on the stage, clutching a microphone with one hand and stabbing at various buttons with the other. Suddenly, triumphantly, she hits another button with a flourish and stamps her feet to the first bars of a very familiar anthem.

'Strewth,' Ros says. 'It's "I Am Woman". Adele thinks she's Helen Reddy!'

And sure enough, she sees that for the first time ever Adele has relaxed her shoulders. More than that, she's rolling them energetically and pumping the air with her free hand. Then, with perfect timing, and in a rich and resonant voice, Adele begins to sing.

'Stone the crows,' Judy says, 'I haven't heard that song in years.'

'Well look at that,' Simone says, turning to Ros. 'She is a woman possessed! And she really can roar!'

A huge lump rises in Ros's throat and she makes no attempt to stop the tears that well in her eyes. 'She sure can,' she says. 'And she is a woman *self*-possessed.'

And when Adele belts out that no one will keep her down again, Ros is on her feet, and Simone and Judy are right behind her, singing with her, swaying as Adele sways, watching her transformed before their eyes, the turquoise jumper enhancing the gleaming chestnut and silver in her hair.

The birthday women are on their feet now, singing and swaying along, and everyone else from the bar staff to the customers is clapping and singing as Adele claims her own strength, her invincibility.

Everyone is on their feet now. Ros, clinging to Simone's arm, sees Adele look at her, and give her a long and meaningful nod, and a smile, before she looks out across the room, pumping her fist in the air again.

'Oh yes Adele,' Ros murmurs, 'you really are a very special woman.'

*

A couple of hours later they catch a taxi home; they agree they can drive Ros's car in to pick up the hire car tomorrow. Back at the house, Adele flops down on the bed and stares up at the ceiling, reliving the event in the pharmacy but also the book club discussion and how she had felt utterly compelled to get up on that small stage and belt out that particular song.

'I always liked it but it never really meant much to me until now,' she'd said to Ros later.

'It always works for me,' Ros said. 'Some people reckon it's a bit daggy these days, but it certainly hit the spot tonight.'

Clarity, Adele thinks, had arrived so simply. Her mind drifts to her daily experience of feeling inferior, powerless, inadequate and sick with anxiety. She wonders how she can have tolerated it for so long. If she had stuck with Astrid, she wonders, who would she be by now? Like Reta, she has allowed all the subtle, and not so subtle, messages and assumptions about women – their reality, their hopes and dreams, their level of competence, and their value – to define her life, her moods, her aspirations. How could she not see all that? How has she never before understood that she can live as the woman she really is?

Chapter Eighteen

*J*udy is a little hungover this morning and when she wanders downstairs at nine-thirty there are no other signs of life and the house seems unusually cold. She pulls her dressing gown tighter around her and from the far side of the lounge room she sees that the front door is wide open. Someone has obviously gone for a walk – Simone probably, she thinks, although last night she'd announced she needed a sleep-in and wouldn't be up for yoga.

'Fried food and gin. Heavenly while you're doing it but there's always a hellish price to pay,' she'd said.

'Shame about yoga, but we could always do it later,' Ros said. 'I'm just beginning to like it!'

But Judy reckons that even after sleeping in Simone would still be the first one up, and that she probably didn't fully close the door behind her. There's a stiff breeze outside; Judy closes the door and goes back through to the kitchen. *Coffee*, she thinks. Tea's not going to do it for her this morning. She fills the kettle and decides to make a big pot – someone else is bound to turn up soon. She looks around the kitchen thinking it feels like home despite the fact they've only been here a few weeks. She wonders what it might be like if they shared a house all the time. No, that would probably be a disaster, but she knows she's not ready for them to go their different ways, and won't be for a while.

Minutes later Adele wanders in, yawning. 'Morning,' she says. 'Oh coffee, you are a saint, Judy, or are you planning to drink all that yourself?'

'I think I probably could,' Judy says, 'but I made it with all of us in mind. How are you feeling this morning?'

Adele slides into a chair at the table, raises one arm in the air and executes a rather floppy punching motion. 'I am powerful,' she says weakly.

'Not very convincing,' Ros says, appearing in the doorway. 'Pretty pathetic in fact, but at least the sentiment is there. We didn't drink that much, did we?'

'We all drank more than we usually do,' Judy says, getting out the mugs. 'I certainly did. And it was a pretty full-on day.'

'Tell me about it,' Ros says.

'I was wondering, Adele, did you hear from Marian about us staying on a bit longer?' Judy asks.

'I did,' Adele says, 'and it's fine.'

'Well it looks like Simone was first up after all,' Ros says. 'Clooney's not around so I suppose she's taken him for a walk.'

Judy leans on the counter waiting until the coffee has brewed long enough, and the other two sit quietly at the table, Adele staring into the middle distance, Ros putting her hands on and off the table, which they all now know she does to check if she can control them. The smell of the coffee wafts through the room as Judy pours it. Adele gets up and takes the milk from the fridge.

'You didn't tell us about your book yesterday, Ros,' Judy says. 'The whole process fell apart, but it was worth it, wasn't it?'

'It really was,' Ros says. 'We'll do it this morning when we're . . . well, when we're better than we are now.'

'Oh my god! Fresh coffee!' Simone says, standing in the kitchen doorway. 'Is there enough for . . . ?'

'There's enough for everyone,' Judy says.

Simone joins them at the table and puts her head in her hands. 'I will never drink gin again, in my whole life, ever.'

'Ha!' Ros says. 'Until the next time. Did you have a good walk?'

Simone looks up, laughs. 'I've only walked from the bedroom to the kitchen, does that count as a good walk?'

Ros stares at her. 'You're wearing a tracksuit.'

'Yes, the house feels unusually chilly this morning.'

'But if you're here, where's Clooney? Has anyone seen him this morning?' Ros asks.

They shake their heads.

'Well who opened the door for him then?' Judy asks. 'It was wide open when I came down.'

They stare at each other.

'Maybe we didn't shut it properly when we came in last night, and that's why it's so cold this morning?' Ros says, and she struggles to her feet. 'And no one's seen him at all?'

'Stay there,' Adele says, getting to her feet and putting a hand on Ros's arm. 'I'll go and look for him. Maybe he's gone downstairs to yoga on his own, you know how he loves squeezing in between us when we're all lined up together.'

Judy finishes pouring the coffee, and sits down at the table. 'He's probably hiding to punish us for leaving him alone for so long yesterday,' she says.

Ros taps her fingers on the table, keeps glancing over her shoulder. 'Where can he have got to?'

Judy and Simone, feeling her tension, wait with her.

Adele appears in the doorway. She has abandoned her dressing gown and is zipping up the jacket of her tracksuit. 'He's not in the house,' she says. 'I've checked everywhere. Was he in your room last night, Ros?'

Ros gets up. 'Yes, he was fast asleep at about four when I got up to go to the loo. But I always leave my door ajar so he can go with Simone in the mornings. Oh my god, he must have wandered off on his own.'

'Okay, I'm going out to look for him,' Adele says.

'Me too,' Simone says.

Ros has gone white. 'I'll come with you,' she says.

'No way,' Adele says, turning back to her. 'Stay here with Judy. He might wander in from somewhere.'

Ros opens her mouth to protest.

'No, Ros,' Adele says firmly. 'Simone and I will go. We'll be quicker on our own.'

Simone gets to her feet. 'I'll have a look in the garden,' she says. 'Best if you stay here, Ros.' She slips out through the back door.

But Ros is determined. She stands up far too quickly and stumbles, and Judy is only just able to stop her from falling. 'Ros,' she says. 'Ros, please just stay here with me.'

Ros is looking wildly around her, her hands shaking furiously, but Judy hangs on to her arm.

'Listen, Ros,' Adele says, 'if you rush around looking for him you could fall, then we'll have to concentrate on you and give up on looking for Clooney. So please stay here.'

'I won't fall over,' Ros says irritably, 'I'm not stupid, and I'm coming with you.'

Judy can see that it is not just Ros's hands that are shaking now; her legs are shaking too. But the rest of her feels rigid with determination, and so she keeps her arm locked firmly in Ros's, resisting her efforts to break away.

'Let them look around the garden,' Judy urges, 'it won't take a minute.'

Ros gives a derisive snort. 'Well I can at least go to the front door and call for him,' she says.

Judy refuses to release her arm and goes with her. They stand by the door for several minutes, with Ros calling desperately for Clooney.

Simone is back first, leaves and twigs in her hair from peering into Clooney's favourite bushes. Then Adele appears from the other side of the house.

'He's not in the garden,' Simone says. She looks up at Adele. 'I think we should go to the waterfall, he loves that walk. If he's not there we might try some of the other paths in Ros's car.'

'Right, good thinking,' Adele says. 'Please stay here with Judy, Ros.'

'I'm not a bloody child,' Ros shouts at her. 'And he's *my* dog.'

'I know you're not a child, but you're behaving like one,' Adele says. 'And I know how much you love him, but please, trust us and don't make it more difficult.' She turns away and seconds later she is racing across to where Simone is heading towards the gate at the bottom of the garden.

'Bloody cheek,' Ros says. 'How dare she.' She wrenches her arm free and heads off after Adele.

'Ros, Ros, stop, please stop!' Judy says, grabbing her again, this time by the back of her dressing gown. But Ros is like a wild animal, waving her arms, her face contorted in fear and anger, tears pouring down her cheeks. 'Ros, for heaven's sake,' Judy shouts, 'stop this. You're just making it worse.'

Judy is surprised by how strong Ros is, and she's angry with her now. She is both shorter and slighter than Ros, but she hangs on, pulling Ros backwards and then pushing her roughly off balance so that she collapses onto the sofa. Judy sits down on top of her and slaps her hard across the face.

*

Simone and Adele jog down the path calling Clooney as they go.

'Ros is having a hissy fit,' Adele says as they slow down on a slippery stretch. 'I don't fancy Judy's chances of holding her back. She's so devoted to Clooney, lord knows what she'll do if we can't find him.'

'We'll find him,' Simone says firmly. 'We have to. I think he could've got through a gap in the fence. Look!' She points to a place where the wire fence has come away from its moorings. 'I bet he got out through there.' She thinks of Ros, so fearful and debilitated by her own condition, and how bereft she will be if something has happened to Clooney. 'Come on,' she says to Adele, dragging open the gate. 'Don't try to run here, the path is too dodgy.' They walk together, briskly and in silence, past the bend and along the narrow final stretch.

Clooney is sitting, or rather lying comfortably on his stomach, head and shoulders up, his large pink tongue hanging out of his mouth, panting happily, enjoying the view of the water cascading over the rocks.

'Clooney,' Simone calls, relief flooding through her. 'Clooney, come on, come here.'

Clooney looks at them, thumps his tail, leaps up and pounds back towards them, perilously close to the edge of the path. Simone turns to Adele.

'Thank god,' she says. 'I was worried he might have gone over the edge.'

'Me too,' Adele says. 'It was the first thing I thought of when you said we should come this way.'

They both bend down to greet him, and Simone pulls some treats out of her pocket.

'Sneaky!' Adele laughs. 'No wonder you top the Clooney popularity poll. I think you are now second only to Ros in his affections.'

Simone smiles. 'I'm not giving him a lot like I was before,' she says, stroking Clooney's head. 'Just a few, very occasionally. Promise you won't report me to Mother Superior?'

Clooney is covered in mud, and dead leaves are tangled in his long furry ears and tail. Simone thinks he's looking rather pleased with himself.

'You're very naughty,' Simone says. 'But we're awfully pleased to see you.' She straightens up. 'Come on, trouble, let's go.'

They walk back in silence, Clooney trotting alongside them, and stop just inside the gate to drag some fallen branches across the hole in the fence.

'I'll ring Gwenda when we get back,' Adele says, 'see if she can get Ray to come up and fix that.'

Simone nods, thinking of Ros, the desperation in her face, the sudden panic and aggression. *Ros really is struggling,* she thinks. *Poor Ros, she tries so hard to be tough and pretend that she's coping, but she's right on the edge.* Perhaps letting off steam might be a good thing for her, but Simone fails to convince herself because the desperation on Ros's face had been utterly heartbreaking.

*

A couple of hours later, Ros lies on her bed exhausted. Clooney, looking a great deal more respectable since Adele and Simone bathed him in the laundry trough, and Simone finished him off with a blow dry, has now crashed out on his bed. Ros feels as though every spark of spirit and energy has been wrung from her. The joy and relief of getting Clooney back was almost as overwhelming as her fear of what might have happened to him. And while she feels calm now, and thankful, she also feels as though something within her has been broken and that it might take a long time to put it back together again.

It's not just about Clooney of course, she knows that, and in fact she is grateful to him for being the trigger to crack open the great mess of emotions that has been building within her. She knows she behaved very badly to people who cared for her, and the return of the wanderer had brought tears and laughter, and many apologies, but she is ashamed now, embarrassed by her own behaviour, shocked in fact that she had been so rude and aggressive. And there, at the root of it all, is her health, her condition, the Parkinson's that, even after admitting it to the others, she has still failed to own, as Simone had urged. She just keeps running away.

But I can see now that I can't do that anymore, she says to James, *it's part of who I am or who I've become. Whatever will I do when I am back home alone, with no plans and no sense of how this might all move on?* She sighs, shifts her position, peers over the side of the bed and reaches down to stroke Clooney, then lies down again. *I have to do better from now on.*

A knock on the door disturbs her. 'Come in,' she says, sitting up abruptly, and reaches for her watch. Two o'clock! Having all missed out on breakfast they'd agreed to a late lunch at two. And then she would hand over her books for Sunday's discussion.

Adele pops her head around the door. 'Ready for lunch, Ros?'

Clooney stretches and gets to his feet, wagging his tail at Adele, and she bends down to stroke him, and looks up at Ros. 'He looks pretty gorgeous with Simone's blow dry, doesn't he?'

'He really does,' Ros says, 'though he runs a mile if I put the hair dryer anywhere near him at home. Simone must have worked some magic on him.' She gets to her feet. 'Thanks for coming to get me, I must have dozed off. Adele, I am so sorry about this morning.'

Adele straightens up. 'You've done all the apologies. It was a horrible thing to happen, we were all on edge and I was rather bossy.'

'You were wonderful.' To her surprise Ros feels her eyes filling with tears again. She blinks them back fiercely. 'Not just this morning, yesterday too. It was remarkable to watch you in the pharmacy, and then later, the karaoke . . .'

Adele laughs. 'What a strange day it was. All I know is that it was right, the time was right, and I suppose I was ready to be different. And you, Ros, have been a big part of that. Anyway, come on down for lunch. You can tell us about the book.'

They sit around the kitchen table eating Judy's vegetable soup with crusty bread that Simone had fetched from the bakery.

'Geoff called,' Simone says. 'Doug is arriving tomorrow and he's invited me there for dinner. Thank goodness it's not tonight or I'd be falling asleep halfway through.'

Ros watches her, trying to imagine how it must feel to be reunited with these people who have been such an important part of her life but from whom she was separated for so long. 'That's going to be a wonderful evening,' Ros says. 'Tears, laughter, and, I imagine, lots of photographs.'

Simone smiles. 'Indeed. And I think there'll be other things as well, but I'm not sure what. Geoff is being very cagey, keeps saying it's better to talk things through when the three of us are together. Anyway, we'll see what tomorrow brings.'

'Book time,' Judy says. 'What have you got for us, Ros?'

Ros hauls up a canvas bag that she had put by her chair, takes out the books and puts them on the table.

'My book is *An Equal Music*, by Vikram Seth,' she says, handing copies around.

'Brilliant!' Adele says. 'I've been meaning to read this for ages.'

'Didn't he write *A Suitable Boy*?' Judy asks. 'I loved that book. But it took me months to read it, it's very long and detailed.'

'That's been compared to *War and Peace*,' Ros says. 'But this one is very different. Much less demanding, and it's set in London. Anyone read it?'

They shake their heads.

'Well this is a love story on several levels, but also a story about music and musicians. I was reading it for the first time in London, but James died before I finished it. For a long time I didn't want to open it again. But some years later I did; I read it all the way through, and loved it, and have read it again twice since then, the last time straight after I got Adele's invitation. It felt right to bring it with me because it's very special to me for all sorts of reasons.'

'It must bring back memories of that time,' Simone says. 'Will that be hard for you, Ros?'

Ros opens her mouth to speak, stops, thinks for a moment, tilts her head to one side. 'I didn't have that in mind when I chose it,' she says, 'but now I think that perhaps it will, and the way I went off the rails this morning makes me feel as though talking about it is something I really need to do.'

Chapter Nineteen

*I*t's Geoff who arrives at six to collect Simone.

'Doug is making Thai chicken curry,' he says as they pull away from the house. 'It's his speciality so I hope you like it, or can pretend to.'

'I love it,' she says.

'I remember your mum's minestrone. I've not tasted anything like it since those days.'

'I'll make it for you,' Simone says, 'from Mama's recipe. It's pretty good but never seems quite as good as hers.'

He drives slowly down the rough driveway and out onto the road. 'Isn't this the most extraordinary thing?' he says. 'You, me and Doug, about to have dinner together after all this time?'

She turns to look at him. 'I'd almost given up,' she says, 'so yes, it feels extraordinary and wonderful.'

They talk about some of the people who had come to the citrus farm. Adults who lived nearby, their own friends from the local school, and later friends of Doug and Geoff whom they had met at boarding school and who came to stay there. There were casual workers too, local people and backpackers, and as they talk, 'Simone feels the past running live through her veins.

'I've been so cut off from it all,' she says as they draw up outside Geoff's house. 'The little wheels of memory are churning up all sorts of stuff now. It's so easy to lose chunks and splinters of the past when you've no one to talk to about it.'

'Good, we can loosen them up some more tonight then,' Geoff says, 'fill in some gaps. I have some excellent champagne and a couple of bottles of really good red to go with the curry. And I have a big box of old photographs.'

Simone groans. 'I drank far too much on Sunday evening and I'm still suffering for it. But photographs, really? How wonderful! I have nothing, only some baby snaps and pictures of me as a toddler before we came to Australia. So I can't wait to see those.'

'Simone! Beautiful as ever,' Doug says a few minutes later, hugging her and then holding her at arm's length, his hands on her shoulders. 'You must have lived a very pure life to have aged so little.'

'You'd probably be surprised *how* pure,' Simone says. 'You're looking pretty good yourself. In fact you both look terrific and I can't imagine that either of you have lived a very pure life.'

'Mine's been pretty conventional really,' Geoff says, opening the champagne. He fills the glasses. 'To us,' he says, 'childhood friends back together again after all these years.'

'To us!' Simone and Doug chorus, and Simone feels the emotion rise in her throat. 'So much to catch up on,' she says, 'this is where I get to find out all your secrets.' She sees them look at each other and look away again. 'You must have some secrets presumably?'

'A few. And so, I imagine, have you,' Geoff says.

'Oh, there were always secrets at home,' Simone says. 'But

I never found out what they were. I just know they must have been pretty substantial because there was always tension, as far back as I can remember, and more so as time went on.'

There is a charged sliver of silence between Doug and Geoff.

'What?' she asks, glancing between them. 'Do you know something?'

'Let's drink our champagne and eat first,' Doug says after a pause. 'You've only been here a few minutes; it's too soon to start raking over our family histories. You have to tell us about Adam, I have to tell you about Steve, and Geoff has to tell you about Eva and his kids. Before we get into the heavy stuff.'

'Oh I see, you're just stirring me,' Simone says, laughing, 'ganging up on me like the old days. Dropping in a word or two, pretending to know stuff to get me bouncing up and down in a frenzy begging you to tell me this incredible secret, which in the end actually turns out to be nothing at all!'

She sees them exchange another glance. 'Something like that,' Geoff says. 'Suffice to say that we know a lot more now than we did back then. Anyway, cheers! Here's to the past and most of all the future.'

They clink their glasses and Simone can see that they too are feeling the same surge of emotion as she is.

'Do you remember when we pricked our thumbs and mixed our blood for lifelong friendship?' Doug asks.

They both nod.

'I do,' Simone says. 'I've thought of it often. And here we are together in our sixties.'

'Almost our seventies, darling,' Doug says. 'Next year's the big seven-oh for Doug and me.'

It's later, after the meal has been cleared away, that Geoff tips the box of photographs onto the table, and they spread them out, picking them up at random, laughing at the images of themselves and each other. Simone sighs with pleasure at the fading black-and-white pictures of long forgotten moments captured on Claire's old Brownie. She remembers Claire lining them up for a photograph, trying to capture them running and jumping, and horse riding on one occasion.

'The horses! I'd forgotten that day,' Simone says. 'Where did we go to ride those horses?' And they argue about when it was and where the horses were.

As they reach their teens the images are clearer: Doug winning a race, Geoff in a tree picking oranges, herself looking shy and self-conscious in a frilly dress blowing out candles on a birthday cake. Simone feels she is bursting with memories as they talk and laugh together. And she is reminded of the expectations she had then, the ambitions, the dreams she dreamed so long ago. Dreams in which all of them were always together.

She picks up a colour photo of a woman sitting on a rough stone wall, a little girl beside her. 'Claire!' she says. 'And Paula?'

Doug nods. 'Cornwall. Paula looks so much like you did the day you arrived at our place. Although she's got more of Carlo in her than you have.'

Simone studies the pictures. 'Does she? I can't tell because I have no photographs from my childhood to compare her with; none at all. I know there *were* some, and I did ask several times over the years, but Papa always said they were difficult to get at, up in the roof, and he'd find them for my next visit. But he never did. I kept thinking that when my parents were both gone I would find a treasure trove of memories. Photographs, old toys, my exercise books and reports from school, maybe even albums with pictures of my grandparents I barely remember from Italy. But when Adam and Stacey and

I went to sort out the house there was nothing. Not a shred of evidence that we had a past in that place at all. It was deliberate, of course. Sometime after Mama died Papa must have gone through and destroyed everything. Not just the family memorabilia but other things, books, pictures, ornaments. I noticed it about eighteen months before he died. I realised that each time I went back things were missing, and I assumed he was packing them in boxes to save me the trouble when he'd gone. Ha! Well I was totally wrong about that.'

They are silent now, staring at the mass of photographs in front of them, and Simone knows that the sadness, which is the underside of her joy at meeting them again, has infected them too.

'What was he doing, d'you think?' Doug asks. 'Cleaning the slate before he died?'

She shrugs. 'Maybe. If so he made a pretty thorough job of it. It was devastating to go back there and feel as though my childhood had just been brushed out of history. It stirred up all sorts of stuff about the time I got home from Paris and you'd all gone, and no one would talk to me about it. You've had each other, and Claire; it must be so wonderful to keep refreshing memories, talking, looking at photographs. My parents never talked about the past. I'd ask them about something and every time I'd hit a wall. In the end I gave up even mentioning it. But it left me confused about things that had actually happened or what I might just have imagined.'

'I . . . we . . . we'd no idea, Simone,' Geoff says, taking her hand. 'I can only imagine how hard that must be and how sad it must make you.'

She nods, picks up the photograph of Claire and Paula again. 'Claire looks so happy here. Happier than I ever remember her. Were you on holiday?'

Doug nods. 'It was a wonderful time, with Mum and our grandparents, and Paula, some years after we'd left Australia.'

'And yet you both ended up coming back.'

'I came back about twelve years later,' Geoff says. 'I'd met Eva in Europe and we got married, but all her family was here, and we wanted to have kids and to have them grow up in Australia.'

'And I came back a lot later,' Doug says. 'Initially just for a holiday with Geoff and Eva, but I fell in love with my nephew and nieces, so I stayed on longer than I'd planned. Then I met Steve, in an underground gay bar in Sydney, and fell in love with him. And that was that.'

'And Claire was okay with that . . . with losing you both to Australia?'

'Well it wasn't ideal, but she was very close to her parents, and her sister and her family who lived nearby. She had missed so much time with them when she married Dad. She was much happier there, and she had Paula, who, by the way, still lives with her.'

Simone looks again at the photograph. 'I'm so glad things worked out for her,' she says. 'Did she never marry again?'

Doug shakes his head. 'No. She had quite a long friendship with a lovely man who *wanted* to marry her. But she wouldn't consider it. You know, Simone, she would be thrilled to see you again. She really loves you, but she always says, "Simone will not want to meet me."'

'But why, why wouldn't I?'

'Because of Carlo, of course.'

She shrugs. 'So they had an affair, it's not –'

'No,' Geoff says, 'no, Simone, they did *not* have an affair.' He glances up at Doug, and Simone sees Doug nod in response. 'It was not an affair, it was not a relationship. It was rape and it was part of a long reign of terror and abuse by Carlo, in an effort to get her to do what he wanted and give him control of the Marshall property.'

*

Adele is making breakfast for everyone. During their evening at the pub they had decided to have a group breakfast today. Adele is wracking her brains to remember why, but she does remember that she'd drawn the short straw. She was first up this morning and was in the games room doing stretches when Judy and Ros rolled up, but there was no sign of Simone.

'She came home really late,' Ros had said. 'She probably needs to sleep. I vote we carry on and do what we can without her.'

Since then Adele has heard Simone go out with Clooney, but she hasn't seen her yet. *Second hangover in three days?* she wonders. That could be a lifetime record for Simone.

'Come along,' she calls up the stairs. 'Breakfast's ready and scrambled eggs wait for no woman.'

Simone comes into the kitchen looking exhausted and as though she has more serious things than breakfast on her mind.

'Good walk?' Adele asks.

'Yep,' Simone replies, picking up Clooney's water bowl. She crosses to the sink, refills it and sets it back in place for him.

'Would you like everything?' Adele asks, indicating the eggs, bacon and tomatoes in the two frying pans.

'Just eggs and toast please.'

Adele glances up at her, opens her mouth to ask about last night's dinner, but something makes her decide against it. Maybe Simone's evening with her friends hadn't worked out well, perhaps it wasn't all champagne, laughter and happy memories, and as she leans over to put a plate in front of her Adele can see that Simone's eyes are red, and she looks not just exhausted, but totally wrecked.

'Are you all right, Simone?' she asks.

'I'm fine, thank you,' Simone says. 'Breakfast looks delicious.'

Adele watches her take a deep breath, straighten her shoulders, and reach for some toast.

'Wow,' says Judy, strolling into the kitchen. 'This looks and smells wonderful, Adele. Nice evening, Simone? No sign of Ros yet?'

'Yes, I'm here,' Ros says, hurrying in. 'Can I help you, Adele?'

'You could rescue the toast from the toaster and add it to the other toast on the table, please,' Adele says.

'Sure thing,' Ros says, peering past her to the frying pans. 'Yum. Delicious, can I have some of everything, please?'

Ros carries the four slices of toast to the table on a plate, tips them into the basket and pops the red-and-white checked cloth back in place.

'Simone, how are you this morning?' she asks, slipping into the seat opposite her. 'Did you have a wonderful time? I heard you come home in the wee small hours – I'm surprised you didn't turn into a pumpkin.'

'Yes, it was quite late,' Simone says, tight-lipped.

Adele senses that they are all poised now, waiting for Simone to tell them about her dinner with Geoff and Doug, but she just reaches for the coffee pot, pours some into the cups and pushes them towards the others. Then she leans back in her chair, staring down at the table. Adele looks at Ros and raises her eyebrows. Ros shrugs, pulls a face and starts tucking into her breakfast.

Judy helps herself to toast. 'You're very quiet, Simone,' she says. 'We're all agog waiting to hear about your dinner, and maybe see some photographs. Did Geoff give you some? I think you mentioned that he said he was getting copies for you.'

Adele and Ros exchange glances again.

'Simone?' Ros says, leaning forward. 'Judy's asked you a question.'

Simone looks up, bewildered. 'Oh sorry,' she says, 'I was miles away.'

'Obviously,' Judy says. 'I was asking about photos, if you have any to show us.' She hesitates. 'Actually, you don't look too well. Would you like me to make you a bloody mary? It's very good for a hangover, the tomato juice soaks up the alcohol molecules. There's some tomato juice in the fridge.'

Simone puts down her knife and fork. 'No thanks, I don't have a hangover,' she says. 'At least not one that can be sorted by a bloody mary.'

'So what sort of hangover *do* you have?' Ros begins gently.

Simone sighs, staring at her plate, pushing the food around with her fork in a desultory way. 'I'm not sure I can describe it,' she says. 'A hangover from the past, I suppose. And the trouble with the past is that there is nothing you can do about it. My past has felt like a great trunk filled with secrets to which I'd never have the key. I was stuck with that and finally came to terms with it, did what we're always being encouraged to do – *moved on.*' She stops, still not looking up.

Adele glances at the others, but like her, they are frozen in awkward silence. 'That's good, isn't it?' she asks cautiously. 'The moving on, leaving things behind you and concentrating on the present and the future?'

Simone turns towards her. 'It does sound good, doesn't it?' she says. 'But as I'm sure *you* know, Adele, you can move on just as you and I have done, but the past is always there in the people we turn out to be. The past as ball and chain, sometimes the size of a marble or an egg, but at other times a cannonball that drags you down.'

She stops again, looking at Adele. 'When I look at you, Adele, I see a woman who has dragged the cannonball all her life, and managed to succeed in spite of it. And then, on Sunday, I saw the cannonball explode, saw you kick your way through the debris and emerge, still as Adele of course, but a . . . well, a new edition, I suppose. Someone even stronger, and brave enough to grasp the change. The marble will always be there but you'll be able to live with it.' She looks away, reaches for her coffee and sips it.

Adele is silent, trying to take in what Simone said, because it feels right. The ball and chain of the past has always held her back. And it does feel different now. *You can't change the past*, she thinks, *but you can change how you view it and how you respond to it, and that means you can also choose to just let it go.*

'And you, Simone?' Ros asks eventually. 'I understand what you're saying and I can see how Adele is a perfect example. But you? You were craving the past, you wanted to fill in the gaps and you reached out to do that. Last night you wanted to step back into it, to honour it. So do you want to tell us what happened?'

Simone nods. 'I do, but it's so hard to start. And while I was walking this morning, I realised that although we're really different we all have the same problem.'

Ah! Adele thinks, *I know what she's doing. This is too hard for her so, being Simone, she can't just blurt it out; she has to find a bigger context for it.* She realises that Simone is trying in some way to theorise whatever it is that has traumatised her, to move it a little further away. But will it work? she wonders, because Simone looks so fragile, so broken.

Judy cocks her head. 'What problem's that?' she asks.

'We're nice. We're all nice women. We are *too* nice. We've spent our lives doing what's expected of us. None of us has really dropped out, committed crimes, been a drain on the community, churned other people's lives upside down or done things to them from which they never recover. We've all done what our parents, the church, or some other authority told us we should do and be. And frankly I don't think that's been good for any of us. You can spend your life doing the right thing, being considerate, stitching up your opinions and feelings in order to support and protect and please other people. We're like Reta in the book. We're just too nice!'

'Whoa,' Ros says, rocking back in her chair, 'that's an awfully big statement, Simone. I don't think anyone would, for example, describe *me* as too nice, or even particularly considerate. Nor as trying to protect or please other people. As you saw a few days ago, even *grumpy old bat* is a bit of a whitewash.'

Adele listens, realising that if this conversation had taken place a couple of weeks ago she would have been frozen with anxiety about what the outcome might be. Now she looks confidently across at Ros.

'But that's *your* view of yourself, Ros,' she says. 'It's who you tell us you are, and then you act to prove it. I think it's who you decided to be, especially after James died, perhaps as a way to manage your loss, make it bearable. Maybe you've always had a bit of it in you, and so it became a persona that would hide your vulnerability. And now that I can see that, I realise it's actually not particularly convincing.'

She looks sideways at Simone and sees that she is nodding; meanwhile Ros is now the one with the stunned mullet expression. And alongside Ros, Judy takes a gulp of her coffee and puts her cup back down on the table.

'I'd say that's just about right, Ros,' Judy says, turning to her. 'I came here not really knowing what to expect from you; you're so smart, so outspoken, sometimes so brutal. And then the first time I reacted you backed off – not completely, just enough to make yourself feel okay about it, I suppose. Since then I've thought that you've created this wall of defence, but the foundations are built on very fine sand.'

Adele has a terrible feeling that any minute now she might burst into laughter and thump Judy on the back. The expression on Ros's face is extraordinary; it seems to be a battle between the fierce urge to be haughty, indifferent or angry, or letting go and working out what's been said. She sees Ros draw herself up, look around at the three of them, search for a middle road.

'Well that's all very interesting,' she says, 'but I thought we were talking about Simone, and about the past. I suggest we put my shortcomings on hold and get back to that. What was it you were about to say, Simone? Something about us being too nice?'

'Yes, too nice,' Simone says. 'I mean, there is a difference between being an essentially good person who knows when to draw the line and put themselves first, and a person who lumbers on doing stuff because they know it's expected of them, and resenting it. That's what we do, it's the way most girls grow up, and we go on doing it, so what we really want and who we want to be gets pushed aside. I did that all my life with my parents. The one occasion when I broke out of that mould created a huge breach in my relationship with both of them and we never recovered from it. But I've still spent the rest of my life trying to be what they wanted me to be: responsible, law-abiding, hardworking, supportive of others, polite . . . And for a lot of that time I was also trying to be a good Catholic. Even when I was furiously angry and upset with my father I was still trying desperately to be the person he'd be proud of.'

Adele nods. Only now is she starting to see the parallels between herself and Simone and the different ways they have managed to live with those parental expectations. She glances across at Ros, who is looking a little more settled now.

'I see what you're saying, Simone,' Ros says. 'It's a really good point and I agree with you. But you're generalising, and I want to understand what has changed for you. Last night you went out to celebrate and you've come home very obviously upset and burdened.'

Simone nods. 'Yes. I'm trying to find a way to talk about it,' she says. 'There was so much that I didn't know . . .' She hesitates now, dropping her eyes to the table again.

Adele can see and feel her pain, her struggle to actually say the words that will describe whatever it is she needs to tell them.

'But what is it, Simone?' Adele asks gently. 'What did you learn last night that has left you so . . . so devastated?'

They wait in silence and then Adele sees Simone draw in her breath, sit up a little straighter.

'Last night,' she says, 'in the company of those dear friends, the trunk that contained the past got blown wide open. I found out that my father was not the hardworking, law-abiding, respectful man, the good Catholic father, I always believed him to be. He was a rapist, a bully and a thief who lied to me about a multitude of things and went to the grave doing so. He bullied Claire Marshall over a long period of time and finally raped her. And my mother colluded in that by doing nothing, presumably because she was also terrified of the man he had

turned out to be. He intimidated Claire, stole from and manipu-
lated her, colluding with a crooked local lawyer in an attempt
to rob her of everything she owned, *everything* . . . including
her home. And so now I have to question everything I thought
I knew about my parents, our past together, everything I took
for granted. And perhaps worst of all, my own complete failure
to confront my father ever again after the night he threw that
bottle at me. Never again through all those years did I demand
an explanation that might have helped me to support my
mother and perhaps to find the Marshalls again.'

Chapter Twenty

Ros, alone in the house on Saturday afternoon, is trying to read the paper but finding it hard to concentrate. Simone has driven over to see Doug and Geoff, and Judy and Adele have gone shopping in town and will probably stop for coffee. She'd thought reading the paper might distract her from thinking about some of the things that have happened this week, specifically those concerning her own behaviour. It seems that everyone has forgiven her for behaving so badly when Clooney went missing, but she still hasn't forgiven herself. And on top of that there was the persona thing that Adele had suggested she'd developed to enable her to cope without James, to mask her vulnerability. Clooney looks up at her adoringly, thumps his tail on the floor and shifts his paws around, indicating that he thinks it's time for a walk. Simone had taken him for a long walk before she went out but Clooney is an opportunist, something that's clearly working for him rather better here than it does at home. Ros gives in and walks with him to the back door.

Clooney bounds out ahead of her into the luscious green

of the garden where the sun and the warmth of the breeze combine to make it feel almost like spring. Ros walks cautiously to the bench, sits, and thinks of Simone struggling to come to terms with the awful reality of her father's treatment of Claire Marshall.

There seems to have been some relief for Simone in the telling, but Ros aches with sympathy for her.

The morning after her dinner with Greg and Doug, once she'd told them everything over breakfast, Simone had sat for ages on the garden seat where Ros is sitting now. She needed to be alone, she'd told them, but all three of them kept watch on her in their different ways. Adele found an urgent bit of trimming and pruning that needed doing not far from where Simone was sitting, and Ros and Judy took their books and mugs of tea out to the back verandah from where they too could easily see her. Later Simone had disappeared to her room, emerging only in the early evening to eat a toasted sandwich made for her by Adele. She looked pale and drawn, and soon went back upstairs saying she needed to sleep again.

It was almost midnight when she knocked on Ros's door just as she was falling asleep.

'May I come in?' Simone asked. And Ros had sat up and shifted across the bed to make room for her.

'Do you need to talk?' Ros asked as Simone, her eyes filled with tears, climbed in next to her.

Simone shook her head. 'I just don't want to be alone,' she said. 'I need to be with someone I trust, and I trust the others too, but somehow . . .' She shrugged as the tears rolled down her face. 'Somehow you got the short straw.'

Ros had held her for a long time until the sobbing slowly receded, and she could see the utter exhaustion in Simone's face.

'I should leave you in peace,' Simone said, eventually moving to sit up.

But Ros stopped her. 'Stay here, Simone,' she said. 'There's plenty of room.'

And Simone had slid down under the doona, closing her eyes, obviously unable to keep them open any longer. Ros, who had not shared a bed with anyone since James died, slipped down beside her and lay stroking Simone's hair until she was sure she was asleep. Several times in the night she woke and listened to her breathing and at seven, when the light sneaked in between the curtains, she slipped out of bed and stood watching her for a moment before going downstairs to let Clooney out and make some tea. Then she climbed precariously back up the stairs, a mug in each unreliable hand.

Simone stirred, stretched and dragged herself into a sitting position as Ros put a mug down beside her and walked around to her own side of the bed.

'I will always remember this, Ros,' Simone said, reaching out for her hand.

'Me too,' Ros said.

Ros thinks now about what Adele had said to her; about her having a protective grumpy persona. *What do you think about it?* she asks James now. *Everyone seems to think it's right, everyone except me. Do you not have one single word to say on the matter? I'm sure you'd have plenty to say if you were here. But I suppose sitting up there at a safe distance you're watching what I do with it. I can almost see that crooked grin of yours just before you say, 'This one's all down to you, sweetheart.'* Ros wonders if Adele is right, if they are all right. What would Leah say? she wonders – after all, she knew Ros when James was still alive. The other person she could ask, of course, would be Donald from the quartet. But then he'd probably tell her anything he thought she wanted to hear.

Clooney, who has been rummaging around among the trees, comes to join her and surprisingly jumps up onto the seat beside her. 'What do you think?' she asks him.

But really she knows the answer, because when she remembers the time after James's death, during that long and lonely flight back to Australia, she'd wondered how she would cope with other people's grief, as well as her own. James was a man with a lot of friends, who went back a long way, colleagues as well as former students, people from his own schooldays. Her mother once told her that when her own mother died she couldn't cope with people coming too close to her in her grief. 'It made me prickly,' she'd said. 'You probably don't remember, but I was very prickly for a long time.' But Ros, who had been in her thirties at the time of her grandmother's death, did remember, and prickly was just the right word. *Is that what I've done?* she wonders now. *Because if it is, it's well past time I stopped. But how am I supposed to cope with all this grief?*

*

'Now that I am fully restored to health,' Judy had said to Adele earlier, 'I think I should take my turn doing the shopping.'

'Oh, I thought I was the chief shopper,' Adele said. 'Are you trying to muscle in?'

'I am,' Judy says.

'It's only a few days since you pinned Ros down on the couch and sat on her. I think that's equivalent to several shopping trips.'

'Well maybe, but you know what I mean. And it's also weeks since I drove a car – I may have forgotten how to do it. Anyway,' she lowered her voice, 'it's all a bit of subterfuge because I was going to ask you to come with me. I just want to chat about the business stuff away from here.'

Adele smiled. 'Lovely,' she said. 'Let's do that. I'll be ready in ten minutes. Can we go for coffee first? I haven't had anything to eat this morning and I feel a croissant moment coming on.'

'It feels really weird,' Judy said later, cautiously driving the hire car onto the side street leading to the main road into town. 'It's amazing how quickly you get out of the habit.'

Now, as they walk out of the car park, she is feeling strong and purposeful. It's not simply that she's getting her health back; indeed, she knows that physically she's still got a way to go. What's changed is all in her head. Since the news of Maddie's death and the moment when she and Ros had talked about conserving emotional energy as a way of conserving themselves, she has felt some of that energy coming back to her. This morning she felt that it was like rising up from under the sea to find herself floating easily on the surface, no longer struggling to survive.

She parks the car and they choose their café. It's a cool but brilliantly sunny day and warm enough, they agree, to sit at a table on the pavement.

'I've made up my mind,' Judy says when the waiter has taken their order. 'And this is the day we agreed to talk it through.'

'So it is,' Adele says. 'I didn't think you'd hold out this long.'

'Nor did I, but I'm glad I did. I'm still convinced that I want to sell the business, but I need to be sure I do it the right way. Just like you said. So would you still be okay to come back to Mandurah with me when we leave here?'

'Of course,' Adele says. 'Time is not a problem for me.'

'Okay, thank you. Because what I've decided is that I should ask Melissa and Pam to stay on for six months until February. If they agree it would be a relief and a safety net, time to sort things out, make new plans. It also means that I could do something else in the meantime, go somewhere different, not even be there for the Christmas rush, because by then it will all be nicely streamlined and easy for them to run. And I can put it on the market next year.'

'That's a *really* good plan,' Adele says. 'Wish I'd thought of it! You'd still own it but not really have to go back into it. Just one thing though: do you think you can be there while we sort things out, and let them run it without constantly interfering? I have an image of Melissa and her mum rolling their eyes in frustration as you turn up at the shop every day and change everything they've done. I think if you do that you'll lose them, and they are very good people to have in there while it's on the market.'

'Adele, I am so over anything at all to do with knitting at the moment. I'm suggesting this based on your advice that if I want to sell it I should take time to get it all sorted, with a transparent system that any buyer can see and feel confident about.'

'Okay, if you're sure.'

'I am,' Judy says. 'The other thing I think I should do when I'm back there is dismantle that stupid knitted town. Get it out of my head. Chuck it in the bin.'

'What!' Adele says – almost shouts. 'Have you gone completely bonkers?'

The waiter, who has just arrived with their coffee and croissants, steps back sharply.

'Whoops, sorry,' Adele says. 'My friend just lost her marbles.'

'No worries,' he says with a genial smile. 'She looks quite sane to me and you only knocked about a year off my life expectancy.' Laughing, he unloads the tray and walks back inside.

Adele turns to Judy. 'Why ever would you do that?'

'Because it means I'm stuck in the past,' Judy says.

'Not necessarily. I think it means you treasure the past. If you want to get over a feeling that you're living in the past then there are better ways of doing it.'

'Such as?'

'Well, you could use some of that free time to go back there for a visit, for a start. That would be one way. But whatever you decide, you should not ever destroy your work. It's unique and beautiful. It's a work of art, women's art, which as you say, quite rightly, is underrated and dismissed. And now that's what you're doing with your own work. Move it out of your house if you want, but give it to some sort of gallery or something. Or better still, send your video of it to the council or the library or the arts centre or whatever in the town – tell them why you created it. I bet they'd be interested; they might even want it for the town. Honestly, Judy, I can't believe you even imagined dumping it!'

*

Simone is sitting on the verandah at the back of Geoff's house watching a cluster of red wattlebirds arguing in the branches of a nearby tree. Geoff is in the kitchen making coffee and Doug, who had been sitting here with her, has got up to take a call from his partner and is talking to him out on the lawn. It feels good being on their territory, silently waiting and observing. It evokes memories of childhood, of sunny days sitting on the front steps of the Marshalls' house watching the boys kicking a ball, or scrambling up the biggest tree in the garden in a race to the top. How blissful it seems in retrospect.

'So how are you feeling now, Simone?' Geoff asks, putting the coffee pot and cups on the table. 'We've been thinking about you a lot. We both felt we handled it badly, dumping everything on you like that. It must have been such a shock. But you took us by surprise.'

'In what way?' she asks.

'We'd taken it for granted that in the years since we last saw each other you would have learned more about Carlo, perhaps seen evidence of who he was, or what he had become.' He hands her a mug of coffee and she holds it in both hands, relishing the warmth of the steam on her face and remembering the warmth she had felt the night she slipped into sleep next to Ros, the comfort of Ros's body close to her, the sound of her breathing, and the knowledge that, for both of them, sharing a bed was no small thing.

'I suppose I always sensed that something in him might explode,' she says, drawing herself back to the present. 'That was the controlling factor in my childhood, the knowledge that by being good, making him proud of me, everything would be okay.' She thinks again of those years, of the tightrope walk of being good and staying out of trouble at home, of the rewards when it all worked and the tense silences or fierce outbursts when it didn't.

'He never laid a finger on me,' she said, 'although I think now that he may have hit Mum. It would explain so much.'

She remembers the time she returned from France, how he had reacted to the way she had grown up in the three years away from home. There had been some pride in it, but also resentment, as though her growing up was something he hadn't expected and didn't really like.

'I started to make life difficult for him when I came home,' she says. 'I asked awkward questions, reacted against things that I'd always accepted: the way he said grace every meal time, his expectation that food would always be on the table ready for him, the dismissive way he talked to Mum. But it was my constant demands to know about you, where you'd gone – that was what really got to him, and of course now I know why.'

'He would certainly have been challenged by your return as an adult,' Geoff says. 'He resented us having come home as grown men, especially when we stood up to him, confronted him with what we knew and made it very clear that his reign of terror was over. I think he must somehow have expected he would be dealing with two teenagers and he was shocked by the reality, by the questions we asked, the way we took control and got stuck into finding out what he was doing. We were both so torn – we wanted to get the law onto him but Mum was adamant. She was terrified, afraid he would attack her or one of us, and that he would say she'd seduced him.'

'There were other things that went on,' Doug says, joining them at the table. 'While we were young, out in the sheds and the orchards, he could be violent. Not with us, but with some of those young guys that helped with the fruit picking and packing. They were teenagers, and he was incredibly hard on them. He'd hit them around the head if they were cheeky, or if he felt they weren't working hard enough.'

Simone sits in the silence, images of the past running through her head. She is finding it hard to believe how ignorant she had been, how she had assumed that she lived on an average regional fruit farm run by a family man who demanded from others the same standards as he set himself. And all the while brutality formed the undercurrent of every day.

'So have you thought any more about coming to London?' Doug asks, dragging her back into the present with a lighter tone.

'I have,' she says, smiling, happy to break her own mood. 'I'd really love to do that. Have you spoken to Claire and Paula?'

'We've spoken to Mum and she'd love to see you. But she's still concerned that you'll be angry with her.'

'Whatever for?'

'Because of Carlo . . . because of Paula.'

'Ha!' Simone says. 'What else could she have done? It would be easy to make judgements but the reality was that he was going to have what he wanted and he used her to get it. She was in an impossible situation. In those days if she'd reported the rape she would probably have been blamed for *leading him on*. Papa always got what he wanted – I knew that about him.'

Simone sips her coffee, letting herself sink back into the pleasure of their company. 'I'm so happy I found you both,' she says. 'Despite everything that I now know, I can't really tell you what it means to me to be sitting here with you like this, to have my brothers back.'

When Geoff had driven her back to the house on Tuesday night, full of delicious food, too much wine and with everything that she'd believed about the past in tatters, she had staggered up the stairs to her room wondering if she would ever get over the anger, the hurt and the disappointment. The conversation at breakfast the next morning had helped a little. But she is still grappling with the grief of learning about the darkness of the past.

'Have you told Adam all this?' Doug asks.

'No,' she says. 'Only that I've found you, and about Paula. He's very caught up in the prospect of having *uncles*, as he's always thought of you, and now an aunt as well. I won't be telling him much more until we can talk face to face. So are you going over to England together?'

'Yes, next month,' Doug says. 'Would that work for you?'

'I'll make it work. I'll join you over there. Let me know when you've organised your travel. When we leave here I want to spend a week or two in Sydney with Ros. She has a studio where I can stay. I think for both of us it will ease the way back into our separate lives. The last few weeks have been challenging for all of us in different ways. We'll have to go back to where we came from as different versions of ourselves. I don't think it will be easy for any of us.'

Chapter Twenty-one

The final Sunday

Ros is walking slowly around the garden with Clooney, thinking about what she's going to say about *An Equal Music*. One of the reasons she had chosen it was that she'd thought it would make it easy to segue from the violinist in the book, who is struggling to get to grips with the fact that she is going deaf, to her own struggle as a cellist trying to get to grips with Parkinson's. But of course the other women know this now, and it's better that it emerged in a more natural way. *I must have been mad*, she thinks, *to imagine I could conceal it from them for weeks.* Thankfully there's so much else in the book to talk about. But the fact that this is the last book they'll discuss here is bearing down on her. So much of what's happened between them in their time in the mountains has been unexpected and significant, and she really doesn't want it to end. 'Come on Clooney,' she calls, 'book time.' He wanders reluctantly towards her and they head back into the house and through to the kitchen where Adele is making tea.

She looks up. 'Oh there you are,' she says. 'I was just thinking how sad I feel; the last book. I don't want to go home, I don't want it all to end.'

'Me neither,' Ros says. 'But you're going back with Judy, aren't you?'

Adele nods. 'Yes, and I'm looking forward to that ... but ... oh well, I guess I should be thankful we've had all this.'

The atmosphere is strangely awkward as they help themselves to tea. Simone and Judy are clearly also in low spirits and their collective energy for talking books is very different from previous Sundays. Ros looks around and is, for once, lost for words, but someone has to kick-start them into a discussion and as this is her book choice the task inevitably is hers.

'Okay,' she says, 'it's clear we're all feeling less than our best, but we came here to read and talk about books, and I'm blowed if I'm going to put up with my choice getting less energy and attention than the others. So let's get into it.'

There is a rustle of movement, shoulder straightening, shifting positions, the clink of cups being put aside. 'So, this is *An Equal Music*,' she continues, 'one of my favourite books for various reasons, some of which are probably obvious to you all. First of all, it's about music, and I really love the way Vikram Seth writes about it, and the way he portrays the musicians, the rehearsals and all the little dramas, triumphs, jealousies and idiosyncrasies. We're all fairly precious about our instruments, and I suspect that most of us have pretty fragile egos even if we manage to hide that. He gets it, and he also gets that we are picky about comparatively small things, and how passionate everyone is about getting it right. I felt I'd lived through all those conversations with the members of the quartet I've played with for many years. It is a very close and interdependent set of relationships that doesn't easily accommodate change. We know each other very well; we rely on each other, know the ways in which each person plays. It's not easy to accept change in a group like that, and it's easy to feel aggrieved or defensive if someone new has to join the group.' She stops suddenly, feeling a lump rising in her throat at the memory of her conversation with Donald.

'Do you think you would go and listen to your quartet play without you, or would that be just too hard?'

'Oh yes, I'll be there whenever I can,' Ros says. 'I love those guys, and I'm really proud to have played with them for so long. But there was an awful finality in that conversation with Donald. We'll always be friends, but what brought us together and sustained our friendship is lost now. I wonder . . .' She stops again, trying to keep her voice steady. 'Someone else will take my place, and because they have to focus on developing that closeness and trust, it will mean that I'll always be an outsider. They lost their musician and I also lost mine.'

It's hard for her to say this, harder still to accept it.

'Will you be able to play for your own pleasure?' Judy asks. 'I'm sorry if it's a silly question, but I don't know much about Parkinson's. I noticed your hands, but they don't shake *all* the time. Can you play at all now?'

'A little,' Ros says. 'About three weeks before we came here I played all the way through a rehearsal. But several times when I've played at home, alone, I've dropped the bow, or haven't been able to maintain the fingering. It seems I have to take things one day at a time, and it may progress very quickly or quite slowly. Anyway, I guess I'm lucky because, unlike Julia in *An Equal Music*, I still have good hearing, so I can at least *listen* to the music I love.'

'That was such a moving element of the book,' Judy says, 'a pianist going deaf. And that character was in her late thirties.

At the beginning I thought Michael was such a lovely character, but he became single minded and selfish. He couldn't really empathise with what Julia was going through.'

'And he helped her to hide it from the other musicians,' Adele says, 'because he was so desperate for her to play with them, or really with *him*. He never seemed to consider how it would be for her if she did play and it all went horribly wrong. That would have been terrible for her. I don't think he ever really entered into what the deafness meant to her. It was all about his need to get her back.'

Ros looks around the room. *Remember this*, she tells herself. *This is us, this is what we do. We talk about books, we make them work in our own lives: walk through the doors they open for us, cross the bridges they lay out for us, and pick and choose what we need to take away from them. They brought us together, and they'll keep us together, too.*

'Michael is *always* very focused on what it all means to *him*,' Simone says. 'At first I was really into him; he seemed so lovely, a kind of tragic hero, and I thought his longing for this woman he'd lost years earlier and yearned for ever since had made him wise and thoughtful, and really sensitive. But once he spots her by chance on that bus, and then she finally calls him, everything begins to change.'

'Yes, it does,' Ros says, 'and I think that's a really interesting part of the book because you don't realise it's happening. It's quite subtle at first and you feel so happy for him, for both of them, that they've met again, and then you . . . well *I* certainly felt that he was trying to invade her life, take over.'

'I think that's very male,' Adele says. 'I'd like to ask Vikram Seth what he actually thinks of Michael, what he intended him to be. Because at the beginning he seemed such a rounded person, someone who had built a well-organised, textured sort of life for himself: the swimming at daybreak in the Thames, his practice rituals, his teaching. He seemed so balanced and genuine, I felt what I have sometimes felt, to my cost, when it comes to men: this is someone I could love and care for and who would love and care for me. But I ended up thinking, actually, Michael, you're a bit of a selfish shit.'

'Exactly,' Ros says. 'Michael can't really hear anything but the wailing of his own neediness, which is why he's able, several times, to simply trample on Julia's relationship with her husband and her son. And to put her under a lot of pressure.'

'So back to the question that I want to ask the author,' Adele says. 'It would be: how does he feel about Michael's behaviour in this respect? I mean, was he writing this consciously, trying to demonstrate the way some men need to colonise the woman they love, attempting to separate them from others? Or does Seth himself not actually understand that, because if he doesn't then of course he wouldn't see it in the character.'

'I think it's deliberate,' Ros says, 'because he writes Julia's resistance to that with such sensitivity. And Michael's the same about the violin, his other great love. It's not his, any more than Julia is his. It's on loan from the woman in Rochdale, Mrs Formby, and in all the years he's been playing it he's never attempted to acquire a violin of his own. I know very well that the instrument you play for years becomes the one you always want to play, plus his livelihood depends on that instrument. It could be gone overnight, and it nearly is in the end, but even then he doesn't really swing into action.'

'He assumes that women will give him what he needs,' Judy says. 'We all thought initially that he was a lovely character, but we all came to the conclusion that he was self-absorbed. He really believes that Julia is going to change her life so he can have what he wants, and that she'll throw her husband's and her child's lives into chaos, for him, because he loves her. Hopeless!'

Ros gets up, walks to the window and looks out into the darkening garden. 'It's interesting, that we all like this book, and we all see the same things in it. I'd like to know what some men think of it. Would they see what we see?' But what she's really thinking about is that because she was only halfway through the book when James died, she was never able to talk about it with him. Another of the many unfinished things between them that can never be completed.

'Did you travel much, Ros,' Simone asks, 'like the quartet does in the story – you know, Venice, Vienna, Prague, all those wonderful cities with links to great composers?'

'We did some tours. Vienna, but not Venice, Prague was magic, Tokyo – oh, and one year we did Paris and London.'

They return to the book, talking again about the characters, about music, about what they most love or dislike. Ros feels flat now, exhausted, almost numb; she has loved the conversation, loved introducing them to this book. But she needs to end it now, there is too much else on her mind. She rallies herself again, struggling to draw some words together.

'I think one of the most wonderful things that novels do is reflect us back to ourselves,' she says slowly, looking down at her shaking hands. She does't know what to say. 'For me . . .' She stops, swallows, starts again. 'For me, this loss of a musician's hearing resonates with my own situation, and I feel a sort of desperation.' She gazes out of the window, then turns to look back at them. She takes a deep breath, feeling weak and almost dizzy, and steadies herself by grasping the back of her favourite chair. 'Desperation . . . yes, desperation about a future in which I am no longer a musician.' *There, I've said it now,* she thinks, *I'm no longer a musician. So who the hell am I?* She sways a little, steadies herself again, sees Simone move as if to go to her but then stop. 'Being with you all has been holding the darkness at bay. But now it's coming to an end and I don't know how to . . . how to go on.' The tears are pouring down her cheeks. It's Adele who gets to her feet now, but Ros holds up her hand to stop her. She feels fragile to the point of shattering. 'I chose this book because I love it, but also because . . . well . . . because I thought I might find some sort of solution by talking about it. But there *is* no solution. It was my music and my belief in *myself* as a musician that has got me through the years since James died, and now that's been taken from me. What's left? What am I now? An old woman on a steep downward slope, losing bits of herself every day . . .' She's struggling to breathe now, spinning as consciousness is sucked out of her. 'Nothing can stop it . . . nothing . . .'

When she opens her eyes the room swims back into focus. She is on the floor, her head in Adele's lap.

'It's okay, Ros,' Adele says, stroking her arm. 'You're okay.'

Ros struggles, wanting to get up.

'No,' Adele says, 'don't try to get up, stay there a moment.'

Simone, on her knees beside her, takes her hand. 'Judy's getting you some water,' she says. 'You fainted, but Adele stopped you from falling, and you've come back so quickly. I'm going to get some more cushions for you. Look, here's Clooney, come to check on you.'

Clooney looks into her face, obviously surprised to find her down there looking up at him. He edges between her and Adele, sniffs her face, licks her forehead and flops down beside her, resting his head on her chest. The warmth and weight of him against her is wonderfully comforting.

'Clooney,' she murmurs, stroking his head. 'What would I do without you?'

Simone reaches for a cushion and Ros lifts her head. 'I can get up . . .'

'Definitely not,' Adele says. 'We'll help you to sit up if you want, but you need to stay here for a while.'

Ros is still slightly dizzy as Simone and Adele support her shoulders and help her to sit, propping her up with cushions.

'Drink this slowly, Ros,' Judy says, returning from the kitchen. 'Don't gulp it. Do you want to hold the glass or shall I hold it for you?'

'No,' Ros says, struggling, wanting to get to her feet. She feels ridiculous now, everyone fussing around her. 'No, I need to get up.'

'Ros!' Adele says, and the force of her tone surprises Ros. 'Stay where you are and drink some water, you grumpy old bat.'

There is a moment of pure silence. Then Ros stops struggling, lets go and leans back. 'I'll drink the water,' she says, looking around at them, and as Judy cautiously puts the glass in her hand, she manages a weak smile. 'I'll do as I'm told. I know not to argue with an invincible woman, let alone three of them.'

*

'Tea and toast,' Simone says, a couple of hours later, carrying a tray into the lounge room and putting it on the coffee table. 'Pity we've run out of crumpets, but I always think toast is comforting.' She looks at Ros, who is sitting on the sofa, her legs up, blanket wrapped around her and Clooney glued to her side. 'You're looking a bit better now, Ros,' she says, 'but still a bit pale.' She takes a mug of tea from the tray and puts it on the small side table where Ros can reach it, along with two slices of toast. 'In fact you're looking rather regal sitting there. Drink your tea and eat some toast, Your Majesty.'

Ros smiles. 'Thanks Simone, I am certainly being royally cared for.' She looks around the room. 'I'm so sorry . . .'

'Oh, do stop apologising,' Judy says, standing beside the fireplace, hands on her hips. 'It's *so* unlike you. We've grown to love our grumpy old bat and now you're going all polite and, well, wet!' They are all laughing now. 'Besides,' Judy continues, 'we have things to do.'

'Do we?' Ros asks, cautiously nibbling the corner of her toast.

'Of course. We need to make a plan for the future. There are ways we can all support Ros –'

'But it's not your responsibility . . .' Ros cuts in.

'It's not about responsibility,' Judy says. 'I'm not saying it's something we're responsible for; it's about commitment to each other, to our friendship. Sisterhood, if you like, Ros, that sounds like your sort of leftie, feminist word. And it's not all about you anyway. As I was about to say when you inter-rupted, we need a plan to support you *and each other*. We're all single and we're all getting older; each of us has had to face something serious since we've been here. That's a bond. This is no longer just a book club. It can be much more; it can have a life long after we leave here. Does anyone have a problem with that?'

'Not me!' Adele says. 'I want this to go on.'

'Me too,' Simone says, looking at Judy, thinking how dramatically she has changed since their drive up here from the airport. 'You're all part of my family now.'

Judy looks at Ros, who gives her a watery smile and nods her head slowly, then more rapidly. 'I'm in,' she says, her voice shaky. 'I'm very much in.'

'There's something else,' Simone says, looking around, wondering how they'll take what she wants to say. 'There are things . . . transitional things we need to do, each one of us.'

'What do you mean, Simone?' Judy asks. 'What transitional things?'

'Well as you just said, Judy, we've all gone through something important. We've all changed in some way; we've faced up to something significant, so none of us can just go back and pick up where we left off. For me it means going to London, meeting Claire and Paula, being with Geoff and Doug again. I can't just go home and pick up my old life again until I've done that. I have to continue what I started when I wrote that message to Geoff the week we arrived.'

'And what about the rest of us?' Judy asks.

'I think it's pretty obvious that you need to go back to Suffolk, Judy. Stand where you stood the day of the king's funeral, assuming it's not been bulldozed and a factory built on it. Say a prayer; see if you can find some people from your past. You know what England's like – full of people doing the same things they've been doing for decades, living in the same places, going to the same church. I bet you'd find a few people you remember and who remember you.'

'Yes, Judy, Simone's right,' Adele says. 'And I need to go and see Jenna. I want to show her who I am now; talk to her about at least a million things. What about you, Ros?'

Ros is silent and Judy sees that she is once again struggling to get her voice under control.

'Well I have to get serious about the Parkinson's, make a self-management plan, as I should have done months ago,' she begins. 'Look at making some changes in the house, get rid of the car . . . all that stuff . . .' She hesitates.

'And before you do that?' Simone asks.

'Before I do that . . .' Ros pauses, then looks up at them. 'Well I think you all know the answer to that. In fact, you all knew it before I did.'

Chapter Twenty-two

London, six weeks later

'So where is it you want me to drop you?' the taxi driver asks.

Ros leans forward to talk to him through the glass. 'As close as possible to the British Library please. I think there's a little café somewhere there,' she says, turning to the others. This is their third day in London and she's starting to get her bearings. 'If not, there will be seats inside the library.'

The traffic moves on slowly and a couple of minutes later the driver pulls up.

'That's the British Library,' he says, pointing across to the other side of the street. 'And you wanted a café, there's one just there, see?'

'Perfect. We'll get out here.' The others pile out onto the pavement while Ros hands over the cash. 'Thanks, you're a star,' she calls back to the driver.

'We aim to please,' he grins and pulls back out into the traffic.

'So let's just check the plan, Ros,' Adele says. 'We'll have a coffee, and when you're ready you'll walk down to the corner, do what you need to do, and then walk back. Okay?'

'That's it,' Ros says, pausing to take a deep breath, and remembering the last time she crossed this street with James on the way to the Library. Clutching her little bunch of hothouse violets she slips her other hand through Adele's arm as the four of them wait for the lights to change and then cross the street together.

It's a bright, chilly morning, but they are all well rugged up; Ros thinks Adele looks particularly striking and sporty in a lime-green puffer jacket she'd bought in Dubai. She had organised this trip for them, using her contacts to get them upgraded to business class, which had made the journey a great deal more comfortable than it would otherwise have been. They settle at an outside table and order coffee.

'Tell them your news, Judy,' Adele says.

Judy blushes and Ros sees that it's obviously good news. When they'd all met at the airport for the flight to London, Ros had been staggered by the change in Judy. Both she and Adele had sent Ros and Simone email updates from Mandurah, so Ros knew that there was now a plan for Judy to exit the business and that she was over the moon at the prospect of freedom. Even so, she hadn't been prepared for the transformation. Judy looked about ten years younger; the tension had gone from her body and her face and she seemed almost giddy with happiness and relief.

'Well,' Judy says now, 'a couple of weeks ago I sent the video of my knitted town to the local council, like Adele suggested. Then I just forgot about it. But guess what? This morning I got an email. Apparently there's quite a significant arts centre there now and they want to talk about the possibility of acquiring it!

So I emailed back and I'm meeting the manager and the mayor when we go to Suffolk on Thursday.'

Ros punches the air. 'Yay! Judy, that's wonderful, good on you, and you too Adele.' And to her dismay tears well in her eyes. 'Oh shit! Am I ever going to stop crying like this at everything? I'm like a bloody sprinkler!' She dabs her cheeks with some tissues and as Simone hugs Judy, Adele beams across at Ros and gives her a thumbs up.

'What are you hiding in your book bag, Adele?' Simone asks as Adele hauls the canvas bag onto her lap.

'Books,' Adele says, 'for next month's discussion.'

'Really?' Ros says. 'I didn't know we'd chosen a book.'

'We didn't,' Adele says. 'I made an arbitrary decision because I thought of a book that would be ideal. So yesterday I rang around and managed to track down four copies, and this morning, while you lot were lying around drinking tea, I popped out in a taxi and picked them up.'

'Impressive,' Simone says. 'Is it a book we had on the list?'

'No,' Adele says. 'I got something else instead.'

They look at her in amazement.

'You actually changed the schedule without consultation?' Ros says. 'I think we've created a monster. First you shamelessly exploit your business contacts to get us here in comfort, and then you start changing the schedule without notice.'

'I know.' Adele laughs. 'It's the new me: ruthless and demanding and I love it! Anyway, I remembered this book and how much I'd loved it, and I think you will too.' She reaches into her bag, pulls out four books and puts them on the table. 'So here it is, *Mrs Palfrey at the Claremont* by Elizabeth Taylor, first published in nineteen seventy-one.'

'Not *the* Elizabeth Taylor, surely?' Judy says, picking up a copy and studying the cover.

'No, another Elizabeth Taylor, one of the finest English novelists of the twentieth century.' Ros says. 'I'd forgotten all about this, but I read it years ago and absolutely loved it.'

'I've read something about her,' Simone says. 'Didn't her first novel come out at the same time as *the* Elizabeth Taylor made her movie debut in *National Velvet*?'

'Yes, and it was a disaster for this writer,' Adele says. 'It completely hijacked the publicity, and all her life she was being confused with the movie star. People would say just what Judy said: "*The* Elizabeth Taylor?" And when the answer was no, they lost interest.'

'So why have you chosen it for us now?' Simone asks.

'It's about an elderly, single woman, a widow, who tries always to be true to herself in difficult circumstances. She's at a crucial point in her life, a sort of threshold, trying to adapt to a big change, and then something happens, something at first quite lovely and . . . no! No! I'm not saying any more. But I guarantee you'll love it.'

'Maybe I'll get a fifth copy for Paula,' Simone muses.

Simone had met Claire and Paula, with Geoff and Doug, the day they arrived in London. She'd slept well on the journey and while the rest of them had been groaning about jetlag she just shrugged it off. A few hours later, when she'd returned to the hotel, where the others were waiting anxiously, she had been exhausted but elated. 'Paula and I connected almost immediately,' she'd told them. 'And when Claire hugged me the past just seemed to melt away.'

Ros holds the book in both hands and strokes the cover, feeling herself retreating somehow from the group, shifting her focus to where she is and why she's here at the heart of all the places she knew with James. She feels calm now, calmer, she realises, than she has felt for a long time, and safe. There is no easy road ahead, but she knows she's not going to have to navigate that alone.

Her phone beeps and she reaches into her bag.

'Oh look!' she says. 'Leah's sent me a video of Clooney.' Adele, who is next to her, leans over and together they watch it, doubling up with laughter as they pass it on to the others. Tim is lying, obviously asleep, on Ros's squishy old sofa. Alongside him Clooney is watching him, fidgeting on his paws in anticipation of a walk. He nudges Tim's arm with his nose. 'Go for it, Clooney,' Leah calls in the background. Clooney tries again, moving to paw Tim's thigh. Tim begins to stir, mumbles something, eyes still closed, and reaches out to pat his head. Clooney, spurred on by success, immediately leaps onto the sofa, clambers over Tim's legs, plants all four paws on his chest and starts furiously licking Tim's face.

'I see my place in Clooney's affections has been usurped by Tim,' Simone sighs when they've finally stopped laughing. 'But just the same, could you send that to me, please Ros? I'd love to have it.'

'Me too,' Adele says. 'I'd like to show it to Jenna and Jean-Claude when I get to Quebec. I've been boring them with Clooney stories on Skype.'

Ros sends on the video and sits quietly for a few moments, watching the others talking and laughing, remembering the day they all arrived at the house and everything that came after. *All those wonderful stories,* she thinks, *where would we be now without those stories and the books that helped us to tell them?* She sighs and gets to her feet.

'Time to do my thing,' she says, picking up her violets.

'I'll just come a little bit of the way,' Simone says, getting up, suddenly serious. They walk together towards the cross street where James had jumped from the bus.

'Thanks, Simone, I'll be all right from here on,' Ros says. 'I won't be long.'

'Be as long as you want,' Simone says. 'We'll be here.' And she gives Ros a hug, then turns and walks away.

Ros walks on to the corner, presses the button for the lights and waits. As she stands there she remembers something Simone said to her on the flight here.

'You and I,' she'd said, 'have to learn to turn our grief into strength. Stop it from dragging us down and use it to make us strong.' Ros stares ahead, thinking of this, willing this small pilgrimage to become something that will finally put her grief to use.

The lights change and she crosses over. She'd imagined sitting on the kerbstone but it's clear she won't be able to do that, there is far too much traffic, and too many pedestrians. But there is a low wall nearby and as the lights change she crosses over and sits on that, feeling very strange, as though she is waiting for something to happen. She shifts her position, closes her eyes to focus, thinking of why she's here, waiting for the right moment.

I hope you're listening, James, she says eventually. I've brought you these violets. Do you remember how much you loved the little bunch I had the day we got married? Well, now I've brought them to help me say goodbye. Not forever of course, just the au revoir I should have said sooner. I'm sorry it's taken me so long, but there was something so final about the thought of it that I just couldn't. But now I'm here I know it's the right thing to do and the right time to do it. I miss you, my darling. I miss you every moment of every day, but I think I've learned to live without you. I didn't do that . . . didn't even want to do that . . . for a very long time. I think I had to open myself to something else before I could leave you in peace. The something else turns out to be these three beautiful women. You'd like them, and they'd love you. I like to think of you up there, looking down, seeing what I'm up to, rolling your eyes, laughing and groaning with embarrassment.

It's a different life without you and I'll never forget how lucky I was to have you in that precious other life. I'm never going to stop missing you, that's never going to change, but there's a right time for closure, don't you think? You can't do it too soon, but I left it too long because I was frightened it would be the end. But it's really about moving forward, isn't it? Moving forward without leaving anyone behind, just leaving them and oneself in peace.

If you know what's going on down here, and I like to think that you do, you'll know I'm okay. Oh dear, I'm useless at this, aren't I? I probably won't be quite so dependent on you in future. Maybe that'll be a relief for you?

And by the way, I really wish you could have waited just a couple more minutes for the bus to stop. Now that I'm here I can see how close the bus stop is to the corner. Why couldn't you have waited? Men, honestly, you're a hopeless lot.

She stops for a moment, inhales deeply, then pulls some tissues from her pocket, wipes away her tears and takes another deep breath before continuing. I'll still keep talking to you, of course, but not so much. In my mind, you'll always remain as the man you were when you left home that morning; the man I loved all those years, and still love in your absence.

It seems a long way from Sydney to London just to say this to you, to bring you these violets. But perhaps the distance itself represents the enormity of what I'm actually doing. I'll leave you to think about that. Thank you for all those wonderful years, my darling, and for . . . well, just for being you and for loving me. You will live for me always, in my heart.

She shifts her position but goes on sitting there for a while, absolutely still, acknowledging, for the first time in all the years she has talked to him in his absence, that there will not be a reply.

Ros eventually gets to her feet, rubs her hands across her teary face, picks up the violets and walks to the corner, just where she imagines James would have jumped, where she thinks his head might have been. His blood might actually be in that stone, she thinks. She crouches down to lay the violets on it, loses her balance, staggers dangerously, and ends up crouched over double in the gutter.

A car swerves to avoid her, the driver blasting out his irritation on his horn.

'All right, keep your hair on,' Ros says aloud.

'Oh my goodness, you poor thing,' a woman says, hurrying over to her, helping her to straighten up, then guiding her back onto the pavement. 'Are you all right? This is such a terrible corner; people are always getting hurt here. My sister fell here last year, shocking bruises she had. I think you should sit down a minute.'

'Yes, thanks,' Ros says. 'I'm all right but I will sit for a minute.' The woman steers her back to the wall and sits down beside her.

'They really should do something about that corner. It's to do with the slope of the kerb or something, and of course people are so impatient, rushing all the time. You're looking a bit better now.'

Ros nods. 'I'll be fine. I'm meeting some friends near the library.'

'That's nice; you'll be able to have a cup of tea, very good for shock. I'll wait with you until you're ready, we can walk together, just in case you feel a bit wobbly. Falling at our age is a worry, isn't it?'

'It is,' Ros says, thinking that this woman is probably

twenty years younger than her.

'I've a good mind to write to the council about this. Plus people are so impatient; they won't wait until the bus turns the corner and stops, so they just jump off, bump into people on the pavement or fall over. D'you know, it's a long time ago now, maybe ten years or more, a man jumped down from the bus in winter and he slipped on the ice and hit his head on the kerb and died before the ambulance got here. How bad is that? Imagine it. Imagine his wife at home thinking he was on his way to work and then finding a policeman at the door.' She shakes her head. 'So sad.'

'Very sad,' Ros says, feeling a small smile twitch at the corner of her mouth. And she glances upwards. *You're famous*, she tells James. *Trust you to hog all the attention. You've become an urban legend.*

'I think I can get going now,' she says to the woman. 'Thank you so much, you've been very kind.'

'Don't mention it. It doesn't take a moment, does it, to stop and help someone? Oh look, are those your violets?' She gets off the wall as if to retrieve them.

Ros puts out a restraining hand. 'It's all right, I don't need them,' she says. 'Just something else to carry.'

'Oh, but . . .'

'Really, let's leave them as . . . well, as a token, let's say, for the man who died here. It feels right, doesn't it?'

She takes the woman's arm, and when the lights change they cross the street and walk on towards the café. And Ros doesn't look back.

Acknowledgements

What a privilege it has been to work on this, my tenth novel, with the wonderful group of people at Pan Macmillan. I'm especially indebted to my publisher, the amazing Cate Paterson, and editors extraordinaire Georgia Douglas and Jo Jarrah. Thank you for your insight, your patience and great ideas, and most of all, for saving me from myself! And thank you, too, to all the other hardworking, efficient and thoughtful people who make sure the books get out onto the shelves and that readers know about them.

Thank you, too, to my wonderful family and friends who put up with me yakking on about what I'm doing, and who boost my spirits when it feels as though it's all falling apart.

And last, but by no means least, thank you to the many loyal readers who write and email and let me know what the books have meant to them. You are an inspiration.